STOLEN GIRL

Also by Marsha Forchuk Skrypuch

Making Bombs for Hitler

The War Below

STOLEN GIRL

A novel by
MARSHA FORCHUK SKRYPUCH

SCHOLASTIC INC.

First published in Canada as *Stolen Child* by Scholastic Canada Ltd., 604 King Street West, Toronto, Ontario M5V 1E1, Canada

While inspired by real events and historical characters, this is a work of fiction and does not claim to be historically accurate or portray factual events or relationships. Please keep in mind that references to actual persons, living or dead, business establishments, events, or locales may not be factually accurate, but rather fictionalized by the author.

ISBN 978-1-338-53871-7

10 9 8 7 6 5 4 3 2 1   19 20 21 22 23

Printed in the U.S.A.   40

First printing 2019

Book design by Yaffa Jaskoll

IN MEMORY OF LIDIA

CHAPTER ONE

1950—COMING TO CANADA

The woman who said she was my mother was so ill on the ship from Europe that she wore a sickness bag around her neck almost the whole time. The man I called father had come over a year before us. He had worked in different places in Canada, looking for one that could be our home. He wrote to us that he'd settled on Brantford, Ontario, because of the trees and the two Ukrainian churches. And a foundry that gave him a job—which meant that we could eat.

Because Marusia was so sick on the ship, she spent most of her time down below. I do not like to feel closed in, so I let her sleep in peace. I was left with lots of time on my own, and I didn't mind. I would run up the stairs to the top deck and lean over the railing, watching the water churn far, far below me. Once, I climbed over the railing and sat on the edge, dangling my legs over the open water and relishing the cool, clean air. I was there less than a minute when a deckhand snatched me by the waist and lifted me to safety. He yelled at me in a language that wasn't Ukrainian or Yiddish or German or Russian. It wasn't English either. I suppose he told me that I was crazy to be doing such a thing. It didn't feel crazy. I was finally alone and out in the open, if only for a moment. It felt like freedom.

When the ship landed at the Port of Halifax, I followed Marusia down the gangplank. I had gotten so used to the rolling of the sea that when my feet touched Canadian soil, I thought it was moving. I had to hold on to a post to stop from falling. Marusia was unsteady on her feet too. She was carrying the suitcase and couldn't reach the post, so I grabbed her hand and steadied her, then we walked to the end of the long, snaking line of immigrants.

At the front of the line stood men in uniform, who interviewed every newcomer. That scared me speechless. What would they ask me about? What could I say?

Marusia squeezed my hand reassuringly. "Remember to call me Mama."

When it was our turn, the officer looked at our documents, then bent down until he was eye level with me. His craggy face was kind, but the uniform terrified me. He said in Ukrainian, "Welcome to Canada, Nadia. Are you glad to be here?"

I don't like to lie, so I didn't answer but just stared at him through my tears. I was glad to finally be out of that terrible displaced persons camp we had been in for five years. In some ways, I was glad to be in Canada because it was so far away from my other life. But there were things about my earlier life that I still yearned for.

The immigration officer tugged on one of my pigtails and then stood up. I listened as he asked Marusia questions about where we came from before the war, and what we did during it. I always noticed how easily Marusia lied.

The officer asked to see the train tickets that the United Nations people had given us. Marusia held them up, not wanting to let them go, but he snatched them from her and examined them carefully. Only when he seemed satisfied did he stamp our papers and hand the tickets and our papers back. Marusia folded them with trembling hands and shoved them through the buttons of her carefully ironed blouse. The man gave her some paper money. "That's five Canadian dollars. For food," he said.

The port was thick with other people who had lost their homelands in the war, just like us. Vendors competed with each other, trying to sell us food. They shouted things like "milk," "apples," and "bread." Marusia had tried to learn some English in the DP camp, and so had I, so we could understand some of the words.

Marusia wanted to buy meat sandwiches and a bottle of milk, but she didn't know the word for sandwich. When she finally got a vendor to understand her, he wanted too much money. We needed to be careful so our money would last. I was hungry and thirsty and thought I would die of heat. But at least we were safe.

"I think that is a food store," I said, pointing to a building with a pyramid of tin cans displayed in the window. The door of the building opened and a man walked out. He carried what looked like a loaf of bread.

"Let us try," said Marusia, pushing me toward the store.

When we opened the door, it was even hotter inside than outside. A rosy-faced man with a barrel belly and a shiny hairless head grinned at us.

"Food . . . ?" said Marusia in English, holding the five-dollar bill up for the man to see.

"Not much left," said the man in English, gesturing with his hands to help us understand.

We looked around the store. He was right. The cans arranged in a pyramid had pictures of different vegetables on them. There were sacks of flour and rice. But no buns or cheeses or sausage or anything that could be eaten without preparation.

"Bread?" asked Marusia.

The storekeeper shook his head sadly.

We were about to leave when the man's face brightened. He crooked his finger and we followed him to the back corner of the store. As he opened up a giant box, a whoosh of lovely icy air enveloped us. He pulled out what looked like a large white cardboard brick. "Ice cream," he said, grinning.

"I scream?" Marusia asked, puzzled.

"No, no," the man said.

I was as confused as Marusia. What did this screaming thing have to do with bread?

The man grabbed the cardboard brick and took it to the front counter. He frowned in concentration as he shuffled through a box under his cash register. Smiling, he held up two flat wooden spoons. "Now you'll see," he said, peeling back a paper layer from the cold brick. A vanilla scent swirled toward us.

"Ice," said the man. Then, "Cream." He took one of the wooden spoons and dragged it across the surface of the brick. A cold ball formed. He poised it on the spoon and held it to my mouth. "Taste," he said.

I clamped my mouth shut.

"I will try," said Marusia in her careful English. The man held the spoon to her open mouth and dropped in the cold ball as if he were feeding a bird. Her eyes widened with shock. I was so glad that I hadn't tried it first. But then she grinned. "Good!" she said.

She rolled a bit onto the other spoon and gave it to me. I touched the strange food with the tip of my tongue. It reminded me of a snowball. I put the entire spoonful into my mouth and shivered at the shock of cold, creamy sweetness. It wasn't just the wonderful taste but the sensation of cold on a hot, sticky day. It was heavenly.

"Five dollars," said the storekeeper.

Marusia blanched. A whole five dollars for this strange new food? She shook her head.

"You eat, you buy," he said sternly.

Marusia reluctantly held up our five-dollar bill. "But this is all we have."

The shopkeeper grabbed it from her fingers.

"Please," she said, tears welling up in her eyes.

The shopkeeper gave us a pitying stare. He reached into his till and took out a one-dollar bill. Marusia took it.

We walked out of the store, Marusia clutching our precious ice cream to her chest. We were barely halfway down the block when she cried, "Oh no. Look!"

Her blouse was covered with thick white liquid. "Hold this," she said, shoving the ice cream container into my hands. She reached through her buttons and took out our precious immigration papers and our train tickets. A corner of one form was wet and a portion of the official stamp was now illegible. The train tickets were damp but not damaged. She waved them in the air, drying them. Meanwhile, I stood there, watching our four-dollars' worth of ice cream melt in the heat. Marusia gingerly refolded the immigration papers and train tickets and shoved them beneath the waistband of her skirt.

"Let us sit there," she said, clutching my elbow to direct me over to a park bench. The minute we sat down she handed me a wooden spoon. We slurped the ice cream as quickly as we could. By the time we were finished, our hands and faces were sticky, but I didn't care. That ice cream was the best thing I had tasted in a very long time. We cleaned ourselves off at a public fountain, but Marusia's blouse no longer looked freshly ironed.

I don't remember all that happened over the next few days. We managed to find our way to the train station. I knew we were traveling west and I remember switching trains in Quebec City. We stopped long enough in Montreal to find a food store. We only had that one-dollar bill. The ice cream had been such a costly treat!

One of the other immigrants traveling on the train suggested that we buy something called Wonder Bread.

"It's cheap," she said. "You could buy three loaves with your dollar."

So we went into a grocery store and asked the red-lipsticked cashier where we would find Wonder Bread. "Down the aisle," she said in a bored voice, pointing with a long red fingernail. An entire shelf was filled with fluffy white loaves wrapped in colorful waxed paper. Marusia took two. We didn't dare buy anything to drink, and besides, there was a water fountain outside. The cashier gave us several coins in change.

When we got back onto the train, Marusia opened up one of the bread packages and drew out a couple of slices for each of us. It looked like perfect white bread, with a soft golden crust. I held it to my face and breathed in. It had no smell. I took a bite. It had no taste. I looked at Marusia. She was chewing slowly, with a puzzled expression on her face. "I wonder why they call this bread," she asked. Then she chuckled sadly. "Wonder Bread."

I felt like crying. Would this be the only kind of bread we could eat in Canada?

Marusia patted my hand. "I'll bake some real bread when we get to our new home."

With the motion of the train and my hunger staved off with Wonder Bread, I drifted off to sleep, dreaming of real bread.

Our train chugged through Ottawa, then we switched trains in Toronto. I was amazed that Marusia could keep it all straight, but each time the train stopped, she would show our tickets to the conductor to make sure we were going in the right direction. These trains were enclosed, with soft chairs and big windows—nothing like the flat-cars in Germany. I stared out the window as the cities flashed by, surprised that there were no bombed-out buildings, no burnt-down cities. Had the war not traveled across the ocean? I guess it was not a world war after all.

By the time the train pulled into Brantford, we had eaten the two loaves of Wonder Bread and I was truly sick of it. At the Brantford train station, I could see Ivan—the man I am supposed to call Father—waiting outside the station for us. His face was freshly shaved, and his hair was combed back and still wet. His hands were shoved deep into the pockets of a carefully pressed pair of worn gray pants.

When we stepped off the train, his face broke into a grin. We were just steps away from the train when he wrapped his arms around Marusia and gave her a loud kiss—right in front of everyone.

I tried to pretend I didn't know them, but then he caught me up in his arms and hugged me close. I tried to push him away, but he held on tight. "You are safe, Nadia," he whispered. "We will not let anyone harm you ever again."

I would not hug him back but instead went limp. I didn't want more of a scene.

Ivan grabbed Marusia's battered old suitcase and put it in the trunk of his big black car. I had no luggage—my few items of clothing had fit easily into Marusia's suitcase. We got into the car, just as if we were a real family. I had not been in a car for a very long time. I settled into the backseat, enveloped in the scent of leather and gasoline . . .

A large black car driven by a man in uniform . . .

"Nadia, open your window a little and let the breeze cool you," Marusia said. Then, turning back to Ivan in the front, "Did you buy this car, Ivashko?"

"No," he replied. "It belongs to my boss. He loaned it to me today so you could have a grand arrival to our new home."

Marusia's eyes crinkled with pleasure and she brushed her husband's cheek with her fingertips. "That was so very thoughtful of him," she said. "It reminds me of when we got married."

I remembered that too. They got married in the DP camp. Not right inside the camp, but in a little Austrian church outside it. The Austrian priest let a Ukrainian priest from the camp do the service. Afterward, we had all taken a taxi back to the camp. That car had been small and old, the leather seats cracked with age.

I settled down for a long ride, but within minutes Ivan turned down a street of mostly older-looking brick houses. I noticed some smaller wooden houses built in between. He pulled up in front of one of these. It looked like it had just been built.

"You bought a house, Ivashko?" Marusia asked with surprise.

"I bought some land, Marusia," he answered. "I am building a house."

Marusia and Ivan got out of the car but I stayed sitting in the backseat. What was the matter with me? All this time, I had wanted the journey to be over. Yearning to be home. But was this really my home?

Ivan opened the back door of the car and held out his hand to me. "Nadia," he said. "I made a swing for you in the backyard."

Twelve-year-olds are too old for swings, I knew that, but I smiled anyway. It was the thought that counted: Ivan tried so hard. I stepped out of the car. Ivan retrieved Marusia's suitcase from the trunk and the three of us walked to the front door.

Ivan opened the door and set the suitcase inside. He turned to Marusia with a grin on his face, picked her up as if she were a child, and carried her through the door. "What are you doing?" she cried. "Put me down!"

"It is a Canadian custom," said Ivan. "It is supposed to bring good luck."

He set her down on the floor just inside and I followed them in, thankful that he didn't carry me over the threshold as well.

On the outside the house looked finished, but inside, only wooden boards—Ivan said they were called studs—stood where walls should have been. The floor was plain sanded wood like you would see in a good barn. There was no furniture.

"Let me take my two girls on a tour of their new home," said Ivan, grabbing each of us by the hand and grinning with excitement. Marusia tried to paint a smile on her face, but her eyes showed the same confusion that I felt.

"This is our living room," he said. Still holding on to our hands, he walked us through an open doorway. "And this is the bedroom."

Was there only one bedroom in this house? The room was tiny. Barely big enough to fit the two bare mattresses on the floor. Neatly folded bedding was stacked on top. If there was just one bedroom, it would be for Marusia and Ivan.

“Will I be sleeping in the living room, then?” I asked. I wouldn’t mind sleeping there. It was more open and airy than this small room.

A look of surprise showed briefly in Ivan’s eyes, but then he answered, “When the house is finished, you will have your very own room in the attic.” He pointed to a small roughed-out area above our heads. “And you can choose the color for your walls.”

How would I breathe in such a tiny space? Thank goodness it wasn’t finished yet. There might be time to change that. “Where will I sleep until then?”

“In the backyard, just like us,” Ivan answered.

In the open. Much better!

“Now let us continue the tour.”

There wasn’t much more to it. Aside from the roughed-out living room and bedroom, there was a kitchen and bathroom and that was it. The bathroom had a sink and a new flush toilet and an old-fashioned iron bathtub with a delicate floral design etched around the edge.

“I got that from the dump,” said Ivan proudly. “Can you imagine that someone threw it out?”

A large chunk of enamel was missing from the bottom of the tub, revealing a gash of black metal and a ring of rust. Other than that, the tub was perfectly usable. What I would have given for a tub like this in the camp.

“That is easily fixed,” said Ivan, following my glance to the chipped part. “Once the house is finished.”

He took us through to the kitchen and we admired the secondhand electric stove with two burners and a freshly painted baby-blue icebox. Stacked neatly on top of it were three clean but chipped dinner plates and three coffee cups, all different. There was an iron frying pan and a knife, fork, and spoon for each of us. Ivan was most proud of the giant kitchen sink and the taps that ran with hot and cold water. “We can do our laundry in that sink too,” he said. “Now, wait until you see our backyard.”

Ivan let go of my hand long enough to open the back door. We stepped out onto cinder blocks that had been stacked up to form a step. In the middle of the tiny backyard was a huge oak tree. Hanging from the strongest branch was a rope swing with a wooden seat.

“That is for you, Nadia.”

I didn’t want to like it, but I couldn’t help myself. “Thank you!” I said, and then I hugged Ivan. I really meant it, which surprised me. I ran out to the swing to see it up close. The wooden seat was as smooth as velvet. Ivan had sanded out every stray sliver.

Marusia and Ivan stood hand in hand on the cinder-block porch. “Try it out,” she said.

I loved the feel of the breeze on my face as I pumped my legs to make the swing go higher and higher. I felt almost free. When the swing was at its highest, I could see into our neighbors' backyards. Two doors down was another swing in a tree. There was at least one other child on this street, and that was good. Maybe this could be home.

CHAPTER TWO
IS BRANTFORD HOME?

That first night, people came to our house with gifts. There was all sorts of food—good rye bread and *holubtsi* and sausage. Marusia was given jars of pickled beets, strawberry jam, and honey, as well as eggs and a sack of flour. Someone brought a bolt of light-blue cloth and Ivan was given a bottle of vodka. The priest gave me a prayer book, and an English lady with a mole on her cheek gave me a package of crayons. Just as most people were leaving, a couple arrived with an angry-looking dark-haired boy in tow.

"This is Mychailo," the woman said to me, pushing the boy forward. "He's a student at Central School."

His parents went into the house, leaving Mychailo with me in our yard.

"What's Central School?" I asked him.

"You'll be going there in September," he said. "You'll hate it."

"Why?"

"They'll make fun of you because you're not Canadian."

"Do they make fun of you?" I asked.

"Not anymore," he said, balling his hands into fists. "I beat them up if they do."

It didn't seem like something that would work for me. Maybe Mychailo would beat people up for me if we became friends?

After everyone left, Ivan said, "I have another surprise for you." He took my hand and walked me to the bushes that acted as a fence between our yard and our neighbor's. "Did you notice what these are?" he asked.

There were no flowers—the bushes looked like they had just been planted—but I recognized the shape of the leaves. "Lilacs!" I said.

"I planted them for you," he said. "They'll bloom next spring and you'll wake up every morning to their scent."

I was so overcome that I could barely croak out a *thank you.*

"This is your home, Nadia," he said, giving my hand a squeeze. "We want you to be happy here."

We dragged out the mattresses and slept in the backyard under the stars. The cool breeze soothed me and I loved being out in the open. The sound of chirping in the night startled me at first, but Ivan explained that it was the frogs singing, even finding a small one to show me. We had frogs back home but I couldn't remember the last time I'd seen one. A frog's song is so very different from the sounds of land mines, artillery fire, bombs. How many nights had I tried to sleep despite all those sounds, all through the war years? And the years in the camp, even without the din of war, we had lived so crowded in with other DPs that all I could hear were snores and grunts and sobs.

As I lay there, looking up at the stars and listening to the frogs, I began to relax—just a little. Maybe everything would be fine. I took deep breaths of the cool evening air and closed my eyes, but sleep wouldn't come. Marusia tossed and turned a little bit. She faced me and began to sing the lullaby I had known all my life.

Kolyson'ko, kolyson'ko
Kolyshy nam dytynon'ku
A shchob spalo, ne plakalo
A shchob roslo, ne bolilo
Ni holovka, ni vse tilo

I could feel the fear leave my body as I listened to the words. I was lulled by the coziness of the mattress and the bedding and being beside the two people who so far had kept me safe.

I fell asleep feeling loved and secure.

I am surrounded by the people whom I love most, snuggled together under a down comforter in a cozy bedroom. Suddenly, there is a banging at the door. I try to wake the people beside me but they have melted away. I am alone. My heart pounds. The door bursts open, but I cannot see who it is.

I woke with my arms flailing, shouting, "Leave me alone!" Strong hands pulled me to a sitting position. I opened my eyes. I was in Brantford, in my own backyard. Marusia sat beside me. I was safe. But even in the darkness I could see the worry on her brow. Ivan was there too, kneeling at my other side.

"Were you having a nightmare?" Marusia asked.

It had seemed so real, but yes, it must have been a nightmare. I nodded.

"Do you want to talk about it?"

"No."

Marusia snuggled up close to me on the mattress and whispered the lullaby into my ear in a low, sweet voice. The words soothed me a little bit and I could feel my heart settle down.

I wanted to sleep but I didn't want to dream again.

Once my breathing slowed, it was easy to convince Marusia that I was all right. She and Ivan needed their sleep.

Marusia settled back on her mattress. I stayed awake, listening to the frogs and the rhythm of Ivan's snores. When I knew that Marusia was also deep in sleep, I sat back up and breathed in some cool night air to try to clear my thoughts. Why did I have that dream? Who was pounding at the door?

I clasped my arms around my knees and rocked back and forth, soothing myself like someone had once soothed me. I chanted the lullaby under my breath. The words made me feel safe and loved. I reached back into my memory to the last time I had felt completely safe. I remembered a time before the camp. I had a bedroom all to myself then, a room with high ceilings and big windows. I had plenty to eat and good clothing to wear.

But had I felt safe? No. Who could feel safe in the middle of a war?

CHAPTER THREE
MISS MACINTOSH

After that nightmare, I tried to stay awake, but exhaustion must have won out, because somehow I slept. When I woke the next morning, I was damp with dew and my neck ached, but I was grateful to be outside and surrounded by clean, fresh air. I sat up and stretched and looked over at the other mattress. Marusia was asleep, but Ivan was not there.

Then Marusia opened her eyes and answered my unspoken question. “He’s gone to work. And I need to find a job too.”

“What will I do?”

“School doesn’t start for two months,” she replied. “The lady who brought you crayons has offered to help you with your English.”

Since there wasn’t a kitchen table, we balanced our breakfast plates of fried eggs, jam, and rye bread on our knees while sitting on the cinder-block steps. We washed with hot water in the bathroom and Marusia combed the tangles out of my hair and rewove it into two tight braids. Then she walked me two doors down the street to the house with the swing in the back. She knocked and we waited.

The door opened. "Good morning, Nadia," said the woman in slow and careful English. "My name is Miss MacIntosh."

"Good morning, Miss MacIntosh," I replied, speaking as carefully as I could in English.

The woman turned to Marusia and, in surprisingly good Ukrainian, said, "Hello, Marusia, I hope you had a good first night in your new home."

While the two chatted at the doorstep, I craned my neck to peek inside, but the curtains were drawn and the room was in shadow. A faint scent of lemons and something else wafted out the door.

Marusia mentioned that she would be looking for a job.

"What did you do in Europe?" asked Miss MacIntosh.

Marusia looked flustered. "You mean during the war?"

"Before that," said Miss MacIntosh.

"I was studying to be a pharmacist," said Marusia. "But I will take any kind of job here."

"It will be difficult for you," said Miss MacIntosh in Ukrainian. "Nadia will be fine with me all day."

What? I knew that Marusia would be looking for a job and that I was supposed to learn more English with this woman. But *all day*? I tugged Marusia's hand and looked at her pleadingly.

"Nadia," said Marusia, "Ivan says that Miss MacIntosh has taught English to several children. You will be fine." And then, with a determination that shocked me, she pulled her hand from mine and stepped away. "Trust me, Nadia," she said. Then she left.

If I had been younger, I might have run after her, but I did not want to make a scene. I took a deep breath and swallowed my tears away. I had lived through the war. I could suffer a day with Miss MacIntosh.

Once my eyes had adjusted to the dimness of her living room, I could see that her floor was wooden like ours, but it was mostly covered with a colorfully braided rag rug. The bits of floor that showed at the edges of the room had been varnished and waxed until they gleamed. Her living room was as tiny as ours, but I was amazed at how much furniture she had in it. Beside the door that led to the kitchen was a tall bookcase stuffed with books. Against the other wall was a fireplace with a photo-covered mantel. In the center was a silver-framed photograph of a sad-looking man in uniform.

"Come and sit here," said Miss MacIntosh, placing her

hand gently on my shoulder and leading me to the overstuffed sofa.

I perched on the edge and Miss MacIntosh drew a book from her shelf and sat down beside me. The book cover was a painting of a girl with blond braids just like mine.

"This is *The Picture Dictionary for Children*," she said, pointing at each word on the cover as she sounded it out.

I love books more than anything. At the camp there were sometimes books in the CARE packages, but not often ones for children. I longed to touch this book, to hold it up to my face and smell it, but instead I sat still on the sofa beside Miss MacIntosh. She opened the book to a marked page. A drawing of a *yabluko*.

"Apple," said Miss MacIntosh, pointing to each letter as she sounded it out.

"Apple," I said.

She flipped to another marked page. A drawing of a big *aftomobile*. "Automobile," she said, grinning. Almost the same word in English and Ukrainian!

We practiced half a dozen words, and then she flipped back to *apple* again and we reviewed them all. We did a few more new ones, and she started back at the beginning again for another review. I knew I wasn't really learning to speak English, I was just learning the English labels for things, but it was fun doing it with the pictures.

When Miss MacIntosh thought I had learned those first words well enough, we went on to the next six, and the next six after that. I have no idea how long we sat there, but it was likely hours because my bottom was getting numb.

I flipped ahead and was startled by the image of a ferocious-looking *pes*. I took a deep breath, then pointed at the letters underneath the picture. "Dog," I said.

"Very good," said Miss MacIntosh, but I think she could tell that the picture had scared me.

"Time for a break," she said as she stood up from the sofa. In Ukrainian, she asked, "Would you like something to eat?"

"Yes, please!" I answered in my best English, getting up from the sofa and stretching. I had no idea how long we had been sitting there. Time had seemed to flash by.

As Miss MacIntosh busied herself in the kitchen, I picked up the silver-framed photograph on the mantel. The uniformed man looked young. His uniform was dark and he wore a cap perched at an angle over his right eye . . .

Another mantel . . . another uniform. This one also dark . . .

An image flitted just beyond my grasp as I put the photo back in its place and turned to the bookcase. Miss MacIntosh's books had colorful spines and the titles were all in English. I longed to pull one out to look at it but didn't want to do that without permission, so I stepped just inside the kitchen and watched her.

"You can sit there," she said, pointing to one of her kitchen chairs.

She set two glasses of milk on the table, two empty soup bowls, and two empty plates. She opened the cupboard and took out a red-and-white can and opened it. She slid the jiggly contents into a saucepan and added a can of water.

Miss MacIntosh didn't have an icebox like we did, but a refrigerator. As she opened it and took out an orange block of something, a bit of the cooled air escaped and enveloped my face.

Miss MacIntosh sliced some pieces off the orange block and arranged the squares on slices of—Wonder Bread! I thought I had seen the last of Wonder Bread, but it was not to be.

"Please, what is that?" I asked in English, pointing to the block of orange.

"Velveeta," answered Miss MacIntosh.

"Velveeta," I repeated, letting the unusual word roll out on my tongue.

"It is a kind of cheese," said Miss MacIntosh in Ukrainian.

"Oh!"

She set slices of Wonder Bread onto a cookie sheet, with the pieces of Velveeta on top, then slid the sheet into the oven. Steam rose from the soup. "It is ready," she said.

She pulled out the cookie sheet and brought it over to the table, then slid an open-faced cheese sandwich onto each of our plates. I watched my bowl fill with red as she ladled out soup for each of us.

This soup was like nothing I had ever seen. Soup was a staple in the camp. Usually it was mostly water with some cabbage and potato, but every once in a while there would be a bit of meat. This soup was thick like gravy. I took a small spoonful and placed it on my tongue. A tangy sweet tomato taste. Not bad, but not really soup either.

I smiled at Miss MacIntosh. "Good!" I said.

She nodded in approval.

The sandwich was another matter. I had never seen cheese quite that color before and the fact that it was on Wonder Bread didn't help. I picked up the sandwich with my fingertips and took a small bite. The bread was toasty from the oven and the cheese had a pleasant, gooey texture. Miss MacIntosh was watching me expectantly. I swallowed down the bite, grateful—as always—for any food . . .

Marusia and I are sprawled on an open flatcar in the blackest part of the night. Other escapees too, all holding on as the train chugs along at an alarming speed. It slows to a stop. I sit up and watch in horror as Marusia jumps off and runs into a farmer's field. She is scrabbling in the dry earth, digging with her bare hands. I hear her hoot for joy. She runs back and jumps onto the flatcar. "Potatoes," she says. "Two of them!"

One of the other fugitives brings a pot out of a tattered bag and someone makes a small fire from gathered twigs in the middle of the flatcar. Another man who has run into the field comes back with his hat filled with muddy water. He dumps it into the pot. Marusia adds her potatoes.

The steam of the cooking potatoes makes my stomach grumble. I have had nothing to eat for days.

This is the first time the train has stopped since we've taken refuge on the flatcar. The potatoes are barely cooked through but we cannot wait. We have no idea how long the train will remain still and we're afraid the smell of fire will bring soldiers.

One man has a spoon tucked away in his frayed coat. He takes it out reverently and dips it into our soup and gives me—the only child—the first spoonful. It is the best soup I have ever tasted. The spoon is passed around like a sacrament. Within minutes, every drop is consumed. The train starts moving just as we're finishing . . .

I felt a hand on my shoulder and was startled back into the present. Miss MacIntosh looked at me with concern.

Tears welled up in my eyes. I rubbed them from my face with the back of my hand and avoided Miss MacIntosh's stare. These random images made me confused and angry with myself.

Miss MacIntosh finished her own soup and sandwich, and then I stacked the dirty dishes and cutlery and began to carry them to the sink.

"You don't have to do that," said Miss MacIntosh, taking the dishes from my hands.

"But I would like to help you," I said, knowing that Marusia would expect nothing less. And the busywork helped me shake away the memory. I stood beside Miss MacIntosh as she filled the sink with hot sudsy water.

"Okay," she said, handing me a dish towel. "You can dry."

I took each plate as she placed it on the rack and dried it carefully, admiring the delicate pattern of matching pink roses as I placed them in her cupboard. The pieces were smooth and light to the touch. Not at all like the mismatched cups and plates that Ivan had found for us.

Miss MacIntosh drained the water from the sink and wiped the counter dry. "There," she said. "All done. I think it's time for a treat." She set out some small brown cookies on a plate. "Gingersnaps," she said, motioning me to sit back down at the table.

"Gingersnaps," I repeated. It was a nice word but didn't exactly roll off the tongue.

They looked like *medvinyky*—honey cookies. I picked one up and sniffed it. They did not smell like honey. They smelled of that other scent that I had noticed when I first arrived at Miss MacIntosh's house. I took a tiny bite. The cookie was crispy like a honey cookie, but its taste was like biting into a memory . . .

The blond woman has her servant make cookies with a sweet yet peppery taste. And they are shaped like men. Gingerbread men. I bite off the head and swallow it down, and then an arm and a leg. I stare at the half-eaten cookie and feel ill. "Eat," the blond woman says.

The gingersnap was a dry lump in the back of my throat. I looked up. Miss MacIntosh was watching me intently again. I tried to swallow but nearly choked. I gulped down some milk and the cookie slid down my throat.

"Good," I said weakly. Miss MacIntosh smiled.

There was a tap-tapping at the kitchen door. Had Marusia given up on her job search and come to get me?

Miss MacIntosh opened the door. It wasn't Marusia. It was that boy from last night—Mychailo.

He looked from Miss MacIntosh to me. He frowned.

"You can come in," said Miss MacIntosh. "I have cookies."

Mychailo stepped in, then plopped himself down in one of the spare kitchen chairs. "Is she teaching you English already?" he asked me in Ukrainian.

"Ask her in English, Mychailo," said Miss MacIntosh.

Mychailo rolled his eyes and reached for a cookie. He popped it whole into his mouth and hardly chewed at all before swallowing. He looked at me and said in painfully slow and loud English, "Are you learning to speak English, Nadia?"

"Tak."

Miss MacIntosh gave me a look.

"Yes," I said. "I am learning to speak English."

Miss MacIntosh nodded with approval. "When you've finished your snack, you two can play in the backyard for a bit if you like."

I didn't know whether I wanted to play with Mychailo. What I longed to do was to go back into Miss MacIntosh's living room and look at her books.

Mychailo gulped down his milk and looked at me. "Let's go," he said in English, pointing to the back door.

Miss MacIntosh's swing was just like mine, but the wood was darker and more worn. Did she swing on this herself? How funny it would be to see a grown woman on a swing!

She was standing at the back door, watching us, so Mychailo said in careful English, "Nadia, sit, and I will push you."

Miss MacIntosh nodded in approval, then went back inside.

I sat down on the swing and pumped with my legs a little to get the rhythm going, and then Mychailo pushed so hard that it took my breath away. "Be gentle," I said in Ukrainian.

"You'll never learn if you keep speaking Ukrainian!" said Mychailo in a voice that mimicked Miss MacIntosh.

"You are hurting me."

Either he didn't understand my English or he didn't care. Each time the swing brought me close to him, he pushed hard on my back. The swing went so high that I was afraid it would loop around and get tangled in the branches of the tree. Yet with each push, I felt the wind in my face and the freedom of flying in the air.

"STOP!"

"If that's what you want," said Mychailo, stepping away from the swing. He plopped down on the lawn and combed the grass with his fingers, ignoring me completely.

I stretched out my feet and dragged them along the ground to slow the swing down, but it was going so fast that I lost one shoe. I panicked and jumped, landing flat on my face on the lawn.

"You are so stupid," said Mychailo. He continued to comb through the blades of grass while I dusted myself off.

The back door opened and Miss MacIntosh stood there. "Lesson time in ten minutes," she said.

I sat on the grass beside Mychailo. "Are you getting English lessons too?" I asked.

"Yes," he said. "I come here every afternoon."

"But your English is already good," I said.

"My parents like me to come, and Miss MacIntosh is a nice lady, so I don't mind. And she makes good cookies."

I mulled this over. Did it mean that I would be coming here every day as well? If I learned quickly, would I only have to come in the afternoons? I also didn't know how I felt about spending so much time with Mychailo.

"Where did you live before the war?" asked Mychailo.

His question took me by surprise. "In . . . in . . . Zolochiv."

Mychailo rolled his eyes. "You are such a bad liar."

He was right. I was lying. But what he didn't realize was that I had lived a lie for so long that I couldn't remember where I had really come from. The lying had come naturally at the camp. If I hadn't done it then, they would have taken me away from Marusia. But something strange had begun to happen since coming to Canada. I was beginning to have flashes from the past, like the ones today, but they were like pieces of a jigsaw puzzle that didn't fit.

"What makes you think I'm lying?" I asked.

"You have a funny accent," he said. "My parents were born in Zolochiv. Ivan is from Zolochiv. But you are definitely from somewhere else."

It scared me to think that this boy knew more about my past than I did. "Was Ivan . . . I mean . . . my father . . . a friend of your parents?" I asked.

"My father was in the Underground with Ivan," said Mychailo. "They fought the Nazis together."

He said nothing more for a while but instead concentrated on raking the grass with his hands. "That's what you remind me of," he said.

"What?" I asked.

"With that hair of yours and those eyes? A Nazi."

And then without a glance at me, he stood up and walked into the house.

CHAPTER FOUR
AM I A NAZI?

I felt strange spending the rest of the afternoon with Mychailo after his Nazi remark. It got me wondering, though. At the DP camp, most people could speak many languages, but no one sounded quite like me. When we first arrived, some people had commented that I didn't sound like my mother and we didn't look like each other, but Marusia would always hush them.

Miss MacIntosh had Mychailo work on his Composition at the kitchen table and she continued to go through the word book with me. I was glad that he wasn't sitting right beside me.

Whenever we paused, I would glance up at the photograph of the soldier on Miss MacIntosh's mantel. Once, she followed my gaze and sighed. "I was going to marry him," she said. "He died in France, fighting the Nazis."

What did Miss MacIntosh think of me? With my blond hair and blue eyes and funny way of talking, did she think I was a Nazi too? That I was responsible for her fiancé's death? My throat choked with tears.

Marusia thought it would be good for me to remember all that I could about the time before we met. She always insisted that I had nothing to feel guilty about. I tried to remember, but all that came to me were bits and pieces. Nothing that made sense. It was all so confusing. I looked up at this kind lady, Miss MacIntosh, and said, "I am sorry he died."

Even though the war hadn't come to Canada, her fiancé had gone to the war. I guess this is why it was called a world war.

The afternoon sped by. I was so caught up in learning the new words that when there was a tapping on the front door, I jumped in surprise. When Miss MacIntosh opened the door, there stood Marusia, looking sad and tired.

Miss MacIntosh let me take the word book home so that Marusia and Ivan and I could all practice our English together. I slipped my hand into Marusia's and gave it a squeeze as we walked down the street. She looked at me, startled. Her eyes filled with tears, but she smiled.

"I will find a job," she said. "Don't you worry."

That made me smile. For as long as I could remember, all I did was live day by day. It meant that I didn't worry. But it also meant that I had stopped hoping.

As we walked down the street hand in hand, Marusia looked at me. "What is the matter, Nadia?" she asked.

I didn't say anything for a bit. We had been through this all before, but then I blurted out, "I'm a Nazi, aren't I?"

Marusia stopped walking. She turned and looked me in the eye. "No, *Sonechko*, you are *not* a Nazi."

"Am I German?"

Marusia shook her head.

"Then why do I look like a Nazi?" I asked. "The other children in the DP camp didn't look like me and they didn't sound like me. Mychailo sounds different from me. *You* sound different from me."

Marusia's eyes filled with tears. "Has Mychailo said something to you?"

I don't like to snitch and I don't like to lie. "He and I don't sound the same."

"You are not a Nazi and you are not German," she said firmly.

"But I remember the place that you stole me from!" I said.

Marusia put one hand on her hip and pointed a finger at me. "Have I ever treated you unkindly?"

"No."

"Have I treated you like anything less than I would if you were my own flesh?"

"No."

"Then trust me when I tell you that I never stole you and you are not a Nazi."

She reached out to grab my hand but I held it behind my back. I was furious with her, although I didn't quite know why. We walked the rest of the way home in silence.

When we got to our house, we saw a truck filled with sheets of plywood parked in front of it. Two men that I recognized from the night before—one of them was Mychailo's father—were unloading wood from the back of the truck. A third man was holding our front door open.

"Come on, let's see what they're doing!" I said to Marusia.

We followed the men into the living room. I blinked in surprise. Just yesterday, this space was nothing more than bare wooden frames, but now plywood sheets had been nailed over the framework, making it an enclosed room. I stepped into the bedroom. Ivan had taken his shirt off and his back glistened with sweat. He was kneeling in the corner, carefully hammering in small nails along one side of a piece of plywood that another man held in place. Three walls of the bedroom were already covered.

Before the walls went up, the house had seemed open and airy and free. I wish it could have stayed like that. But I breathed in deeply the scent of fresh sawdust and pasted a smile onto my face for Ivan.

He looked up when he heard us step in. "Here are my girls," he said, grinning.

"You are such a fast builder!" said Marusia.

"I wanted to have the walls up before you got to Brantford," said Ivan. "But I've been working overtime the past few weeks and the days got away from me." He gestured toward the other men. "What would I do without my good friends?"

"You all must be hungry," said Marusia. "We shall make you something to eat."

The sound of nails echoed through the kitchen as I helped Marusia put something quick together. Once the men had eaten and finished up their work, they left, promising to be back the next day.

Ivan and Marusia sat on the cinder-block step, sipping mugs of tea after everyone had left. I sat on my swing and listened to their conversation.

"When do you sleep, Ivashko?" Marusia asked, brushing his forehead with her fingertips. "You barely closed your eyes last night before it was time for you to get up."

"I will sleep once the house is finished," said Ivan.

"Can you take a rest now?" asked Marusia. "Why don't you lie down on the mattress?"

"It's still light out," he protested. "I can get some more work done on the house."

"Come." Marusia took his hand. "We'll lie down for a few minutes together. Just to rest our eyes."

I wanted to give them some time on their own. After all, they hadn't been married for very long, and they had been apart for a year. I got up from the swing and headed toward the front yard.

"Where are you going?" called Marusia.

"Exploring," I called back, trying hard to look happy.

"Stay in the neighborhood," she said. "And come home before it gets dark."

I smiled to myself at that. Did Marusia really think I would go very far? I sat on the front steps for a while and looked up and down the street. Maybe I would just sit here for an hour. I could hear children playing in the distance and a car or two passed. Once, a man wearing a suit and carrying a lunch box walked by. He tipped his hat to me and smiled, so I smiled back. That small gesture made me feel safer, I don't know why. Maybe this new life we had invented would be all right.

Mychailo had said that Central School was down the street from me. It couldn't be very far. I took a deep breath and stood up. *I am a Canadian girl now*, I told myself. *And Canadian girls walk down the street by themselves without fear.*

I forced myself to walk away from the house and down the street. I felt a little bit scared to be doing this, but I was proud of myself too. And the soft breeze on my face felt good. I walked past Miss MacIntosh's house until I got to George Street and then I saw what had to be the school: a huge old yellow brick building two and a half stories high, with a circular driveway in the front and a huge lawn.

There weren't many buildings this big left standing in Germany. It felt eerily safe to be walking in this unfamiliar area all by myself. There were no bombs, no men in uniform, no burnt-out buildings, no barbed wire.

I walked up to one of the windows and peered in. It was a classroom with rows of desks and various posters pinned to the wall. This one had a portrait of King George above the chalkboard—I recognized him from some of the coins I'd seen.

Which rulers had been on the walls of my other classrooms? I drew a blank. I sat down in the grass and leaned against the wall of the school. It wasn't time to go home yet. Perhaps I could walk just a bit farther? Three blocks away was a beautiful park, a church, and some rich-looking buildings across the road.

The building beside the church caught my eye. It had four marble pillars and a set of white steps leading up to fancy double doors on the second floor. I walked up the steps and stood on my toes so I could peer through the glass. I could see a marble entranceway, and beyond that, a room lined with books. How I longed to touch those books. To smell them . . .

"It's the library," said a familiar voice behind me.

"Why did you creep up on me like that?" I said, turning to face Mychailo.

He had a silly look on his face. "I didn't," he said. "You just didn't hear me."

I tried to stare him down but then noticed that he was holding a thick book.

"Did you get that from in there?" I asked.

"It is a library," he said. "What do you think?"

"How much did it cost?"

"It's free for me to read," he said. "As long as I return it."

"Who gets to use the library?" I asked.

"Anyone," he said. "You just have to fill out a form and they give you a library card. Then you can take out books as often as you want, as long as you return them after you've read them."

"Who decides what books you can read?"

"It's not like that in Canada," said Mychailo. "You can

read any book in the children's department, as long as you have a library card."

"Can I go in now?"

"It just closed," he said. "But do you want to go tomorrow after our class with Miss MacIntosh?"

I was beginning to warm to Mychailo. He could be rough and rude, but that could be said of any boy. This one liked books.

CHAPTER FIVE
EVA

I would have liked to sleep outside under the stars again, but angry clouds had formed in the sky just as the sun was setting. We swept up the sawdust, and Ivan dragged one mattress out to the middle of the living room.

"It's almost like you're outside," said Marusia. "This is a big room. And if you need us, we're right in there." She pointed to the bedroom. The look in her eyes told me that she was exhausted, and I knew that Ivan was even more tired, so I smiled and said that I would be fine. I took Miss MacIntosh's word book to bed with me and looked at the pictures and tried to sound out the words until it got dark.

The rain pounding on the rooftop muffled the sound of the frogs—or maybe frogs slept inside during the rain too? The rain was comforting, but the distant grumbling of thunder reminded me of gunfire.

The windows were bare, so when a car passed, strange

shapes played across the walls. I closed my eyes and concentrated on breathing deeply and hoped I would fall asleep quickly.

I am snuggled under a down comforter, surrounded by people who love me. I hear pounding on my door. I try to snuggle in and hide behind the others, but they've melted away. I am alone. More pounding at the door. A child's voice asking me to open up. Who is that child, and why does her voice terrify me?

I sat up with a jolt. Where was I? A frog chirped. I looked around in the darkness and saw moonlight coming in through the window. Rain still pounded on the rooftop. I was in Ivan's house in Brantford. This room had no furniture and smelled of freshly sanded wood. I was safe here. I wrapped my arms around my legs and rocked myself back and forth. I felt like screaming but I didn't know why. I closed my eyes and chanted the *kolysanka* under my breath.

Who was the girl I had dreamed of? I did not want to go back to sleep and I did not want to wake up Ivan and Marusia, so I tiptoed into the kitchen and poured myself a glass of water. I sat down at the table and watched the raindrops on the kitchen window. I wanted to remember that time. If I could figure out the puzzle, maybe the nightmares would go away. Marusia said I had nothing to be ashamed of. But how could she know that for sure? I stared out the window again, still thinking of that girl . . .

I am in the bedroom with the high ceiling. Raindrops trickle outside pink-curtained windows and I see the beginning of daylight peeking around the edges. There is a tap-tapping on the door.

It flies open and Eva bounds in. "Sister, you should be up by now!" She scrambles up onto my bed. "Wear your new pink dress," she says. "Then we'll match."

I watch her chubby feet as she slides off the bed and skips out the door. No one looking at us together would ever think that we match, even if we are both dressed in pink. I stay in bed for a moment longer. Why do I not feel safe in this room? It is all a girl could hope for, with its pink ruffled curtains and soft four-poster bed. A wooden box in the corner brims with stuffed toys. On the wall across from the bed is a high shelf holding a row of perfectly blond, blue-eyed dolls—all gifts from Vater. I do not like them.

As I get out of bed, one foot lands on the sharp corner of a book. I bend down and pick it up: Der Giftpiltz—The Poisonous Mushroom. *Another gift from Vater that I do not like. It slips out of my hands and crashes back to the floor. I brush the wrinkles out of my nightgown and walk barefoot to the bathroom. The air is damp and the mirror is covered with steam. Mutter must have just gotten up herself. She is probably waiting in the dining room for Eva and me.*

I grab my toothbrush, smear it with toothpaste, and give my teeth a quick brushing. I splash water on my face, making sure to dampen my soap bar so it looks like I used it, and then dry off with the pink towel that is stitched with the initials GH, *just like my other towels.*

A crack of thunder jolted me out of the past. For just a second, the kitchen was daylight-bright from lightning. The scene in my mind was still so vivid that I could almost feel the grit of toothpaste on my tongue. I took a slow sip from the glass of water on the table in front of me and tried to remember more, but the moment had passed. Was that girl—Eva—my sister? Why did I not love her?

There was nothing in that memory that was frightening, so why did it scare me so? And what did *GH* stand for? I did not want to go back to sleep, so I stayed sitting at the table and watched the rain and more lightning through the kitchen window. I'd had enough food and fine clothing back then. I'd had Mutter and Vater and Eva. Why was I not happy?

It was still dark when I heard the creak of footsteps on the wooden floor and the sound of the bathroom door swinging open—Ivan was getting ready for work. Through the kitchen window there was now a bare glimmer of morning light. I could see the outline of the swing, shimmering with rain. I remembered how happy Ivan was when he surprised me with it. Maybe I could surprise him now. I walked over to the sink and filled the kettle with water for tea and put it on a burner. I found the frying pan, set it on the other burner, took out some bacon from the icebox, and placed it in the frying pan. As the bacon sizzled, I cracked two eggs into the pan.

By the time the bathroom door opened, breakfast was waiting on the table at Ivan's spot.

He came into the kitchen in his work shirt and pants, smelling of soap and with his wet hair combed back. "Nadia," he said, glancing first at me and then at the plate of food. "What a surprise."

I could tell from the look in his eyes that he had a thousand questions. "I couldn't sleep," I told him. "And I wanted to do something special for you."

Ivan walked up behind my chair. He hugged my shoulders and kissed the top of my head. "You are such a sweet girl," he said. "Thank you."

"Eat," I told him, swallowing back tears. "It will get cold."

Ivan ate quickly and gulped down his tea. I knew that he didn't want to be late for work. After he left, I washed the dishes and prepared breakfast for Marusia and myself.

I took the word book with me when Marusia dropped me off at Miss MacIntosh's house after breakfast and we practiced new words and phrases. Mychailo came after lunch, just as he'd done the day before, but he seemed somehow nicer. He sat at the kitchen table with a workbook while I sat in the living room with Miss MacIntosh. Hours flew by.

"You learn so quickly, Nadia," Miss MacIntosh said with a smile. She took the word book from my lap and closed it, then set it on the coffee table. "Would you like to take this book home again with you?"

"Yes, please," I said.

"Why don't I bring Nadia to the library today?" Mychailo said from the kitchen. "Then she'd get to practice her English with different books."

Miss MacIntosh's face brightened. "What a lovely idea, Mychailo. If Marusia comes back before you two are finished at the library, I'll tell her where you are."

Mychailo didn't take me directly to the library. Instead, we walked around downtown for a bit. He showed me the movie theater, the market square, and the city hall. There was a long gray car parked out in front of city hall. "I think that's the mayor's," said Mychailo.

When we got to the library, we went up the big white steps to the glass doors and opened them. I was enveloped by a whoosh of cool air and the scent of books and furniture polish.

"The children's department is this way," said Mychailo, taking me to a set of inside stairs that went down to the basement. We walked up to a long counter in the middle of the main room. For a library, this room had surprisingly few books. The walls were wood-paneled and empty of shelves.

"Can't we go in there?" I said, pointing to the room on the left that was filled with books.

"We've got to find Miss Barry first," said Mychailo. "You need to get a library card."

Just then a pretty woman with blond curls and blue-framed glasses came in. "Good to see you, Mychailo," she said. "So you've brought a friend."

"This is Nadia."

I did a little curtsy and said, "Hello, Miss Barry."

"Nadia needs a library card," said Mychailo. "I can help her with the form."

Miss Barry went behind the counter and looked through the drawers. She handed me a pencil and a sheet of paper with questions and lines on it. "I need a phone number and address."

My heart sank. "We do not have a phone," I said. Did that mean that I couldn't have a library card?

Mychailo took the form from my hand. "I'll fill it out," he said. "And I'll put in the phone number of the foundry where your father works—my father works there too, so I know the number."

"Thank you, Mychailo!"

He led me into the room on the left. "These are good ones to start with," he said.

I gasped as I stepped into the room. All four walls were covered with shelves of books, and there were aisles of books as well . . .

A long-ago room filled with books, so many books, but I was forbidden to touch them . . .

"You should try this book," Mychailo said. He handed me one and read the title out loud, *The Little Engine That Could.* "I'll be in the other room for a while, so come and find me if you get bored."

I held the book up to my face and breathed in its lovely scent of ink and glue. It seemed hard to believe that I would be allowed to take a book home from this place. I opened it up. The images in this story niggled at my memory. *A train chugging along . . . boxes of toys . . . a blond doll with blue eyes . . .* Maybe this wasn't the book for me. I put it back on the shelf and pulled out one that had a painting of three little kittens on the front. Using the pictures as clues, I read as much as I could while I stood there . . . *kittens, mittens, cry.*

I did the same with a few more books. How would I ever choose? I put them all back on the shelf and wandered into the other room. These books were thicker and they didn't have as many pictures. I found Mychailo sitting in a corner, surrounded by books.

"Which one are you going to take out?" I asked him.

He looked up at me and then back down at the books on the floor. "I think I'll take *Tom Sawyer* today," he said. "Aren't you getting one?"

"I can't decide," I said.

"I'll show you some that I liked when I first came to Brantford," he said. He stacked the books from the floor and set them on a wheeled cart. With *Tom Sawyer* tucked in the crook of his arm, he walked to the picture-book room with me following close behind.

"Here's a good one," he said, reaching up and grabbing an oversized book from a shelf at the back. "It will help teach you the words for numbers in English."

It was a counting book very similar to Miss MacIntosh's word book. "Thanks, Mychailo," I said. "This is perfect."

When I got back home, Ivan was stretched out on the floor in our living room, carefully tapping nails into a narrow strip of wood along the bottom of the wall. "Can I get you anything?" I asked him.

Ivan looked up from his work and smiled. "I would love some water."

I went into the kitchen and set my library book on the table. I filled a glass with tap water and brought it out to the living room for Ivan. He drank it down quickly and handed the glass back to me.

When I took it back to the kitchen, I stood for a moment and stared out the window. I could see my own reflection there. My face, my eyes, my braids . . .

I am wearing the pink dress. The sight of it makes me feel sick.

When I get downstairs, Mutter is at the dining room table. Cook has served her porridge and Eva is halfway through hers. On the table is a crystal serving dish filled with berries, apples, and grapes.

Cook places a bowl in front of me, sprinkled with cinnamon and sugar. Even so, I hate it.

"The rally is in less than an hour," says Mutter, her eyes sparkling with excitement. "Eat quickly."

Eva shovels the last of her porridge into her mouth and swallows it down. She puts her spoon on the table with a clatter and stands up. "I'm finished!"

"Go get your hairbrush," says Mutter. "I'll fix your hair as soon as your sister and I finish our breakfast."

I swallow the cereal as quickly as I can, not caring so much what it tastes like but just to get it over with. Eva comes back with pink hair ribbons and a hairbrush and a hand mirror.

Mutter brushes out the tangles from Eva's dark blond hair until it hangs down her back in shiny waves. She expertly makes two braids, finishing off each with a pink ribbon.

When it is my turn, Mutter tugs at my hair and braids it up more tightly than she needs to. "There," she says with a cold edge in her voice. She hands me the mirror. "Don't you look lovely?"

The face that looks back at me is the same one as always. I never think of myself as lovely.

A long black car with a small swastika flag on each side of the hood idles in the driveway as we walk outside. A uniformed man opens the back door. Mutter gets in first, then Eva, then me. The upholstery is lush black leather that gleams from a fresh buffing. The car door is closed with a firm click and we speed away.

It takes half an hour of fast driving to get into the city. The streets narrow. Our driver slows down so we can wave to the blocks and blocks of cheering crowds.

When we get within walking distance of the stage, the car stops. Soldiers push the crowd away so we can get out, and then they lead us to the steps on the side of the stage. Most of the chairs are taken by Nazi officers, but there are a few other mothers and children as well. We take our spots in the front row, behind the podium.

The crowd roars as another long black car pulls up. When the führer steps out, the crowd goes wild. Vater gets out of the car just behind the führer.

The crowd chants "Heil Hitler! Heil Hitler!" *as the führer steps onto the stage, but it is as if he doesn't notice. He walks up to me and crouches down until we are eye level. He is so close to me that I can see his nose hair and smell the slightly spicy scent of his hair pomade.*

"What a perfect specimen of Aryan youth you are, my dear," he says, pinching my cheek. I smile. What else can I do? Vater stands behind the führer, bursting with pride, but Eva looks like she is about to cry and Mutter's lips are a thin white line. Vater sits down between Eva and Mutter. Vater grabs Mutter's hand and kisses it.

The führer walks to the podium and begins to . . .

"Nadia, what are you doing?"

I nearly jumped out of my skin at the sound of Marusia's voice. The empty glass almost shot out of my hand. I blinked twice. I was standing in front of the window in the kitchen of the Brantford house.

I turned to Marusia. She stood by the table, with Ivan beside her, his hammer in one hand and a look of concern on his face.

I shook my head, desperate to clear away the image of Hitler's face. If I'd met Hitler—*Hitler* himself—then I must be a Nazi. What secret was Marusia keeping from me? Who *was* I?

My face was wet with tears, but I couldn't remember crying. My legs felt wobbly, so I set the glass beside the sink and sat down at the table.

Marusia walked behind my chair. She wrapped her arms protectively around me and rested her head on my neck.

Ivan knelt beside us.

"Are you all right?" he asked. His eyes were round with fright.

"I was just thinking," I told them.

"You were shouting, '*Heil Hitler*,'" said Ivan, a troubled look in his eyes.

"What were you thinking about?" asked Marusia.

"The farmhouse and that family," I said. "But there was more."

"Do you want to talk about it?" she asked.

"No!" Couldn't she understand how ashamed I was? Marusia insisted that I wasn't a Nazi, but that's not what my memory was telling me. How I wished I could wash away that horrible past.

"You need to air these memories, Nadia," said Ivan. "And until you remember it all, you'll keep on having nightmares."

Was Ivan right? Maybe he was . . .

"Would it help if I told you about what happened to *me*

during the war?" he asked. He straddled the chair facing me and looked into my eyes.

Ivan's offer surprised me. He never talked about his past. "I would like to hear what you did during the war," I told him.

For a minute he said nothing and I saw his eyes fill with tears as his memories came drifting into his mind. He blinked the tears back and took a breath. "My story is one like so many others. The Soviets killed my father and brother in 1941. They were killing thousands of the men, even some of the women and children. I wasn't arrested with them—I thought at the time that I was lucky—but then the Nazis came."

Ivan's eyes met mine and I could feel my face flush with shame. He looked up at Marusia, who still stood behind me, her arms wrapped around me. Ivan gave a ragged sigh. "I thought nothing could compare to the Soviets, but I was wrong. The Nazis were just as bad. My sister was captured in a Nazi slave raid. My mother was sent to a concentration camp. I was the last of my family. I joined the Underground. Sometimes we fought the Nazis and sometimes we fought the Soviets. It depended on which front was closest. I escaped to a DP camp just as the war was ending."

So much sadness in so few words.

"I am sorry, Ivan." I could feel tears spilling down my cheeks.

"I needed to say that out loud," said Ivan. "And you should talk to us about what *you* remember." He gave me a long bear hug.

Maybe he was right. I just couldn't do it yet.

We were silent for a long time, each of us wrapped in our own thoughts. As I sat there, I tried to piece together what I now remembered about my past. The rich farmhouse and a bedroom filled with toys. A pink dress that I hated—why would I hate it so? Towels stitched with *GH*. What did *GH* stand for? Were Mutter, Vater, and Eva my real family? The scene of meeting Hitler face-to-face was etched in my brain—how I wished I could scrub that away, but it was vivid, right down to his smell.

Ivan hated the Nazis. Look what they'd done to his mother and sister. If I was a Nazi, then how could Ivan love me? How could anyone love me?

But how could I argue with these flashes from the past? My name wasn't really Nadia, but something starting with *G*. The farmhouse, the long black car, and Hitler—these images were like photographs in my mind.

I knew how easily Marusia could lie. Was she lying to me about my past?

CHAPTER SIX
LILACS

Summer went by quickly. Marusia got a job picking strawberries. When strawberry season was over, the same farmer hired her to work on his other crops. My days were taken up with lessons at Miss MacIntosh's house and visits to the library with Mychailo. Miss Barry grinned whenever she saw us. She would let us look at the new arrivals and would point out books that she thought we might like. The routine of the summer seemed to settle my mind. The flashbacks and nightmares seemed to go away.

On Saturday nights, if Ivan wasn't too tired, he, Marusia, and I would walk to the hall on Dundas Street. It was a rented building shared by all the Ukrainians in town—Catholic and Orthodox alike. Marusia especially loved it when we went out like this. For working on the farm, she wore a used pair of men's overalls and she would change into a secondhand housedress when she got home.

But for Saturday nights, she wore her one nice blouse and skirt.

Sometimes people at the hall would get together a band and there would be a dance. Other times, people would sit at tables and talk. Marusia would sit with a group who were writing letters to relief organizations, trying to find lost loved ones. They would update each other on their progress and compare notes.

I liked to go because there were other children who spoke Ukrainian. Mychailo would often be there. I was devastated to learn that none of the other Ukrainian children except for Mychailo would be attending Central School. There weren't that many of us and we were spread all over the city. There were two sisters who had been born in Canada. Their Ukrainian was not good. They went to Grandview. And a tall boy with glasses who spoke Ukrainian with a Polish accent was going to start at St. Basil's School.

Early each Sunday morning we would dress again in our good clothing and walk to the Ukrainian Catholic church on Terrace Hill Street, which was one block closer than the hall. It was a small church and there were so many people who attended that we had to get there early if we wanted to get a pew. The only inside place where I felt completely safe was sitting in that church. Few parishioners could sing on key, but that didn't bother me. I loved being enveloped in the hymns and I loved the smell of the incense. It made me feel protected.

Ivan worked on the house every day after work, and by the last week in August, it was finished. Each morning, Marusia got picked up by a truck to take her to the farm in Burford. Her hands were swollen from the long hours of working in the fields, but the money was needed.

I knew it was more than just her hands and the long hours that bothered her, though. Whenever the postman delivered mail, she looked through the envelopes with a hungry eye, but he never seemed to bring whatever she was waiting for. I asked her about it once, but her eyes filled with tears. "I cannot talk about it now," was all she told me. I think she was hoping to get news from the Red Cross about a relative. At the hall, when someone got one of these letters, everyone gathered round to hear it read aloud. Sometimes the news was bad, but when it was good, we all hooted for joy.

Marusia had once studied to be a pharmacist, but as a slave laborer during the war, she'd worked in a factory. Later on, she was forced to work as a cook at the German farm where we met. How awful it was for her to have to do hard labor again, even though she was supposed to be free. I would see a troubled look come over her face from time to time. Whenever I asked her what was wrong, she'd paste on a smile and say, "Nothing, Nadia. I was just thinking."

As often as we could, the three of us would sit down together on the cinder blocks in the backyard and pore over the books from the library and from Miss MacIntosh. Marusia's dream was to learn English well enough to get a job in a store or maybe even a pharmacy. Ivan's spoken English was good, but he had no way of learning how to write it. I think he was looking forward to me starting school because then I could teach him everything I learned.

The week before school was to start, Ivan greeted me at the door when I came in from Miss MacIntosh's. He had a grin on his face. "The day has come to choose the color of your room."

No, no, no. I had become used to sleeping in the living room on cold or rainy nights, and outside when the weather was hot.

"I don't need a bedroom," I said. "Why don't I sleep in the living room always?" Ivan looked at me with one eyebrow raised. "Then you could use that upstairs room for storage."

He shook his head. "Nadia, you need your own room."

I said nothing. Ivan caught my hand in his and led me out the door. "You'll see," he said. "In time you'll like having a bedroom again."

The paint store was on Colborne Street—two big blocks around the corner from the library. Ivan held the door open with one hand and made a sweeping motion with his other. I stepped in. The wet-paint smell tugged at the edges of my memory but, thankfully, no images came.

Shiny metal cans were stacked against the walls and in the aisles. I expected to see different colors, but the cans were mostly covered with white labels. On a stand beside the cashier's counter was a book of color chips. Ivan led me to it. He flipped it open at random and the page revealed shades of yellow and gold. He looked at me expectantly, but I shook my head. Yellow meant sunshine and I loved sunshine, but yellow made me sad . . .

I am in that long black car. It is just me and Vater and the chauffeur. We are taken to a cluster of buildings surrounded by barbed wire. The sign at the entrance says Work Shall Set You Free. *The gates open and the chauffeur drives in. I feel sick. Vater grabs my hand and pulls me out of the car as he gets out.*

He leads me past a snaking line of hungry-eyed women and children. Some wear heavy clothing and others are dressed for summer. They all wear one thing in common: a yellow hand-stitched star. A girl my age is in a yellow dress that once was beautiful. Maybe her mother thought a yellow star wouldn't show on a yellow dress. As we pass, the girl looks me in the eye.

"Don't stare at them," says Vater, pulling me by the hand. We step into a storage area beyond the lineup. Crates and boxes brim over with fancy clothing: fur coats, blue satin slippers, a tiara—even what looks like a new wedding gown. A well-fed man sitting behind a desk doesn't get up when we enter, but he nods as if he is expecting us. My heart pounds with fear. Is Vater angry with me? Is he leaving me here? I have no yellow star.

The man grins at me as he looks me up and down. His teeth are yellow and his uniform collar is so tight that his neck bulges. "You must be Gretchen," he says.

I am too frightened to speak.

"You'll need better clothes than that," he says, looking at my blue tunic and white blouse. He turns to Vater. "I will find her something good."

We walk back out, past the women and children with the yellow stars. I can feel more than one pair of eyes like heat on my back . . .

"What about this one?" said Ivan.

Gretchen . . .

I blinked once.

Gretchen Himmel. *GH.* My name was Gretchen Himmel.

I blinked again. I was back in the paint store with Ivan. I looked down at the color he was pointing to. A pale buttery yellow. "No," I said. Yellow meant death. I could never sleep in a yellow room. I flipped the page so quickly that I nearly tore it.

"Careful," said Ivan, smoothing down the crease in the glossy paper.

My mind was still swirling between past and present. I clutched onto the side of the counter so I wouldn't fall.

Ivan looked at me strangely. "What's wrong, Nadia?"

I took a deep breath and tried to clear my thoughts. "I am fine," I said. I wanted to get this over with. "Let's look at some other colors."

Next were pinks and reds—everything from the palest blush of that long-ago pink brocade dress to the violent red of blood. *No, no, no.*

The next page showed blues. My hand reached out of its own accord and touched a pale mauve. A wisp of scent tickled the edge of my brain. Lilac bushes in a much-loved garden.

"You'd like your room to be that color?" Ivan asked. And I surprised myself. Yes, I did want that color. Lilac would make me feel safe. I still wasn't happy about the thought of being closed up in a small room all night, but the color would be soothing. And maybe I could convince Ivan to leave the door off.

He handed a lilac paint chip to the clerk and ordered one can. We walked home, carrying the can between us.

Ivan and I painted the room together. It didn't take long. It was a small room, after all. But I still slept in the living room for the next few days to give the walls a chance to dry.

I was a bundle of nerves that first night in my own bedroom. But Ivan had found a secondhand lamp for me and he set it on the wooden crate that was my nightstand. "If you get scared, turn on the light," he whispered. He sat at the edge of my mattress and sang the *kolysanka* until I fell asleep. I dreamed of lilac bushes on a sunny, windy day . . .

CHAPTER SEVEN
SCHOOL

I didn't see much of Marusia in those last weeks of summer. Some days she worked such long hours at the farm that she wouldn't get home until after dinnertime. The task of making an evening meal had fallen to me, but I didn't mind. I reveled in all the farm produce that Marusia would bring home, depending on the day or week—lettuce, cucumbers, corn, tomatoes, peaches, onions. In the camp, we ate rice, rice, and more rice. Now our dinners were a big salad or corn, boiled potatoes, and maybe a bit of sausage.

On the morning that I was to start school, Marusia woke me up early and said, "I have a surprise for you."

When she did it and how she found the time, I do not know, but she had made me a blouse and skirt from that bolt of blue cloth that one of the ladies had brought on our first day here. She had edged the collar with white hand-stitched daisies and had ironed smartly creased pleats into the skirt. I looked up at her through my tears.

"Put it on, *Sonechko*. You don't want to be late on your first day."

I slid my arms into the sleeves and as I did up each small white button, I noticed the delicate white stitches that circled each buttonhole. The skirt fit perfectly. Marusia gave me a new pair of white knee socks. Then, with a grin, she pulled out black shiny shoes from a paper bag. I tugged the socks up to my knees and then slipped my feet into the shoes.

"They're almost new," said Marusia. "I hope you like them."

I usually tried to stay dignified with Marusia. She was not my mother, after all. But I felt the love she had put in every pleat and the affection of each stitch in this new blouse. I looked at the frayed corner of her own carefully pressed blouse and the lines of weariness under her smiling eyes. I scrambled onto her lap and hugged her fiercely. I could feel hot tears spilling down my cheeks.

"Nadia, my Nadia," Marusia said, drying my tears with the back of her hand. "I wanted to make you happy."

I tried to answer but I could not speak. I just nodded, hoping she realized how much I appreciated all that she did for me. I splashed cold water on my face to calm my swollen eyes, and then Marusia braided my hair.

Instead of doing it the usual way, she coiled it up like a crown and then topped it off with a huge white bow. I looked at myself in the mirror—seeing another me in another mirror. A younger me wearing a pink dress, my eyes red from crying . . .

"You look like you've seen a ghost," said Marusia.

I blinked. That younger me was gone like a wisp of smoke.

Marusia walked me to Central School. We were the first to arrive.

She pushed the door open and we stepped into the empty hallway. "Your room is down here," she said, tugging at my hand as she turned and walked down a corridor to the left. She knocked on the door, and when no one answered she turned the knob. The door opened. "Good luck," she said. She put her fingertips to her lips and blew a kiss to me as she walked out of the school. It wasn't until she was gone that I realized her walking me to school meant she had missed her ride to work.

I stepped inside the empty classroom. I had peered

into this very classroom when I had taken my first walk around the neighborhood. A large blackboard and a big desk were at the front. Rows of desks filled the rest of the room. Which one should I take? Would the teacher be upset if she came in and found me in the wrong place? I took a chance and sat in a desk in the back corner, then waited for the others to arrive.

In the camp, one of the men who had been a professor before the war taught the few older children a bit of history. A woman who knew English had held classes for the adults as well as children. We sat on benches and used our laps as desks. On the wall had been a paper poster of Taras Shevchenko, Ukraine's most famous poet. I don't know where the picture came from. I can't imagine anyone escaping the war with it. Maybe it arrived in a CARE package from Canada or the United States. I also had a vague recollection of lessons in German from a stern-faced woman in a one-room schoolhouse, but when this was I could not remember.

I looked down at the beautiful blue outfit that Marusia had made for me. I ran my fingers lightly over the fabric, loving that each stitch had been made just for me . . .

Vater in the drawing room cuts an imposing figure in his black uniform. I see that his tall leather boots are covered with mud. No matter. There are slaves to clean up after him. He sets a package on top of the table and sits down. Mutter sits across from him, with her back rigid on the divan, a stiff smile on her lips. She pats the spot beside her. Eva scrambles to sit there. I sit beside Eva.

"This is for you, Gretchen," he says.

At first I am excited. I lean over and touch the brown paper lightly with one finger.

"Open it!" says Eva.

I look at her and see that she is almost bursting with excitement.

I pull the package to my lap and tear it open. A beautiful pink brocade dress. It is not like anything I have ever had before. I know I am supposed to be happy, but the sight of this dress makes me feel ill. I look up at Vater and put a smile on my face.

"Thank you," I say.

Vater grins. "Now the entire Himmel family will look nice at the rallies."

I take it to my room. I hold it to my shoulders and turn to the mirror. I look like someone else.

That night, I cannot sleep. I turn on my bed lamp and get the dress. It smells of fresh laundry soap and a faint scent of something else. Sweat? I turn it inside out and examine it for clues. I notice an extra ribbon of cloth attached along the side of the back zipper. I fold it over. A name tag. Tiny embroidered letters: Rachel Goldstein.

A sudden image of that girl in the lineup, the one in yellow.

I push the dress away from me.

Children's voices coming through the classroom window, laughing and calling, sounding excited, yanked me back to the present. Tears welled in my eyes, so I took a deep breath and tried to calm myself.

I could tell from the sounds outside that other children were getting closer, but none of them came into the classroom. Maybe I should have waited outside instead of coming into this room? But just then a woman with straight hair cut to her chin walked in and I was trapped.

She smiled at me and said, "You must be our new student, Natalie Kraftchuk."

I stumbled to my feet and bowed my head to her, and in my best English I said, "Good morning, Mrs. Teacher. My name is Nadia Kravchuk."

She held out her hand to me. "I am Miss Ferris. The other children will be coming in soon."

I shook her hand. She turned and left the room, so I sat back down.

I heard a loud bell and nearly jumped back out of my seat. Within minutes, the hallway buzzed with children's voices. Miss Ferris came back into the classroom. Behind her was a line of children.

CHAPTER EIGHT
HUMILIATION

A gangly boy with short hair was the first to enter the classroom. He gazed around, then his eyes locked on mine. I could feel my embarrassment rising like heat as he stared at my shoes, my outfit, the bow in my hair. And then he laughed. I would have crawled under my desk if I could. He elbowed the boy who was coming in after him and pointed at me. That boy grinned. Next came a girl. She was dressed in a skirt and blouse, but nothing fancy. Her hair fell in loose curls to her shoulders. No bow. No braids. She glanced in my direction and then quickly looked away as if she hadn't seen me. She took a seat as far away from me as she could. Other students came in after her. Not one said hello and each scrambled to get a desk far away from me.

The last student to enter was a girl with golden skin and a glossy black braid that reached down almost to her waist. There was nowhere else to sit except beside me, so she did. She turned to me and smiled—she had a gap between her two front teeth and her eyes were friendly.

"Hi," she said. "My name is Linda. What's yours?"

Linda. What a beautiful name. I could have cried from relief.

"Nadia," I said. I wanted to ask if she lived in the neighborhood, but I was such a bundle of nerves that the English words left me. Instead, I smiled stupidly at her.

"Children!" Miss Ferris stood at the front of the room and clapped her hands. "We have two new students this year. Natalie and Bob, please stand up."

Why was she calling me Natalie? I stumbled to my feet. A boy at the opposite side of the room also stood up, the tips of his ears turning red from the attention.

"Children, let us all welcome Natalie Kravchuk and Bob Landry."

"Welcome to Central School, Natalie and Bob," the students called out in ragged unison.

We both sat down. Bob's entire ears were now red, as was his face. I'm sure I was just as red. Miss Ferris took attendance and then passed out new workbooks and thick pencils. Then she had each of us stand up one by one and tell the class what we had done over the summer.

Because I was at the back of the class, my turn was last. That gave me time to prepare, but it also gave me time to get nervous. I had no idea how to explain what I did over the summer. I could do it in Ukrainian or Russian or Yiddish or German . . . but English? Finally, it was my turn. I stood up.

"I am *Nadia* Kravchuk. I moved to Canada this summer," I said slowly and carefully.

There were rumblings of chuckles around me. I was about to sit down, but Miss Ferris said, "What did you do when you got here, Natal—Nadia?"

"I learned English."

One of the boys at the front of the class burst out laughing. "Not very well," he called out.

"Yeah," someone else said, "and she looks like a Nazi."

I could feel my face go hot with shame. My last name had been Himmel. I'd had a sister named Eva. I called my parents *Mutter* and *Vater*. Wasn't I a Nazi?

Marusia had told me again and again that I wasn't, but what about my memories? Her words and my memories didn't seem to match.

Miss Ferris rapped a ruler hard on her desk and shouted, "Silence!" She pointed at the two boys. "David and Eric, go to the principal's office. *Now*." I sat down, wishing I could disappear. It was bad enough that I looked and dressed differently from everyone else, but my accent made me stand out too.

I'm not quite sure what else Miss Ferris taught us that morning. All I could think about was getting home so I could change my clothes and comb out my hair. How I wished I could change my accent!

I dutifully copied down the things that our teacher wrote on the board and I murmured thanks under my breath when she didn't call on me to say anything more. After what seemed like too many hours, a bell rang. I watched the others put their workbooks away. Thank goodness. My torture was over.

I closed up my books and shoved them into the desk and then followed the other students out the door. Linda, the one friendly student, was close behind me. As soon as the freshness of the outside air hit my face I felt a sense of relief. It had been like a prison in there. I began to walk out of the schoolyard and toward my house.

Linda trotted beside me and tugged on my arm. "You can't leave school property!"

I turned to her in confusion. The bell had rung, after all. "But the bell . . ."

Her mouth widened in its gap-toothed smile. "That was just the recess bell. You can't go home until the lunch bell."

“I cannot stay here.”

“They’ll send the truant officer after you!”

“The what?” I asked.

“The police. You can’t go home during school.”

Even the thought of police didn’t stop me from leaving. Linda stood at the edge of the schoolyard with shock on her face, but I kept on going, picking up speed as I got farther from the school. The dressy shoes pinched my heels, but I didn’t slow down. By the time I got to our house I had a stitch in my side. I flipped the welcome mat at the front door and grabbed the key, opened the door, and hurried in.

I had rarely been in the house alone and was struck by its eerie quiet. It was almost like the house was watching me with silent disapproval. I kicked off my shoes and ran upstairs, taking comfort in the sound of my feet thumping against the wooden steps. I threw myself onto the bed, punching my pillow in anger. How could I go back to that school? The other children hated me.

I shrieked at the top of my lungs and that felt good, because only the house could hear me and I could be as miserable as I wanted. Once the tears began, they wouldn’t stop. I cried out of pity for myself as the new kid at school. I cried in anger for feeling so helpless. But mostly I cried out of shame for the girl that I must have been in the past.

Did I really belong here? Was I a Nazi? Maybe I didn't deserve to be safe. Where *did* I belong?

I don't know how long I cried, but my eyes got so puffy I could barely open them. I looked down at the beautiful outfit that Marusia had made me and realized that it was now wrinkled and damp. What an ungrateful, horrible person I was. How would Marusia feel about me now? Would she send me back to that other family, the one I had tried to push out of my memory?

I unbuttoned my blouse and tried to shake out the wrinkles. I hung it on a hanger and put it on the hook on the back of my door. I undid the skirt and stepped out of it, being careful not to damage it further. I folded it and smoothed out the wrinkles with my hands and then carefully set it in my top dresser drawer. I took out the oldest skirt and blouse that I could find and put those on instead.

"It's all you deserve, you ungrateful thing."

It was *my* voice saying it, but it sounded like something I had heard long ago. I tried to undo my braids. I was able to get the elastics out from the bottom, but I couldn't undo the elaborate knot on the top of my head because Marusia had wrapped my braids together so tightly with the big white bow. My arms ached from the effort. I lay back down on the bed. I wanted to sleep but couldn't, so I stared at the ceiling.

A scene from my past slid into my mind . . .

The men were separated from the women. I stood on my toes to see where they were going but it was too crowded. I thought of that girl in the yellow dress with the yellow star, standing in a lineup just like this.

"Remove all of your clothing," said a uniformed woman in a bored voice.

I turned to Marusia in alarm, but she was already unbuttoning her tattered and filthy blouse. She threw it on the pyramid of burning clothing. She took off her skirt and threw it in the fire as well. "Hurry, Nadia," she said.

My outfit had once been a pink party dress, but now it was blackened with grease and grass and sweat. How many flatcars had we ridden on and how many ditches had we hidden in to get to this place? The days blurred in my memory. I tried to undo my once-delicate ribbon belt, but it was shredded so badly that I couldn't find the beginning of the knot. And I couldn't reach the zipper at the back of the dress.

Marusia put her hands at the collar of my dress and with a single motion ripped it off me. She threw it into the fire.

"Undergarments too," said the woman.

We threw it all into the fire and then stood in the next line.

A woman with a large pair of shears cut off my braids, then snipped away until my scalp was bare. I watched my filthy hair fall onto the ground in clumps.

Marusia's face remained still as her hair was cut away. We stepped into line with the other refugees waiting for showers. At the door a woman sprayed us with something awful. I screamed.

"It will be all right," said Marusia. "That's just to kill the lice."

We crowded into the white-tiled room and were enveloped in scalding streams of water. I watched black trickles of grime and dead lice swirling down the floor drain.

I was glad to be free of that pink dress and all that it stood for. We were given sheets to cover our nakedness when we exited the shower. The sheets had lice, but we wrapped ourselves in them anyway.

Next came the interview. We stood in line yet again, shivering and damp, but cleaner than we had been since our escape. I stood on my toes to see what was happening at the front of the line. A uniformed man sat at a table, taking notes. He stamped a paper and sent the refugee in either one direction or another.

Marusia bent down and whispered in my ear. "Tell them you're my daughter. Your name is Nadia. You were born in Lviv . . ."

I knew that if they found out where I really came from, the Soviets would take me and I would be sent to Siberia. But where did I really *come from? That I didn't know. Did Marusia?*

A loud banging at the door snapped me back to the

present. Linda had said it was against the law to run away from school. Were the police after me? I was too terrified to move.

Another banging. "Nadia!" A familiar woman's voice.

I peeked out the edge of my window. It was Miss MacIntosh. Maybe I could pretend that I wasn't home. But just as I was thinking that, she saw me. "Open the door!" she called. She didn't look happy.

I walked down the stairs but still didn't open the door. I ran to the bathroom and looked at my face in the mirror. My eyelids were puffed out and red and my face was swollen. What would Miss MacIntosh think? I ran cold water over a cloth and held it to my face. The coolness was soothing, but when I looked back in the mirror, the same puffy eyes looked back at me. It was no use.

The knocking on the door was more insistent than ever now. "Nadia!" Miss MacIntosh called. "I know you're in there."

I opened the front door. The expression on Miss MacIntosh's face transformed in an instant from annoyance to concern. She stepped in and shut the door behind her.

"What's happened to you?"

I looked down at my feet and didn't answer. I was afraid that if I tried, it would be sobs, not words, that would come out.

All at once I felt Miss MacIntosh's warm arms envelop me and she picked me up like I was nothing more than a baby. She hugged me close and I felt myself go limp. I didn't know whether it was relief or resignation. She carried me into the kitchen and sat down on a wooden chair, still holding me in her arms. She rocked me on her lap, even though my legs were almost as long as hers and my feet could touch the floor. She murmured, "It's going to be fine, Nadia."

I almost started to cry again, but something deep inside told me that it was time to stop. So instead, I took a deep breath and let it out slowly. I got myself out of Miss MacIntosh's arms and stood up.

"Why are you here?" I asked.

"You ran away from school," she said. "You need to come back."

"I cannot." I folded my arms and tried to look defiant.

"You don't have a choice," said Miss MacIntosh. "It's against the law to run away from school."

So what Linda had told me was true. Would the police be coming next?

Miss MacIntosh must have noted the panic on my face. She said, "If you come back this afternoon, everything will be fine."

"But how can I go back, looking like this?"

"Be strong, Nadia," Miss MacIntosh said sternly. "I'm

not even supposed to be here right now. I have yard duty. But when Linda told me you had run off, I had to check on you."

She stood up and opened our icebox. She took out two apples. "Hold these on your eyes. It will make the swelling go down."

As I did that, I could hear her making kitchen sounds—slicing bread and frying eggs. The aroma of sizzling butter and eggs made my stomach grumble. I heard a plate clatter onto the table.

"Eat," said Miss MacIntosh.

I took an apple off one eye. She was sitting across from me, eating an open-faced egg sandwich with a knife and fork. I set both apples down and devoured my own lunch. I was surprised at how hungry I was.

I took both plates to the sink and rinsed them when we were finished.

"We need to leave in fifteen minutes," said Miss MacIntosh. "I want to fix your hair."

We went into the bathroom together, and I watched in the mirror as Miss MacIntosh carefully undid Marusia's elaborate braids from the top of my head. "It was a beautiful hairdo," she said. "Just not right for school."

As she combed out my hair, a strange expression appeared on her face. "You've got a black mark here," she said. "Right at the hairline."

I inhaled sharply. My tattoo. I turned my left palm upward and stared at the same mark on my inner wrist, but I turned it back down before Miss MacIntosh saw it. Both tattoos were so plain that most people didn't notice.

"It must be a mole," I lied.

I watched Miss MacIntosh's face in the mirror. She was about to say something but then changed her mind. Sometimes I wondered if she knew more about my past than I did. She gently combed out the tangles. The comb in my hair reminded me of another woman who had tackled my tangles, but with the tug of resentment, not care. With it came another flicker of that pink brocade dress . . .

Miss MacIntosh didn't walk to school with me, which I was thankful for. She must have sensed how humiliating it was for me to go back at all, and arriving with a teacher would be that much more unbearable.

My eyes were still red from crying when I got back to school. The first bell had rung and students were just forming into lines. Some of the kids in my class looked up at me, then quickly turned away. Maybe Miss Ferris had said something to them. But then I heard Eric mutter, "The Hitler girl's back."

I stepped in behind Linda. "Good to see you!" she whispered.

I sat down in the same desk and tried to act as if nothing had happened. As Miss Ferris droned on with her lessons, I tried to sort out my recent memories. Why was it all coming back to me now? When we were in the DP camp, I'd just pushed my thoughts out of my mind. I tried that on the ship, and it had mostly worked. But when we got to Brantford, the nightmares started up and the memories came back. Why wouldn't the sadness leave me alone?

Once we were all seated, I stared at the back of Eric's head a few seats in front of me. Why did he call me the Hitler girl? It was such a mean thing to do. I noticed that his brown hair was carefully trimmed short around the ears and was left a bit longer on top. He probably hadn't combed it since the morning, but it looked perfect. I was sure that it was a barber who had cut it, not a soldier. Had he ever had his hair hacked off for lice? Could he even imagine such a thing? How dare he judge me.

I looked up and down the rows of children in front of me. Each boy and girl looked well fed and clean. No one was dressed in rags. They probably all had parents. My heart ached with jealousy. How I wished I lived a simple life that had never been touched by war.

CHAPTER NINE
MYCHAILO

I knew that Mychailo was the only other Ukrainian student at Central School, but I didn't see him until afternoon recess. He was tossing coins against a wall with some other boys and caught my eye. He nodded and went back to his game.

I saw him later walking home about a block behind me. I waited for him, but he was with the boys from earlier. He walked right past me as if he didn't know me, so I walked the rest of the way home by myself.

Since I was the first one home, I began to peel some potatoes for supper. I had just filled a pot with water when there was a knock on the front door. It was Mychailo, a sheepish expression on his face.

"So, suddenly you know who I am?" I said.

"Come on," he said, shuffling his feet. "You didn't expect me to talk to you when I'm with a bunch of guys, did you?"

“I don’t see why not.” I left the door open, but walked back to the sink. He followed me in and sat down on a kitchen chair, watching me peel the potatoes.

“Want to go to the library?” he asked.

I did want to go to the library, but I was still angry, so I didn’t answer.

“Are you going to cook them on low while we’re gone?” he asked.

I shook my head but still didn’t say anything.

“You are going to go with me, aren’t you?”

I liked that. It sounded a little like an apology. I finished peeling the last potato, rinsed them all off, and put them in the pot of water. I didn’t turn it on. Marusia had told me never to do that.

“I can go to the library for a short visit,” I said. “I’ll boil the potatoes when I get back.”

Mychailo was silent for the first few minutes of our walk, then he said, “Sorry for not talking to you before.”

I didn’t say anything. I knew why he didn’t talk to me. He didn’t want to be teased. But it felt awful to have him treat me like a stranger.

When we got to the library, Mychailo went right to a trolley of books that were waiting to be reshelved. “I discovered this a few days ago,” he said. “All the best books are right here on this trolley." His eyes lit up as he pulled out a dog-eared novel called *Black Beauty*. "You'd like this," he said. "I read it last year."

I took it from him and flipped through the pages. All text and no pictures. And the text was small. "I can't read this," I said. He should have known. I had only taken out picture books so far.

"It will take you a while to read it," he said, "but I think you would like the story." He grinned at me then and said, "It's a girly book."

"But you liked it."

He blushed a little bit at that, then shot back with, "It's got good action too."

He shuffled through the other books and found one on hockey, one on rocks, and another novel.

"What's the novel?" I asked, grabbing it out of his hand. It took me a bit to sound it out, and even once I did, I couldn't understand it. "*Freddy Goes to Florida*? What does *Freddy* mean?"

"Freddy," he said, "is a name, like Mychailo or Nadia. This particular Freddy is a talking pig."

"A talking *pig*?" That made no sense at all. "And what is *Florida*?"

"It's a place," he said, as if he couldn't understand my confusion.

"It doesn't make sense," I said. "Pigs don't talk and pigs don't go places unless they're taken by humans."

Mychailo rolled his eyes. "Maybe you should read one," he said. "*Freddy Goes to Florida* is the first in the series. Then you'd understand. They're hilarious. I've been trying to borrow this one for quite a while."

"I bet you don't take those books to school with you."

"You're right about that," he said. "The hockey book is for taking to school."

I set *Black Beauty* down. It had too many words. "Can I try a Freddy book too?"

"Sure," said Mychailo. "Let's see if there are any on the shelf."

There were a few, so Mychailo drew out a copy of *Freddy the Detective*. "This was the first one I read," he said. "And it's really good."

I flipped through it. Even though it was a bit thicker than *Black Beauty*, the print was big and there were some pictures. Not quite a picture book, but not as daunting as *Black Beauty*. I breathed in deeply the wonderful scent of ink on paper and ran my hand across a page. Even the *feel* of this book made me happy . . .

I am in my four-poster bed in the German farmhouse. I should be asleep but I am woken by the rumble of voices from downstairs. I get out of bed. Shivering in my bare feet and thin nightgown, I slip down the stairs to see where the voices are coming from. The double doors of the library are open. Vater is seated with a brandy in one hand. Other men, their uniform jackets unbuttoned, sit around the table, telling each other stories and laughing. These are SS men. I know that because they have the very same badges on their collars as Vater.

But that is not what catches my eye. After all, I've seen them so often—at rallies in the city, and here for dinner parties. What I notice this time is the room they are in. It is usually closed. This room is lined from floor to ceiling with books, mostly in German, but some in other languages too. Fat books, thin books, some with gold lettering on their spines. I love books. I long to hold them. But I am not allowed to touch these books.

I walk back up to my room and pull out from under my bed the one book Vater has allowed me: Der Giftpiltz. *I turn the pages. The paintings are colorful and the print is large and clear. I want to love this book but I cannot. It talks about Jews and how they are poisonous toadstools but Germans are wholesome mushrooms. Something deep inside me tells me this is wrong. I think of that girl who wore the yellow star and my heart aches. I close the book and shove it back under my bed.*

"We should be going," said Mychailo. "Don't you have to put supper on?"

Suddenly, I was back in the library in Canada. In Brantford. I looked at Mychailo, then up at the clock on the wall. We had been at the library for an hour.

We walked to the checkout counter, him with his three books and me with the one novel. I still felt a little bit like I was in a dream world.

An older boy who looked vaguely familiar from today's recess was standing in line in front of us. He turned, caught Mychailo's eye, and nodded in greeting. He didn't seem to notice me, and that was fine with me. A few more people stood behind us in line. I didn't know most of them but recognized Linda. She was with a girl who looked like an older version of herself. It had to be her sister. Once my book was stamped, I waited for Linda and her sister to be checked through.

Mychailo tugged on my sleeve. "Come on," he said. "I thought you had to cook the potatoes."

"This will only take a minute." I knew he didn't want to be seen with me, but this wasn't a boy from school, it was two girls, so what was the harm? He stood impatiently by my side as Linda and her sister had their books stamped.

"Hi, Nadia," said Linda. She glanced at Mychailo, then back at me. "This is my sister, Grace."

Grace was taller than Linda, but she had the same golden skin and glossy hair. "So you are Nadia," she said, holding out her hand to me. "Good to meet you." She smiled at Mychailo, then tilted her head so she could read the spines of the books he was holding. "I didn't know you were a Freddy fan, Mychailo."

"You know each other?" I asked.

"Grace and I are in the same class."

Grace noticed the copy of *Freddy the Detective* in my hand. "How can *you* read *that*?"

I looked at her in surprise. What had Linda said about me to her sister? I knew my English wasn't perfect, but did she think I was stupid? "Slowly," I said, forcing my lips into a smile.

We stood chatting for a few minutes longer. "I've got to get home and turn on the potatoes before Marusia gets home," I said.

We walked up the half flight of stairs together and out the children's entrance. Linda and Grace walked with us as far as Sheridan Street, where Mychailo and I turned and they continued. Mychailo dropped his library books off at home and then we both went back to my place.

Once inside, I turned on the potatoes. Then we went out to the backyard and sat on the cinder blocks.

"You have to remember to call Marusia and Ivan your

mother and father when you're talking to non-Ukrainians," Mychailo said.

My heart skipped a beat. "I always call them that."

Mychailo rolled his eyes. "You're so stupid you don't even know what you're saying."

I was about to yell at him, but I stopped. He was right. Didn't I just use Marusia's name with Linda and Grace? I would have to watch myself.

"Not everyone is perfect like you, Mr. Smarty-Pants," I replied.

"This is serious," said Mychailo. "I don't know where you really came from, but if you want to stay in Canada, you had better get used to calling Marusia and Ivan your mother and father."

I didn't say anything to that. I knew he was right and I was surprised at myself for slipping up. At the DP camp, I never let my guard down, but now that we were safely in Canada, my past was forcing itself to be remembered and my thoughts seemed to get all jumbled.

Just then we heard a truck stop in front of the house and Marusia's voice calling out a good-bye to the other farm workers.

"I should be heading home," said Mychailo. "Don't say hi to me at school, okay?"

I shrugged instead of answering. Maybe I would say hi to him just to get him angry.

A few seconds later, Marusia came around to the back. She was carrying a heavy paper bag so I scooted over and grabbed it from her and we both walked inside.

She took the bag from my arms when we got inside and tipped it over onto the table, spilling out a few giant tomatoes, then onions, a small cabbage, and some green peppers. At the bottom were half a dozen big, beautiful apples. "I'll make apple squares for dessert," she said, her eyes sparkling.

She seemed to notice what I was wearing for the first time. "You've changed," she said.

Then she looked at my unbraided hair. "And you took your hair down."

We put the vegetables and some of the apples away in silence, and Marusia prodded the boiling potatoes with a fork to see how done they were. "How was your first day at school?" she asked.

I took a deep breath and held it. I needed to tell her right now what had happened. To clear the air and not hurt her feelings. But I couldn't get the words out.

Marusia's forehead crinkled in a frown, then she took a paring knife from the drawer and began to peel one of the apples. I watched the peel of apple skin grow. I had seen her skin an entire apple by paring off a single long tendril. Ivan couldn't do that. Neither could I.

The silence between us grew. I got the dishrag and wiped off the counter. I got out the broom and swept the floor even though it was already clean.

Marusia broke the silence. "I was telling the girls at the farm today about the outfit I made for you."

I didn't trust myself to say anything, so I caught her eye and tried to smile.

"They told me that students don't dress like that in Canada," she said. The apple was peeled, so she set it down on the counter and wiped her hands with a cloth. "Did you have trouble today?"

"I . . . I . . . love the new clothing." I stared at the floor and couldn't say any more. My throat was choked with tears.

Marusia stepped toward me, took the broom from my hands, and set it against the wall. She held me tight. I exhaled. I could feel the tension and worry leave with that long-held breath. I rested my head on her chest and wrapped my arms around her waist, sinking into her warmth and the scent of apples, sweat, and straw. I breathed in deeply, but I still couldn't speak.

She rocked me gently and murmured, "It's fine, Nadia. Don't worry. You're safe now, *Sonechko*."

The words soothed me. And with them came an image of another mother holding me and soothing me. Another time I thought I was safe . . .

That night in bed, I tried to remember more about the other time and another mother, but it was like trying to catch my shadow. I couldn't fall asleep, so I turned on my lamp, squinting at the sudden brightness. Once my eyes got used to it, I grabbed the Freddy novel and propped myself up on my pillow. On the cover was a pig wearing a cap, looking through a magnifying glass. Page one began, *It was hot* . . . That much I could read.

I tried to sound out more. The story seemed to be about two ducks looking at a house in the heat. It didn't make sense. Maybe if I wasn't so tired it would make sense. I set the book down and got *The Picture Dictionary for Children*. I had gone through the whole book four times, and each time I did I would find something new.

This time as I flipped through it, I kept on noticing the same couple of pictures that were used for various words. For example, the words *automobile*, *drives*, and *parks* were all illustrated with a fancy car. It wasn't colored in, but in my imagination, it was a shiny black car. The picture for *burn* was a house burning down, and the same burning house was used to show both *destroy* and *fire*.

My nostrils filled with the memory of smoke. How many times had I seen burning buildings? It was so familiar. Yet who was I and where was I when these things had happened? This was yet another piece of the puzzle that didn't fit.

I closed the book and waited for my heart to stop pounding. I didn't turn off the light.

I am in the backseat of a long black car, dressed in pink finery. The doors are locked and the windows rolled up tight.

I look out the window and through the haze of smoke. Girls and women running from a burning building. One girl glances my way. It is like looking into a mirror. She calls something to me but she's pushed away by a man in uniform. I pound at the window and pound at the door. Let me out, let me out!

The book slid off my chest and fell to the floor with a thunk. I jumped awake. The lamp was still on. I was safe in my bedroom in Canada. My head still swam with the nightmare. I rubbed my eyes and the image disappeared. I had been safe in the car and the fire was outside. Why had I wanted to get out? And who was that girl who looked like me? Was it just a trick of a dream, or did this really happen?

CHAPTER TEN

LINDA

Those first few weeks of school were better than the horrible first day. Miss MacIntosh taught one of the higher grades and she'd nod to me when we passed in the hallway. Knowing she was in the building gave me comfort. It was the same with Mychailo. For all anyone could tell, we were strangers, but we were the only DP kids there and we had a special bond.

After school he would often drop by. He even helped me with homework once. If the other boys ever knew that, he would be teased. But I had Linda to play with at recess, and each day English seemed easier. I was grateful that Miss Ferris would not tolerate me being called "the Hitler girl" in her presence. But that didn't stop Eric and David from whispering it behind my back.

One recess as Linda and I were walking around the schoolyard pretending to be interested in watching the other children play, she turned to me and asked, "Would you like to come to my place after school today?"

I was delighted with the invitation but had to say no. "Marus—Mama wouldn't know where I was," I told her. "Can you come to my house instead?"

Linda grinned. "I could do that. I'll let Grace know and she can tell Mom and Dad where I am."

It felt nice walking all the way home with someone to talk to. Linda loved the swing Ivan had made for me. I showed her through the house as well. When I opened the doors to each of the rooms, I tried to see it through Linda's eyes. Would she think that we were extremely poor? What would she think of the chipped tub in the bathroom and the repainted icebox in the kitchen? She hadn't commented on the cinder blocks that we used as back-door steps, but I noticed her looking at them.

When we got up to my bedroom, she sat on the bed and tested the springs. "Comfy," she said. "And I love the lilac-colored walls. Everything here is so fresh."

I looked at her face to see if she was making fun of me. I was sure that most of the kids at school had nicer homes than mine, but she seemed sincere.

"You must love it here," she said.

I was beginning to get used to my new home, and Canada was growing on me. Did I love it? Maybe. "The place I lived in before was much nicer than this," I said. The words were out before I knew it.

"Where was that?" asked Linda, flopping down on the bed.

"In Europe," I said, my heart starting to hammer. Why had I started this conversation?

"If you had a nicer place, why did you come here?"

I said nothing. I wished I could take back the words I had already let out.

"Doesn't make sense," said Linda.

"It was because of the war." I hoped that would end the conversation.

She looked at me strangely. "If you had a nicer place, were your parents well off?" she asked.

I opened my mouth to reply but then closed it again. *Why* had I started this conversation?

"I was kidding," I told Linda. "We were just regular people."

Mychailo had warned me to never let Canadians know that Marusia and Ivan weren't my real parents, because the government could take me away from them. Marusia had warned me too, all those years at the camp, and on the ship.

I was so mad at myself for coming so close to betraying them. The last thing I wanted was to be separated from the only two people who had ever cared for me. I smiled at Linda and shrugged, hoping she'd brush off my comment.

"Nadia? I'm home!" The sound of the front door creaking open and Marusia's footsteps on the wooden entranceway made me practically jump out of my skin.

"I'm up here," I called down. "With a friend."

I could hear Marusia walking into the kitchen on the level below us, and the rustling of a grocery bag as she set it on the table. Then I heard her footsteps on the stairs.

In a few seconds, she appeared in the doorway of my bedroom. "There you are, Nadia." She looked from me to Linda. "Are you going to introduce me to your friend?"

"Ma—Mama, this is Linda. Linda, this is my mother."

Linda scrambled to her feet and held out her hand. "Glad to meet you, Mrs. Kravchuk."

Marusia shook Linda's hand. "Come on downstairs in a couple of minutes. I'll go make you a treat." She turned and walked back down the stairs.

When we could hear her down in the kitchen again, Linda whispered to me. "What did she do in the war?"

I didn't know how to answer that. Why hadn't I been quiet about it like Mychailo had warned me to? "I'll tell you about it later. Let's go get our snack," I said, hoping she would forget about all of this.

When we went downstairs, Marusia had sliced an

apple in a bowl for each of us and drizzled them both with honey. "You can take it outside to eat if you like," she said. "But bring the bowls back when you're finished."

The swing was just wide enough to hold us both if we squeezed on together, and Linda's legs were long enough to keep it steady, so that's where we sat together and ate our snack.

"This is yummy," said Linda, crunching with satisfaction.

I loved the gooey treat too. It wasn't something Marusia had ever made just for us. I guess she wanted to serve something special for my friend. She always tried so hard to make things good for me. It made me feel guilty for the things I had said to Linda.

Linda looked over to the house and whispered to me. "She can't hear us from inside, can she?"

"I don't think so."

"So what did she do during the war?"

I slowly swallowed the piece of apple that sat on my tongue. "I was just being silly." I said. "She was a factory worker."

"What about you?" asked Linda. "It must have been exciting to grow up in the middle of a war."

Exciting? I had never thought of it that way. So terrifying that I couldn't remember half of it, that's what it was to me. "I was young," I said. "It's all jumbled in my mind."

"Tell me what you remember, then."

So I told her about Marusia and I escaping and our arrival at the displaced persons camp. Linda's eyes went wide as I told her some things. I held back the ones about the German family.

The back door opened and Marusia stuck her head out. "You two are cozy on that swing," she said, grinning. "Finish up your apples. Linda, Nadia and I will walk you home."

"I can walk home myself," said Linda.

"We would like to walk you home," said Marusia.

She washed and polished some apples and put them in a paper bag to take with us. I was puzzled at first but then realized what Marusia was up to. She wanted to meet Linda's parents. The apples were a gift.

Linda's one-story yellow brick house was on Usher Street—behind the railway station and one street closer than the Ukrainian church. I had passed by it on the way to church but never realized she lived there.

"Would you like to come in?" Linda asked.

"That's not necessary," said Marusia. "I just wanted to make sure that you got home safe."

Linda knew as well as I did that the real reason for this

little walk home was to check out her family. "Wait here," she said. "I want my mom to meet you."

She ran ahead of us and flew in the front door of her house. A moment later a careworn woman drying her hands on a blue apron stepped out onto the front step and greeted us, Linda peeking out from behind her. "I'm Rita Henhawk, Linda's mother."

"I'm Marusia Kravchuk, and this is my daughter, Nadia. Here are some apples," she added, holding the bag out to Mrs. Henhawk. "I picked them today."

Mrs. Henhawk took the bag and smiled. "Are they from your own tree?"

"No," said Marusia. "I work at a farm."

Mrs. Henhawk nodded in understanding. "Can you come in for a cup of tea?" She opened the door wide. A striped cat darted between her legs and ran out onto the road.

I was about to chase after him, but Linda's mother said, "Don't worry. He'll be back. Joe never misses his supper."

We stepped inside the house and were enveloped by warmth and a savory scent of something cooking. "Excuse the mess," said Mrs. Henhawk. "I've been making corn cakes."

There was no mess. The front door led directly into a living room that had only a few pieces of furniture in it.

They had a worn sofa, two hardback chairs, and a wooden chest that served as a coffee table. There were no bookshelves and the wooden floor was bare, but it was a tidy room. I could tell that the Henhawks were poor but proud like us. So Linda had been sincere about the nice things she'd said about our house. That made me feel so much better.

Beyond that was a kitchen with a red linoleum floor, so newly mopped it was still glistening. A carved wooden bowl covered with a checkered cloth sat on one end of the kitchen table. Linda's older sister sat on a chair at the opposite side of the table, a textbook and binder spread out before her and a half-finished glass of milk close at hand. Grace looked up when we stepped in, gave a bit of a wave, and went back to her homework.

"Make yourselves comfortable," Mrs. Henhawk said, indicating the sofa. "I'll put the kettle on."

"That would be lovely," said Marusia. She sat down on the sofa and patted the spot beside her. I sat down.

"And some milk for you, young lady?" Mrs. Henhawk asked me.

I wasn't thirsty, but Marusia nudged me in the ribs, so I too said that would be lovely. Linda went into the kitchen to help. In a few moments she came back out, carrying two glasses of milk and two mugs of tea on a tray. Her mother came out of the kitchen with a platter of small golden cakes.

I held my corn cake in both of my hands and blew on it to cool it down. Marusia took a bite of hers. Smacking her lips with delight, she said, "This is delicious."

I bit into mine and had to agree. It was like butter, corn, and bacon all mixed together.

"It's an old family recipe," said Mrs. Henhawk. "I'm glad you like them."

Marusia and Mrs. Henhawk made small talk while Linda and I sat impatiently waiting for them to finish. I would have liked to explore the neighborhood with Linda. Or at least explore the house. But I knew this step was necessary. Marusia was very protective of me.

Finally, Marusia finished her tea and set down the cup. "It was so good to meet you," she said. We both stood.

"They seem like nice people," said Marusia, as we walked back home. "You can go there after school sometimes, but you've got to let me know the day before."

CHAPTER ELEVEN
GHOSTS

I had a friend in Linda, parents who loved me, and a roof over my head. The weeks marched by, and before the first frost, Ivan had finished all the painting and had installed the inside doors. Marusia and I planted tulip and daffodil bulbs by the front walk. I looked forward to seeing them bloom the following spring. I was lucky to be loved by Marusia and Ivan.

It wasn't all perfect. Eric still called me "the Hitler girl" whenever he saw me at recess or on the way home—and he made a point of seeing me often. Thank goodness that other boy had tired of the game. My memories of the past had stopped coming at me so quickly and I was able to sort some of them out, but there were still huge blanks in my memory.

On the last Sunday evening in October, I sat between Marusia and Ivan on the cinder-block steps at the back of our house. Someone in the neighborhood must have been burning leaves, because there was a haze in the air and I could smell smoke. Marusia brewed a pot of chamomile tea with honey and we each sipped a mug of it. As I sat there between the two people who had changed their lives to protect me, I looked at the swing that Ivan had made for me. I saw the lilac bushes that he had planted for me. I thought of Marusia protecting me in the camp and of the skirt and blouse that her farm-worn hands had stitched with love. I began to cry.

"Sonechko," said Marusia, leaning her head onto my shoulder. "What is the matter?"

My throat was filled with sobs. "Nothing . . . it's fine, it's fine . . ." I tried to stop the tears but they had a mind of their own.

"Did you have another nightmare?" asked Ivan.

I shook my head. "I am happy," I said. "I don't know how you can love me, but I'm glad that you do . . ."

"Nadia, Nadia," cooed Marusia. "You may not be the daughter of my blood, but you are the daughter of my heart. I love you and Ivan loves you."

"But I don't deserve to be loved," I sobbed. "You say I'm not a Nazi, but my memories say I am."

Ivan pulled a handkerchief out of his pocket and dried

my tears. "Tell us everything you know, Nadia. Maybe we can help you make sense of it all."

My memories tumbled out. I told them about Eva and the pink dress and where I thought it came from. I told them about the books I was forbidden to read and the one I was forced to read. I told them about meeting Hitler. It seemed like Marusia had known some of this, but not all. Ivan sat listening in silence, his lips set in a thin grim line. When I finished, I was empty of tears.

"Do you remember when we met?" Marusia asked.

I closed my eyes and thought hard. Marusia was so much a part of my life, but *exactly* when we met? I drew a blank. Marusia and I escaping on the flatbed of the train was a vivid memory. And the day we arrived at the DP camp. On the edge of my dreams was an image of Marusia with that same German family at that same farm in the countryside. I didn't know how she fit in, but she was somehow there and so were lilac bushes. Marusia back then was like a once familiar song now forgotten.

"Do you want me to tell you about it?" she asked.

I began to shake. I had no idea why. "Not now."

Marusia lightly touched my forearm with her fingers. "I don't mean to push you," she said. "But it is important for you to fill in those forgotten parts of your life. Otherwise, we'll never find out who you really are."

That is what scared me the most. Did I *want* to know who I really was? What if I didn't like that person? That was the thought I fell asleep to . . .

I pull at the handle of the door but it won't open and the window won't roll down. I pound on the glass. "Let me out, let me out." Outside, the world is filled with smoke. I hear sirens. See a face that looks like mine.

The front door clicked softly open and shut. I bolted out of bed and scrambled to the window. Ivan. I knew it was Ivan on his way to the foundry in the darkness of the early morning. Why did this sound scare me so?

I rubbed the sleep out of my eyes and thought of the dream that was still a fragment of fear in my mind. Why did I dream I was trying to get out of a safe car when a building was burning outside? It made no sense. And how could I be outside and inside that car at the same time?

I tiptoed downstairs and slipped out to the backyard. I sat on my swing in the darkness and breathed in the faint scent of burned leaves. The smell reminded me of something that happened long ago, something I *did* remember . . .

The long black car idled beside the smoking ruin of a newly bombed factory. Vater got out. "I won't be long," he said to Mutter as he closed the door.

"You'd better not be," Mutter said, more to herself than to Eva or me. "We can't be late for this rally."

Yet another rally. It was hot in the car and my pink dress felt itchy. My hair was pulled so tightly into a braid that my scalp ached. Eva's hair cascaded loosely down her back and her dress was made of cool pink muslin, yet she couldn't sit still. The buckle of her shoe nearly caught on my skirt as she clambered over me to get to the window. I smoothed it back down and sighed.

"Sit down, Eva," said Mutter, reaching over me to tug at Eva's dress, but Eva stayed where she was.

"It's hot in here, Mutti." Eva rolled down the window and a cool, smoky breeze drifted in.

"We're going to smell like smoke," said Mutter.

"At least we won't smell sweaty," said Eva.

Had I said that, I would have been slapped. I arched my neck so I could see what was happening at the factory. I knew that this one made weapons for the war and that was why it was attacked.

One long wing of the building was bombed flat and smoke curled out of the remains. Anyone who had worked in that part of the factory would have died.

Vater was giving orders to boys who wore swastika armbands. Frightened women in gray rags limped out of billowing smoke. Everything was in shades of gray except for the slashes of blood on clothing where sharp fragments of blasted brick had cut forearms and shoulders. Blood dried a sticky brown in tangles of blond and black and chestnut hair where shrapnel had hit scalps.

"Why aren't they wearing the yellow stars?" asked Eva.

Mutter leaned over to get a better look at the women. I did the same. These ones were wearing white-and-blue badges saying OST.

"They're the eastern workers," said Mutter.

"Are they animals like the Jews, Mutti?"

"Yes, dear, that's why they work in the munitions factory. You wouldn't want Germans to get bombed, would you?"

I squinted at individual faces in the sad and tattered crowd of OST workers. One girl had hair not quite as fair as my own. As if she could feel my stare, she looked up.

It was like I was seeing an older version of myself.

Our eyes met and her mouth formed a wide O of shock. She tried to call something to me but then one of the Hitler Youth stepped in front of her and pushed her away . . .

The back door opened with a squeak. I blinked once, and then again, and looked around. It was daylight and I was on my swing. My feet were blue with cold. I looked to the back door and Marusia was standing there, clutching a thin housecoat around her shoulders.

"Nadia," she said. "I had no idea you were out here. You are going to catch your death."

I stumbled a bit on frozen legs as I got off the swing. Marusia wrapped a blanket around me when I got inside. She busied herself at the stove, then set a mug of scalding cocoa on the table in front of me. It warmed my fingers as I raised it to my lips. Flashes and flakes of that memory still seemed as real as my cocoa. That girl who'd looked like me—I knew now that it wasn't me. And the OST badge she wore—where had I seen one before?

"Did you remember something more?"

"Not about when we met," I said. "I remembered about that black car and I know why there was smoke."

I told her about the bombing and the girl who looked like me. She reached out and took one of my hands. She didn't say anything for a bit. It was like she was trying to figure out what to say. "Millions from Ukraine and Poland were taken as *Ostarbeiters*—OST workers."

I had an image of Marusia in a worn gray dress with an OST badge stitched to her chest. I set my cocoa down so quickly that some of it sloshed onto the table. I covered my face with my hands, but the image wouldn't go away. "You were an OST worker too, weren't you?"

"Nadia," Marusia said. "Your memory is coming back. Do you remember when we met?"

"Were you at that bombed-out factory? Was it you I saw?" But even as I asked the question, I knew that I was wrong. Looking at Marusia was not like looking at an older version of me.

"We met at the farm, Nadia. Try to remember."

Parts of it came back to me . . . *The military truck stopping in our drive. A soldier unlatching the back door and an OST woman tumbling out onto the gravel. From the stench I could tell she'd been traveling for a long time. Marusia trying to stand, but her legs so wobbly that she falls back down. Looking up and seeing me. Then me feeling so guilty of my finery and of who I was, and running back into the farmhouse to hide in shame.*

"I remember, Marusia," I said in a small voice. "I remember now. Where did you come from?"

"Zelena," said Marusia. "A small village in eastern Ukraine. The Germans came and ordered everyone my age to come to the village square. Anyone who didn't come was rooted out and shot. They sorted through us. I was loaded into the back of a truck." She brushed a tear from her cheek with the back of her hand. "It wasn't heated and we weren't given food. Some people had bits of food with them and we shared it. We traveled for many days."

"And then you were taken to the farm?"

"No," said Marusia. "I was sent to work at the Ford Werke factory in Cologne."

Wisps of the past drifted into my mind. The bombed-out weapons plant . . . "I'm glad they didn't have you making bombs," I whispered.

"In that way I was lucky," said Marusia. "But we were still slaves."

"How did you get to the farm?" I asked.

"At the car factory, they locked us into a big barracks at night," said Marusia. "But I escaped. I was caught and sent back, but the factory didn't want me back. They said I was undependable, so I was sent to a concentration camp. But I convinced them that I was a good cook. I was given to General Himmel, who gave me to his wife."

I stared at my cocoa. The man whom I knew as Vater, Marusia knew as General Himmel. The thought of what she had been through made my stomach churn.

"It is good that you're beginning to remember," she said. "As you remember more, you will understand why you have nothing to feel guilty about."

"Why don't you just tell me everything you know about my past?" I asked her. "Wouldn't that be simpler?"

"I don't know your whole past," said Marusia. "I'm afraid that if I tell you what I know, it could influence your memories. It's best for you to air this out as the memories surface."

"That's easy for you to say," I told her angrily. "You don't have to live with these nightmares."

Marusia was silent for a moment. She brushed away a tear from her eye, then reached out her hand and placed it on top of mine. "I am living with my own ghosts, *Sonechko*."

CHAPTER TWELVE
RED INK

At school later that morning, I tried to pay attention, but as Miss Ferris wrote notes on the board, the words seemed to blur and blend together. I kept on thinking about that girl who looked like an older me. Who was she and why did she appear in my nightmares? I was so absentminded that I didn't hear the bell for morning recess. Linda touched my arm and I nearly jumped out of my seat.

"Sorry!" she said. "You look like you've seen a ghost."

I blinked a couple of times to try to clear the images from my mind. Maybe that girl who looked like me was just a ghost of my imagination? "Let's go outside," I said.

Linda sped down the hallway in front of me and pushed open the door. I followed her on legs that felt like rubber.

"You're acting strange today," said Linda, once we were outside.

"Sorry," I said. "I don't feel very well."

"Maybe the fresh air will do you some good."

Except the air wasn't fresh. It smelled of burning leaves. We walked past a group of girls from our class who were clustered together chatting quietly. I overheard bits of their conversation. Halloween was tomorrow and they were talking about what costumes they would be wearing for the class party—a witch, a ghost, a nurse . . .

Others were playing double Dutch with the younger students, but none of them called to Linda or me to ask us to join them. Most of the boys were out in the field tossing around a football. How I wished that I could be like these other students. Wouldn't it be wonderful to not have a past?

When we got back into the classroom, I noticed an envelope sticking out of the corner of my workbook. I had a moment of panic. Had Miss Ferris noticed that I wasn't paying attention this morning? Maybe it was a note sending me to the principal's office. I pulled the envelope out of my workbook and breathed a sigh of relief. A big childish *N* was written on the front in red ink and the writing didn't look at all like Miss Ferris's tidy script. Could this be an invitation to a birthday or Halloween party? I looked over to Linda's desk. There was no envelope on hers. I couldn't possibly go to a party if she hadn't also been invited.

Most of the other students had returned to their desks by this time, but class hadn't begun and Miss Ferris still sat at her desk at the front of the room, marking papers. I held the envelope on my lap so Miss Ferris wouldn't see me opening it. I ripped it open as quietly as I could and pulled out the piece of paper—a crude drawing of a girl with yellow braids—covered in red swastikas. Underneath, someone had written, *Nazi Nadia, go back to Hitler-land!*

"Nadia, what are you reading?" Miss Ferris asked in a sharp voice. She stood at the front of the room with her hands on her hips. "You know we don't pass notes in class."

I shoved the paper into my desk, but the envelope fluttered to the floor. Several of my classmates turned to watch me. Eric was grinning and David covered his mouth to keep from laughing out loud.

"Noth-nothing . . ." I said. "I was just getting out my workbook."

"Your workbook is on your desk," said Miss Ferris sternly. "Stand up, and share with us what you find so interesting."

I stumbled to my feet but didn't take the horrible note out of my desk. I could feel my heart pound in my chest. How could I possibly read it out loud?

"Get the note, Nadia. We would all like to hear it."

I stood there, frozen. Miss Ferris marched down the aisle and knelt at my desk. She pulled the offending piece of paper out and unfolded it.

Her face became still. "Sit down, Nadia," she said, resting her hand gently on my shoulder. She walked to the front of the classroom and held up the hideous drawing for everyone to see. A hush fell over the room. Someone giggled. I crouched down in my seat. If only I could disappear.

"Who did this?" she almost shouted. No one raised a hand. "You will all have a detention if the guilty party does not step forward."

This time she did shout. No one raised their hand. I stared at the back of Eric's head. He sat rigid, with his hands folded neatly on his desk. I was sure he was no longer grinning. I couldn't be sure if it was him or David. It could have been anyone. I felt embarrassed and small.

"Hands on your desks, everyone," Miss Ferris said sternly. "Palms up." She marched up one aisle and down the next, examining everyone's hands for red ink. When she got to David's desk she stopped. She grabbed one of his hands and twisted it back and forth. "Red ink," she said. "Empty your desk. Now!" David reached into his desk and emptied it of books and notebooks and pens and pencils. Miss Ferris looked through each item carefully for more evidence and then tossed it to the floor.

"That's all I have," he said with an innocent look on his face. Miss Ferris reached inside his desk and rooted around. She pulled out a pad of paper and a fountain pen filled with red ink. She flipped through the paper. More sickening sketches of "Nazi Nadia." I crouched farther down in my seat.

"Get up," said Miss Ferris. She grabbed David by the ear and marched him out of the room. Once the door slammed shut behind them, a couple dozen pairs of eyes turned to stare at me.

I convinced Marusia and Ivan to let me stay home from school on Halloween. I did not feel like dressing up in a silly costume and pretending that I was having fun just a day after David's nastiness. Doing chores around the house was preferable.

"Let us not make this a habit," Marusia warned me.

I was at the kitchen sink, scrubbing grass stains out of one of her work shirts, when I spied Mychailo at the back door. He wasn't wearing a costume. "It's open," I called through the window.

"Didn't your class have a party this afternoon?" I asked him as he stepped inside.

"We did," said Mychailo. "I just put a sheet over my head and called myself a ghost."

That made me smile.

He rooted through his pockets and pulled out a candy kiss. "Here," he said, holding it out for me. "Now you can say you've been kissed by a boy."

That made me blush. "Thanks," I said. "Put it on the table." My hands were still soapy. I rinsed Marusia's shirt, wrung it out, and then hung it on the laundry line outside. I opened up the candy kiss and popped it into my mouth.

"Are you going trick-or-treating tonight?" Mychailo asked. "You can go with me if you want."

I hadn't planned on going trick-or-treating. After the incident at school yesterday, I didn't even feel like going outside. The whole thing was so shameful. Besides, this custom of Halloween seemed strange to me—and a little bit scary.

"I don't have a costume."

"You can go as a ghost," he said. "Or a hobo." He looked at me with impatience. "Those costumes are easy. Don't you want free candy?"

I had to admit that the thought of free candy was exciting. And if I did go trick-or-treating, I would feel safe going with Mychailo. "I'll ask Mar—*Mama* and *Tato* if I can go," I said.

"Great," he said. "I'll come by just as it starts to get dark."

Ivan was pleased that I had decided to go out trick-or-treating and he was especially happy that I was going with Mychailo. "You need to be a child more often," he said. And he helped me put together a costume. I was a scarecrow, with itchy long grass from the far edges of the backyard stuffed into a flannel shirt of Ivan's. I wore a pair of Marusia's overalls that were so old they were patched on the patches. Ivan used Marusia's red lipstick to paint on a scarecrow face. We had no candy to give out, but we did have a bowl of apples from Marusia's farm that she had polished to a glossy sheen.

I could tell by the expression in Marusia's eyes that she was less sure about me going out, but she pretended to be happy. She gave me an extra-long hug good-bye when I left with Mychailo.

"Stay on this street," she said. "And be home in an hour."

One nice thing about living on a street with close-together houses is you can get to a lot of them in an hour. My pillowcase was soon full of treats: candy apples and caramel corn, bubble gum and peanuts. I dumped all of my candy out on the kitchen table when I got home. Ivan, Marusia, and I ate far too much of it. I went to bed with a stomachache. I tossed and turned all night and had a long and scary dream. In the morning I could only remember bits and snatches.

CHAPTER THIRTEEN
MANSION

I got into the habit of going to Linda's house on Tuesdays after school and she came to my house on Thursdays. It was hard to find a place to play inside. Linda shared a bedroom with Grace on the second floor. They had bunk beds and a bookshelf crammed with old novels. I longed to look through that bookshelf, but the bedroom itself made me feel like I couldn't breathe. I think part of it was because Grace was always there. She'd either be reading, propped up on a pillow on the top bunk, or she'd have a friend over and they'd be doing a project for school or something.

There wasn't much of a place to play in Linda's backyard either. It was nothing more than an overgrown strip of land on a hill with wild bushes along either side and a laundry line down the middle. Linda had a deck of cards and we tended to play Crazy Eights or Concentration at the kitchen table, but then one Tuesday she brought out a board game called Monopoly.

With the cards, we could play several games in the space of an hour or two, but Monopoly was a much longer game. Marusia would get dropped off at Linda's house on Tuesdays after finishing at the farm, but once we started playing Monopoly, the game would just be getting interesting when Marusia would arrive and it was time for me to leave.

"Can you come to my house on Saturday?" asked Linda. "Mom said you could stay even if the game takes all day."

Marusia and Ivan agreed. Linda's mother suggested I come early on Saturday morning and she invited me to stay for lunch.

Ivan was doing some yard work at the Ukrainian church, so he walked me to Linda's house, and we decided that once I was finished, I would walk over to the church to meet him and we'd head home together.

When I got to Linda's, it was just before nine. Mrs. Henhawk was in the kitchen making applesauce.

"Linda will be down in a minute," she said. She offered me an apple, but I had just eaten breakfast. "Take a seat beside George." She pointed to the chair next to her husband. "He won't bite."

I sat down and Mr. Henhawk lowered his newspaper, caught my eye, and gave me a wink. He seemed as friendly as Mrs. Henhawk was.

I must have let a fly into the house when I came in through the back door. It kept buzzing around my head. I waved it away but it kept coming back. Suddenly, I felt the whack of a newspaper against the side of my head.

I blinked once and then again. Why would Mr. Henhawk hit me like that? I barely heard what he was saying to me now . . .

"Don't stuff yourself, Eva," Mutter is saying as she tries to pull the plate away, but Eva grabs it with two hands and pulls it back.

"They're my favorite, Mutti, and you know it," says Eva, cutting off a giant portion of apple-filled Eierkuchen *and shoving it into her mouth. A chunk of apple falls out and lands on the table. She picks it up and pops it back into her mouth.*

"If only that *one would eat half as much as you." Mutter looks at me. "If the führer hears we've starved his little darling, it will be the end of us."*

I look at the plate in front of me and pick up my knife and fork. I cut one bite and hold a piece of Eierkuchen *to my mouth, but the greasy smell of it makes me feel sick. I think of the women and children with the yellow stars. How can I eat this when it seems they have nothing? I push the plate away.*

Mutter slaps me hard across the face.

"Nadia, are you all right?"

Mr. Henhawk's voice pulled me back to the present. I was standing by the table in the Henhawk kitchen, a chair upended beside me. I lifted my hand to my cheek. I could almost feel the tingle of that long ago slap from Mutter.

"I'm fine," I told him.

But I didn't feel fine. These scenes from the past made me queasy and confused.

Linda appeared in the kitchen doorway holding the Monopoly box. "Nadia, you don't look so good."

The kitchen was humid, with an overwhelming smell of apples. I felt like I was going to be sick. "Would you mind if we played outside instead?" I asked.

"Sure," said Linda. She set the Monopoly box on the kitchen table. "We'll be outside, okay?" she said to her parents.

"Stay in the neighborhood," said Mr. Henhawk.

I gulped in fresh air as we stepped out to Linda's narrow, overgrown backyard.

"Let's go to the park," she said.

I didn't know that there was a park. I walked beside Linda as she stayed on her own side of Usher Street and headed west. As we got farther from where she lived, I noticed that the houses seemed to get shabbier. Usher curved into Rushton Street and I spotted a fancy wrought-iron gate almost hidden by bushes. It looked like something from a storybook. Was I dreaming, or was this real? I went up to touch the gate.

"Come this way and I'll show you something better," said Linda, grabbing my hand.

So it was real.

We walked around the curve. Through the bushes I could see that the gate was attached to a long fancy fence, also almost completely hidden by leaves. But all at once there was a break in the bushes. I was so shocked by what I saw that I grabbed Linda's shoulder to steady myself. A rundown mansion on top of a hill. It seemed out of time and place, like something from a dream—or a nightmare. It felt a little sinister, with paint peeling from the lattice-work and ragged curtains hanging limp inside shattered windows.

"That's Yates Castle," said Linda. "I don't think anyone lives there anymore, except maybe hobos."

Something about the vast abandoned mansion tugged at my memory, but why? It looked nothing like the large, well-kept farmhouse I had lived in with Eva and Mutter and Vater. And there was no building like this in the DP camp, of course. Hot bile rose up in my throat and I doubled over, gagging.

"Nadia, are you all right?" asked Linda.

I took a few heaving breaths and tried to calm myself. After a couple of minutes I was able to stand up straight again. "I'm . . . fine," I managed.

"What's wrong? Does the house scare you?" she asked.

I couldn't answer.

"Does it remind you of something during the war?"

"It must," I told her. "But I don't know what."

"Come on," she said, grabbing my hand again. "Let's get away from here."

As we walked past the mansion—or castle or haunted house, whatever it was—I couldn't tear my eyes from it. It was awful and beautiful at the same time . . .

I am being carried, kicking, screaming, up white-painted steps. "Baba! Baba! I want my baba!" *I am put in a room all by myself. I try to open the door but it's locked. I pound until my knuckles bleed but no one answers.*

Linda was saying my name, but I ran down the block, pulling her with me. I had no idea where I was going but I had to get away from that house.

"Slow down!" she cried, tugging on my hand. "I've got a stitch in my side."

When I stopped running, I realized that I was huffing for breath and covered in sweat. I felt Linda's hand take mine and she led me up a pathway through the trees. We stepped out onto tidy grass on a hill. It was open and airy and not scary at all. It was hard to believe that such a nice park was hidden from anyone strolling down Usher Street.

She led me to the middle of the open space and we both flopped onto the grass. For long minutes, we lay there side by side, watching the clouds and not saying a word.

Then Linda asked, "What did Yates Castle remind you of?"

A feeling of dread came over me. I sat up and looked at Linda. I had confided some things about my other past to her already. I longed to talk to her about those scenes that would flash into my mind. But would she understand? More important, would she tell anyone else? Mychailo had warned me about talking to Canadians. But Linda was my best friend, after all. I had to tell her something.

"All I remember is being locked up in a fancy house," I said. "That, and how frightened I was."

"Who would have locked you up?" she asked, a puzzled expression on her face.

"I don't know."

"Was it your parents?"

"No!" It was hard to even think of Marusia or Ivan doing anything like that to me.

I didn't say anything more, so Linda dropped the subject. We played a few games, like I Spy, and finding shapes in clouds, and then she said we should go to the church to find Ivan. "After the scare you've had, I'm sure you want to go home."

I looked at Linda with new appreciation. What a kind friend she was.

"Do we have to go past that house again?" I asked her.

"We don't have to," she said. She pointed up the hill. "That's Terrace Hill Street. We can go up that way to your church."

"Are you sure you don't mind us not playing Monopoly?"

"Nadia," said Linda. "Of course I don't mind. We can always play another day."

Once we got up the incline to Terrace Hill Street, we had a beautiful view of the train station and beyond. You could see almost all the way to my house, yet the castle was hidden by trees.

As we walked down Terrace Hill Street, I was surprised at how close the Ukrainian church was, and I was disturbed to realize that Yates Castle and the church were actually back to back. In fact, along the side of the church and extending down to the castle was a set of steps and a carriage road. My heart tightened. That little church had been one of the few places I had felt truly safe, but now that I realized how close it was to that creepy house, I wondered if the church would ever feel like a safe place again.

Ivan was raking the leaves off the lawn in front of the church. I noticed that Mychailo was helping his father plant a row of shrubs along the church walkway. When we got there, Ivan looked at me with surprise. "You've finished your game already?"

"We're not finished, but . . ." I looked to Linda.

She caught my eye and nodded. "We got bored," she said, shrugging. "We'll play another day."

Ivan looked at the pile of leaves he had raked up and then gazed at the rest of the lawn. "I won't be finished here for at least another hour."

"I could help you," I said

"So could I," said Linda. "Do you have any more rakes?"

I looked at her and smiled in thanks.

Ivan grinned. "It won't take long at all with three of us working."

When we were finished with the yard work, Ivan took my hand and began to walk toward those dreaded steps that led down to Usher Street alongside Yates Castle.

"This is a quick way to Linda's," he said. "And I want to show you an interesting house."

Ivan knew about it! Of course he did. He had been doing yard work at the church. How could he miss seeing a castle behind the church? I was just surprised that I had never noticed it through the trees before.

I didn't budge from my spot on the sidewalk. "That place scares me."

Ivan's forehead crinkled in surprise. He looked at me, then at Linda. She shrugged her shoulders. "So you don't want to go down that way?" he asked.

"No."

We walked down Terrace Hill Street and then to Main and dropped Linda back home.

Once it was just the two of us walking home, Ivan asked, "Does that big old house remind you of something?"

I nodded.

"The German house in the country?"

I shook my head.

"Are you sure you don't want to go look at it with me?"

"I'm sure."

"That's too bad," said Ivan. "Because it's an interesting place and I thought you'd enjoy seeing it up close."

I shivered at the thought of it.

"It was built in the eighteen hundreds by the man who owned the railroads," he said. "He wanted it to look like—"

I squeezed Ivan's hand so hard that he looked at me and stopped talking mid-sentence.

CHAPTER FOURTEEN
STOLEN

One Saturday morning, Marusia burst through the front door with a grin on her face and a grocery bag in her arms. I had been at the library all morning and had just gotten home a few moments before.

"You will never guess what happened today," she said, taking off her winter coat.

"You got a new job?"

Marusia's face fell. After harvest finished, she hadn't been able to find another full-time job. Since the beginning of December she had been working four mornings a week at the laundromat that had opened up downtown, but it didn't pay nearly as much as what she had made at the farm.

"Not that." She dug her hand deep into her coat pocket and pulled out three small stubs of paper. "Tickets to the movies—for tonight," she said. "One of my customers gave them to me."

How exciting! I had walked past the movie theater with Mychailo, but never dreamed that I could ever go. "What movie will we see?"

"*Cinderella* is playing," said Marusia. "It's the English version of *Popelyushka*."

Popelyushka was a fairy tale that tugged at my memory. It seemed that I had known the story for my whole life.

Ivan was working at the church, but as soon as he got home, we told him the good news. We had a quick supper, then we bundled up for our special evening out. It took only a few minutes to get to the theater. A line had formed, but Ivan walked up to a man wearing a red hat and showed him our tickets. He waved us inside.

The first room we stepped into was a huge open area decorated with old-fashioned paintings on the ceiling and red velvet curtains. One wall was plastered with old movie posters. There was a dark-haired woman with red lipstick on the poster for a movie called *Gone with the Wind*. I tugged Ivan's hand and pointed. He grinned. Marusia looked just as pretty this evening, with her hair combed out and her lipstick on.

We walked through the opening in the curtains and into the theater itself. The seats were filling quickly, but I pointed to the front row. It was nearly empty. We hurried before others noticed, and got the three seats in the exact center. I snuggled into my chair and leaned way back so I could see the whole giant screen above me.

Cinderella started with a big book being opened and a voice saying, "Once upon a time in a faraway land there was a tiny kingdom . . ."

I felt like I had stepped inside a storybook. Never before had I seen a movie made with drawings instead of people, and never before had I watched a movie in "Technicolor." The movies that Vater took us to were all about Hitler and how he was a hero. They were very serious and not interesting. *Cinderella* was nothing like that. It had songs and dances and happy things, even though the story was sad in parts. Cinderella's bare bedroom in the big mansion at the beginning of the movie made my stomach flip. Did the bedrooms in Yates Castle look like this?

After the movie was over, the three of us walked home in the dark. Ivan had his arm around Marusia's waist and I walked a few steps ahead of them, my hands shoved into the pockets of my winter coat. As we walked, I thought of the song that Cinderella sang, about a dream being a wish your heart makes. I had never thought of dreams like that before. Was my heart trying to tell me something in my dreams? It didn't seem like a wish to me. It was more like a fear.

• • •

Marusia and Ivan sat in the kitchen together and chatted when we got home from the movies. I wanted to give them time with each other, so instead of sitting with them, I went up to my bedroom. I sat on my bed and looked at my beautiful room with new appreciation. I had an attic bedroom like Cinderella's, but mine was cozy and warm. The lilac-painted walls made me feel safe and my wooden crate nightstand was simple, but it held my library books and my lamp. What more did I need? How lucky I was to be loved by Marusia and Ivan. I drew out a library book and hugged it to my chest . . .

Dark shadows dance on the scuffed white walls. Someone else's fingernail scratches are etched around the glass doorknob and there are tiny splinters of wood fraying from the door itself. The one window is too high to peer out of so I grab onto the bars and try to hoist myself up. For a few trembling moments I look out at the dirt-trampled snow far below. My arms give out and I fall back down to the floor. Why am I a prisoner in this house?

My throat is raw from screaming and my fingernails are bloodied from scrabbling at the doorknob. I lie on the wooden floor and stare up at the bare light bulb. I can hear nothing but my own gasping breaths. Then a thump-thumping of hard shoes just outside my door. Shuffling. A struggle. A child screams down the hallway. A door slams shut.

Another stolen child.

I pray for the door to open. I pray for a way to escape.

Hours or days pass and I hear something at my window. How can this be? I am on the second floor. Have I died and is it an angel tapping there? But then I realize that someone is throwing stones at the window. I get up off the floor and grip the window bars. With my bare feet flat against the wall, I climb up to the window like I'm climbing a mountain. I get my feet onto the ledge and hoist myself up.

A woman. Eyes swollen nearly shut from weeping. Head covered with a faded kerchief. She sees me through the window-pane and waves frantically at first, but then realizes that I am not the child she is looking for. How many stolen children are in this place?

"Help me!" I scream. I pound on the window.

A soldier nudges her with his rifle.

From a room down the hallway, I hear a child cry, "Mama!" That child pounds on the window too.

Why can I hear the child scream and pound but the woman cannot? She turns and scans the windows one last time and the soldier hits her in the face with his rifle, knocking her to her knees.

I hear the door open behind me. A woman dressed in white comes into the room and orders me away from the window, but I stay where I am. "Help!"

The nurse is beside me now and she wraps an arm around my waist. I kick and thrash. I feel a cold sting on my shoulder. Suddenly, I feel weak. I cannot hold onto the bars any longer. I fall into the woman's arms.

The library book slipped out of my hand and landed on my toe. I rubbed my eyes and looked around. I was standing in my own lilac bedroom in the house that Ivan built on Sheridan Street in Brantford. It was dark outside but my lamp was on. No bars on the window. The door open. I was safe. My heart felt like it would explode.

I didn't want to be alone, so I walked down the stairs. Marusia and Ivan were no longer in the kitchen drinking tea. I poked my head into their bedroom. Ivan was softly snoring and Marusia was sound asleep. We still had no living room furniture so I sat in the middle of the floor and stared out our front window.

My flashes of the past before this had been short. This one had been terrifyingly long. I struggled to remember more bits about the building . . . A rich person's home in the city that had been transformed into something horrible. Tall white steps leading to an elegant entryway with a vaulted ceiling. Stairs on either side leading up up up. I remembered being carried like a sack of grain up those stairs. Being locked in a room. Others were locked in rooms beside me. What had I done to deserve this punishment? What happened before that . . . and what happened after? My mind was a blank.

A warm hand rested on my shoulder. It took me a few moments to realize I was back in the present. Marusia was kneeling at my side. "Nadia . . . Nadia . . . Are you all right?"

"I have remembered more."

"Do you want to talk about it?"

I didn't say anything for a few minutes, but instead tried to breathe slowly to calm down my heart. "I dreamed of being locked in a big house."

"The German farmhouse?" Marusia asked.

"No," I said. "This was a fancy house in the city."

Marusia's brow furrowed. "How old were you?"

"I don't know . . . too short to see out the window."

"So this is a memory from before you lived with the Germans . . ." Marusia said, as much to herself as to me.

"*Before* I lived with the Germans? What does that mean?" I asked. I could feel her trembling beside me. I think she was weeping in the darkness but didn't want me to know it.

"I have told you that you are not German," she said. "That was not your birth family."

If that family wasn't my birth family, who were they? And who *was* my birth family?

I knew Marusia and Ivan were not my birth parents, but I knew they loved me. It felt right that the Germans weren't my parents. Mutter never treated me the same as Eva. But how did I get there and who were my *real* parents? None of this made sense.

"Then who am I?"

Marusia shook her head. "I don't know exactly who you are, but you are Ukrainian. I know that for a fact."

"But—how can you know?"

"Small things that you did without knowing it," she said.

"Like what?" I asked.

"The way you crossed yourself after a prayer," she said. "And you would sing the *kolysanka* to yourself when you thought no one was listening."

"I thought it was my secret song."

"Yes," said Marusia, hugging me. "I know you thought that. You also didn't look like anyone else in that German family."

I nodded in agreement.

"And you spoke German with a Ukrainian accent," she said with a smile.

"I did?"

"Very much so."

It was a jumble in my head, but I was comforted to know that those people weren't my family. Every time a student at school would taunt me, calling me a Hitler girl or Nazi Nadia, I felt a tug of shame. I had met many kind Germans, both in Canada and during the war. I felt sorry for Mutter because she was always sad, but she was not kind to me. And Vater was almost a stranger. A cold, hard stranger. After the war, when I heard about the many evil things that Hitler had done, it made me feel ashamed of who I might be.

And that one big question still hung over me. *Who am I?*

I didn't want to go back to my room and I was too shaken to be alone. Ivan only had a few more hours to sleep before it would be time for him to get up so Marusia tiptoed back to the bedroom and got a blanket and pillows and we slept on the floor in the middle of the living room, hugging each other tightly.

I couldn't get to sleep. I didn't want to think about that house. I thought about Cinderella and how she could dream about what her heart wished for. As I drifted toward sleep again, a memory of another mother long ago appeared in my mind . . .

I sat on her warm lap in the dark with my arms around her waist, and breathed in her faint scent of lilac. I did not want to let her go. She cooed the kolysanka *in my ear. A warm tear splashed on my cheek. I looked up. Despite the darkness I saw tears on her face . . .*

But who was she?

It was almost Christmas, and a soft blanket of snow covered the streets and houses. I got out of the habit of going to Linda's house. We were still friends, but the thought of being close to Yates Castle made me uncomfortable. Going to church wasn't the same either. The smell of incense no longer gave me comfort.

One day, after school and before Ivan or Marusia got home, I sat on my swing in the backyard and closed my eyes and tried very hard just to think of my past. So often, the memories would come to me unexpectedly. How I would love to be able to think of them on purpose so I could sort it all out. I could hear someone banging a hammer in the distance and the sound reminded me of mortar fire. Big, soft snowflakes hit my head and shoulders. I closed my eyes and held my face to the sky. As each flake tickled my face, I tried to remember the past.

"Boo!"

I screamed and nearly fell off the swing.

"Hey, I really scared you," Mychailo said. "You should see your face."

"That wasn't very nice," I snapped at him. My heart was still pounding.

"Do you want to go to the park?" he asked.

"It's too cold," I said.

Mychailo rolled his eyes. "If the snow bothers you, why are you sitting out here on the swing getting snowed on?"

"Fine, let's go to the park," I said. Going to the park might be just the thing to clear my head. I wrote a note for Marusia and Ivan and propped it on top of the icebox.

We got to the park, but then Mychailo didn't want to stop because there were some boys from the school horsing around with a toboggan.

"We can just walk around," I told him. "Or maybe go to the library."

We walked past our school and the library, through Victoria Park, and all the way to the market square without saying a word to each other. It wasn't a market day so the square was empty. I gazed into store windows filled with toys and perfumes and other things for Christmas—there was so much choice.

Mychailo finally asked, "What are you thinking about?"

"Nothing," I answered.

"That's not true," he replied. "You've got a sad look on your face. Are you thinking about your old home?"

I looked up at him in surprise. “What do you mean?”

“What I mean is pretty simple,” he said. “Don’t you ever think about the home you left behind?”

“It’s such a jumble,” I told him. “But I do think about it a lot.”

Mychailo must have had some similar experiences. He had lived in a camp just like us. He had lived through the war. But this was something that we never talked about. I wasn’t sure if it was because it was too painful for him, or if it was because his mind wouldn’t let him remember, like what happened to me.

“What do you remember about the war?” I asked him.

“Everything,” he said, kicking at a stone with the tip of his shoe. “Sometimes I wish I could forget.”

“Can you tell me what you remember?” I asked. “Maybe it will help *me* remember.”

“Smells, most of all,” he answered. “Gunpowder and rot and blood.”

Even as he said the words, my nose wrinkled at the memories.

“The nicest thing about Canada is that they don’t have those smells here.”

Mychailo was right. In Canada, everything smelled like it had just been washed.

We walked to the library in silence. Mychailo pulled open the heavy side door that led directly to the children's department. As I stepped in I took a deep breath, savoring the scent of furniture polish, soap, and books. Much better than the smell of war.

When I got back home, Marusia and Ivan were there, but I felt like being alone. I sat on my swing in the snow and thought about the smells that haunted Mychailo. I had started to remember so much of my past. I willed myself to think about my escape with Marusia, first remembering the parts that came easily to me, and then thinking about what happened next, starting with our last days before reaching the DP camp . . .

I remembered. The train had stopped. We'd huddled together on the flatcar with many other escapees. Rain poured down but one man took off his frayed greatcoat and tried to cover us all.

A jeep pulled up. Soviet soldiers piled out. There was a fight, gunshots, screams. Marusia gripped my hand as we and the other escapees scattered. We ran. Another gunshot. I felt a bullet whiz past my shoulder. We were the only ones not caught.

We ran and ran. My ribs ached but we kept on going until it was the blackest part of night, and we reached a deserted village. The Soviets had already been here. My nose wrinkled at the familiar stink of blood and smoke. Where once a house had stood, now there was just a hole in the ground—the remains of a root cellar. Marusia stumbled down first and then lifted me in.

I shivered from the cold and the wet; the dirty rag that had once been my pink dress did not keep me warm. How long Marusia and I huddled together in the rubble on the floor of the cellar I did not know. We tried to cover ourselves with leaves. Tried to sleep.

The next morning, I woke with a start when Marusia screamed and rolled on top of me. I could not get my breath and pushed at her to get her off me, but she wouldn't move. I heard a whoosh, then saw a pitchfork. It missed my head by an inch. Standing above us was a woman shriveled and bent with age. She reached down to grab the handle of the pitchfork, but Marusia swung around and held onto the blades.

"Please don't hurt us," Marusia pleaded in German.

The woman blinked in surprise. "A woman and child!" she murmured. "I thought you were more Russian soldiers."

"We have been running from them," said Marusia.

"Are you Germans?"

"No," said Marusia. "We are foreign workers."

"Why don't you go back with them?" the woman asked, pointing in the direction of the Soviets' advance.

"They're as bad as the Nazis," said Marusia.

"Come on, then," said the woman, turning her back on us.

I helped Marusia to her feet. She gripped the handle of the pitchfork and we climbed out of the root cellar.

The old woman assumed our obedience and did not look back. Now that it was light, I could see the charred ruins of cottages lining the street. We followed her to what used to be the village square. All was rubble except for the corner of a church. The burnt wood and glass shards had been shoved to one side of the church floor. Within the protection of where the two remaining walls met, the floor was covered with a filthy bedsheet. On it lay a young woman slashed with blood and bruises. At first I thought she was dead, but then I noticed a slight movement of her face.

"My granddaughter survived," said the old woman. "But just barely. I need you to watch her while I look for food."

We stayed there for several days. The old woman shared with us the food she managed to scrounge. Marusia cleaned the granddaughter's wounds and disinfected them with a tincture she made from leaves and stalks. When we left, the old woman pointed us in the direction of the nearest displaced persons camp . . .

That night, in Brantford, I dreamed the scent of manure and gunpowder, blood and dirt. And lilacs.

CHAPTER FIFTEEN
INSPECTOR SUTTON

"Students, look smart," Miss Ferris said the next morning. "We're having a visitor after recess and I want you all to be on your best behavior."

I looked over to Linda. She arched an eyebrow. When Miss Ferris turned to write something on the blackboard, Linda leaned toward my desk and whispered, "It's probably the inspector."

I didn't know what that meant. I noticed that many of the students seemed on edge and Miss Ferris herself spoke with a half-strangled voice. Whoever this inspector was, I didn't look forward to seeing him.

I finally got my chance to ask Linda about the visitor once the recess bell rang. "They send a boss a couple of times every year," she explained. "If a teacher isn't doing a good job, she can get fired."

"What about the students?" I asked.

“An inspector can cause trouble for students too,” said Linda. “If you’re late for school a lot or if you’re absent too many times, the inspector wants to see you. I dread it when they come.”

I thought of my horrible first day of school and how I had left the yard without permission. “Do you think I’ll be in trouble because of leaving school on the first day?” I asked.

She paused to consider. “If you were going to get into trouble, it would have happened by now. That was months ago.”

Her words made me feel slightly less frightened about the inspector’s visit, but like everyone else, I was not looking forward to it.

As we were lining up to go back into school after the recess bell rang, a black taxi pulled up. All I could see through the back window were the head and shoulders of a woman.

I nudged Linda with my elbow and whispered, “Is that the inspector?”

Linda looked doubtful. “I’ve never seen a lady inspector.”

Miss Ferris came out and made us step neatly in line. We marched into our class and took our seats. She rapped a ruler on her desk to get our attention.

"Inspector Sutton is here," she said, a look of panic on her face. "When she comes in, I shall clap my hands twice and you will say, in unison, 'Good morning, Inspector Sutton.'"

Just then the door flew open and an unsmiling woman carrying a black satchel strode in. Her gray hair was pulled into a loose bun at the nape of her neck and she wore a brown tailored suit over a white men's-style shirt. When I had seen her in the taxi, I was nervous, but now seeing her in front of me, I was terrified. It wasn't a normal kind of terror. Something deep inside told me that this woman was going to harm me. I had a panicked urge to bolt from the classroom, but the inspector was standing in front of the only exit. It was all I could do to stay seated. I gripped the sides of my desk to keep from shaking.

Miss Ferris was also nervous. Was she feeling the same as me? Her face was drained of color. She forgot to clap her hands, so some students jumped out of their seats, but not everyone. I was the last to get to my feet. A few straggling voices called out, "Good morning, Inspector Sutton."

The inspector put her satchel on the floor and her hands on her hips. "Is that the best you can do?"

"GOOD MORNING, INSPECTOR SUTTON!" we shouted out in unison.

"Good morning, class," she said. Then, using her hands like the conductor of an orchestra, she motioned for us to sit down.

"Now, Miss Ferris." The inspector turned away from us and gazed upon our teacher. "What poem can your students recite for me?"

"Um . . . Miss . . . Inspector Sutton . . . we haven't practiced recitations recently." Miss Ferris clutched her ruler as if it were a lifeline.

"Can they sing a song for me?"

Miss Ferris brightened. "They can sing 'The Maple Leaf Forever.'"

"Very good," said Inspector Sutton. "Let's hear it."

Miss Ferris got us all to stand up again and we sang the song. Most of us seemed to be on key and we kept fairly good time with each other, I thought. Miss Ferris looked expectantly at Miss Sutton.

"Good," said the inspector.

She walked behind Miss Ferris's desk and grabbed the back of her chair, dragged it across the floor, and positioned it to face us, then sat down. "That's better," she said. She drew a pair of wire-rimmed spectacles out of her suit pocket and perched them on the end of her nose. She took a black notebook out of her satchel, then pointed to one student at a time. Each was made to stand and answer a single question and then sit down. She jotted down notes about each of us. They weren't difficult questions, but it was terrifying nonetheless. My question was, "What is your favorite color?" When I told her it was lilac, she smiled and said that my English was good for a newcomer.

After she was finished, Inspector Sutton put Miss Ferris's chair back behind the desk and walked to the door. I was so relieved that she was leaving. She hadn't said anything about me running away from school on that first day. Linda had been right.

I was almost starting to breathe again when the inspector paused. It was like she had just remembered something. She opened her satchel and took out the black notebook, flipping through the pages with a frown on her face. "The new girl . . . Nadia?" She looked over her spectacles and surveyed the class yet again.

I stood up.

"Come here," she said with a smile. "You can carry my bag."

The thought of going near that woman made me feel like I was going to be sick to my stomach. I took one deep calming breath and began to walk over to her. She smelled like mothballs.

Her bag was surprisingly heavy and I needed both hands to carry it. She walked out of the room and I stumbled after her. She was waiting at the door to the grade one class when I caught up with her.

"Thank you," she said. "That bag gets so heavy to carry around all day. Here's a little something for your trouble."

She pulled a cellophane-wrapped hard candy from her pocket and held it out to me.

I stared at that candy on her outstretched palm. Without knowing why I was doing it or where I was going, I bolted down the hallway. All I knew was that I had to get away. I pushed open the outside door and kept on running. It was cold and I was without my winter coat and boots, but that didn't stop me. The chill against my face felt like freedom.

"Nadia, come back!" Inspector Sutton called.

I didn't stop running but turned to look. She was standing in the entranceway with a look of shock on her face. I was grateful that she wasn't following me. When I turned a moment later to check, she was gone.

I didn't know where I was going, but a feeling deep inside me told me that my life depended on getting away from that brown-suited woman. I didn't want to go home. Wouldn't that be the first place she would look for me?

My legs took me on my usual route to the library. I hid behind a snowbank when I heard a car. I could see the children's entrance, but there was a group of mothers with little children in strollers chatting in front of it. I ran up the steps to the main doors, painfully aware that I was in full view of anyone passing by. Luckily, none of the chatting mothers noticed me. When I got to the top, I opened the door just a crack. My face was blasted with warm air as I peered in. No one was there, so I stepped inside. I didn't realize how chilled to the bone I was until the warmth of the inside air wrapped around me. I could hear voices coming out of the main library room, so I slipped down the steps to the children's department.

It was story time in the picture-book room, but the novel room looked empty. I sat on the floor in the corner farthest from the door and wrapped my arms around my legs and rocked my body back and forth, chanting the *kolysanka*. My whole body trembled—not just from being out in the cold, but from my memories. Images of a brown-suited woman invaded my mind. I tried to think of other things but it was no use. I was frightened beyond words.

CHAPTER SIXTEEN

BROWN SISTERS

I shiver at the foot of our bed, my arms wrapping around my knees for warmth. We layer our clothing, but the cold always seeps through. We have one threadbare wool blanket that is too worthless to barter for food. I tuck it lovingly around my baba*, but her lips are still blue. Lida walks into the bedroom holding a chipped bowl in her hands. It contains what we like to call soup, but we both know there is little nourishment in it: water, faint flavor from bones boiled dozens of times, scraps of potato or cabbage, and anything else we can find to put in it.*

She sets the bowl down on the nightstand and props up Baba's head and shoulders with a pillow. Baba's eyes flicker open. She looks at me and then at Lida. "My granddaughters," she says. "Don't waste this food on me. I am not long for this world."

Lida and I both know what Baba says is true, but how can we not try to save her? She is all the family we have left. Tato was taken by the Soviet police in early summer, like so many of the other Ukrainian men. Weeks after that, Mama was taken by the Nazi police. Old people and children don't get ration cards. Baba's hoarded bits got us through the fall. But now that it is the dead of winter, we are desperate. We have burned most of our furniture for warmth and bartered our precious books. Even our beloved lilac bush has been hacked to pieces and burnt as firewood.

Lida leans on the edge of the bed and offers a spoonful of soup, but Baba refuses to open her lips. Lida sighs. "What if we share?"

Baba nods. "You eat first."

We pass the spoon around, sharing the watery soup one sip at a time.

Once Baba falls back to sleep, Lida and I go out to the street to beg. First we sit in front of the bakery. When Sarah and her parents were alive, they would always find something for us—even if it was just a stale bun. But they were among the first that the Nazis took.

The woman who comes out now speaks German. She pushes us away with a broom. We sit on the steps in front of the boarded-up church, huddling close together for warmth. I remember a time when we could go inside. Mama and Tato were still with us. The smell of incense made me feel safe. But people don't come here anymore. Besides, there are too many beggars and not enough food. We are given not even a crust of bread.

I notice that a snaking lineup of children has suddenly formed outside the gates of what used to be the synagogue. Whenever a line forms, we know to run to it. Does it matter what is being given out? It will be better than nothing.

When we get closer we see two women dressed in brown suits with white collars and cuffs. "Maybe they're nuns," I say hopefully.

Lida looks at me with surprise. "The Nazis got rid of the sisters long ago."

One of the women writes notes in a black leather book. The other dips her hand into a large paper bag and brings out candies. My stomach rumbles at the sight. I cannot remember the last time I have eaten anything other than maggoty bread or watery soup.

I stand on my tiptoes and see that Sofia from down the street is talking to the brown sisters now. She does a little whoop for joy when she gets candy. Finally, it is my turn. Lida stands behind me, her hands resting on my shoulders.

"What lovely blond hair you have," the woman says to me in German. She crouches down until her face is level with mine. "And blue eyes."

I smile politely. My blond hair often helps when begging from Germans.

"Girls, are you sisters?" the woman taking notes asks.

"Yes," I say.

"Where do you live?" she asks.

"In that house." I point to our whitewashed cottage at the end of the street.

"Is she telling the truth?" the woman asks Lida with a smile.

"Yes."

The other woman reaches into her bag and draws out three candies. She gives all of them to me. The look of hope on Lida's face crumbles. The woman reaches back into the bag and draws out three more sweets. She holds them just under Lida's nose. "Tell me how old you are and how old your little sister is."

"Larissa is five," Lida says. "And I am eight."

The woman grins. She puts the three candies into Lida's palm.

Lida grabs my hand and we run back home, giggling. Baba is asleep when we get there. Lida and I each put one of our candies on her nightstand, and then we sit together, leaning against our cold hearth, and savor our candies.

The three of us sleep together in the big bed for warmth. Usually, Baba hugs us tight and sings the kolysanka. *But since she is already asleep, Lida and I sing it softly to ourselves.*

When I first hear the banging, I think it is a dream. I know it is real when Baba sits up in bed and wraps her bony arms around us. "Do not open the door," she hisses.

The three of us sit in the dark, clinging to each other and praying that whoever is on the other side will go away. But the banging continues. The door bursts open. A beam of light darts through the main room, then finds the bedroom. The doorway fills with the silhouette of two soldiers; one holding a flashlight and the other pointing a rifle at us. When my eyes get used to the brightness, I see a third person—the woman in brown who gave us candy.

She comes to the bed and grabs me roughly by the arm, but Baba won't let go. The woman turns to the soldiers. "Take her."

Baba holds on with such strength that I have bruises on my rib cage for days after, but in the end she is no match for two armed men. One throws me over his shoulder. The other does the same with Lida.

"Baba!" I scream as they carry us out the door.

Baba falls back on the bed amid torn bedclothes, a trickle of blood on her cheek. Her arms extend toward us and the look on her face makes my heart crumble. Just before the flashlight clicks off, I notice the two candies sitting at her nightstand. Untouched.

Lida and I are thrown into the back of a truck. It smells like urine. Other children are weeping. Lida and I find each other in the darkness and clutch each other in fear and desperation.

I felt a hand on my shoulder. Then a voice came.

"Nadia, are you okay?" Miss Barry.

I rubbed my eyes, blinked twice, and looked around me. I was crouched in the corner of the novel room in the children's department of the public library. In Brantford. I was safe. That girl was my sister. Lida. Where is she now?

I am not Nadia. I am not Gretchen. *Larissa.* My name is Larissa!

I felt something warm cover my back and shoulders. "You're shivering," said Miss Barry. "Where is your coat?"

I looked at her but didn't answer. My mind was still filled with images from the past.

"Let's get you into the staff room," she said. "There's a sofa for you to lie down on."

She gently picked me up and carried me into the other room. "I am going to get in touch with your parents." I watched as her lips continued to move, but I didn't understand anything more that she said. My mind had returned to the past . . .

I am in a large white room with bright lights. Maybe a hospital room, but the children are frightened, not sick. When it is my turn, the nurse makes me remove everything but my underwear. My face is hot with shame. I scream when she holds a metal instrument up to my face. "Tsk tsk," she says, then in German, "This is a caliper—for measuring. Nothing to be afraid of."

Her words do not comfort me. As she measures and takes notes, a different woman takes photographs of me—from the front, the side, the back.

What are they doing? What does this mean?

My nose is measured in three places. "Turn around," she says. I feel the cold metal prongs dig into the sides of my head.

She writes more numbers in her book. She measures my legs and my arms and waist. Throughout all of this, I stand there, too frightened to move.

When she is finished, she grips my left palm upward and I watch in fear as she carefully injects pinpricks of black into my wrist. Is this poison? When she's finished, I hold it up to my face. It looks like a tiny mole.

She grabs my hair roughly and I feel a pinprick behind my ear. "There," she says. "You are a Lebensborn."

What is a Lebensborn? *I know of the children who disappear. One day they are begging on the street and the next day it's as if they never existed. Are they* Lebensborn *too?*

Lida's turn is next. She is measured and photographed but isn't marked with black.

When all the children are measured, we are sorted into two groups: those with black marks and those without. I am in one. Lida is in the other. Her group is marched to the door.

"Please!" I scream. "Let me go with my sister!"

"You are the lucky one," says the woman in white.

"Lida!" I scream.

Lida turns and looks. Her eyes are filled with despair. She is shoved out the door. I try to run after her but they hold me back.

Days blur. Children marching. Children saluting the führer. We are given small rations of plain food. At first I gobble it down, but then I feel guilty that I can't save some to give to Baba or

Lida. The thought of eating this food makes me feel ill. I speak Ukrainian to one of the other children, but a woman in white slaps my face. "You are German!" she says. "Speak German."

The next time I speak my own language, I am dragged away. They kick me down a flight of wooden stairs and I land on the dirt floor. It is dark and all I can see are the glowing eyes of rats. I clasp my arms around my knees and try to stay warm. When the women in white come to get me, the brightness from outside almost blinds me.

I take classes with the other children. A woman who does not smile teaches us the rules we are to live by. Ukrainians and Poles are subhuman. Those who are allowed to live will be slaves to the Aryans. "You are Aryans," she tells us. "The people you think were your parents are thieves. They stole you from your Aryan parents and now we will give you back."

I know she speaks lies.

"Jews are rats," she continues. "None deserve to live."

I think of Sarah and her parents. They were Jewish and they were taken away. Sarah's mother had always found me bread. Sarah's father never hurt a soul.

"You are wrong!" I cry.

I cover my mouth, but it is too late.

The other students regard me with round-eyed horror.

I am put in a truck and taken away from the other children. A soldier throws me over his shoulder and carries me up a tall set of white steps and into a mansion. I pound on his back and scream for my baba. *I am locked into a bare white room and given no food or water. I pound on the door but no one comes. The next day I call in German. Someone brings water . . .*

I was suddenly aware of the blanket that was draped over my shoulders. It had the faint scent of lavender and talcum powder. I snuggled into it, thankful for its warmth. The rush of memory faded and I looked around me. I was lying on a sofa in a room near Miss Barry's desk. She sat on a stool in front of me, her hands gripped around a glass of water. All at once, the image of the school inspector filled my mind.

"Please don't send me back to school!"

"You're safe with me," said Miss Barry. "I phoned your father at the foundry. He asked me to sit with you until he can get here."

She held the glass of water out to me. I took grateful sips. My mouth felt like sawdust. I closed my eyes.

CHAPTER SEVENTEEN
GRETCHEN

Gretchen Himmel. With a flash of understanding, I remembered *becoming* Gretchen Himmel.

At first I only pretended to believe that I was German. But the more I lied, the more real it became. I first spoke German to make the punishment stop, but soon I was thinking in German. Marching with the other children, reciting long poems and songs about Hitler and the Reich. We were born to rule the world. I was proud to be one of the chosen.

Larissa disappeared and Gretchen emerged . . .

Gretchen knows that the woman I called Baba is not my grandmother. She stole me from my parents, who are decent German farmers. The man who called me daughter is a bandit. The woman I called mother is a spy. That girl Lida is not my sister. She is an evil slave and she was trying to trick me. She is being punished for her crimes.

Jews are rats. They deserve to die. I can hardly wait to go back home, to my real parents. My name is Gretchen. I've seen my birth certificate and it says Gretchen Himmel. *It is a relief to leave the confusion behind.*

I am bathed, then dressed in a crisp white blouse and blue tunic and shoes that pinch at the heel. My hair is clean and combed and braided. I sit by myself in the backseat of a long black car and breathe in the clean scent of freshly polished leather. The car stops at a huge farmhouse in the country. The fields around it go on for miles and are tended by slaves. The driver is a soldier in a dove-gray uniform and he opens the door for me with a smile. He says, "I am sure you are glad to be home, Gretchen."

I step out of the car and gulp in the country air. A blond girl in a pale pink dress pushes open the door of the house and runs to me. A sad-eyed blond woman follows close behind.

"My big sister has finally arrived!" the little girl says.

Before I know it, she has wrapped her arms around my waist. She is crying or laughing, I don't know which. "I am so glad you're home," says Eva in German.

Is this my home? I don't remember it. But I don't remember many things. I am relieved to be safe, in a place called home.

Eva tugs me by the hand, pulling me to the open door of the big farmhouse. The blond woman walks a few steps behind us. She has barely greeted me, but Eva tells me she's our mutti. *I watch her through the corner of my eye and see that she's wiping a tear away from her cheek.*

The door of the house opens up to a big entryway that smells of bleach. My heart pounds, but Eva squeezes my hand.

She leads me into a room just beyond the entryway and I gasp. Two walls are lined from floor to ceiling with books, most in German, but some in other languages too. I hunger to touch them. The books call to me. Above the fireplace is a huge portrait of Hitler, our leader and savior. On the mantel is a framed picture of a sad-looking young man in a dark uniform.

"That's our Geert," says Eva.

"He is very handsome," I say.

The woman who is supposed to be our mother stands behind us and regards the photo. I can hear her sniffle. "Your brother was handsome," she says. "And brave. He died while fighting for the Fatherland."

She leaves the room and Eva and I are alone. "Mutti has been so sad since Geert died. Maybe she'll cheer up now that you've come."

I don't remember Geert, and now he's gone. That makes me feel guilty. "I too am sad that our brother died."

Eva looks at me strangely, then blinks. "You'll like it here," she says. "There's lots of food."

"Your father is on his way," said Miss Barry.

I blinked once, slowly, and looked around. I was on the sofa in the staff room at the library. I looked down and saw that I was holding a glass of water. I took a sip. Miss Barry brushed a wisp of hair out of my eyes. It was such a gentle gesture that I almost wept . . .

Eva is right. There is a lot of food. Apples and mushrooms and noodles and sauce, meat and stuffing. Mutter places it all on the dining room table. But whatever I put in my mouth sits like a lump of coal on my tongue. Mutter makes chocolate cake with icing to entice me. She makes biscuits in the shape of men and draws on a face in white icing. Eva loves it all and gulps down every bit. I force myself to eat even when it makes me feel ill. I want the hurt to go away from Mutter's eyes.

I have my own room with a giant four-poster bed, but I cannot sleep. Dark-uniformed men dine at our table and talk together until the wee hours of the morning. I hear the clinking of glasses and roars of laughter. I rarely see Vater except at these meetings. Eva and I put on our prettiest dresses and go downstairs to greet the guests. Vater introduces us as his "two flowers for the Fatherland."

When I am finally able to go back to my room, I sing a song of nonsense words to block out the noises, but I cannot sleep.

In spring, the OST woman arrives at the farm in the truck. She smells bad and I do not like her, but the next time I see her she no longer wears the OST badge and she is clean. Mutter tells us to call her Cook. Eva and I play outside together. We collect lilacs to give to Mutter. She puts them in a vase and sets them in the middle of the kitchen table. She says Cook will like them. Mutter prefers bought ones for the dining room.

We are not allowed to go into the fields where the slaves are. I see a slave come to the door. Cook bandages his wound. Mutter doesn't see that. Neither does Eva. I should tell Mutter about it, but for some reason, I don't.

Mutter begins to take Eva on errands but leaves me at home. When they are gone, I open up the book room and breathe in the scent of old paper. It makes my heart ache to smell it, but somehow it makes me happy too. I climb up on the desk and draw out a book with gold lettering on the spine. The one beside it crashes to the ground, bending the pages.

My heart pounds when I hear footsteps. It is only Cook. She picks up the book and puts it back on the shelf. She takes the one I am holding and puts it away too. She examines the books. Her eyes light up and she takes one down and hands it to me.

"You can look at this storybook until they come home," she says.

The title is not in German. "Popelyushka!" *I say. Cook smiles.*

Another time, I sit under the lilac bushes and whisper my nonsense song under my breath. Cook comes up to me. I notice that her hands are red with work and her eyes look tired and sad. I feel sorry for her even though she is an animal. I say in German, "Would you like to hear me sing?"

She nods.

I sing again my secret song. Cook weeps. On the second verse, with a tear-filled voice, she joins in. She sings the entire song with me.

How can she know my secret language? "You know my kolysanka,*" I say. She tries to hug me but I push her away. Mutter has told me to stay away from the slaves.*

Cook swallows back her tears, and then in harsh, precise German she says, "This is not your home."

I am shocked speechless.

But she isn't finished. There is more. "I will protect you."

The harsh ringing of a telephone jarred me back to the present. I blinked and looked around. The past was so real, yet here I was, lying on a sofa in the staff room of the library. I could hear Miss Barry's voice talking to someone on the other end of the telephone. Then her voice faded . . .

When Mutter and Eva come back from their errands, I am bursting to tell them what Cook said. She should be punished for her crime. But for some reason I say nothing. The next time Eva and Mutter go away, Cook invites me to share a meal in the kitchen with her. It is slave food—a thin soup with black bread. I take one spoonful of the thin broth and begin to weep. I try to remember what the soup reminds me of, but my memory has been washed clean.

We are to go to a rally and Mutter has told me to be ready for when they get back. I put on my pink dress and Cook braids my hair. I wait. And wait. And wait.

I walk through the house and see that drawers have been left open and belongings are scattered on the floor. I feel the ground tremble.

"The Soviets are coming," whispers Cook. "We must leave this place."

I do not want to go. This is my home. The room of books is here. The lilac bush is here. Mutter told me to wait. Cook picks me up and carries me out the door. I scream and pull her hair. She drops me on the ground and I fall hard on my back. "Come with me if you want to live," she says. And she begins to walk away.

I follow her, begging her to wait up. I run after her through the fields and I see that the slaves are all gone. When I mention this, Cook turns on me, her face red with fury. "Slavs," she says, "Not slaves. Those people are Ukrainian. They're just like you."

I don't believe her, but this is not the time to argue. She tells me her name is Marusia, not Cook.

We hide behind bushes as Soviet soldiers comb the fields, rooting out the other Slavs—the other stolen people. We are to be brought back to the Soviet Union and punished for letting ourselves be stolen by the Germans.

We walk through forests and countryside studded with land mines. We see villages burning and hear bombs exploding. I do not expect to live.

We join a group of ragged survivors. "Your name is Nadia now," Marusia tells me. "You will never be Gretchen again."

"But why Nadia?" I ask her.

"The name means hope," she says. "It was the middle name of my little sister. She was stolen by the Nazis too."

CHAPTER EIGHTEEN

LARISSA

"Nadia . . . *Nadia*. You are safe."

The scent of apples and laundry soap. It had to be Marusia. I opened my eyes. It was Marusia, in her work clothes. I blinked and looked around, trying to get my bearings. I was still in the library staff room, bundled up in Miss Barry's blanket. A shiver ran deep in my bones. I felt unbearably sad and so very cold.

Marusia's arm was around my waist. Ivan was sitting cross-legged on the carpet, his brow creased with concern. There was no one else here, just me, Marusia, and Ivan.

How much trouble was I in for running away from school a second time? Ivan seemed to know what was on my mind. "We told the inspector that you were ill," he said.

I could feel my throat filling with tears—of relief, but also guilt. How long had I been here?

"What time is it?" I asked.

"It's after six," said Ivan. "We have been sitting here with you for hours."

Money was so scarce for us, and I had made them miss work.

I had no control over it—the tears flowed. "I am so sorry," I said. "I didn't mean to cause so much trouble."

"You are not trouble," said Ivan.

Marusia said nothing. I could tell by her gulps of air that she was weeping. I realized it wasn't just me she was weeping about. She had lost another Nadia—her own sister—years ago. Just as I had lost my family. She held me tight and rested her head on my shoulder. I hugged her back. Ivan leaned forward and wrapped his arms around both of us. We wept together.

I don't know how long we stayed like that, but I was suddenly aware that we were still in the library.

"Can we go home?" I asked.

We untangled our arms, but when I tried to get up, my joints were so weak that my knees buckled. Marusia was wobbly too.

"Let's get my girls home," said Ivan. He took the blanket off my shoulders and held my coat open so I could slip it on. He must have gone to the school to get it. He wrapped one arm around my waist and another around Marusia's, giving us each support.

When we got home, Marusia warmed up some homemade soup and sliced a few pieces of rye bread. Before, a meal like this would have caused confusing memories and nightmares. But now that my memory was back—parts of it, at least—I was able to think of that last bowl of soup I had shared with my grandmother and sister. It was a sad time, but also a cherished one. How I missed them both.

I still had not pieced together all the details of my life before my parents disappeared. The ache of their loss was like a wound in my heart. I must have been very young when they were taken away. And I realized now that they weren't just taken away. They were dead. Tato was killed by the Soviets and Mama was killed by the Nazis. My teeth chattered—not from the cold but from the realization of all that I had lost.

I wrapped my arms around my chest and rocked back and forth in my chair. Back and forth, back and forth, trying to remember the last time my parents had held me.

But I also knew that Mama and Tato had loved me. Flecks and shadows of scenes from the past told me that. When I thought hard now about Tato, I could remember his warm smile and the last time he tucked me into bed . . .

Mama, dear Mama. Her lilting voice as she sang the *kolysanka*.

And Baba? What strength she had. But she couldn't have survived the shock of losing me and Lida.

Lida.

The dark-haired girl in my dream who tried to grab my hand . . . The OST girl in the bombed-out factory who met my gaze. That was Lida. I knew it now.

Marusia brushed her fingertips lightly on my forearm. "Are you ready to tell us about it?"

I was. At least, about as much as I remembered. It was a relief to say the details out loud.

At first it was all jumbled, but as I continued, my memories began to fall more and more into place. I sorted through the parts of my life when I was Gretchen, and the earlier parts when I was myself.

It was a weight taken from my shoulders to know for sure that Vater and Mutter were not my real parents. The thought of Vater in particular made bile rise in my throat. I had a twinge of worry about Eva, though. She wasn't my sister, but she was just a child. Where was she now? Was she safe? Did she ever think of me?

Marusia nodded as I spoke. She knew my history from when we met at the farm. Of my earlier life, she had guessed some of it. Ivan must have heard from Marusia all that she knew, but still he sat spellbound.

"I always wondered what your real name was," said Marusia. "Larissa is a beautiful name. And you have a sister named Lida."

"Yes."

My sister. My dear big sister, Lida. I started to cry again. "Do you think she still might be alive?" I managed to ask.

"With the memories that you've pieced together, maybe we will be able to find what became of her," said Marusia.

"We'll write to the Red Cross," said Ivan. "We can always hope."

AUTHOR'S NOTE

I FIRST HEARD about the *Lebensborn* program from my mother-in-law, the late Lidia (Krawchuk) Skrypuch. The Nazi front passed through her city of Zolochiv twice and soldiers took over her house. She and her parents became prisoners in their own home. One day she overheard bits of conversation from the Nazi officers. Something was happening at her school the next day. Her parents kept her home. When she did go back to school, all of her blond and blue-eyed female classmates had disappeared. She heard they had been taken for the *Lebensborn* program. I asked her what that meant.

The *Lebensborn* Program

The Holocaust—the Nazi murder of over six million Jews during World War II—is well documented. Most people are not as aware of the Nazis' plans for other people. Hitler and the Nazis believed that the Germanic peoples of Central Europe were the descendants of "Aryans"—members of a "master race" whose destiny was to rule the world. Other ethnic groups were sorted into a pecking order, based on how much "Aryan blood" they supposedly had. Most of the peoples of Northern Europe, Great Britain, and the Low Countries, as well as parts of France, were considered mostly or partly Aryan. Other groups, especially in the south of Europe, were judged less pure but acceptable as neighbors and allies. At the very bottom of this hierarchy were the Jews, along with the Roma (Gypsies). The Nazi goal was to exterminate every Jew and Rom in the world. The Nazis also planned to kill people they deemed mentally or physically unfit.

Nazi policy regarding the Slavs—who include the Russians, Ukrainians, and Byelorussians, as well as the Poles, Czechs, and many others—was less consistent. Slavs were categorized as racially inferior, and Hitler declared that most of their lands in Eastern Europe belonged to Germany as *Lebensraum* ("living space") for the expansion of the Aryan race. Although the Nazis did not call for a Holocaust-style eradication of the Slavs, they treated civilians in Eastern Europe far more harshly than they did civilians elsewhere in Europe. Historians estimate that at least 10 million civilian Slavs were killed by the Germans in Poland and the USSR.

In order to free up "living space" for Aryans, Slavs were to be deported en masse from their homelands. Others were to be sent to Germany as slave laborers. People from the eastern part of Ukraine made up the bulk of these slave laborers. British intelligence reports indicate that the rate of deportation from Soviet Ukraine at times approached 15,000 to 20,000 a day. Soviet cities were full of what the Nazis considered "superfluous eaters"—and death by starvation was common.

Hitler wanted more Aryans to be born, but German women weren't having babies quickly enough. In 1936, Hitler's secret police, the SS, created the *Lebensborn* (Fount of Life) program to increase the number of Aryan children, so that the master race could populate more of Europe. In the beginning, the *Lebensborn* program concentrated on making sure more Aryan babies were produced in Nazi-occupied parts of Europe. But between 1940 and 1942, the Germans also turned their attention to the blond, blue-eyed Polish and Ukrainian children from Eastern Europe, children who also looked Aryan. They began to steal these children from their parents.

There were two methods of rounding up children. The

first was to take every child of a certain age in random villages or towns and sort through them, sending some to be killed, assigning others for slave labor, and yet others for adoption by Nazi families.

Method two involved using specially trained Nazi women known as Brown Sisters to go through a town searching for children with Aryan features. An Aryan-looking child would be offered candy, giving the Brown Sister the chance to ask questions. The child's home would then be raided in the middle of the night and the child taken away.

The stolen children were put through tests, including the measurement of sixty-two body parts, to ensure that they were "racially valuable." Any tiny shortcoming meant the difference between an adoptive home and either a concentration camp or a slave labor camp.

The final round of racially valuable children was then sent to special homes where the children were brainwashed into thinking that they were German. Some were told that their parents were dead, or had only been spies and liars. Children who were still young—under the age of eight—were then placed with their new Nazi families. Older children were put in Nazi Youth boarding schools or fostered out.

The Nazis went to great lengths to destroy the records of these children when it became clear that Germany would lose the war, so it is hard to know exactly how many were stolen in this way, although it is estimated to be about 250,000 Polish and Ukrainian children alone. The Nazis were so successful with this program that after the war, most of the stolen children refused to leave their German parents, even if their birth parents were still alive and could be located.

The *Ostarbeiters*

The Nazis didn't just steal children. They also forced millions of young adults into forced labor. Those from Eastern Europe were called *Ostarbeiters* (Eastern Workers). They were treated harshly—often worked to death. They were required to wear a badge stitched with the letters *OST* and most lived behind barbed wire in guarded camps. There were 3 to 5.5 million *Ostarbeiters* in Nazi Germany. Most were Ukrainian. Many were forced to work in German munitions factories because the Nazis realized that these factories were prime targets for bombing by the Allied nations. Many *Ostarbeiters* died in Allied bombing raids.

Ukrainian Identity

Before World War II, the land where Ukrainians had lived for more than a thousand years had become part of Poland and the Soviet Union. Since wartime statistics identified people by their citizenship, not ethnicity, Ukrainians were identified as Polish or "Soviet" (which was often inaccurately presumed to be Russian). The fall of the Soviet Union in 1991 has made long-suppressed archival information more available to researchers, and has also heightened public awareness of ethnic distinctions among the peoples of Eastern Europe and the former Soviet Union. Both developments have allowed a truer picture of the Ukrainian experience of World War II to emerge. The nation of Ukraine declared its independence in 1991.

READ MORE ABOUT LIDA IN

MAKING BOMBS FOR HITLER

A novel by MARSHA FORCHUK SKRYPUCH

CHAPTER ONE

LOSING LARISSA—1943

The room smelled of soap and the light was so white that it made my eyes ache. I held Larissa's hand in a tight grip. I was her older sister, after all, and she was my responsibility. It would be easy to lose her in this sea of children, and we had both lost far too much already.

Larissa looked up at me and I saw her lips move, but I couldn't hear her words above the wails and screams. I bent down so that my ear was level with her lips.

"Don't leave me," she said.

I wrapped my arms around her and gently rocked her back and forth. I whispered our favorite lullaby into her ear.

A loud crack startled us both. The room was suddenly silent. A woman in white stepped in among us. She clapped her hands sharply once more.

"Children," she said in brisk German. "You will each have a medical examination."

Weeping boys and girls were shoved into a long snaking line that took up most of the room. I watched as one by one, kids were taken behind a broad white curtain.

When it was Larissa's turn, her eyes went round with fright. I did not want to let go of her, but the nurse pulled our hands apart.

"Lida, stay with me."

I stood at the edge of the curtain and watched as the woman made Larissa take off her nightgown. My sister's face was red with shame. When the woman held a metal instrument to her face, Larissa screamed. I rushed up and tried to knock that thing out of the nurse's hand, but the nurse called for help and someone held me back. When they finished with Larissa, they told her to stand at the other end of the room.

When it was my turn, I barely noticed what they were doing. I kept my eyes fixed on Larissa. She was standing with three other girls. Dozens more had been ordered to stand in a different spot.

When the nurse was finished with me, I slipped my nightgown back on. I was ordered to stand with the larger group—not with Larissa's.

"I need to be in that group," I told the nurse, pointing to where Larissa stood, her arms outstretched, a look of panic on her face.

The nurse's lips formed a thin flat line. "No talking."

She put one hand on each of my shoulders and shoved me toward the larger group.

A door opened wide. We were herded out into the blackness of night.

Larissa screamed, "Lida! Don't leave me!"

I looked back into the room, but could not see her. "I will find you, Larissa!" I shouted. "I promise. Stay strong."

A sharp slap across my face sent me sprawling onto the cold wet grass. I scrambled up and tried to break through the sea of children. I had to get back to Larissa.

Strong arms wrapped around my torso and lifted me up. I was thrown into blackness. With a screech of metal, the door slammed shut.

Blackness.

I dreamed that I was lying in a sea of humming bees. We were swaying back and forth and I sang the lullaby under my breath, imagining that I was being rocked in Mama's arms.

I opened my eyes. It was so dark they took a few minutes to adjust.

I was crammed inside a hot metal room that smelled like a dirty barn. It was so stuffy and stinky and crowded that I could barely breathe. I realized with a shock that we were moving. This was not a room after all, but a train car—the kind for cattle. It swayed back and forth. The sound was not the humming of bees, but the whispers of frightened children and the thrumming of the train on its tracks. At least the sound of war was muffled out.

"Does anyone know where we're going?" I asked.

The whispers stopped. A lone thin voice answered. "To Germany, I think."

My heart sank. If they took me to Germany, how would I ever find Larissa? Wherever she was, she must be feeling so frightened, so alone.

I tried to stand, but with the movement of the car and the hazy light, I fell backward, one of my bare feet landing on a girl's chest.

"Ow!" she cried.

"I'm sorry."

It was pointless to try standing, so I sat up and tried to get my bearings. In the dim light I could see a tangle of limbs and tufts of hair. Kids were packed in so tightly that each overlapped the next. Something smelled bad and a sloshing sound came from one corner.

"What is that over there?" I asked no one in particular.

"That's our bathroom," said the girl I had stepped on. "A pail."

I wrinkled my nose. All these people and one pail for a bathroom? No wonder it smelled so bad.

I crawled as far away as I could get from the stinky pail, moving slowly and being careful not to hurt any of the kids who were crammed in my way. When I got to the other side of the car, I saw there was a thin seam of light framing a panel in the siding. It was a door. I pounded and screamed with all my might. The children who were propped up against it scooted to the side.

"It won't do you any good," said a boy's voice. "We've already tried to open it."

I looked over to him in the dim light and saw a silhouette of wild hair. There was a trickle of dark on his cheek. Was he bleeding?

Using the ridges in the siding to help me balance in a standing position, I felt a long lever across the door. I pushed it down hard. It moved and sprang back up, but the door didn't open.

"It's locked from the outside," a girl's voice said.

I pounded on it again with my fists. Nothing happened.

ABOUT THE AUTHOR

MARSHA FORCHUK SKRYPUCH is a Ukrainian Canadian author acclaimed for her nonfiction and historical fiction, including *Making Bombs for Hitler* and *The War Below*, both companions to this novel. She was awarded the Order of Princess Olha by the president of Ukraine for her writing. Marsha lives in Brantford, Ontario, and you can visit her online at calla.com.

TOP 10 PARIS

MIKE GERRARD & DONNA DAILEY

DK

EYEWITNESS TRAVEL

Left **Glass Pyramid, Musée du Louvre** Right **Crypt vaults, Sacré-Coeur**

DK

LONDON, NEW YORK,
MELBOURNE, MUNICH AND DELHI
www.dk.com

Printed and bound in China by Leo Paper Products Ltd

First American Edition, 2002
14 15 16 17 10 9 8 7 6 5 4 3 2

Published in the United States by DK Publishing,
345 Hudson Street, New York, New York 10014

Reprinted with revisions 2003, 2004, 2005, 2006, 2007, 2008, 2009, 2010, 2011, 2012, 2013, 2014

Published in Great Britain by Dorling Kindersley Limited.

A catalog record for this book is available from the Library of Congress

ISSN 1479-344X
ISBN: 978-1-46541-001-6

Within each Top 10 list in this book, no hierarchy of quality or popularity is implied. All 10 are, in the editor's opinion, of roughly equal merit.

Floors are referred to throughout in accordance with French usage; i.e. the "first floor" is the floor above ground level.

MIX
Paper from responsible sources
FSC™ C018179
FSC www.fsc.org

Contents

Paris Top 10

The information in this DK Eyewitness Top 10 Travel Guide is checked annually.
Every effort has been made to ensure that this book is as up-to-date as possible at the time of going to press. Some details, however, such as telephone numbers, opening hours, prices, gallery hanging arrangements and travel information are liable to change. The publishers cannot accept responsibility for any consequences arising from the use of this book, nor for any material on third party websites, and cannot guarantee that any website address in this book will be a suitable source of travel information. We value the views and suggestions of our readers very highly. Please write to: Publisher, DK Eyewitness Travel Guides, Dorling Kindersley, 80 Strand, London, Great Britain WC2R 0RL, or email: travelguides@dk.com.

Cover: All photographs specially commissioned except: Front – **Corbis**: Scott Stulberg c; **Dorling Kindersley**: Max Alexander clb. Spine – **Dorling Kindersley**: Robert O'Dea b. Back – **Dorling Kindersley**: cra; Max Alexander ca; Eric Meacher cla.

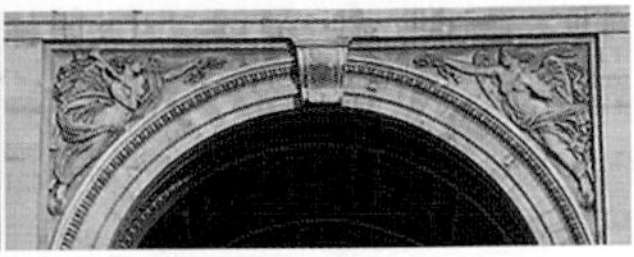

Left **Rose window, Notre-Dame** Right **Stone carvings, Arc de Triomphe**

Around Town

Streetsmart

Left **Bois de Boulogne** Right **Montmartre**

PARIS TOP 10

PARIS TOP 10

TOP 10 Paris Highlights

From Notre-Dame to the Eiffel Tower, Paris holds some of the world's most famous sights and these ten attractions should be top of the list for any first-time visitor. With the exception of the overtly modern Pompidou Centre, they have been landmarks of this elegant and romantic capital for centuries and remain awe-inspiring sights, no matter how often you visit the city.

1 Musée du Louvre

The world's most visited museum also contains one of the world's finest collections of art and antiquities (up to 1848). To complete the superlatives, the building was once France's largest royal palace *(see pp8–11)*.

2 Musée d'Orsay

This former railway station is one of the world's leading art galleries *(above)* and, for many, reason alone to visit Paris *(see pp12–15)*.

3 Eiffel Tower

Over seven million visitors a year ascend to the top of this most famous Paris landmark for the spectacular views. It was erected for the Universal Exhibition of 1889 *(see pp16–17)*.

4 Notre-Dame

This great Gothic cathedral, founded on the site of a Gallo-Roman temple, is a repository of French art and history. It also represents the geographical "heart" of France *(see pp18–21)*.

5 Sacré-Coeur

The terrace in front of this monumental white-domed basilica in Montmartre affords one of the finest free views over Paris *(see pp22–3)*.

6 Arc de Triomphe

Napoleon's triumphal arch, celebrating battle victories, stands proudly at the top of the Champs-Elysées and, along with the Eiffel Tower, is one of the city's most enduring images *(see pp24–5)*.

7 Centre Georges Pompidou

Home to France's National Museum of Modern Art, the building itself is a work of contemporary art. There are also extensive research facilities *(see pp26–7)*.

8 Panthéon

The great and the good of France are buried in the Panthéon *(above)*, including Voltaire *(see pp28–9)*.

9 Sainte-Chapelle

Called "a gateway to heaven", this splendid medieval church *(left)* was built to house the relics collected by St Louis on his many Crusades *(see pp30–31)*.

10 Hôtel des Invalides

The glowing golden dome of the Hôtel des Invalides church *(right)* is unmistakable across the rooftops of Paris *(see pp32–3)*.

For guided tours in Paris **See p165**

Top 10 Musée du Louvre

One of the world's most impressive museums, the Louvre contains some 35,000 priceless objects. Built as a fortress by King Philippe-Auguste in 1190, Charles V (1364–80) was the first king to make it his home. In the 16th century François I replaced it with a Renaissance-style palace and founded the royal art collection with 12 paintings from Italy. Revolutionaries opened the collection to the public in 1793. Shortly after, Napoleon renovated the Louvre as a museum.

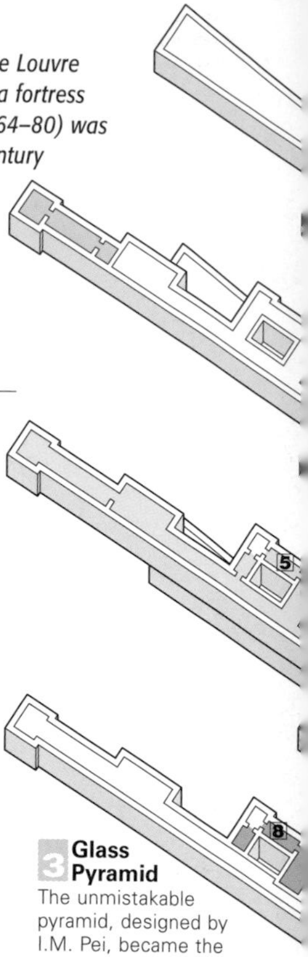

Musée du Louvre façade

Try out Le Café Marly in the Richelieu Wing or the food court in Carrousel du Louvre. For a special option make a reservation at the Grand Louvre restaurant below the pyramid.

Beat the queues and buy tickets online or at machine kiosks at the Porte des Lions entrance at the west end of the Denon Wing (except Friday).

- *Musée du Louvre, 75001*
- *Map L2*
- *01 40 20 53 17*
- *www.louvre.fr*
- *Open 9am–6pm Mon, Thu, Sat & Sun, 9am–9:45pm Wed & Fri; closed Tue & public hols*
- *Admission €11 (subject to change); free 1st Sun of month; under 18s free; under 26s (EU only) free* • *Partial disabled access*

Top 10 Sights

1. Venus de Milo
2. Mona Lisa
3. Glass Pyramid
4. Marly Horses
5. The Raft of the Medusa
6. The Winged Victory of Samothrace
7. The Lacemaker
8. Slaves
9. Medieval Moats
10. Perrault's Colonnade

1 Venus de Milo

The positioning of this statue, dramatically lit at the end of a hallway, enhances its beauty. Believed to represent the goddess Aphrodite, it dates from the end of the 2nd century BC and was discovered on the Greek island of Milos in 1820.

2 Mona Lisa

Arguably the most famous painting in the world, Leonardo's portrait of the woman with the enigmatic smile *(see p11)* has been beautifully restored. Visit early or late in the day.

3 Glass Pyramid

The unmistakable pyramid, designed by I.M. Pei, became the Louvre's new entrance in 1989. Stainless steel tubes form the 21-m-high (69-ft) frame *(below)*.

4 Marly Horses

Coustou's rearing horses being restrained by horse-tamers were sculpted in 1745 for Louis XIV's Château de Marly. Replicas stand near the Place de la Concorde.

For more Paris museums **See pp34–5**

5 The Raft of the Medusa

A shipwreck three years earlier inspired this early Romantic painting *(right)* by Théodore Géricault (1791–1824) in 1819. The work depicts a moment when the survivors spot a sail on the horizon.

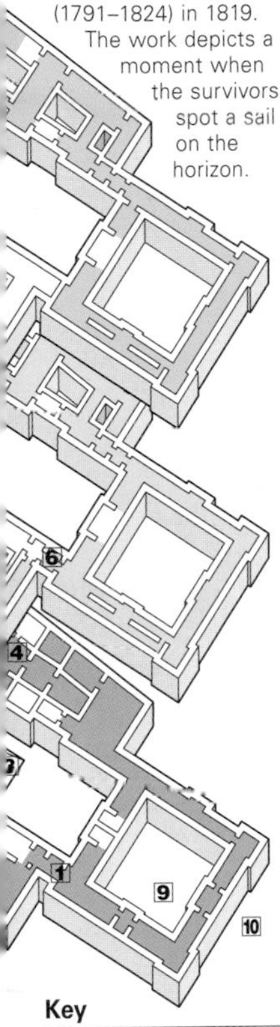

Key

- Ground floor
- First floor
- Second floor

6 The Winged Victory of Samothrace

This Hellenistic treasure (3rd–2nd century BC) stands atop a stone ship radiating grace and power. It commemorates a naval triumph at Rhodes.

7 The Lacemaker

Jan Vermeer's masterpiece *(below)*, painted around 1665, gives a simple but beautiful rendering of everyday life and is the highlight of the Louvre's Dutch collection.

8 Slaves

Michelangelo sculpted these two slaves (1513–20) for the tomb of Pope Julius II in Rome. The unfinished figures seem to be emerging from their "prisons" of stone.

9 Medieval Moats

An excavation in the 1980s uncovered the remains of the medieval fortress. You can see the base of the towers and the drawbridge support.

10 Perrault's Colonnade

The majestic east façade by Claude Perrault (1613–88), with its columns *(below)*, was part of an extension plan commissioned by Louis XIV.

Gallery Guide

The foyer is under the pyramid. Visitors who have tickets are given priority access at the pyramid. Alternatively, buy tickets at the Carrousel du Louvre entrance (99 rue de Rivoli) and Porte des Lions. The Sully, Denon and Richelieu wings lead off from the foyer. Painting and sculpture are displayed by country, plus galleries for *objets d'art*, antiquities, prints and drawings. Don't miss the temporary shows, contemporary and tribal art (Pavilion des Sessions, Denon).

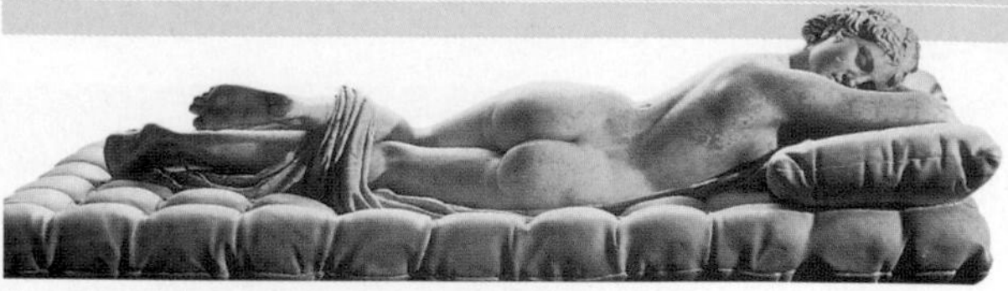

Above **Sleeping Hermaphrodite, Greek Antiquities**

TOP 10 Louvre Collections

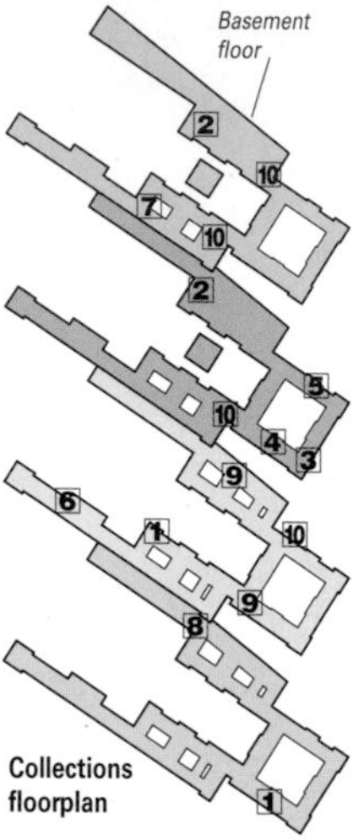

Collections floorplan

1 French Paintings

This superb collection ranges from the 14th century to 1848 and includes works by such artists as Jean Watteau, Georges de la Tour and JH Fragonard.

2 French Sculpture

Highlights include the Tomb of Philippe Pot by Antoine le Moiturier, the Marly Horses *(see p8)* and works by Pierre Puget in the glass-covered courtyards.

3 Egyptian Antiquities

The finest collection outside Cairo, featuring a Sphinx in the crypt, the Seated Scribe of Sakkara, huge sarcophagi, mummified animals, funerary objects and intricate carvings depicting everyday life in Ancient Egypt.

Akhenaton and Nefertiti, Egypt

4 Greek Antiquities

The wondrous art of Ancient Greece here ranges from a Cycladic idol from the third millennium BC to Classical Greek marble statues (*c*.5th century BC) to Hellenistic works (late 3rd–2nd century BC).

5 Oriental Antiquities

A stunning collection includes a re-created temple of an Assyrian king and the Codex of Hammurabi (18th century BC), mankind's oldest written laws.

6 Italian Paintings

French royalty adored the art of Italy and amassed much of this collection (1200–1800). There are many works by da Vinci including the *Mona Lisa*.

7 Italian Sculpture

Highlights of this collection, dating from the early Renaissance, include a 15th-century *Madonna and Child* by Donatello and Michelangelo's *Slaves (see p9)*.

8 Dutch Paintings

Rembrandt works take pride of place in this section, along with domestic scenes by Vermeer and portraits by Frans Hals.

9 Objets d'Art

The ceramics, jewellery and other items in this collection span many countries and centuries.

10 Islamic Art

This exquisite collection, which spans 13 centuries and three continents, is covered by an ultra-modern glass veil.

For more Paris museums **See pp34–5**

Top 10 Louvre Residents

1. Charles V (1364–80)
2. Henri II (1547–49)
3. Catherine de' Medici (1519–89)
4. Henri IV (1589–1610)
5. Louis XIII (1610–43)
6. Louis XIV (1643–1715)
7. Anne of Austria (1601–66)
8. Guillaume Coustou, sculptor (1677–1746)
9. Edmé Bouchardon, sculptor (1698–1762)
10. François Boucher, artist (1703–70)

Leonardo da Vinci and the Mona Lisa

***Mona Lisa*, Leonardo da Vinci's enigmatic portrait**

Born in Vinci to a wealthy family, Leonardo da Vinci (1452–1519) first took up an apprenticeship under the Florentine artist Andrea del Verrocchio, then served the Duke of Milan as an architect and military engineer, during which time he painted the acclaimed Last Supper *mural (1495). On his return to Florence, to work as architect to Cesare Borgia, he painted his most celebrated portrait, the* Mona Lisa *(1503–06). It is also known as* La Gioconda*, allegedly the name of the model's aristocratic husband, although there is ongoing speculation regarding the identity of the subject. The masterpiece, particularly the sitter's mysterious smile, shows mastery of two techniques:* chiaroscuro*, the contrast of light and shadow, and* sfumato*, subtle transitions between colours. It was the artist's own favourite painting and he took it with him everywhere. In 1516 François I brought them both to France, giving da Vinci the use of a manor house in Amboise in the Loire Valley, where he died three years later. The* Mona Lisa *is a rare surviving work of portraiture by the Renaissance master.*

Leonardo da Vinci

A Renaissance man extraordinaire, Leonardo was not only an artist but a sculptor, engineer, architect and scientist. His many achievements included the study of anatomy and aerodynamics.

TOP 10 Musée d'Orsay

This wonderful collection covers a variety of art forms from the 1848–1914 period, including a superb Impressionists section. Its setting, in a converted railway station, is equally impressive. Built in 1900, in time for the Paris Exposition, the station was in use until 1939, when it was closed and largely ignored, bar its use as the location for Orson Welles' 1962 film, The Trial. *It was later used as a theatre and as auction rooms, and in the mid-1970s was considered for demolition. In 1977, the Paris authorities decided to save the imposing station building by converting it into this striking museum.*

Musée d'Orsay façade

The busy restaurant is open for lunch, plus dinner on Thursdays; closed Monday. For a snack or a drink try the upper level café (Café Campana) or the self-service mezzanine café just above.

Regular music concerts are held. Call 01 40 49 47 50.

- *1 rue de la Légion-d'Honneur, 75007*
- *Map J2*
- *01 40 49 48 14*
- *www.musee-orsay.fr*
- *Open 9:30am–6pm Tue–Sun (Thu till 9:45pm); closed 1 Jan, 1 May, 25 Dec*
- *Admission €9 (under 18s free, under 26s EU only free), €6.50 18–25s non-EU. Tickets can be bought online*

Top 10 Features

1. The Building
2. Van Gogh Paintings
3. Le Déjeuner sur l'Herbe
4. Olympia
5. Blue Waterlilies
6. Degas' Statues of Dancers
7. Jane Avril Dancing
8. Dancing at the Moulin de la Galette
9. La Belle Angèle
10. Café Campana

1 The Building

The former railway station which houses this museum is almost as stunning as the exhibits. The light and spacious feel when one first steps inside, after admiring the magnificent old façade, takes one's breath away.

2 Van Gogh Paintings

The star of the collection is Vincent Van Gogh (1853–90) and the most striking of the canvases on display is the 1889 work showing the artist's *Bedroom at Arles (below)*. Also on display are self-portraits, painted with the artist's familiar intensity (Middle Level).

3 Le Déjeuner sur l'Herbe

Edouard Manet's (1832–83) controversial painting (1863) was first shown in an "Exhibition of Rejected Works". Its bold portrayal of a classically nude woman *(below)* enjoying the company of 19th-century men in suits brought about a wave of criticism (Room 29).

For more Paris museums **See pp34–5**

4 Olympia

Another Manet portrayal (1865) of a naked courtesan, receiving flowers sent by an admirer, was also regarded as indecent and shocked the public and critics, but it was a great influence on later artists (Room 14).

5 Blue Waterlilies

Claude Monet (1840–1926) painted this stunning canvas (1919) on one of his favourite themes. His love of waterlilies led him to create his own garden at Giverny to enable him to paint them in a natural setting. This experimental work *(below)* inspired many abstract painters later in the 20th century (Room 36).

6 Degas' Statues of Dancers

The museum possesses an exceptional collection of works by Edgar Degas (1834–1917). Focusing on dancers and the world of opera, his sculptures range from the innocent to the erotic. The striking *Young Dancer of Fourteen* (1881) was the only one exhibited in the artist's lifetime *(right)* (Room 31).

7 Jane Avril Dancing

Toulouse-Lautrec's (1864–1901) paintings define Paris's *belle époque*. Jane Avril was a famous Moulin Rouge dancer and featured in several of his works, like this 1895 canvas *(below)*, which Toulouse-Lautrec drew from life, in-situ at the cabaret (Room 10).

8 Dancing at the Moulin de la Galette

One of the best-known paintings of the Impressionist era (1876), this work was shown at the Impressionist exhibition in 1877. The exuberance of Renoir's (1841–1919) work captures the look and mood of Montmartre and is undeniably one of the artist's masterpieces (Room 32).

9 La Belle Angèle

This portrait of a Brittany beauty (1889) by Paul Gauguin (1848–1903) shows the influence of Japanese art on the artist. It was bought by Degas, to finance Gauguin's first trip to Polynesia (Room 72).

10 Café Campana

As a rest from all the impressive art, the Musée d'Orsay's café, renovated by the Campana Brothers, is delightfully situated behind one of the former station's huge clocks. A break here is an experience in itself and the food is good too.

Gallery Guide

As soon as you enter the gallery, collect a map of its layout. The ground floor houses fine works from the early to mid-19th century, as well as striking Oriental works, decorative arts and a bookshop. The middle level includes Naturalist, Symbolist and Post-Impressionist paintings and sculpture terraces. The upper level is home to the Impressionist galleries. The museum also features temporary exhibits focusing on 19th-century artists, such as Manet and Degas.

For more Paris art galleries **See pp36–7**

Left ***Blue Dancers* (1890), Degas** Right ***La Belle Angèle* (1889), Gauguin**

Musée d'Orsay Collections

1 The Impressionists
One of the best Impressionist collections in the world. Admirers of Manet, Monet and Renoir will not be disappointed.

2 The Post-Impressionists
The artists who moved on to a newer interpretation of Impressionism are equally well represented, including Matisse, Toulouse-Lautrec and the towering figure of Van Gogh.

3 School of Pont-Aven
Paul Gauguin *(see p13)* was at the centre of the group of artists associated with Pont-Aven in Brittany. His work here includes the carved door panels known as the *House of Pleasure* (1901).

4 Art Nouveau
Art Nouveau is synonymous with Paris, with many metro stations retaining entrances built in that style. Pendants and bottles by René-Jules Lalique (1860–1945) are among the examples.

5 Symbolism
This vast collection includes works by Gustav Klimt (1862–1918), Edvard Munch (1863–1944) and James Whistler's (1834–1903) 1871 portrait of his mother.

6 Romanticism
The Romantics wanted to heighten awareness of the spiritual world. One striking work is *The Tiger Hunt* (1854) by Eugène Delacroix (1798–1863).

Floorplan: the collections

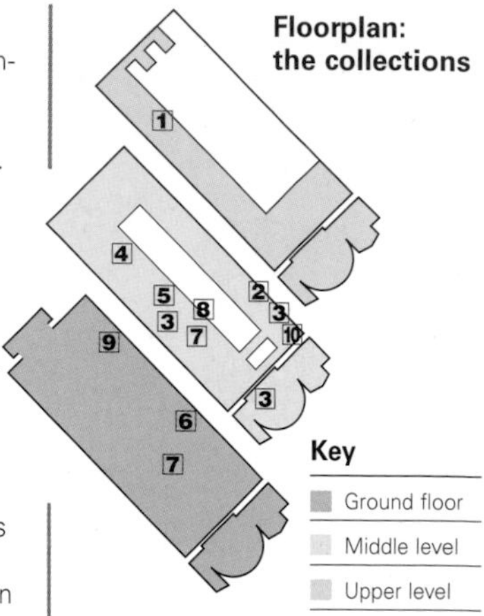

7 Sculpture
The collection includes pieces by Rodin *(see p111)* and satirical carvings of politicians by Honoré Daumier (1808–79).

8 Naturalism
Naturalist painters intensified nature in their work. *Haymaking* (1877) by Jules Bastien-Lepage (1848–84) is a fine example.

9 Nabis
The Nabis Movement moved art into a more decorative form. Pierre Bonnard (1867–1947) is one of its exponents.

10 Photography Collection
Some 10,000 early photographs include work by Bonnard, Degas and photographer Julia Margaret Cameron (1815–79).

Top 10 Impressionists

1. Claude Monet (1840–1926)
2. Edouard Manet (1832–83)
3. Auguste Renoir (1841–1919)
4. Edgar Degas (1834–1917)
5. Camille Pissarro (1830–1903)
6. Alfred Sisley (1839–99)
7. James Whistler (1834–1903)
8. Walter Sickert (1860–1942)
9. Mary Cassatt (1844–1926)
10. Berthe Morisot (1841–95)

(Prices for Impressionist paintings are considered a financial barometer for the art world. One of Monet's Waterlily paintings fetched almost US$80 million in 2008.)

The Impressionist Movement

Regarded as the starting point of modern art, the Impressionist Movement is probably the best-known and best-loved art movement in the world – certainly if prices at auction and the crowds in the Musée d'Orsay's galleries are anything to go by. The movement started in France, and almost all its leading figures were French, including the Parisian-born British artist Alfred Sisley. Impressionism was a reaction against the formality and Classicism insisted upon by the Académie des Beaux-Arts in Paris, who were very much the art establishment and decided what would or would not be exhibited at the Paris Salon. The term "impressionism" was actually coined by a critic of the style, who dismissed the 1872 Monet painting Impression: Sunrise, *which is now on display at the Musée Marmottan* (see p153). *The artists themselves then adopted the term. The style influenced painters such as Van Gogh and was to have a lasting influence on 19th- and 20th-century art.*

***Cathedral at Rouen* (1892–3), Claude Monet**

***Dancing at the Moulin de la Galette* (1876), Renoir**

Top 10 Eiffel Tower

The most distinctive symbol of Paris, the Eiffel Tower (Tour Eiffel) was much maligned by critics when it rose on the city's skyline in 1889 as part of the Universal Exhibition, but its graceful symmetry soon made it the star attraction. At 312 m (1,023 ft) high, it was the world's tallest building until it was surpassed by New York's Chrysler Building in 1930. Despite its delicate appearance, it weighs 10,100 metric tons and engineer Gustave Eiffel's construction was so sound that it never sways more than 9 cm (3.5 in) in strong winds.

Eiffel Tower from the Trocadéro

There are restaurants and snack bars on levels 1 and 2 and a champagne bar on level 3, plus food kiosks around the base.

Beat the queues by booking your visit in advance either by phone or online.

• Champ-de-Mars, 7e • Map B4 • 08 92 70 12 39 • www.tour-eiffel.com • Open: Lift 9:30am–11:45pm daily; last adm for top 10:30pm (mid-Jun–1 Sep: 9am–12:45am; last adm for top 11pm); Stairs 9:30am–6:30pm daily; last adm 6pm (mid-Jul–1 Sep: 9am–12:45am; last adm midnight) • Admission: €5 (stairs); €8.50–€14 (lift) • Disabled access first and second levels only

Top 10 Features

1. Viewing Gallery
2. Ironwork
3. Lighting
4. View from the Trocadéro
5. Gustave Eiffel's Office
6. First Level
7. Second Level
8. Hydraulic Lift Mechanism
9. Bust of Gustave Eiffel
10. Champ-de-Mars

1 Viewing Gallery

At 276 m (906 ft), the view is stupendous, stretching for 80 km (50 miles) on a clear day. You can also see Gustave Eiffel's sitting room on this level.

2 Ironwork

The complex pattern of the girders, held together by 2.5 million rivets, stabilizes the tower in high winds. The 18,000 metal parts can expand up to 15 cm (6 in) on hot days.

For more on the Eiffel Tower Quarter **See pp110–17**

3 Lighting
A 200,000-watt lighting system makes the Eiffel Tower a spectacular night-time sight. It sparkles like a giant Christmas tree for five minutes every hour from dusk until 1am.

4 View from the Trocadéro
Day or night, the best approach for a first-time view of the tower is from the Trocadéro *(see p136)*, which affords a monumental vista from the terrace across the Seine.

5 Gustave Eiffel's Office
Located at the top of the tower is Gustave Eiffel's office, which has been restored to its original condition. It displays wax models of Thomas Edison and Eiffel himself.

6 First Level
You can walk the 345 steps to the 57-m- (187-ft-) high first level and enjoy a meal at the restaurant 58 Tour Eiffel. The Eiffel Tower Epic tells the tower's story in photos and interactive displays.

7 Second Level
At 116 m (380 ft) high, this is the location of the Jules Verne Restaurant, one of the finest in Paris for both food and views *(see p117)*. It is reached by a private lift in the south pillar.

8 Hydraulic Lift Mechanism
The 1899 lift mechanism is still in operation and travels some 103,000 km (64,000 miles) a year. The uniformed guard clinging to the outside is a model.

9 Bust of Gustave Eiffel
This bust of the tower's creator, by Antoine Bourdelle, was placed below his remarkable achievement, by the north pillar, in 1929.

10 Champ-de-Mars
The long gardens of this former parade ground *(right)* stretch from the base of the tower to the École Militaire (military school).

Caricature of Gustave Eiffel with his tower

The Life of Gustave Eiffel

Born in Dijon, Gustave Eiffel (1832–1923) was an engineer and builder who made his name building bridges and viaducts. Eiffel was famous for the graceful designs and master craftsmanship of his wrought-iron constructions. He once remarked that his famous tower was "formed by the wind itself." In 1890 he became immersed in the study of aerodynamics, and kept an office in the tower until his death, using it for experiments. In 1889, when the Eiffel Tower was erected, its creator was awarded the Légion d'Honneur for the achievement.

TOP 10 Notre-Dame

The "heart" of the country, both geographically and spiritually, the Cathedral of Notre-Dame (Our Lady) stands majestic on the Ile de la Cité. After Pope Alexander III laid the foundation stone in 1163, an army of craftsmen toiled for 170 years to realize Bishop Maurice de Sully's magnificent design. Almost destroyed during the Revolution, the Gothic masterpiece was restored in 1841–64 by architect Viollet-le-Duc. Some 130 m (430 ft) in length with a high-vaulted nave and double side aisles, it also contains France's largest organ.

Notre-Dame seen from the River Seine

There are cafés opposite the Square Jean XXIII.

Free organ recitals on Sunday afternoons.

• 6 Parvis Notre-Dame-Place Jean-Paul II, 75004 • Map N4 • 01 53 10 07 00 (towers); 01 42 34 56 10 (cathedral)
• Open: cathedral 7:45am–6:45pm daily (to 7:30pm Sat–Sun); towers Apr–Sep: 10am–6:30pm daily (to 11pm Sat–Sun Jun–Aug); Oct–Mar: 10am–5:30pm daily
• Adm (towers): €8.50 (€5.50 18–25s, under-18s free, free 1st Sun of month)

Top 10 Features

1. West Front
2. Portal of the Virgin
3. Flying Buttresses
4. The Towers
5. Galerie des Chimières
6. The Spire
7. Rose Windows
8. Statue of the Virgin and Child
9. Choir Stalls
10. Treasury

1 West Front

The glorious entrance to the cathedral *(right)* is through three elaborately carved portals. Biblical scenes, sculpted in the Middle Ages, represent the life of the Virgin, the Last Judgment and the Life of St Anne. Above is the Gallery of Kings of Judaea and Israel.

2 Portal of the Virgin

The splendid stone tympanum *(left)* was carved in the 13th century and shows the Virgin Mary's death and glorious coronation in heaven. However, the Virgin and Child carving seen between the doors is a modern replica.

3 Flying Buttresses

The striking buttresses supporting the cathedral's east façade are by Jean Ravy. The best view is from Square Jean XXIII.

4 The Towers

The towers are 69 m (226 ft) high; climb the 387 steps of the north tower for great views. In 2013 new bells rang here to celebrate the cathedral's 850th birthday.

For more Paris churches **See pp40–41**

Galerie des Chimères

5 Lurking between the towers are the famous gargoyles *(chimères)*, placed here by Viollet-le-Duc to ward off evil.

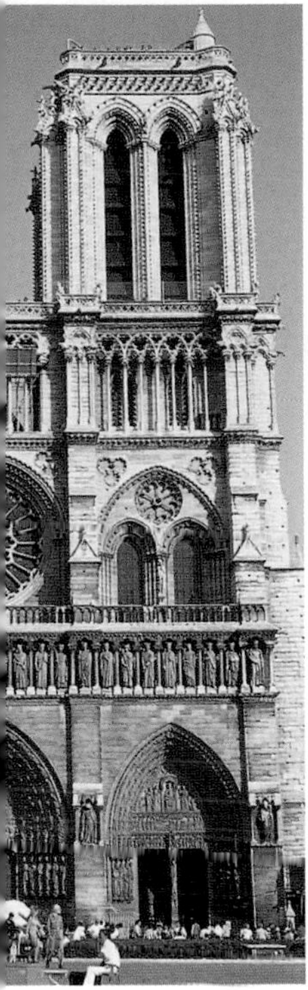

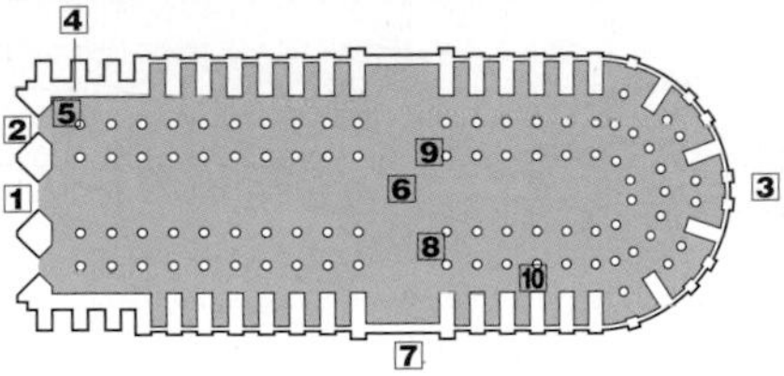

Floorplan of the Cathedral

The Spire

6 The 96-m (315-ft) spire was added by Viollet-le-Duc. Next to the Apostles statues on the roof is one of the architect, admiring his work.

Rose Windows

7 Three great rose windows adorn the north, south and west façades, but only the north window *(below)* retains its 13th-century stained glass, depicting the Virgin surrounded by figures from the Old Testament. The south window shows Christ encircled by the Apostles.

Statue of the Virgin and Child

8 Also known as Notre-Dame de Paris (Our Lady of Paris), this beautiful 14th-century statue was brought to the cathedral from the chapel of St Aignan. It stands against the southeast pillar of the transept, at the entrance to the chancel.

Choir Stalls

9 More than half of the original stalls commissioned by Louis XIV survive. Among the beautifully carved work on the 78 stalls are scenes from the Life of the Virgin.

Treasury

10 Ancient manuscripts, reliquaries and religious garments are housed in the sacristy. The Crown of Thorns is on public view on the first Friday of every month.

Cathedral Guide

Enter through the West Front. The stairs to the towers are outside to your left. Ahead, the central nave soars to a height of 35 m (115 ft), while 24 side chapels line the walls. These contain the "May" paintings by Charles le Brun, donated by the goldsmiths' guild each May in the 17th–18th centuries. The fine transept across the nave is the best place to admire the three rose windows. Remnants of the 14th-century stone screen can be seen on the north and south bays of the chancel. Nicolas Coustou's *Pietà* stands behind the high altar, flanked by statues of Louis XIII by Coustou and Louis XIV by Antoine Coysevox.

Left **Joan of Arc** Centre **Empress Josephine** Right **Napoleon**

Top 10 Famous Visitors to Notre-Dame

1 Joan of Arc
The French patriot Jeanne d'Arc (1412–31), who defended her country against the invading English, had a posthumous trial here in 1455, despite having been burnt at the stake 24 years earlier. At the re-trial she was found to be innocent of heresy.

2 François II and Mary Stuart
Mary Stuart (1542–87) (Mary Queen of Scots) had been raised in France and married the Dauphin in 1558. He ascended the throne as François II in 1559 and the king and queen were crowned in Notre-Dame.

3 Napoleon
The coronation of Napoleon (1769–1821) in Notre-Dame in 1804 saw the eager general seize the crown from Pope Pius VII and crown himself emperor and his wife Josephine, empress.

4 Josephine
Josephine's (1763–1814) reign as Empress of France lasted only five years; Napoleon divorced her in 1809.

5 Pope Pius VII
In 1809 Pope Pius VII (1742–1823), who oversaw the Notre-Dame coronation, was taken captive when the emperor declared the Papal States to be part of France. The pope was imprisoned at Fontainebleau, 50 km (30 miles) south of Paris.

6 Philip the Fair
In 1302 the first States General parliament was formally opened at Notre-Dame by Philip IV (1268–1314), otherwise known as Philip the Fair. He greatly increased the governing power of the French royalty.

7 Henry VI of England
Henry VI (1421–71) became King of England at the age of one. Like his father, Henry V, he also claimed France and was crowned in Notre-Dame in 1430.

8 Marguerite of Valois
In August 1572, Marguerite (1553–1589), sister of Charles IX, stood in the Notre-Dame chancel during her marriage to the protestant Henri of Navarre (1553–1610), while he stood alone by the door.

9 Henri of Navarre
As a Protestant Huguenot, Henri's marriage to the Catholic Marguerite resulted in uprising and massacres. In 1589 he became Henri IV, the first Bourbon king of France, and converted to Catholicism, declaring that "Paris is well worth a mass".

10 Charles de Gaulle
On 26 August 1944, Charles de Gaulle entered Paris and attended a Magnificat service to celebrate the liberation of Paris, despite the fact that hostile snipers were still at large outside the cathedral.

For more historic events in Paris **See pp44–5**

Top 10 Events in Notre-Dame History

1. Construction of the cathedral begins (1163)
2. St Louis places the Crown of Thorns here temporarily (1239)
3. Construction is completed (1334)
4. Re-trial of Joan of Arc (1455)
5. Crowning of Emperor Napoleon (1804)
6. Publication of Hugo's novel *The Hunchback of Notre-Dame* (1831)
7. Completion of 23-year restoration programme (1864)
8. Mass for the Liberation of Paris (1944)
9. De Gaulle's Requiem Mass is held (1970)
10. Visit of Pope John Paul II (1980)

The Man Who Saved Notre-Dame

Novelist Victor Hugo

By 1831, when Victor Hugo's novel Notre-Dame de Paris (The Hunchback of Notre-Dame) *was published, the cathedral was in a sorry state of decay. Even for the crowning of Emperor Napoleon in 1804, the setting for such ceremonious state occasions was crumbling and had to be disguised with wall hangings and ornamentation. During the Revolution, the cathedral was even sold to a scrap dealer, but was never actually demolished. Hugo was determined to save the country's spiritual heart and helped mount a successful campaign to restore Notre-Dame before it was too late; the man chosen to design and oversee the restoration was Eugène Emmanuel Viollet-le-Duc (1814–1879). Paris-born, Viollet-le-Duc had already proved his skill in restoration work, as evidenced by the cathedrals in Amiens and Laon, and on the spectacular walled city of Carcassonne in southern France. Work began in 1841 and continued for 23 years until the building was finished more or less as we see it today. Viollet-le-Duc later went on to restore Sainte-Chapelle nearby* (see pp30–31).

The Hunchback of Notre-Dame
Hugo's 1831 novel tells the story of Quasimodo, a hunchbacked bell-ringer at Notre-Dame, who falls in love with gypsy girl Esmeralda.

For more novels set in Paris **See pp46–7**

Top 10 Sacré-Coeur

One of the most photographed images of the city, the spectacular white outline of Sacré-Coeur (Sacred Heart) watches over Paris from its highest point. The basilica was built as a memorial to the 58,000 French soldiers killed during the Franco-Prussian War (1870–71). It took 46 years to build and was finally completed in 1923 at a cost of 40 million francs (6 million euros). Priests still pray for the souls of the dead here, 24 hours a day, as they have since 1885. People flock here for the panoramic views – at sunset, in particular, there are few sights in Paris more memorable.

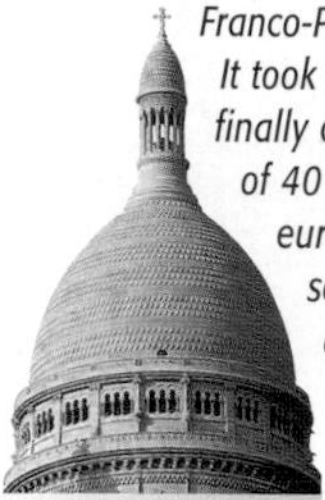

Sacré-Coeur dome

Avoid the crowds and head to 23 rue des Abbesses and grab a bite at the St Jean or try Café Arrosé at 123 rue Caulaincourt.

An evocative sung Mass takes place on Sundays at 11am.

- *Parvis de la Basilique du Sacré-Coeur, 75018*
- *Map F1*
- *01 53 41 89 00*
- *www.sacre-coeur-montmartre.com*
- *Open 6am–10:30pm, last entry 10:15pm (basilica), 9:30am–5:30pm (dome) daily. Crypt opening times vary.*
- *Admission €8 (dome and crypt only)*

Top 10 Features

1. Great Mosaic of Christ
2. Crypt Vaults
3. Bronze Doors
4. Dome
5. Statue of Christ
6. Bell Tower
7. Equestrian Statues
8. Stained-Glass Gallery
9. Façade
10. The Funicular

1 Great Mosaic of Christ

A glittering Byzantine mosaic of Christ *(right)*, created by Luc Olivier Merson between 1912–22, decorates the vault over the chancel. It represents France's devotion to the Sacred Heart.

2 Crypt Vaults

The arched vaults of the crypt house a chapel containing the heart of Alexandre Legentil, one of the advocates of Sacré-Coeur.

3 Bronze Doors

The doors of the portico entrance are beautifully decorated with bronze relief sculptures depicting the Last Supper *(right)* and other scenes from the life of Christ.

For more Paris churches **See pp40–41**

4 The Dome

The distinctive egg-shaped dome of the basilica is the second-highest viewpoint in Paris after the Eiffel Tower. Reached via a spiral staircase, vistas can stretch as far as 48 km (30 miles) on a clear day.

5 Statue of Christ

The basilica's most important statue shows Christ giving a blessing. It is symbolically placed in a niche over the main entrance, above the two equestrian statues.

6 Bell Tower

The *campanile*, designed by Lucien Magne and added in 1904, is 80 m (262 ft) high. One of the heaviest bells in the world, the 19-ton La Savoyarde hangs in the belfry. Cast in Annecy in 1895, it was donated by the dioceses of Savoy.

7 Equestrian Statues

Two striking bronze statues of French saints stand on the portico above the main entrance, cast by H Lefèbvre *(below)*. One is of Joan of Arc, the other of Saint Louis.

8 Stained-Glass Gallery

One level of the great dome is encircled by stained-glass windows. From here there is a grand view over the whole interior.

The Franco-Prussian War

In 1870, as Prussia made moves to take over Germany, France was also threatened by its military power. Two Catholic businessmen in Paris vowed to build a church dedicated to the Sacred Heart if France were spared the Prussian onslaught. France declared war on Prussia in July, but she was ill-prepared and in September Napoleon III was captured. Parisians held fast, however, defending their city with home-made weapons and eating dogs, cats and rats. But by January 1871 they surrendered.

Captured French soldier taking leave of his wife

9 Façade

Architect Paul Abadie (1812–1884) employed a mix of domes, turrets and Classical features in his design. The Château-Landon stone secretes calcite when wet and bleaches the façade white.

10 The Funicular

To avoid the steep climb up to Sacré-Coeur, take the *funiculaire* cable railway and enjoy the views at leisure. It runs from the end of rue Foyatier, near Square Willette.

TOP 10 Arc de Triomphe

The best day to visit the world's most familiar triumphal arch is 2 December, the date that marks Napoleon's victory at the Battle of Austerlitz in 1805, when the sun, setting behind the Champs-Elysées and the Arc de Triomphe, creates a spectacular halo around the building. Work began on the 50-m (164-ft) arch in 1806 but was not completed until 1836, due, in part, to Napoleon's fall from power. Four years later, Napoleon's funeral procession passed beneath it, on its way to his burial in Les Invalides (see pp32–3). *Today the arch is a focal point for numerous public events.*

Arc de Triomphe pediment

Try to get here early, as the morning light shows the golden tone of the stone-work at its best.

Enjoy a coffee and the old-world charm of Le Fouquet (99 ave des Champs-Elysées) – expensive, but worth the treat.

• Place Charles-de-Gaulle, 75008 • 01 55 37 73 77 (enquiries) • http://arc-de-triomphe.monuments-nationaux.fr • Map B2 • Open Apr–Sep: 10am–11pm daily; Oct–Mar: 10am–10:30pm daily (last adm 45 mins before closing); closed 1 Jan, 1 May, 8 May (am), 14 Jul (am), 11 Nov (am), 25 Dec and for major events • Admission €9.50

Top 10 Features

1. Viewing Platform
2. Tomb of the Unknown Soldier
3. Museum
4. Departure of the Volunteers in 1792
5. Frieze
6. Triumph of Napoleon
7. Battle of Austerlitz
8. Battle of Aboukir
9. General Marceau's Funeral
10. Thirty Shields

1 Viewing Platform

Taking the elevator or climbing the 284 steps to the top of the Arc de Triomphe *(below)* gives visitors a sublime view of Paris and a sense of the arch's dominant position in the centre of the Place de l'Etoile. To the east is the magnificent Champs-Elysées *(see p103)* and to the west is the Grande Arche of La Défense *(see p151)*. There are another 40 steps after the lift.

2 Tomb of the Unknown Soldier

In the centre of the arch flickers the eternal flame on the Tomb of the Unknown Soldier, a victim of World War I buried on 11 November 1920. It is symbolically re-ignited every day at 6:30pm.

For more historic buildings in Paris **See pp42–3**

3 Museum

Within the arch is a small but interesting museum which tells the history of its construction and gives details of various celebrations and funerals that the arch has seen over the years. The more recent of these are shown in a short video.

6 Triumph of Napoleon

As you look at the arch from the Champs-Elysées, the relief on the left base shows the restored *Triumph of Napoleon.* This celebrates the Treaty of Vienna peace agreement signed in 1810, when Napoleon's empire was in its heyday.

7 Battle of Austerlitz

Another battle victory is shown on a frieze *(above)* on the arch's northern side. It depicts Napoleon's heavily outnumbered troops breaking the ice on Lake Satschan in Austria, a tactic which drowned thousands of enemy troops.

8 Battle of Aboukir

Above the *Triumph of Napoleon* carving is this scene showing Napoleonic victory over the Turks in 1799. The same victory was commemorated on canvas in 1806 by the French painter Antoine Gros and is now on display at the Palace of Versailles *(see p151)*.

9 General Marceau's Funeral

Marceau died in battle against the Austrian army in 1796, after a famous victory against them only the previous year. His funeral is depicted in this frieze *(right)*, which is located above the *Departure of the Volunteers in 1792.*

4 Departure of the Volunteers in 1792

One of the most striking sculptures is on the front right base *(right).* It shows French citizens leaving to defend their nation against Austria and Prussia.

10 Thirty Shields

Immediately below the top of the arch runs a row of 30 shields, each carrying the name of a Napoleonic victory.

5 Frieze

A frieze running around the arch shows French troops departing for battle (east) and their victorious return (west).

The Great Axis

The Arc de Triomphe is at the centre of three arches and together they create a grand vision of which even Napoleon would have been proud. The emperor was responsible for the first two, placing the Arc de Triomphe directly in line with the Arc de Triomphe du Carrousel in front of the Louvre *(see pp8–11)* which also celebrates the 1805 victory at Austerlitz. In 1989, the trio was completed with the Grande Arche at La Défense. The 8km-long (5-mile) *Grand Axe* (Great Axis) runs from here to the Glass Pyramid at the Louvre.

10 Centre Georges Pompidou

Today one of the world's most famous pieces of modern architecture, the Pompidou Centre opened in 1977, when architects Richard Rogers and Renzo Piano startled everyone by turning the building "inside out", with brightly coloured pipes displayed on the façade. Designed as a cross-cultural arts complex, it houses the excellent Musée National d'Art Moderne (Modern Art Museum) as well as a cinema, library, shops and performance space. The outside forecourt is a popular gathering-spot for tourists and locals alike.

Centre Georges Pompidou façade

The centre's café is pleasant and has free Wi-Fi access. For something grander, head to Georges, the roof-top brasserie.

Buy tickets online to avoid the queues.

• Place Georges Pompidou 75004 • Map P2 • www.centrepompidou.fr • 01 44 78 12 33 • Open 11am–9pm Wed–Mon (11pm Thu); closed 1 May • Adm (museum) €9–14; Brancusi's Studio free (open 2–6pm Wed–Mon). Free 1st Sun of the month, under 18s free, under 26s free (EU only)

Top 10 Features

1. Escalator
2. Top-Floor View
3. The Piazza
4. Stravinsky Fountains
5. Pipes
6. Bookshop
7. Brancusi's Studio
8. Man with a Guitar
9. Violinist at the Window
10. La Baigneuse

1 Escalator

One of the building's most striking and popular features is the external escalator *(right)*, which climbs, snake-like, up the front of the centre in its plexi-glass tube. The view gets better and better as you rise high above the activity in the Centre's forecourt, before arriving at the top for the best view of all.

2 Top-Floor View

The view from the top of the Pompidou Centre is spectacular. The Eiffel Tower is visible, as is Montmartre in the north and the Tour Montparnasse to the south. On clear days views can stretch as far as La Défense *(see p151)*.

3 The Piazza

Visitors and locals gather in the open space in front of the Centre to enjoy the variety of street performers and changing installations of monumental sculptures, which are often related to shows at the Centre.

4 Stravinsky Fountain

This colourful fountain in Place Igor Stravinsky was designed by Niki de Saint-Phalle and Jean Tinguely as part of the Pompidou Centre development. Inspired by composer Stravinsky's ballet *The Firebird* (1910), the bird spins and sprays water!

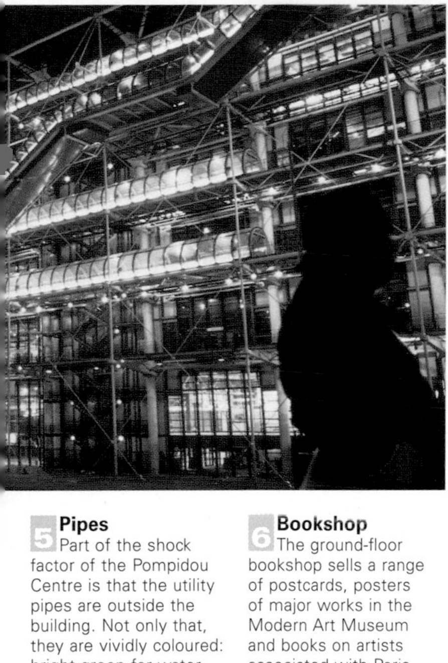

5 Pipes

Part of the shock factor of the Pompidou Centre is that the utility pipes are outside the building. Not only that, they are vividly coloured: bright green for water, yellow for electricity and blue for air conditioning.

6 Bookshop

The ground-floor bookshop sells a range of postcards, posters of major works in the Modern Art Museum and books on artists associated with Paris.

7 Brancusi's Studio

The studio of revolutionary Romanian sculptor Constantin Brancusi (1876–1957) is to the north of the centre, displaying his abstract works.

8 Man with a Guitar

Within the Modern Art Museum, this 1914 work by artist Georges Braque (1882–1963) is one of the most striking of the Cubist Movement.

9 Violinist at the Window

French artist Henri Matisse (1869–1964) was one of the proponents of the short-lived Fauvist Movement, which advocated the use of bold, strong colours. *Violinist at the Window* was painted in 1917–18 and can be interpreted as a self-portrait.

10 La Baigneuse

Joan Miró (1893–1983) was born in Barcelona but moved to Paris in 1920. His simplistic yet evocative *La Baigneuse (The Swimmer)* (1924) depicts an immense blue ocean, watched over by a crescent moon. A woman's form is almost lost amid the waves; her tendrils of yellow hair reflect their serpentine lines.

Centre Guide

The Centre is home to various institutions. The Museum of Modern Art (Mnam) is on levels 4 and 5, the cinema on level 1. Check at the information desk or on the website for details about the temporary shows, rehangs of works on level 5 and the contemporary art "happenings". Displays at the Mnam often change and some works are now shared with its sister institution in Metz.

TOP 10 The Panthéon

Today Paris's beautiful Panthéon building is a fitting final resting place for the nation's great figures. However, it was originally built as a church, on the instigation of Louis XV to celebrate his recovery from a serious bout of gout in 1744. Dedicated to Sainte Geneviève, the structure was finished in 1790 and was intended to look like the Pantheon in Rome, hence the name; in fact it more closely resembles St Paul's Cathedral in London. During the Revolution it was turned into a mausoleum, but Napoleon gave it back to the church in 1806. It was later deconsecrated, handed back to the church once more, before finally becoming a public building in 1885.

Panthéon façade

Crêpes à Gogo (12 rue Soufflot, open 7am–11pm) is an ideal pit stop for a crêpe, coffee and an ice cream.

Ticket sales stop 45 minutes before closing time, so arrive on time.

• Place du Panthéon, 75005 • Map N6 • 01 44 32 18 00 • http://pantheon.monuments-nationaux.fr • Open Apr–Sep: 10am–6:30pm daily; Oct–Mar: 10am–6pm daily; closed 1 Jan, 1 May, 25 Dec • Admission €7.50 (under 25s €4.50, under 18s and EU under 25s free) • No dis access

Top 10 Features

1. Dome
2. Dome Galleries
3. Crypt
4. Frescoes of Sainte Geneviève
5. Foucault's Pendulum
6. Monument to Diderot
7. Façade
8. Pediment Relief
9. Tomb of Voltaire
10. Tomb of Victor Hugo

1 Dome

Inspired by Sir Christopher Wren's design of St Paul's Cathedral in London, as well as by the Dôme Church at Les Invalides *(see p32)*, this iron-framed dome *(below left)* is made up of three layers. At the top a narrow opening only lets in a tiny amount of natural light, in keeping with the building's sombre purpose.

2 Dome Galleries

A staircase leads to the galleries immediately below the dome, affording spectacular 360-degree panoramic views of Paris. The pillars surrounding the galleries are both decorative and functional, providing essential support for the dome.

3 Crypt

The crypt is eerily impressive in its scale compared to most tiny, dark church crypts. Here lie the tombs and memorials to worthy French citizens, including the prolific French writer Emile Zola *(see p47)*.

For more Paris burial sites **See p156**

4 Frescoes of Sainte Geneviève
Delicate murals by 19th-century artist Pierre Puvis de Chavannes, on the south wall of the nave, tell the story of Sainte Geneviève, the patron saint of Paris. In 451 she is believed to have saved the city from invasion by the barbaric Attila the Hun and his hordes due to the power of her prayers.

6 Monument to Diderot
French philosopher Denis Diderot (1713–84) is honoured by this grand 1925 monument by Alphonse Terroir.

7 Façade
The Panthéon's façade was inspired by Roman design. The 22 Corinthian columns support both the portico roof and *bas-reliefs*.

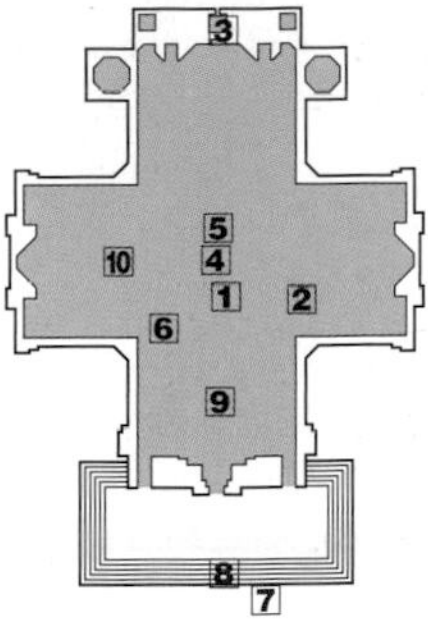

Panthéon Floorplan

9 Tomb of Voltaire
A statue of the great writer, wit and philosopher Voltaire (1694–1788) stands in front of his tomb.

10 Tomb of Victor Hugo
The body of the French author *(see p46)* was carried to the Panthéon in a pauper's hearse, at his own request.

5 Foucault's Pendulum
In 1851 French physicist Jean Foucault (1819–68) followed up an earlier experiment to prove the earth's rotation by hanging his famous pendulum from the dome of the Panthéon. The plane of the pendulum's swing rotated 11° clockwise each hour in relation to the floor, thereby proving Foucault's theory.

8 Pediment Relief
The *bas-relief* above the entrance *(below)* shows a female figure, representing France, handing out laurels to the great men of the nation – the same way that Greeks and Romans honoured their heroes.

Louis Braille

One of the most influential citizens to be buried in the Panthéon is Louis Braille. Born in France in 1809, Braille became blind at the age of three; at nine he attended the National Institute for the Young Blind in Paris and proved to be a gifted student. He continued at the Institute as a teacher and, in 1829, had the idea of adapting a coding system in use by the army, by turning words and letters into raised dots on card. Reading braille transformed the lives of blind people forever. Its inventor died in 1852.

Sainte-Chapelle

This Gothic masterpiece, built by Louis IX (1214–70) as a shrine for his holy relics of the passion and completed in 1248, is considered the most beautiful church in Paris, not least for its 15 stained-glass windows soaring 15 m (50 ft) to a star-covered vaulted roof. The church was damaged during the 1789 Revolution but restored in the mid-19th century.

Sainte-Chapelle façade

For a little 1920s-style elegance, try Brasserie des Deux Palais on the corner of boulevard du Palais and rue de Lutèce.

A pair of binoculars comes in handy if you want to see the uppermost glass panels.

- *6 blvd du Palais, 75001*
- *Map N3*
- *01 53 40 60 97*
- *Open Mar–Oct: 9:30am–6pm (mid-May–mid-Sep: till 9pm Wed); Nov–Feb: 9am–5pm; closed 1 Jan, 1 May, 25 Dec*
- *Admission €8.50, €5.50 for under 25s (free 1st Sun of month Nov–Mar). €12.50 joint adm to Conciergerie (see p69). Temp exhibitions €1.50 extra. Ticket sales stop 30 mins before closing*
- *Restricted disabled access (48 hrs advance notice for wheelchairs)*
- *http://sainte-chapelle.monuments-nationaux.fr*

Top 10 Features

1. Upper Chapel Entrance
2. Rose Window
3. Window of Christ's Passion
4. Apostle Statues
5. Window of the Relics
6. The Spire
7. Main Portal
8. St Louis' Oratory
9. Seats of the Royal Family
10. Evening Concerts

1 Upper Chapel Entrance

As you emerge, via a spiral staircase, into this airy space *(right)*, the effect of light and colour is utterly breathtaking. The 13th-century stained-glass windows, the oldest extant in Paris, separated by stone columns *(below)*, depict Biblical scenes from *Genesis* through to the Crucifixion. To "read" the windows, start in the lower left panel and follow each row left to right, from bottom to top.

2 Rose Window

The Flamboyant-style rose window, depicting St John's vision of the Apocalypse in 86 panels, was replaced by Charles VIII in 1485. The green and yellow hues are at their brightest at sunset.

For more Paris churches **See pp40–41**

3 Window of Christ's Passion
Located above the apse, this stained-glass depiction of the Crucifixion is the chapel's most beautiful window.

4 Apostle Statues
Beautifully carved medieval statues of 12 apostles stand on pillars along the walls. Badly damaged in the Revolution, most have been restored: the bearded apostle *(right)*, fifth on the left, is the only original statue.

5 Window of the Relics
Another striking window *(below)*, this tells the story of St Helena and the True Cross and of St Louis bringing his many relics to Sainte-Chapelle.

6 The Spire
The open latticework and pencil-thin shape give the 75-m (245-ft) *flèche* (spire) a delicate appearance. Three earlier church spires burned down – this one was erected in 1853.

Relics of the Passion
Louis IX, later St Louis, was the only French king to be canonized. While on his first Crusade in 1239, he purchased the alleged Crown of Thorns from the Emperor of Constantinople, and subsequently other relics, including pieces of the True Cross, nails from the Crucifixion and a few drops of Christ's blood, paying almost three times more for them than for the construction of Sainte-Chapelle itself. The relics reside in Notre-Dame and are only displayed on religious holidays.

7 Main Portal
Like the Upper Chapel, the main portal has two tiers. Its pinnacles are decorated with a crown of thorns as a symbol of the relics within.

8 St Louis' Oratory
In the late 14th century Louis XI added an oratory where he could watch Mass through a small grille in the wall. The chapel originally adjoined the Conciergerie, the former royal palace on the Ile de la Cité *(see p69)*.

9 Seats of the Royal Family
During Mass, the royal family sat in niches located in the fourth bays on both sides of the chapel, away from the congregation.

10 Evening Concerts
Sainte-Chapelle has excellent acoustics. From March to November classical concerts are held here several evenings a week.

TOP 10 Hôtel des Invalides

The "invalides" for whom this imposing Hôtel was built were wounded soldiers of the late 17th century. Louis XIV had the building constructed between 1671 and 1678, and veterans are still housed here, although only a dozen or so compared to the original 4,000. They share their home with arguably the greatest French soldier of them all, Napoleon Bonaparte, whose body rests in a crypt directly below the golden dome of the Dôme Church. Other buildings accommodate military offices, the Musée de l'Armée and smaller military museums.

Musée de l'Armée façade

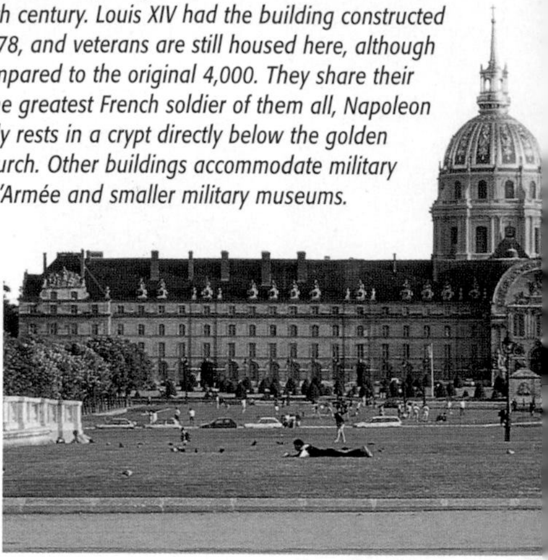

Le Café du Musée, between the Varenne metro station and the Musée Rodin ***(see p111)*** **is a lovely spot for a drink.**

A ticket provides access to all attractions.

- *129 rue de Grenelle, 75007*
- *Map D4*
- *08 10 11 33 99*
- *www.invalides.org*
- *Open Apr–Sep: 10am–6pm daily, until 9pm Tue (Oct–Mar: until 5pm); closed first Mon of month (except Jul–Sep), 1 Jan, 1 May, 1 Nov, 25 Dec*
- *Admission €9.50 adults; €7.50 concessions; under 18s free; under 26s (EU only) free*
- *Limited disabled access*

Top 10 Features

1. Napoleon's Tomb
2. Golden Dome
3. Musée de l'Armée
4. Dôme Church Ceiling
5. Hôtel des Invalides
6. Church Tombs
7. St-Louis-des-Invalides
8. Invalides Gardens
9. Musée de l'Ordre de la Libération
10. Musée des Plans-Reliefs

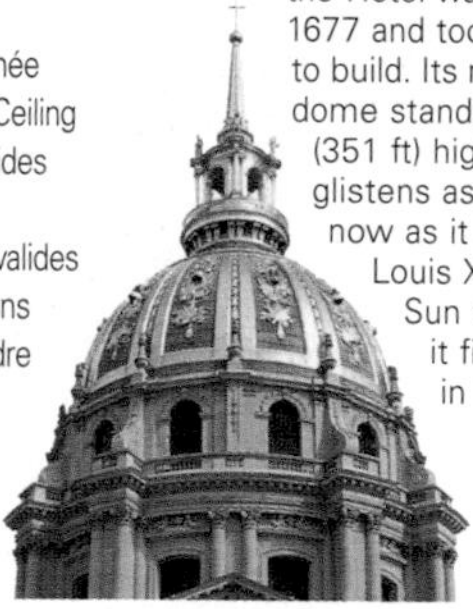

2 Golden Dome

The second church at the Hôtel was begun in 1677 and took 27 years to build. Its magnificent dome stands 107 m (351 ft) high and glistens as much now as it did when Louis XIV, the Sun King, had it first gilded in 1715.

1 Napoleon's Tomb

Napoleon's body was brought here from St Helena in 1840, some 19 years after he died. He rests in splendid grandeur in a cocoon of six coffins *(left)*, almost situated "on the banks of the Seine" as was his personal wish.

3 Musée de l'Armée

The Army Museum is one of the largest collections of militaria in the world. Enthusiasts will be absorbed for hours, and even the casual visitor will be fascinated. The "Department Moderne", which traces military history from Louis XIV to Napoleon III, has been revamped and is especially worth a visit *(see p111)*.

For the Invalides Quarter **See pp110–17**

4 Dôme Church Ceiling

The colourful, circular painting on the interior of the dome above the crypt is the *Saint Louis in Glory* painted in 1692 by the French artist, Charles de la Fosse. Near the centre is St Louis, who represents Louis XIV, presenting his sword to Christ in the presence of the Virgin and angels.

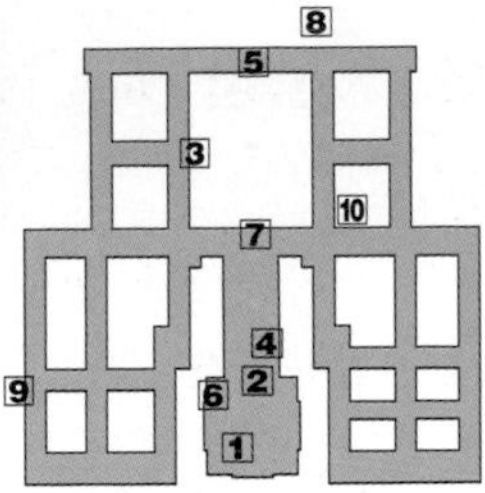

Hôtel des Invalides Floorplan

9 Musée de l'Ordre de la Libération

The Order of Liberation, France's highest military honour, was created by Général de Gaulle in 1940 to acknowledge contributions during World War II. The museum details the history of the honour and the wartime Free French movement.

5 Hôtel des Invalides

One of the loveliest sights in Paris *(above)*, the Classical façade of the Hôtel is four floors high and 196 m (645 ft) end to end. Features include the dormer windows with their variously shaped shield surrounds.

7 St-Louis-des-Invalides

Adjoining the Dôme Church is the Invalides complex's original church. It is worth seeing for its 17th-century organ, on which the first performance of Berlioz's *Requiem* was given.

10 Musée des Plans-Reliefs

Maps and models of French forts and fortified towns are displayed here and some of them are beautifully detailed, such as the oldest model on display, of Perpignan in 1686.

6 Church Tombs

Encircling the Dôme Church are the imposing tombs of great French military men, such as Marshal Foch and Marshal Vauban, who revolutionized military fortifications and siege tactics.

8 Invalides Gardens

The approach to the Hôtel is across public gardens and then through a gate into the Invalides Gardens themselves. Designed in 1704, their paths are lined by 17th- and 18th-century cannons.

Hôtel Guide

Approach the Hôtel des Invalides from the Seine for the best view, and then walk around to the south side (by the Dôme Church) to reach the ticket office. You will need a ticket for the museums and to see Napoleon's Tomb. If time is short, concentrate on the Musée de l'Armée, before walking through to the front of the buildings and reaching the impressive cobbled courtyard that is directly in front of the Dôme Church.

Left ***Mona Lisa*, Musée du Louvre** Centre **Musée Carnavalet** Right **Cannons, Musée de l'Armée**

TOP 10 Museums

1 Musée du Louvre

French and Italian sculpture, Greek and Roman antiquities and paintings from the 12th to the 19th centuries are just some of the highlights of the world's largest museum *(see pp8–11)*.

2 Musée Carnavalet

Housed in a grand Marais mansion, this museum presents the history of Paris. The collection includes painting, sculpture and antique furniture, re-creating private residences of the 16th and 17th centuries. There is also a collection of mementoes from the Revolution as well as a wonderful French garden.

3 Musée des Arts Décoratifs

Set over nine levels, adjoining the west end of the Louvre's Richelieu Wing, this decorative arts museum showcases furniture and tableware from the 12th century to the present. The breathtaking anthology of pieces includes Gothic panelling and Renaissance porcelain, to 1970s carpets and chairs by Philippe Starck. Also in the museum is the Musée de la Mode et du Textile, which mounts fashion exhibitions and the Musée de la Publicité, which has exhibitions on advertising *(see p95)*.

4 Musée National du Moyen Age

This splendid museum dedicated to the art of the Middle Ages is known by several names, including the Musée de Cluny after the beautiful mansion in which it is housed, and the Thermes de Cluny after the Roman baths adjoining the museum. Highlights include the famous "Lady and the Unicorn" tapestries, medieval stained glass and exquisite gold crowns and jewellery *(see p120)*.

Muséum National d'Histoire Naturelle garden

5 Muséum National d'Histoire Naturelle

Paris's Natural History Museum in the Jardin des Plantes contains a fascinating collection of animal skeletons, plant fossils, minerals and gemstones. Its highlight is the magnificent Grande Galerie de l'Evolution, which depicts the changing interaction between man and nature during the evolution of life on Earth *(see pp60 & 129)*.

6 musée du quai Branly

In a city dominated by Western art, this museum housing 300,000 artifacts (of which 3,500 are on display at any one time) tips the balance in favour of arts from Africa, Asia, Oceania and the Americas. Must-sees include the African instruments. The striking Jean Nouvel-designed building is an attraction in itself *(see p112)*.

7 Musée de l'Armée

France's proud military history is on display in this museum, housed in a wing of the Hôtel des Invalides. Exhibits include military art and artifacts from ancient times through to the 20th century, with a large modern exhibit devoted to World War II. Napoleon's campaign tent, his stuffed dog, and suits of armour and weapons from medieval times are among the many highlights *(see p111)*.

8 Musée Cognacq-Jay

The Hôtel Donon is a fine setting for this superb collection of 18th-century art, furniture, porcelain and other decorative arts, amassed by the wealthy founders of the Samaritaine department store. Paintings by Rembrandt, Reynolds and other masters alone are worth the visit *(see p85)*.

Venus with Doves, Musée Cognacq-Jay

9 Cité de l'Architecture et du Patrimoine

In the east wing of the Palais Chaillot, the Cité de l'Architecture and the Musée des Monuments Français showcase French architectural heritage and has become one of the world's great architectural centres. The Galeries des Moulages houses models of great French cathedrals *(see pp135–6)*.

10 Musée Jacquemart-André

Set in an elegant private mansion, this museum was once the home of Edouard André and his artist wife Nélie Jacquemart. The museum houses their spectacular personal art collection, which features works by Boucher, Botticelli, Rembrandt and Fragonard, as well as excellent temporary exhibits *(see p105)*.

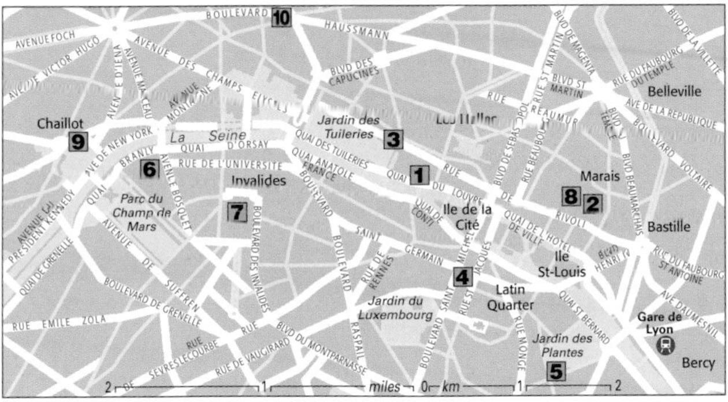

For Paris art galleries **See pp36–7**

Left ***Bedroom at Arles* (1889), Van Gogh, Musée d'Orsay** Right **L'Orangerie**

Top 10 Art Galleries

1 Musée d'Orsay

See pp12–15.

2 Musée Picasso

A favourite of Parisians and visitors alike. The beautifully restored Hôtel Salé *(see p90)* in the Marais is a splendid setting for this extensive collection of paintings, sculptures, drawings and other works by Pablo Picasso (1881–1973), including works from his Cubist period. Large sculptures also adorn the garden and courtyard. There are more than 500 pieces of Picasso's work on display across the four floors *(see p85)*.

3 Musée Rodin

On a sunny day, head straight for the gardens of the Musée Rodin, next to the Hôtel des Invalides complex, where you can enjoy some of the French sculptor's most famous works, including *The Thinker* and *The Burghers of Calais*, while strolling among the shady trees and rose bushes. Then go inside the beautiful 18th-century mansion, the Hôtel Biron, where Auguste Rodin (1840–1917) lived and worked for nine years, until his death. An extensive collection of his works from throughout his career is on display, plus temporary exhibitions *(see p111)*.

4 Musée National d'Art Moderne

The revolutionary Pompidou Centre is the perfect home for France's outstanding Modern Art Museum. It features some 1,400 works on two levels, one focusing on the artists and movements of the first half of the 20th century, the other featuring art from the 1960s to the present day. The museum often rotates changing displays of works *(see pp26–7)*.

Pl Georges Pompidou, 75004 • Map P2 • Open 11am–9pm, Wed–Mon • Admission charge

5 Jeu de Paume

This gallery is one of the finest exhibition spaces in the city, being set within a 19th-century real tennis court *(jeu de paume)*. It is a showcase for outstanding photography, film and video.

1 pl de la Concorde, 75008 • Map D3 • Open noon–9pm Tue, noon–7pm Wed–Fri, 10am–7pm Sat, Sun • Closed 1 Jan, 1 May, 25 Dec • Admission charge

***The Thinker*, Musée Rodin**

For more on Paris artists **See p144**

6 Musée de L'Orangerie

The prime exhibits here are eight of Monet's huge waterlily canvases *(see p13)* and the gallery, located in a corner of the Tuileries, was renovated to improve their display. The Walter-Guillaume collection covers works by Matisse, Picasso, Modigliani and other modern masters from 1870 to 1930.

Jardin des Tuileries, 75001 • Map D3 • www.musee-orangerie.fr • Open 9am–6pm Wed–Mon • Admission charge

7 Espace Montmartre Salvador Dalí

This underground museum with its black walls, lighting effects and soundtrack features some of Dalí's lesser-known works, including bronzes and book illustrations *(see p141)*.

Lip Sofa, Salvador Dalí

8 Musée Marmottan-Claude Monet

The Impressionist paintings of Claude Monet are the star attraction at this museum, featuring some 165 works donated by his son and perhaps the finest collection of his works in the world. They include a series of his late waterlily paintings. Other Impressionist and Realist painters are also represented, and there is a fine collection of illuminated medieval manuscripts *(see p153)*.

9 Musée Maillol

Works of the French artist Aristide Maillol, including his drawings, engravings, paintings and plastercasts, are the focal point of this museum which was created by his model, Dina Vierny. Other major artists feature in temporary exhibitions *(see p121)*.

10 Maison Européenne de la Photographie

If you're a photography fan, don't miss this splendid gallery in the Marais. Its exhibitions range from portraits to documentary work, retrospectives to contemporary photographers *(see p87)*.

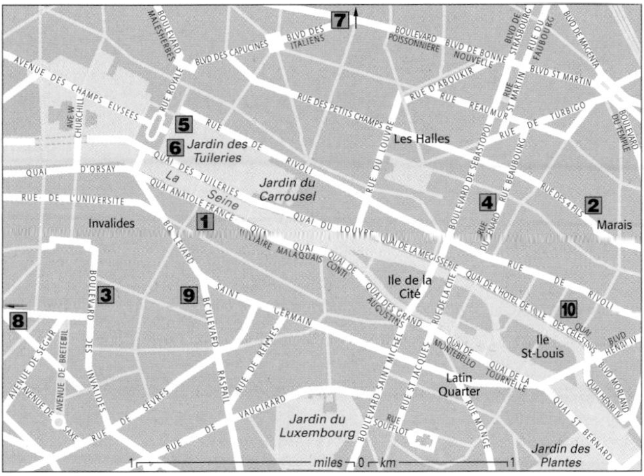

Left **Jardin du Luxembourg** Centre **Jardin des Plantes** Right **Bois de Boulogne**

TOP 10 Parks and Gardens

1 Jardin du Luxembourg
Parisians love this centrally located park, set around the Palais du Luxembourg. The sweeping terrace is a great place for people-watching, while locals sunbathe around the Octagonal Lake or sail toy boats in the water. Statues are dotted throughout the grounds, and there is a café *(see p119)*.

2 Jardin des Tuileries
Now officially part of the Louvre, these gardens were laid out in the 17th century as part of the old Palais de Tuileries. They stretch along the Seine between the Louvre and Place de la Concorde. The walkways are lined with lime and chestnut trees. Statues include bronze figures by Aristide Maillol *(see p95)*.

3 Jardin des Plantes
Established as a medicinal herb garden for the king in 1635, these vast botanical gardens are a wonderfully tranquil spot. Paths are lined with statuary and mature trees, including the oldest in Paris, grown from the stump of an *Acacia robinia* dating from 1636 *(see p129)*.

4 Bois de Boulogne
At the weekends, Parisians head for this vast park on the western edge of the city, with a boating lake and paths for cycling, jogging and strolling. There are three formal gardens, lakes and waterfalls, and even two horse-racing tracks. A good spot for a break from the city bustle *(see p152)*.

5 Bois de Vincennes
Another great escape from the city, this park is to the east of Paris what the Bois de Boulogne is to the west. A former royal hunting ground, it was landscaped in the 1860s. Now it features ornamental lakes and waterfalls, a zoo, a funfair and horse-racing tracks *(see p151)*.

6 Parc Monceau
The most fashionable green space in Paris, full of well-heeled residents of the nearby mansions and apartments. The lush landscaping dates from the 18th century, and some architectural follies, such as the Classical colonnade, survive *(see p153)*.

Bois de Boulogne

7 Jardins du Palais-Royal

These lovely gardens are enclosed by the 18th-century arcades of the Palais-Royal *(see p96)*. Contemporary sculptures include Daniel Buren's controversial striped columns. *Pl du Palais Royal, 75001 • Map L1*

8 Versailles

There are gardens galore at this famous royal palace, from the formal French gardens with their geometric paths and shrubberies, to the wandering paths through the rural-style English garden north of the Petit Trianon. In summer, you can row boats on the lovely cross-shaped Grand Canal *(see p151)*.

9 Parc Montsouris

Located south of Montparnasse, this is the second-largest park in central Paris and very popular with city residents. It was laid out in the English style atop an old granite quarry by landscape architect Adolphe Alphand between 1865 and 1878. Hemingway *(see p47)* and other writers and artists frequented the park in the mid-20th century. It has a jogging path, lake and a bandstand. *Blvd Jourdan, 75014 • Metro Cité Universitaire*

10 Parc des Buttes Chaumont

The great city planner Baron Haussmann created this wonderful retreat northeast of the city centre in 1867, from what was formerly a rubbish dump *(see p61)*. His architects built artificial cliffs, waterfalls, streams and a lake complete with an island crowned by a Roman-style temple. There is also boating available, a café and lovely views of Sacré-Coeur *(see pp22–3)*. The park is currently being renovated. *Rue Manin, 75019 • Metro Buttes-Chaumont*

Top 10 Fountains

1 Agam Fountain
Jewish architect Yaacov Agam designed this fountain of water and lights. *La Défense • RER La Défense*

2 Four Seasons Fountain
Paris looks down on figures representing the Seine and Marne rivers, designed in 1739 by sculptor Edme Bouchardon. *Rue de Grenelle • Map C4*

3 Fontaine des Innocents
Carved by Jean Goujon in 1547, this is Paris's only Renaissance fountain. *Square des Innocents • Map N2*

4 Medici Fountain
This ornate 17th-century fountain with a pond was built for Marie de Médicis. *Jardin du Luxembourg • Map L6*

5 Molière Fountain
This 19th-century fountain honours the French playwright. *Rue de Richelieu • Map E3*

6 Observatory Fountain
Four bronze statues representing the continents hold aloft a globe. *Jardin du Luxembourg • Map L6*

7 Châtelet Fountain
The two sphinxes of this 1808 fountain commemorate Napoleon's victory in Egypt. *Pl du Châtelet • Map N2*

8 Stravinsky Fountain
Birds squirt water from this colourful fountain *(see p27)*.

9 Trocadéro Fountains
Spouting towards the Eiffel Tower, these fountains are illuminated at night *(see p17)*.

10 Versailles Fountains
The fountains at Versailles *(see p154)* flow to music at weekends in spring and in summer.

Left **Notre-Dame** Centre **Sacré-Coeur** Right **Sainte-Chapelle**

TOP 10 Places of Worship

1 Notre-Dame
See pp18–21.

2 Sacré-Coeur
See pp22–3.

3 Sainte-Chapelle
Although the chapel is no longer used for worship, the soaring stained-glass windows encourage reverence *(see pp30–31)*.

4 Eglise du Dôme
The final resting place of Napoleon Bonaparte is the beautiful Dôme Church in the Hôtel des Invalides complex – an elaborate monument to French Classical style. Built as the chapel for the resident soldiers of the Invalides, its ornate high altar is in stark contrast to the solemn marble chapels surrounding the crypt, which hold the tombs of French military leaders. Its golden dome can be seen for miles around *(see pp32–3)*.

5 Panthéon
Patterned after the Pantheon in Rome, this domed late 18th-century church only served as a house of worship for two years, before becoming a monument and burial place for the great and the good of the Revolution era. Later distinguished citizens are also buried here *(see pp28–9)*.

6 St-Eustache
For centuries, this monumental Gothic edifice was the "market church" serving the traders of Les Halles. Taking more than 100 years to build, it was finally completed in 1637 and its cavernous interior displays the architectural style of the early Renaissance. Popular Sunday afternoon organ recitals and other classical concerts take place in this wonderfully atmospheric setting *(see p75)*.

Baptism of Christ, La Madeleine

7 La Madeleine
Designed in the style of a Greek temple in 1764, this prominent church in Paris's financial district, on the edge of the Opéra Quarter, is one of the city's most distinctive sights, spectacularly surrounded by 52 Corinthian columns. The church was consecrated to Mary Magdalene in 1845. The bronze doors, which include *bas-reliefs* of the Ten Commandments, and the *Last Judgment* on the south pediment are exterior highlights, while the ornate marble and gold interior has many fine statues, including François Rude's *Baptism of Christ*. It is also a popular venue for classical concerts.
Pl de la Madeleine, 75008 • Map D3 • Open 9:30am–7pm daily (services vary) • Free

8 Grande Synagogue de la Victoire

Built in the late 19th century, this elaborate synagogue is the second-largest in Europe. The building is open only to those wishing to attend services and to groups who have arranged a visit in advance. Other smaller synagogues can be found in the Marais, which has a large Jewish community, including one at 10 rue Pavée, built in 1913 by Hector Guimard, the architect who designed the city's Art Nouveau metro stations. *44 rue de la Victoire, 75009 • Map E2*

9 Mosquée de Paris

The city's Grand Mosque was built during the 1920s as a tribute to North African Muslims who gave military support to France during World War I. It features beautiful Moorish architecture, executed by craftsmen brought over from North Africa, and a peaceful interior courtyard *(see p129)*.

10 St-Sulpice

Outstanding frescoes in the Chapel of the Angels by Eugène Delacroix are the highlight of this 17th-century church's otherwise sober interior. With more than 6,500 pipes, its organ, designed by Jean-François Chalgrin in 1776, is one of the largest in the world. The novelist Victor Hugo married Adèle Foucher here in 1822 *(see p119)*.

St-Sulpice façade

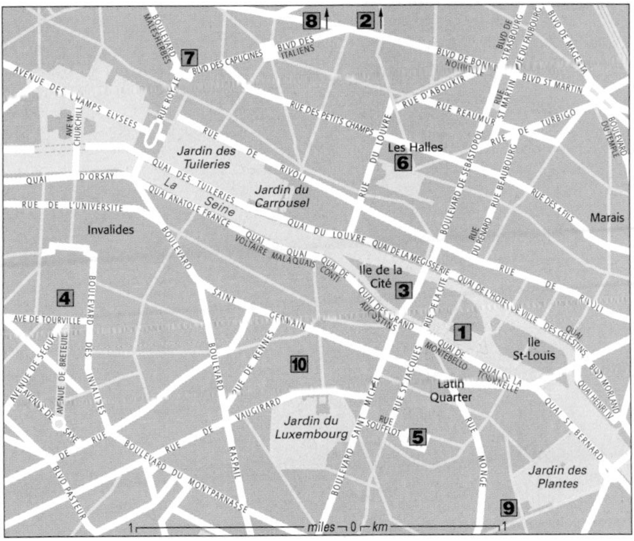

Left **Conciergerie** Right **Hôtel de Ville**

TOP 10 Historic Buildings

1 Hôtel des Invalides
See pp32–3.

2 Versailles
Louis XIV turned his father's old hunting lodge into the largest palace in Europe and moved his court here in 1678. It was the royal residence for more than a century until Louis XVI and his queen Marie-Antoinette fled during the Revolution *(see p151)*.

3 Conciergerie
Originally home to the caretaker and guards of the Palais de Justice, the Conciergerie was turned into a jail at the end of the 14th century. It took its place in history during the Revolution, when more than 4,000 citizens (including Marie-Antoinette) were held prisoner here, half of whom were guillotined. It remained a prison until 1914 *(see p69)*.

4 Palais de Justice
The enormous building that now houses the French law courts and judiciary dates back to Roman times and was the royal palace until the 14th century, when Charles V moved the court to the Marais. During the Revolution, thousands were sentenced to death in the Première Chambre Civile, allegedly the former bedroom of Louis IX *(see p70)*.

Palais de Justice

5 Hôtel Dieu
The Hôtel Dieu, now the hospital for central Paris, was built on the site of a foundling home in 1866–78; the original 12th-century building on the Ile de la Cité was demolished during the urban renewal schemes of the 19th century. A monument in the courtyard commemorates a courageous battle here in 1944 when Paris police held out against the Nazis. *1 pl du Parvis Notre-Dame, 75004 • Map N4*

6 Palais de l'Elysée
This imposing palace has been the official residence of the President of the French Republic since 1873. It was built as a private mansion in 1718 and subsequently owned by Madame de Pompadour, mistress of Louis XV, who extended the English-style gardens to the Champs-Elysées. Napoleon signed his abdication here in 1815 *(see p105)*.

7 Hôtel de Ville
Paris's city hall sports an elaborate façade, with ornate stonework, statues and a turreted roof. It is a 19th-century reconstruction of the original town hall, which was burned down in the Paris Commune of 1871

(see p45). Though the pedestrianized square in front is pleasant now, it was once the site of gruesome executions: Ravaillac, assassin of Henri IV, was quartered alive here in 1610. ✆ *4 pl de l'Hôtel de Ville, 75001 • Map P3 • 01 42 76 40 40 • Open for group tours only (booking essential: 01 42 76 54 04) • Free*

8 Palais-Royal

This former royal palace now houses State offices. Built by Cardinal Richelieu in 1632, it passed to the Crown on his death 10 years later and was the childhood home of Louis XIV. The dukes of Orléans acquired it in the 18th century. ✆ *Pl du Palais Royal, 75005 • Map L1 • Closed to the public*

9 La Sorbonne

The city's great university had humble beginnings in 1253 as a college for 16 poor students to study theology. France's first printing house was also established here in 1469. After suppression during the Revolution it became the University of Paris *(see p119)*.

10 Palais du Luxembourg

Marie de Médicis had architect Salomon de Brosse model this palace after her childhood home, the Pitti Palace in Florence. Shortly after its completion she was exiled by her son, Louis XIII. It was seized from the Crown during the Revolution to become a prison and it now houses the French Senate. Nearby is the Musée du Luxembourg. ✆ *15 rue de Vaugirard, 75006 • Map L6 • 01 44 54 19 49 • Open for reserved tours only; gardens open dawn-dusk*

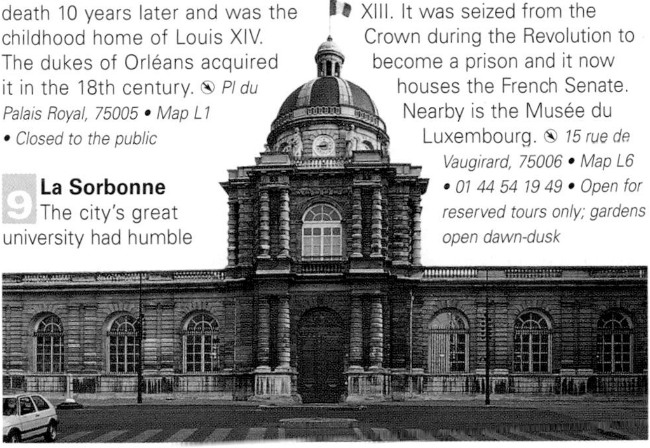

Palais du Luxembourg

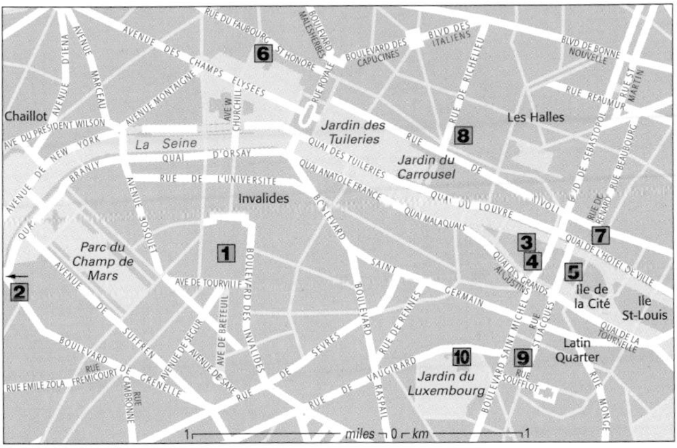

Left **Charlemagne crowned as Holy Roman Emperor** Right **Paris Commune burning of the city**

TOP 10 Historical Events in Paris

1 Arrival of the Parisii

Although the remains of Neolithic settlements have been found dating back to 4500 BC, the first inhabitants are considered to be a Celtic tribe called the Parisii, who settled on the Ile de la Cité in the 3rd century BC. Hunters and fishermen, they named their village Lutetia, meaning "boatyard on a river". The tribe minted their own gold coins and a pagan altar was found beneath Notre-Dame.

2 Roman Settlement

The Romans conquered the Parisii in 52 BC and destroyed their city. After rebuilding it as their administrative centre, they founded their own town on the Left Bank. The baths in the Hôtel de Cluny *(see p34)* and the amphitheatre in rue Monge are the only remains. In AD 360 the Roman prefect was declared emperor and Lutetia was renamed Paris, after its original inhabitants.

3 Founding of France

Roman rule weakened under Barbarian attacks. In 450 the prayers of a young nun, Geneviève, were credited with saving the city from invasion by Attila the Hun. She became the patron saint of Paris. But in 476 the Franks captured the city, Christianity became the official religion and Paris the capital of their new kingdom, France.

Succession of Louis XIII

4 Charlemagne, Holy Roman Emperor

In 751 the Carolingian dynasty became rulers of France when Pepin the Short ascended the throne. His heir Charlemagne was crowned Holy Roman Emperor in 800 and moved the capital to Aix-La-Chapelle (Aachen). Paris fell into decline until Hugues Capet became king in 987, moving the capital back to his home city.

5 St Bartholomew's Day Massacre

Catherine de'Medici, Henri II's queen, bore three French kings and one queen, Marguerite de Valois, who married the Protestant Henri of Navarre in August 1572. Many Protestants came to Paris for the wedding and Catherine plotted their massacre. The killings began on 24 August and thousands died. Henri of Navarre survived and later became Henri IV, the first Bourbon king.

6 French Revolution

Following decades of royal excess and the growing gulf between rich and poor, Paris erupted with the storming of the Bastille prison in 1789 *(see box)*.

7 Napoleon's Coronation
As Paris rose from the ashes of the Revolution, a young general from Corsica, Napoleon Bonaparte, saved the city from a royalist revolt, then led military victories in Italy and Egypt. He crowned himself Emperor of France in Notre-Dame in 1804 *(see p20)*.

8 The Second Empire
In 1851, Napoleon's nephew, Louis-Napoleon, seized power as Emperor Napoleon III. He appointed Baron Haussmann to oversee massive building works that transformed Paris into the most glorious city in Europe. The wide boulevards, many public buildings, parks, sewer system and the first department stores date from 1852 to 1870.

9 The Paris Commune
Following France's defeat in the Franco-Prussian War in 1871 *(see p23)*, many citizens rejected the harsh terms of the surrender and a left wing group revolted, setting up the Paris Commune. But, after 72 days, government troops marched on the city. In a week of street fighting (21–28 May), much of the city burned and thousands of rebellious citizens were killed.

10 Liberation of Paris
The occupation of France by Germany during World War II was a dark period for Paris. However, the city was also the centre for the French Resistance. Allied forces liberated Paris on 25 August 1944; just two days earlier, the German commander Von Choltitz had ignored Adolf Hitler's order to burn the city.

Top 10 Events in the French Revolution

1 14 July 1789
Storming of the Bastille prison, a symbol of repression, launches the Revolution.

2 4 August 1789
The abolition of feudalism, and the right of everyone to be a free citizen is declared.

3 26 August 1789
Formal declaration of the Rights of Man and the Citizen, which incorporated the ideals of equality and dignity, later incorporated into the 1791 Constitution.

4 October 1789
Citizens march on Versailles and the royal family returns to Paris as prisoners in the Tuileries Palace *(see p95)*.

5 20 June 1791
The royal family try to escape but are spotted in Varenne and return as captives.

6 10 August 1792
A mob storms the Tuileries and the royals are imprisoned in the Temple..

7 21 September 1792
The monarchy is formally abolished and the First Republic is proclaimed.

8 1792–4
"The Terror" reigns, under the radical Commune led by Robespierre, Danton and Marat. Thousands are executed by guillotine.

9 21 January 1793
Louis XVI is found guilty of treason and executed. His queen Marie-Antoinette follows him to the guillotine on 16 October.

10 28 July 1794
Robespierre is guillotined, ending the Terror, and the Revolution draws to a close.

Left **Plaque on Victor Hugo's house** Right **Film still from *A Tale of Two Cities***

Historical Novels set in Paris

1 Les Misérables

The 1862 novel by Victor Hugo (1802–85) is an all-too-vivid portrayal of the poor and the dispossessed in early 19th-century Paris. At its centre is the tale of nobleman Jean Valjean, unfairly victimized by an unjust system. The younger character of Marius is based around Hugo's own experiences as an impoverished student.

2 The Hunchback of Notre-Dame

Better known by its English title, which inspired a film of the same name, Victor Hugo's Gothic novel was published in France in 1831 as *Notre-Dame de Paris*. Set in the Middle Ages, it tells the strange and moving story of a hunchback bell-ringer Quasimodo and his love for Esmeralda *(see p21)*.

3 A Tale of Two Cities

The finest chronicler of 19th-century London life, Charles Dickens (1812–70) chose to set his 1859 novel in London and Paris, against the background of the French Revolution *(see p45)*. His description of conditions in the Bastille prison makes for grim reading.

4 Le Père Goriot

Honoré de Balzac (1799–1850) chronicled Paris life masterfully in his 80-volume *La comédie humaine* series, and this 1853 novel is certainly among the finest. Balzac's house at 47 rue Raynouard in the 16th *arrondissement*, where he lived from 1840–47, is open to the public *(see p137)*.

5 Sentimental Education

Gustave Flaubert (1821–80) studied law in Paris but illness disrupted his chosen career and he devoted himself to literature. This work (*L'education sentimentale* in French), first published in 1870 in two volumes, stands alongside his greatest novel, *Madame Bovary* (1857), and marks the move from Romanticism to Realism in French literature.

6 Bel-Ami

Guy de Maupassant (1850–93) published this, one of his best novels, in 1885, criticizing the get-rich-quick Parisian business world of the *belle époque* (Beautiful Age). Maupassant is known as one of the world's greatest short-story writers, and he is buried in the cemetery at Montparnasse *(see p152)*.

Guy de Maupassant

7 A la Recherche du Temps Perdu

The master work of Marcel Proust (1871–1922) was written in 13 volumes, the first novel appearing in 1913. Proust lived on boulevard Haussmann, and his epic tale is the fictionalized story of his own life, and of Paris during the *belle époque*. Proust is buried in Père Lachaise cemetery in eastern Paris *(see p153)*.

8 Nana

Perhaps the greatest Parisian chronicler of them all, Emile Zola (1840–1902) was born, lived and died in the city, although he spent part of his youth in Aix-en-Provence in southern France. *Nana* was published in 1880 and tells a shocking tale of sexual decadence, through the eyes of the central character, a dancer and prostitute.

9 L'Assommoir

Published in 1877, Zola's *L'Assommoir* (The Drunkard) shows a side of Paris that many at the time would have preferred to ignore – the alcoholism of the working classes. It is one of the author's series of 20 linked books known as the *Rougon-Macquart* sequence, which depict life in every quarter of society, through the eyes of two branches of the same family.

10 Thérèse Raquin

Here Zola focuses on the secret passions that lurk behind a single Paris shopfront, opening up to reveal a tale of obsessive lust that ultimately leads to a brutal murder. It was published in 1867 and, only his second novel, shows the author's astonishing maturity and unflinching examination of all aspects of 19th-century life.

Top 10 Foreign Writers who Lived in Paris

1 Ernest Hemingway

The US author (1899–1961) wrote *A Moveable Feast* as an affectionate portrait of his time in Paris from 1921–1926.

2 F. Scott Fitzgerald

Like Hemingway, US writer Fitzgerald (1896–1940) lived in Montparnasse and frequented the bar La Coupole *(see p125)*.

3 George Orwell

The English novelist (1903–50) tells of his shocking experiences living in poverty in *Down and Out in Paris and London* (1933).

4 Samuel Beckett

Born in Ireland in 1906, the playwright lived in Paris from 1928 until his death in 1989.

5 Anaïs Nin

US novelist Nin (1903–77) met her lover, fellow American Henry Miller, in Paris. Her *Diaries* tell of her time here.

6 Albert Camus

Algerian-born Camus (1913–60) moved to Paris in 1935 and lived here until his death.

7 Henry Miller

Miller (1891–1980) showed the seedier side of Paris in his novel *Tropic of Cancer* (1934).

8 Diana Mitford

Controversial fascist sympathiser and authoress, Mitford (1910–2003) spent her dotage in Paris.

9 James Joyce

Joyce (1882–1941) lived in Paris from 1920 to 1940. *Ulysses* was published here in 1922 by Shakespeare and Co.

10 Milan Kundera

Czech-born Kundera (b.1929) moved to Paris in 1978 where he wrote *The Unbearable Lightness of Being*.

For literary haunts **See p125**

Left **Palais de Chaillot** Centre **Liberty Flame** Right **Pont Alexandre III**

TOP 10 Riverfront Sights

1 Eiffel Tower

Although the top of the Eiffel Tower can be seen above rooftops across the city, one of the best views of this Paris landmark is from the Seine. The Pont d'Iéna lies at the foot of the tower, bridging the river to link it to the Trocadéro Gardens. The tower, illuminated at night, is a highlight of a dinner cruise on the Seine *(see pp16–17)*.

Eiffel Tower

2 Palais de Chaillot

The curved arms of the Palais de Chaillot encircling the Trocadéro Gardens can be seen from the Seine. In the centre of the gardens the magnificent fountains spout from the top of a long pool lined with statues, while two huge water cannons spray their charges back towards the river and the Eiffel Tower on the opposite bank *(see p135)*.

3 Liberty Flame

A replica of the Statue of Liberty's torch in New York was erected in 1987 by the *International Herald Tribune* to mark their centenary and honour the freedom fighters of the French Resistance during World War II. It is located on the right bank of the Pont de l'Alma, the bridge over the tunnel where Diana, Princess of Wales, was killed in an automobile crash in 1997. The Liberty Flame has now become her unofficial memorial and is often draped with notes and flowers laid in her honour.
Map C3

4 Grand Palais and Petit Palais

Gracing either side of the Pont Alexandre III are these two splendid exhibition halls, built for the Universal Exhibition of 1900. The iron Art Nouveau skeleton of the Grand Palais is topped by an enormous glass roof, which is most impressive when illuminated at night. The Petit Palais is smaller but similar in style, with a dome and many Classical features *(see p103)*.

5 Pont Alexandre III

The most beautiful bridge in Paris is the Pont Alexandre III, a riot of Art Nouveau decoration including cherubs, wreaths,

For Paris boat trips **See p164**

lamps and other elaborate statuary. Built for the Universal Exhibition of 1900, it leads to the Grand Palais and Petit Palais. There are wonderful views of the Invalides complex and the Champs-Elysées from the bridge *(see p104)*.

6 Dôme Church

An impressive view of the Eglise de Dôme in the Hôtel des Invalides complex can be had from the Pont Alexandre III. The golden dome beckons visitors down the long parkway lined with streetlamps and statues *(see pp32–3)*.

7 Musée du Louvre

This grand museum stretches along the river from the Pont Royal to the Pont des Arts. The Denon Wing, seen from the Seine, was largely built during the reigns of Henri IV and Louis XIII in the late 16th and early 17th centuries *(see pp8–11)*.

8 Musée d'Orsay

The view of this modern art gallery from the Right Bank of the Seine is one of its finest angles, showing off the arched terminals and grand façade of this former railway station. Architect Victor Laloux designed it specifically to harmonize with the Louvre and Tuileries Quarter across the river *(see pp12–15)*.

9 Conciergerie

This huge and imposing building, which served as a notorious prison during the Revolution, commands the western end of the Ile de la Cité. The building retains some of the few medieval features on the island, including the torture chamber, clock and twin towers which rise above the quai de l'Horloge *(see p69)*.

10 Notre-Dame

The great cathedral is never more majestic than when viewed from the Left Bank of the Seine. It rises at the eastern end of the Ile de la Cité above the remains of the ancient tribes who first settled Paris in the 3rd century BC *(see pp18–21)*.

Notre-Dame

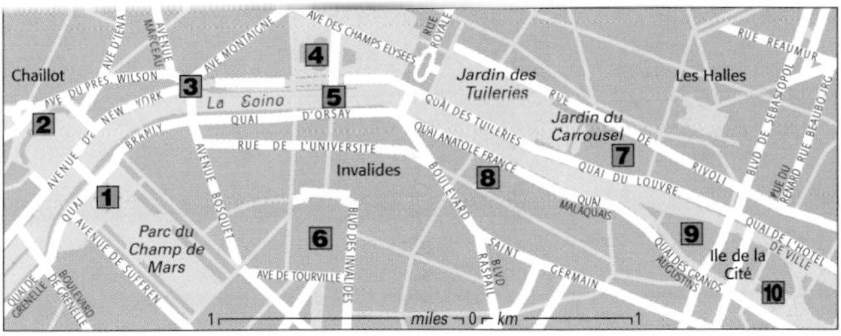

Left **Jardin des Tuileries** Right **Bois de Boulogne**

Top 10 Walks in Paris

1 Jardin des Tuileries

A stroll through the beautiful Tuileries Gardens is one of the must-dos of Paris. Before the Revolution this was a prime spot for the aristocracy to show off their latest fashions. The gardens are now part of the Musée du Louvre *(see p95)*.

2 The Left Bank

A very Parisian walk, particularly on a Sunday, is along the Left Bank (Rive Gauche) of the Seine. The riverside quays of the Latin Quarter have been lined with second-hand bookstalls *(bouquinistes)* for centuries. The books are mostly in French, but you'll also find stalls selling prints and postcards *(see p122)*.

3 Montmartre

The steep streets of the Butte are a good place to get some exercise after indulging in the irresistible French cuisine. Although this famous artists' quarter is more touristy than Bohemian these days, its old charms can still be found in the winding back streets and small squares *(see pp140–43)*.

Montmartre

4 The Marais

With inspiring art galleries, delectable delis, and shop after shop filled with contemporary fashions and *objets d'art*, a walk in the Marais is great fun, even if you only window-shop. The beautiful mansions are a great backdrop for your stroll and there are plenty of cafés and bars for sustenance *(see pp84–7)*.

5 Jardin des Plantes

In this historic botanical garden you can escape the bustle of the city and lose yourself on the shady tree-lined avenues, amid colourful flowerbeds, or the hothouses and exotic gardens. Or simply relax on the lawns *(see p129)*.

6 Jardin du Luxembourg

Napoleon designated this the "garden of children", and whether or not you have little ones in tow you'll enjoy a walk through this favourite haunt of the Latin Quarter. After you've seen the octagonal pond and the Medicis Fountain, seek out the miniature Statue of Liberty and the statues of French queens *(see p119)*.

7 The Passages

These covered arcades around the Grands Boulevards were built at the end of the 18th century to shelter elegant shoppers from bad weather. Now lined with speciality and antiques shops, they

For more on getting around Paris **See p164**

are wonderfully atmospheric places to explore. Most are in the 2nd *arrondissement*, and connecting passages Verdeau, Jouffroy and Panoramas together form the longest in Paris. *Map H5*

8 Ile St-Louis
Although you could walk end to end in about 10 minutes, the Seine's smaller island demands a more leisurely stroll. You'll discover superb little art galleries, trendy boutiques, and a village-like atmosphere within this up-market enclave *(see p68)*.

9 Bois de Boulogne
Come here at the weekend if you want to join the locals in the "great escape", and you'll have 8.65 sq km (3.34 sq miles) from which to choose your path. The Bagatelle Gardens are a fine place for a walk in spring and summer, when a stunning array of roses and other flowers are in bloom *(see p152)*.

Boulevard St-Germain

10 Boulevard St-Germain
There's no better way to enjoy the Latin Quarter than to do as the Parisians do – stroll the Boulevard St-Germain, preferably late on a Sunday morning. After your walk, honour the birthplace of café society with a coffee at either Les Deux Magots or Café de Flore, two of the city's most famous literary and intellectual haunts *(see p120)*.

Top 10 Outdoor Activities

1 Walking
Paris is a compact city so you can easily combine sightseeing with exercise.

2 Roller-blading
A fad which shows no sign of abating, skaters weave their way through traffic and pedestrians alike.

3 Cycling
Head for the Bois de Boulogne and Bois de Vincennes to escape the Paris traffic, or grab a Vélib' *(see p164)*.

4 Boating
Boating lakes in the Bois de Boulogne and Bois de Vincennes allow you to flex your rowing muscles.

5 Jogging
You can get your aerobic fix along the pathways of Paris's parks and gardens.

6 Table Tennis
Try your luck at the outdoor concrete tables found in several parks and squares.

7 Sunbathing
De rigueur on the *quais* beside the Seine, especially during "Paris Plages" in July and August *(see p57)*.

8 Swimming
There are 38 public pools in Paris, but hours are restricted during school terms. Or try the pool at the Forum des Halles.

9 Football
France's football team has many young imitators in parks, gardens and streets.

10 Boules
A sport dominated by older men, but anyone can enjoy a game of *pétanque* wherever there's a sandy stretch in a park or garden.

Left **Café de Flore** Centre **La Closerie des Lilas** Right **Café Marly**

TOP 10 Cafés and Bars

1 Café de Flore

A hang-out for artists and intellectuals since the 1920s, its regulars have included Salvador Dali and Albert Camus. During World War II Jean-Paul Sartre and Simone de Beauvoir "more or less set up house in the Flore". Although its prices have skyrocketed, its Art Deco decor hasn't changed and it's still a favourite with French filmmakers and literati *(see p125)*.

2 Les Deux Magots

Rival to the neighbouring Flore as the rendezvous for the 20th-century intellectual élite. Hemingway, Oscar Wilde, Djuna Barnes, André Breton and Paul Verlaine were all regulars, and Picasso met his muse Dora Maar here in 1937. Similarly pricey, with outside tables facing the boulevard and the square *(see p125)*.

3 Le Petit Vendôme

The search for the best sandwiches in Paris stops here, with bread from the award-winning Julien bakery and just the right slathering of butter with cured ham or goat's cheese. Good hot dishes are served too. *8 rue des Capucines, 75002 • Map E3 • 01 42 61 05 88 • €*

Les Deux Magots

4 Café Marly

Superbly situated in the Richelieu wing of the Louvre *(see p9)*, the café offers simple but expertly prepared brasserie fare (steaks, salads, steak tartare, club sandwiches) as well as delicious desserts. The dining room has plush decor and velvet armchairs, but the best spot is under the arcade overlooking the glass pyramid and the cour Napoléon. *93 rue de Rivoli, 75001 • Map L2 • €€€*

5 Café de la Paix

A grand Parisian café with prices to match, but it's worth a visit to enjoy the frescoed walls and sumptuous surroundings, designed by Charles Garnier, architect of the Opera House across the square *(see p97)*. This is another Paris landmark with a string of famous past patrons, and arguably the best *mille-feuille* cakes in town. *12 blvd des Capucines, 75008 • Map E3 • €€€€€*

6 La Closerie des Lilas

The main restaurant here is expensive, but the bar is a good spot to soak up the atmosphere of this historic site where artists and writers from Baudelaire to Archibald MacLeish have drunk since 1808. Look out for the famous names of visitors etched

For more places to eat in Paris **See pp64–5**

on the tables in the bar. The busy brasserie also has live piano music in the evenings and attracts a chic crowd *(see p157)*.

7 Le Fumoir

There are many reasons to drop into this café-bar-restaurant next to the Louvre whether it be to people-watch from the terrace out front or hide out with a martini and game of backgammon in the comfy library at the back. The hot chocolate is heavenly, cocktails are expertly made and the bistro cooking shows Italian and Swedish influences. *6 rue de l'Amiral de Coligny, 75001 • Map F4 • 01 42 92 00 24 • €€€€€*

Café de la Paix

8 Chez Jeannette

Although the owners haven't touched the scruffy vintage decor, this café near Gare de l'Est has now become one of the hottest hang-outs in Paris with a crowd outside to prove it. Inside, the high ceilings, mirrors and old-fashioned booths, as well as reasonably priced food, create a lively atmosphere. *47 rue du Faubourg-Saint-Denis, 75010 • Map G2 • 01 47 70 30 89 • No disabled access • €€*

9 Le Café de l'Industrie

Unpretentious but stylish, the Bastille café with three large rooms is decorated with everything from spears, to old film star publicity stills. The simple food, such as onion soup, is good value. Non-stop service from noon to midnight *(see p92)*.

10 Bistro Mélac

This friendly wine bar off the beaten track is full of character, with a rustic beamed ceiling hung with country hams and a vine growing around the walls. The owner is an enthusiastic wine lover and aims to please with his reasonably priced cellar. A fun harvest of the bar's vine is held on the second Saturday of September. *42 rue Léon-Frot, 75011 • Metro Charonne • 01 43 70 59 27 • Closed Sun, Mon, Easter, Aug and last week Dec • €€*

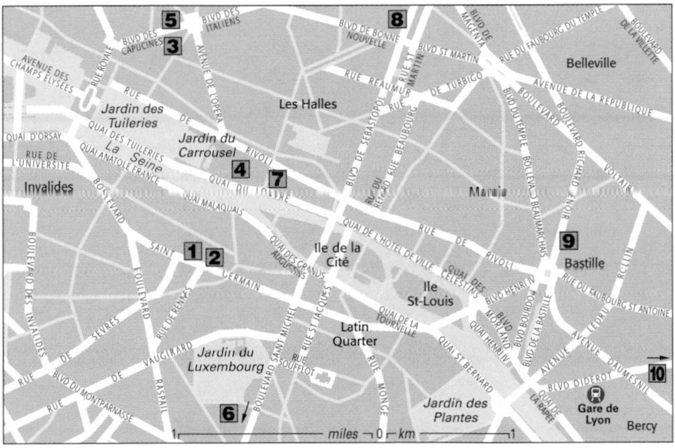

For price guides to Paris restaurants **See p73**

Left **Au Printemps** Right **Rue de Buci**

Top 10 Shops and Markets

1 Flower and Bird Markets

Dating from 1808, the colourful Marché aux Fleurs (flower market) on the Ile de la Cité is the oldest and one of the largest flower markets in Paris. Its blooms brighten up the area between the stark walls of the Conciergerie and Hôtel Dieu from Monday to Saturday – everything from orchids to orange trees. On Sundays it is joined by the Marché aux Oiseaux (bird market) with equally colourful, caged species. *Pl Louis-Lépine, 75004 • Map P4*

2 Au Printemps

One of Paris's two top department stores, Printemps opened in 1864. Its goods range from designer clothing and accessories, to middle-of-the-range labels and funky fashions, home decor and furniture. The sixth-floor brasserie is crowned with a lovely Art Nouveau stained-glass cupola. *64 blvd Haussmann, 75009 • Map E2*

3 Galeries Lafayette

Printemps' great rival store opened in 1894 and is a monument to Parisian style, topped by a glorious steel-and-glass dome. Along with designer clothes, there's a fabulous food hall. The seventh floor has great views. *40 blvd Haussmann, 75009 • Map E2*

4 Bastille Market

Every Thursday and Sunday morning, this market stretches along the tree-lined boulevard that separates the Marais from the Bastille. Sunday is the best day, when locals come to socialize as well as shop for foods such as fish, meat, bread and cheese. Some stalls sell North African and other international fare. *Blvd Richard-Lenoir, 75011 • Map H5*

Marché aux Fleurs (flower market)

5 Place de la Madeleine

This is a gourmand's delight. Some of the most delectable speciality food shops in Paris are dotted around the edges of this square, including the famous Fauchon food hall and the smaller Hédiard. There's Maille for mustard, Kaspia for caviar, Marquise de Sévigné for chocolates and La Maison de la Truffe for truffles *(see p98)*.

6 Rue de Buci

The artist Picasso reputedly did his shopping at this daily morning market in the heart of

St-Germain. The huge fruit and vegetable stalls are of high quality but of greater interest are the food shops opening on to the street, which sell specialist and regional fare. You can also buy prepared Italian dishes and delicious pastries. ✎ *Map L4*

7 Rue Mouffetard

One of the oldest street markets in Paris winds downhill through the Latin Quarter every Tuesday to Sunday morning. Although this formerly cheap and Bohemian market has been discovered as a tourist spot, it retains its charm, the narrow streets lined with food stalls and speciality shops. there are also good restaurants in the quieter side streets. ✎ *Map F6*

8 Le Bon Marché

Paris's first department store was founded on the Left Bank in 1852, its structure partially designed by Gustave Eiffel *(see p17)*. Today it's even more hip than its competitors, with an in-store boutique featuring avant-garde fashions. It also has designer clothes, its own line of menswear and the enormous La Grande Epicerie food hall. ✎ *22 rue de Sèvres, 75007 • Map D5*

Marché aux Puces du St-Ouen

9 Aligre Market

Away from the tourist bustle, this Bastille market, dubbed the "Notre-Dame of markets", retains an authentic Parisian atmosphere. Every morning from Tuesday to Sunday North African traders hawk inexpensive produce in the open-air market, and there's an adjacent flea market and a covered market selling top-quality fare. ✎ *Pl d'Aligre, 75012 • Map H5*

10 Marché aux Puces de St-Ouen

Every Saturday to Monday the largest antiques market in the world comes alive. There are actually several markets here: the oldest, Marché Vernaison, is the most charming; Marché Malik sells vintage clothing. Others offer furniture, jewellery and paintings. ✎ *Porte de Clignancourt, 75018 • Metro Porte de Clignancourt*

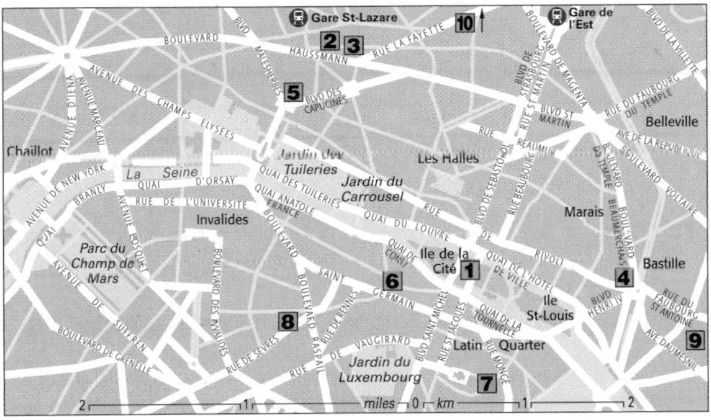

For more on shopping in Paris **See p169**

Left **Fête du Cinéma** Right **Tour de France**

TOP 10 Festivals and Events

1 Nuit Blanche

Paris held its first Nuit Blanche in 2002 and the all-night contemporary art event now attracts more than 1,500,000 people each year. Its goal is to give a fresh perspective on Paris with installations and exhibitions in several different neighbourhoods, and to make contemporary art more accessible to all. *First weekend Oct*

2 Fête du Cinéma

Film buffs should be sure to verify the exact dates of this annual event, held each June. For just three days, cinemagoers pay full price for the first film that they see, but can then see as many other films as they choose, for a few euros each. *www.feteducinema.com*

3 Paris Jazz Festival

Paris is home to jazz all year round *(see pp62–3)*, but every summer there is a major jazz festival in the city. Acts from all over the world come to play in the Parc Floral de Paris in the Bois de Vincennes *(see p151)*, but there are many lesser venues involved as well. *Jun–end Jul • www.parcfloraldeparis.com*

4 Grandes Eaux Nocturnes

A true midsummer night's dream with superb illuminations and installations in the gardens of Versailles, plus a spectacular firework display over the Grand Canal. *Dates in Jun, Jul and Aug*

5 Tour de France

Don't miss this summer highlight if you really want to understand the French passion for cycling. Towards the end of July each year, the world's greatest and most gruelling cycle race approaches Paris. On the final laps the riders pass the Louvre, race along the banks of the Seine, go down the rue de Rivoli and, of course, the Champs-Elysées. Thousands of fans pack the streets to cheer the riders home and see who will win the Yellow Jersey. *www.letour.fr*

6 Festival d'Automne à Paris

This major festival promotes contemporary arts across the board in Paris, encouraging all walks of life to see and enjoy performances of dance, music, film and drama. *mid-Sep–Dec • www.festival-automne.com*

Paris Jazz Festival

7 Fêtes des Vendanges

Paris used to be one of the country's major wine producers, but these days only the vineyards at Montmartre remain *(see p142)*. These produce just under 600 litres (5 barrels) of wine each autumn, but great fun is had at the Fêtes des Vendanges with wine, food stalls and a street parade. *Oct: first Fri (for five days)*

8 Fête de la Musique

To celebrate the summer equinox, professional and amateur musicians take to the streets of Paris. Major shows are held in Place de la République and other concert venues, but the most fun is to be had wandering through residential neighbourhoods and dropping into locals' bars. *21 Jun*

9 Paris Plages

Launched in 2002 by the mayor of Paris, Bertrand Delanoë, this hugely popular summer event transforms a stretch of the Seine *quais* and the Canal du l'Ourcq into a mini Cannes, with tons of soft sand, sunbeds, parasols and palm trees. There are also events and attractions for children. *mid-Jul–mid-Aug • www.paris.fr*

10 Mois de la Photo

Paris reveres the art of photography and every alternate November (in even-numbered years) it hosts the "Month of the Photo". Galleries, museums, shops, cultural centres and many other venues all give space to exhibitions, workshops and lectures on all aspects of the art. For anyone interested in photography, it is the most exciting time to visit Paris. *Nov • www.mep-fr.org*

Top 10 Sports Events

1 Tour de France

This great cycle race reaches its climax in Paris.

2 Prix de l'Arc de Triomphe

This world-renowned horse race attracts the city's *crème de la crème*. *Longchamp racecourse • Oct: first weekend*

3 French Tennis Open

Paris's legendary clay-court tournament. *Stade Roland Garros • end May–1st week Jun*

4 Gucci Masters

Show-jumping fans and competitors descend on Paris. *Paris Nord Villepinte • Dec*

5 Six Nations Rugby

The French team plays against England, Scotland, Ireland, Wales and Italy in this Feb–Mar tournament. *Stade de France*

6 Paris Marathon

Runners start at the Champs-Elysées and end at avenue Foch. *Apr*

7 Football Cup Final

The biggest club event in French football. *Stade de France • mid-May*

8 Prix de Diane

Parisian high society flocks to this upmarket horse race *Chantilly • Jun: second Sun*

9 Top 14 Rugby Final

Some of the world's finest rugby players take part in the final for the French Rugby league. *Stade de France • May/Jun*

10 Ice-Skating Grand Prix

The Trophée Eric Bompard is the Parisian leg of the International Grand Prix. *Palais Omnisports de Paris-Bercy • Nov*

Left **The Lido** Centre **Le Crazy Horse Paris** Right **Théâtre de la Ville de Paris**

Top 10 Entertainment Venues

1 Opéra National de Paris Garnier

Not just a night out, but a whole experience, opera has now returned to its original Paris base after the theatre had a spell as a dance-only venue. The vast stage can hold a cast of 450, and the building itself is an example of excessive opulence, complete with grand staircase, mirrors and marble *(see p97)*.

2 Folies-Bergère

The epitome of Parisian cabaret, the Folies were, for a time, no more than a troupe of high-kicking, bare-breasted dancers. Today, the musical shows have largely returned to the nostalgic days when Maurice Chevalier and Josephine Baker *(see p63)* performed here. ✆ *32 rue Richer, 75009 • Map F2 • 08 92 68 16 50 • www.foliesbergere.com*

Folies-Bergère

3 The Lido

Home to the world famous troupe of long-legged dancers, the Bluebell Girls, the fabulous special effects include aerial ballets and an on-stage skating rink. There are many who regard this dinner-cabaret as an essential Parisian experience. ✆ *116 bis ave des Champs-Elysées, 75008 • Map D3 • 01 40 76 56 10 • www.lido.fr*

4 Moulin Rouge

The original home of the Can-Can, the theatre's dancers were immortalized on canvas by Toulouse-Lautrec during the *belle époque* and are on display in the Musée d'Orsay *(see p13)*. The show still has all the razzamatazz that has been dazzling audiences since 1889. The pre-show dinner is optional *(see p142)*.

5 Le Crazy Horse Paris

More risqué than the other big-name cabaret shows, the Saloon has a reputation for putting on the most professional as well as the sexiest productions. Striptease features, along with glamorous dancing girls and other cabaret acts. The computer-controlled lighting effects are spectacular. ✆ *12 ave George V, 75008 • Map C3 • 01 47 23 32 32 • www.lecrazyhorseparis.com*

6 Le Cirque d'Hiver

Worth visiting for the façade alone, this whimsical listed building, dating from 1852, plays host to the traditional Cirque Bouglione, complete with acts such as trapeze artists, clowns, jugglers and tame tigers. ✆ *110 rue Amelot, 75011 • Map H3 • 01 47 00 28 81 • www.cirquedhiver.com*

For more Paris cabarets and clubs **See p146**

7 Comédie Française

Paris's oldest theatre was founded in 1680 and is still the only one with its own repertory company, staging both classical and modern drama (in French). The current building dates from the 18th century. Around the corner from the main box office, a special window opens 45 minutes before curtain-up, selling reduced price tickets for under-27s and concessions. *1 pl Colette, 75001 • Map L1 • 08 25 10 16 80 (+33 1 44 58 15 15 from abroad) • www.comedie-francaise.fr*

8 Opéra National de Paris Bastille

Opened in 1992 as the largest opera house in the world, this modern building was heavily criticized, not least for its acoustics and poor facilities. However, this is still the best place to see opera in Paris. *Pl de la Bastille, 75012 • Map H5 • 08 92 89 90 90 (+33 1 71 25 24 23 from abroad) • www.operadeparis.fr*

9 Théâtre du Châtelet

The city's largest concert hall and fourth-largest auditorium was built in 1862. The repertoire covers classical music, ballet and opera, Broadway shows and popular Sunday morning chamber music concerts. *1 pl du Châtelet, 75001 • Map N2 • 01 40 28 28 00 • www.chatelet-theatre.com*

10 Théâtre de la Ville

Once known as the Sarah Bernhardt Theatre, in honour of the great Parisian actress who performed here and managed the theatre in the 19th century, today it puts on an eclectic range of modern dance, music shows and some classical theatre. *2 pl du Châtelet, 75004 • Map N2 • 01 42 74 22 77 • www.theatredelaville-paris.com*

Top 10 Films set in Paris

1 Les Enfants du Paradis
The city's underworld is shown in this 1944 classic.

2 Everyone Says I Love You
Woody Allen's 1996 movie included many scenes shot around Notre-Dame and the Left Bank.

3 A Bout de Souffle
French New Wave director Jean-Luc Godard's 1959 film stars Jean-Paul Belmondo as a car thief on the run.

4 French Can-Can
The Jean Renoir classic (1955) tells the story of how the famous dance was created in Montmartre clubs.

5 Last Tango in Paris
Controversial, erotic 1972 film starring Marlon Brando.

6 The Trial
Orson Welles used the then empty Gare d'Orsay (now the Musée d'Orsay) to create a convincingly huge and anonymous office for his 1962 version of Kafka's novel.

7 Subway
The metro was the star in this 1985 Luc Besson film about a man who seeks refuge at night in its stations.

8 Les 400 Coups
Gritty Paris streets feature in this 1959 François Truffaut film about a boy on the run.

9 Amélie
Jean-Pierre Jeunet's 2000 sensation about a girl's quest for love features numerous scenes in Montmartre.

10 Midnight in Paris
Woody Allen returns to Paris in this 2011 popular eulogy to 1920s bohemia.

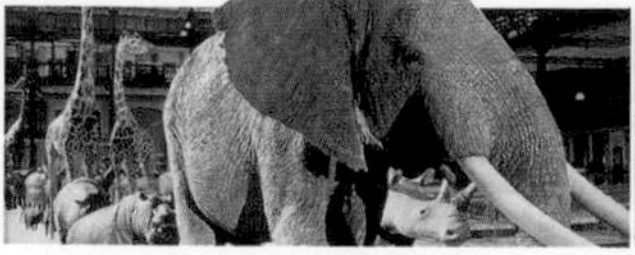

Left **Grande Galerie de l'Evolution** Right **Jardin d'Acclimatation**

Top 10 Children's Attractions

1 Disneyland® Paris

Formerly known as Euro-Disneyland, the French offspring of America's favourite theme park is a clone of its parent, and has now been joined by the Walt Disney Studios® complex. Both have big queues, so arrive early. There are rides for children of all ages and most adults are equally enchanted *(see p151)*.

2 Parc de la Villette

One of the city's top children's attractions, with activities for all ages. The Cité des Sciences et de l'Industrie, a high-tech hands-on science museum, gets star billing, while the Cité des Enfants is a science and nature attraction for younger children. Kids also love the Argonaute, a real submarine that voyaged around the world 10 times, the Géode with its IMAX screen and the futuristic outdoor playground *(see p152)*.

Parc de la Villette

3 Eiffel Tower

A trip to the top is one of the most memorable activities for children in Paris *(see pp16–17)*.

4 Grande Galerie de l'Evolution

The most exciting and imaginatively designed section in the Natural History Museum is the Great Gallery of Evolution. Elephants, giraffes and other stuffed animals rise out of a re-created savannah, a huge whale skeleton hangs from the ceiling, while special displays help tell the story of the development of life on earth. Nature workshops are also held for children during school holidays *(see p129)*.

5 Musée de la Magie et des Automates

Kids are enchanted by this museum of magic, located in the cellars of the former home of the Marquis de Sade. Magicians conjure up shows every half hour involving optical illusions, card tricks and lots of audience participation. Exhibits include working automata and memorabilia from master magicians such as Houdini (1874–1926). *11 rue St-Paul, 75004 • Map R4 • 01 42 72 13 26 • Open 2–7pm Wed, Sat, Sun (daily during school holidays, except Jul & Aug) • Admission charge • www.museedelamagie.com*

6 Parc Astérix

Dozens of attractions including one of Europe's longest roller coasters, an adventure playground and a replica of Albert Uderzo's original comic book village. *Plailly, 60128 • RER B to Roissy CDG1, then shuttle from bus stop A3 • 08 26 30 10 40 (+33 3 44 62 31 31 from abroad) • Open Apr–Aug: 10am–6pm Mon–Fri, 9:30am–6pm Sat, Sun; Sep–Oct: 10am–6pm Sat, Sun • Admission charge • www.parcasterix.fr*

7 Jardin d'Acclimatation

This amusement park at the north end of the Bois de Boulogne *(see p152)* has roller coasters, pony rides and puppet shows. An electric train, "le Petit Train", runs here from Porte Maillot. *Bois de Boulogne, 75016 • Map A2 • Open 10am–7pm daily (summer); 10am–6pm daily (winter) • Admission charge • www.jardindacclimatation.fr*

8 Grévin

This waxworks museum was founded in 1882. Celebrity-spotting from the world of pop music and film can be the most fun for kids, but there are also wonderful tableaux from French history. *10 blvd Montmartre, 75009 • Map F2 • 01 47 70 85 05 • Open 10am–6:30pm Mon–Fri, 10am–7pm Sat, Sun & public hols (last admission 1 hour before closing) • Admission charge • www.grevin.com*

9 Jardin du Luxembourg

The park has tennis courts, puppet shows, donkey rides and a good playground (for a fee). But most fun of all is the Parisian pastime of sailing model boats in the fountain and riding the 19th-century carousel. *Jardin du Luxembourg • Map E5 • Open dawn–dusk*

10 Parc des Buttes Chaumont

The highest park in Paris is great for a family picnic. Kids will enjoy the suspended bridges, waterfalls, pony rides and puppet shows. *Parc des Buttes Chaumont, 75019 • Map H2 • Open 7am– 10pm daily (9pm Oct–Apr) • Free*

Lift, Eiffel Tower

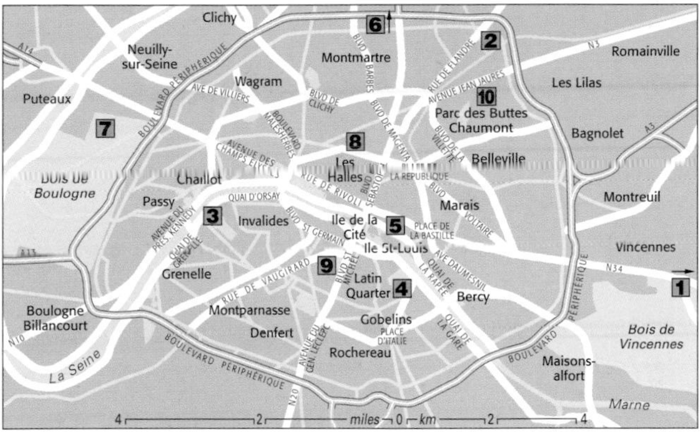

Left **Jazz Club Etoile** Centre **Au Duc des Lombards** Right **Le Baiser Salé**

TOP 10 Jazz Clubs

1 Sunset-Sunside

This club offers a double serving of late-night jazz – acoustic and modern at street level (Sunside) and electric, fusion and groove in the vaulted cellar room (Sunset). On Sunday afternoons there's a "jazz and tea" session for families. *60 rue des Lombards, 75001 • Map N2*

2 Au Duc des Lombards

The Left Bank may be the traditional home of jazz clubs but this sleek, modern club is firmly on the Right Bank, in the Les Halles district *(see pp74–7)*. The memorabilia of the "greats" who played here may have disappeared during refurbishment but the club's policy is still to bring in the best overseas jazz artists to play alongside home-grown talent. Good food is served day and night. *42 rue des Lombards, 75001 • Map N2*

3 Le Baiser Salé

Jazz, blues, Latin and African music are the mainstays at this tiny cellar club, which is low on space but high on volume. The Baiser was promoting World Music long before the phrase had been invented, and the eclectic approach has led to a relaxed and friendly atmosphere. It's also cheaper than many other clubs. *58 rue des Lombards, 75001 • Map N2*

4 Caveau des Oubliettes

The ground floor is a pub, but the tiny jazz club in the vaulted basement below, which used to be a prison and dates back to the 12th century, is the main draw here. It's open until late and there's a concert on from 10pm every night except Mondays. There's no cover charge but drinks are expensive. *52 rue Galande, 75005 • Map F5*

5 Autour de Midi et de Minuit

Halfway up La Butte, this atmospheric joint has added some welcome buzz to the slopes of Montmartre. It's jazz all the way, mostly swing but some modern jazz as well, performed in a vaulted cellar below the excellent bistro. *11 rue Lepic, 75018 • Map E1*

Caveau de la Huchette

6 Jazz Club Etoile

Formerly known as the Jazz Club Lionel Hampton, the Etoile serves up a wide range of sounds, including blues, rock and even gospel music. There's an emphasis on visiting African-American musicians

For more Paris entertainment **See pp58–9**

(Oscar Peterson and BB King have played here). Its Jazz Club Lounge offers a Jazzy Brunch on Sundays. ✆ *Hôtel Le Méridien-Etoile, 81 blvd Gouvion-St-Cyr, 75017 • Map A2*

7 New Morning

Seating up to 300 people, this large club's policy of embracing all kinds of music (jazz, blues, Latin, soul and the unclassifiable), not to mention inviting performers up from the floor, has led to a relaxed crowd of regulars. ✆ *7–9 rue des Petites-Ecuries, 75010 • Map F2*

8 Le Petit Journal Montparnasse

This is the club that barely sleeps – the doors close at 2am, but open up again five hours later. You can just drink, or have a meal while listening to the live music, which is mainly big band jazz but on some nights takes in salsa, blues or rock. ✆ *13 rue du Commandant-Mouchotte, 75014 • Map D6*

9 Le Petit Journal St-Michel

Older brother of the Montparnasse branch, this club opened in 1971 and concentrates on New Orleans-style swinging jazz. There's a fun atmosphere in this Latin Quarter cellar, together with a pleasant dining room in which to have a meal, just off the main stage area. ✆ *71 blvd St-Michel, 75005 • Map M5*

10 Caveau de la Huchette

Don't be fooled by its tourist-trap setting in the heart of the Latin Quarter – this venue is worth every penny of the entrance price. The building was once home to the Knights Templar, and jazz has been played under the medieval vaults since 1947. ✆ *5 rue de la Huchette, 75005 • Map N4*

Top 10 Musical Artistes in Paris

1 Edith Piaf
Discovered as a street singer in Paris, the diminutive Piaf (1915–63) became known as the "Little Sparrow".

2 Maurice Chevalier
The Parisian singer/actor (1888–1972) is, for many, *the* voice of France. In 1958 he won an Academy Award for his role in *Gigi*.

3 Django Reinhardt
Belgian gypsy guitarist Reinhardt (1910–53) first found fame in Paris in collaboration with Stephane Grappelli.

4 Lionel Hampton
US bandleader Hampton (*b.* 1909) regularly played in the Left Bank jazz clubs.

5 Sidney Bechet
US jazz virtuoso Bechet (1897–1959) settled in Paris in the 1940s and wrote his great tune "Les Oignons" in 1949.

6 Jacques Brel
Belgian singer/songwriter Brel (1929–78) moved to Paris in 1953, where audiences loved his melancholy songs.

7 Stephane Grappelli
Paris-born Grappelli (1908–97) studied classical violin, but later innovatively adapted the instrument to jazz.

8 Josephine Baker
The African-American dancer (1906–75) gained notoriety for dancing semi-nude at the Folies-Bergère.

9 Miles Davis
US trumpet-player Davis (1926–91) was a favourite in Paris for his "cool jazz" style.

10 Coleman Hawkins
US bebop saxophonist Hawkins (1904–69) played Paris many times in the 1930s.

Left **Guy Savoy** Centre **Le Jules Verne** Right **Taillevent**

TOP 10 Places to Eat

1 L'Astrance

There is probably no table in Paris that is more coveted than one in this sober 25-seat dining room, with its set menus at €70 (for lunch) or €310 (for dinner), orchestrated by young culinary genius Pascal Barbot. You'll need to book a month ahead for lunch, two months for dinner. *4 rue Beethoven, 75016 • Map B4 • 01 40 50 84 40 • Closed Sat–Mon, Feb, Aug, 1 week Oct (call to check) • No disabled access • €€€€€*

2 Guy Savoy

Artichoke and truffle soup is one of star chef Guy Savoy's signature dishes, in his chic and smart restaurant (jacket and ties required for male diners). One of the city's best dining experiences *(see p109)*. To sample Savoy's cooking at more affordable prices, try the bistro-style Les Bookinistes in the St-Germain quarter *(see p127)*.

Brasserie Bofinger

3 Les Papilles

The setting – a wine shop lined with wooden tables – barely hints at this restaurant's remarkably sophisticated cooking, from a chef who once worked at Taillevent. Pick your wine straight off the shelves to accompany the bargain set menu *(see p127)*.

4 Taillevent

Taillevent's atmospheric oak-panelled dining room is frequented by a mix of businessmen and romantic couples. Dishes such as rex rabbit with Cremona mustard and black radish feature on the seasonal menu and there's an exceptional wine list. You need to book well ahead to dine here *(see p109)*.

5 Le Jules Verne

Now in the perfectionist hands of world-famous chef Alain Ducasse, this restaurant on the second floor of the Eiffel Tower has entered the 21st century. It has been revamped with a futuristic brown decor and there is a suitably luxurious menu, replete with truffles in winter. Service is excellent and the panoramic views are breathtaking, but book in advance *(see p117)*.

6 Brasserie Bofinger

One of Paris's oldest brasseries, dating from 1864, is worth a visit for the original wood and glass decor and leather banquette seating. Alsatian specialities include sauerkraut and paté. *5–7 rue de la Bastille, 75004 • Map H5 • 01 42 72 87 82 • No disabled access • €€€€€*

7 Le Chateaubriand

One of the best restaurant's in Paris, Le Chateaubriand provides a relaxed setting and offers affordable gastronomic cuisine. Basque chef Iñaki Aizpitarte creates innovative and award-winning dishes for a daily changing menu. Book in advance. *128 ave Parmentier, 75011 • Map H3 • 01 43 57 45 95 • €€€€€*

8 Pierre Gagnaire

Famous French chef Pierre Gagnaire creates culinary dishes at this formal diner. Try the foie gras, oysters and ginger served with tamarillo sorbet and Paris mushrooms. *6 rue Balzac, 75008 • Map B2 • 01 58 36 12 50 • No disabled access • Closed Sat, Sun L, Aug • €€€€€*

9 L'Arpege

Alain Passard's three-star restaurant is one of the most highly regarded in Paris. Dishes include turnip tatin with honey and roasted rapeseed. *84 rue de Varenne, 75007 • Map D4 • 01 47 05 09 06 • No disabled access • Closed Sat & Sun • €€€€€*

10 L'Atelier de Joël Robuchon

Take a seat at the lacquered bar to experience a top French chef's take on contemporary cuisine. Signature dishes are the merlan Colbert (fried whiting), and carbonara with Alsatian cream and bacon. *5 rue de Montalembert, 75007 • Map E4 • 01 42 22 56 56 • €€€€€*

L'Atelier de Joël Robuchon

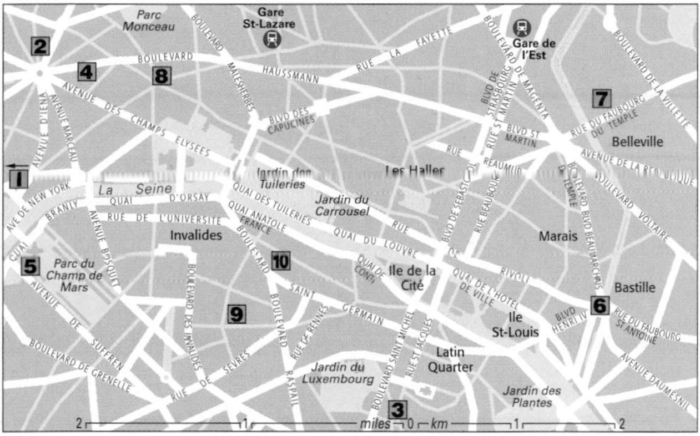

For a price guide to Paris restaurants **See p73**

AROUND TOWN

Left **Notre-Dame** Right **Salle des Gens d'Armes, Conciergerie**

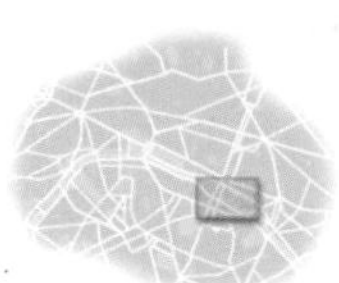

Ile de la Cité and Ile St-Louis

PARIS WAS BORN ON THE ILE DE LA CITÉ. *The first settlers came to this island on the Seine in 300 BC* (see p44) *and it has remained a focus of church and state power through the centuries, with the great cathedral of Notre-Dame and the law courts of the Palais de Justice commanding the island. This tiny land mass also has the honour of being the geographical heart of the city – all distances from Paris are measured from Point Zéro, just outside Notre-Dame. While the Ile de la Cité seems overrun with tourists, the smaller Ile St-Louis, connected to its neighbour by a footbridge, has a village-like feel and has been an exclusive residential enclave since the 17th century. Its main street is lined with shops, galleries and restaurants and is a wonderful place for a stroll.*

TOP 10 Sights

1. Notre-Dame
2. Sainte-Chapelle
3. Conciergerie
4. Marché aux Fleurs
5. Crypte Archéologique
6. Pont Neuf
7. Palais de Justice
8. Place Dauphine
9. St Louis-en-l'Ile
10. Square du Vert-Galant

Angel detail, Sainte-Chapelle

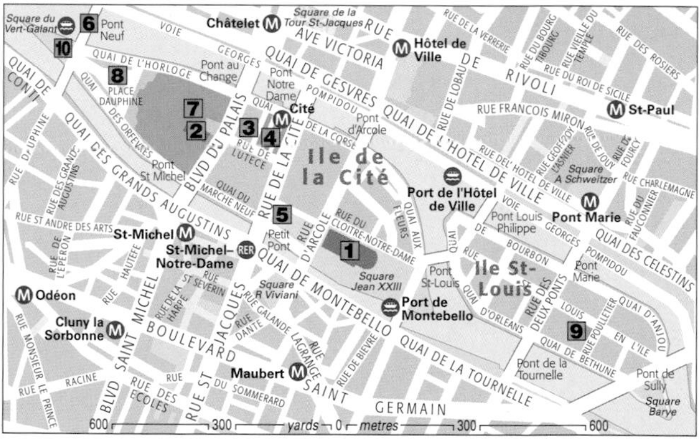

1 Notre-Dame

See pp18–21.

2 Sainte-Chapelle

See pp30–31.

3 Conciergerie

This imposing Gothic palace, built by Philippe le Bel (the Fair) in 1301–15, has a rich history. Parts of it were turned into a prison, controlled by the concierge, or keeper of the king's mansion, hence the name. Ravaillac, assassin of Henri IV, was tortured here, but it was during the Revolution that the prison became a place of terror, when thousands were held here awaiting execution at the guillotine. Today you can see the Salle des Gardes and the magnificent vaulted Salle des Gens d'Armes (Hall of the Men-at Arms), the medieval kitchens, torture chamber, the Bonbec tower, and the prison. The cell where Marie-Antoinette was held and the history of other famous Revolution prisoners is on display. Outside, look for the square Tour de l'Horloge, erected in 1370, which houses the city's first public clock, still ticking away. *2 blvd du Palais, 75001 • Map N3 • Open 9:30am–6pm daily • Admission charge*

Sainte-Chapelle

4 Marché aux Fleurs

One of the last remaining flower markets in the city centre, the beautiful Marché aux Fleurs is also the oldest, dating from the early 19th century. It is held year-round, Monday to Saturday, in place Louis-Lépine, filling the north side of the Ile de la Cité with dazzling blooms from 8am to 7pm. There is also a bird market here on Sundays, which sells some rare species *(see p54)*. *Map N3*

5 Crypte Archéologique

Fascinating remnants of early Paris dating back to Gallo-Roman times were discovered in 1965 during an excavation of the square in front of Notre-Dame in order to build an underground car park. The archaeological crypt displays parts of 3rd-century Roman walls, rooms heated by hypocaust, as well as remains of medieval streets and foundations. The scale models showing the evolution of the city from its origins as a Celtic settlement are particularly interesting. *Place du Parvis-Notre-Dame, 75004 • Map P4 • Open 10am–6pm Tue–Sun • Admission charge*

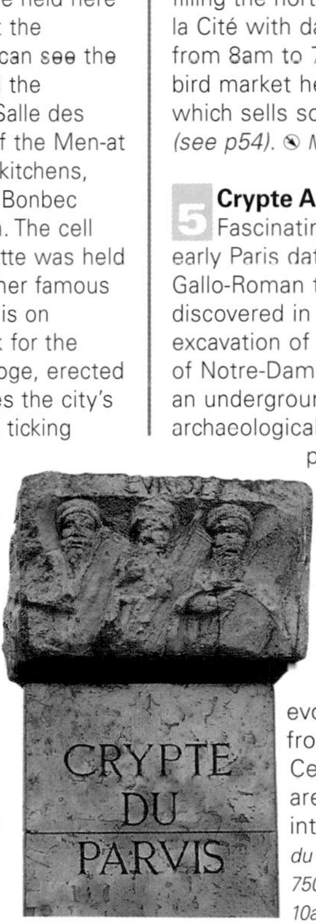

Crypte Archéologique

The Guillotine

Dr Joseph Guillotine invented his "humane" beheading machine at his home near the Odéon and it was first used in April 1792. During the Revolution some 2,600 prisoners were executed on the places du Carrousel, de la Concorde, de la Bastille and de la Nation, after awaiting their fate in the Conciergerie prison.

6 Pont Neuf

An incongruous name (New Bridge) for the oldest surviving bridge in Paris. Following its completion in 1607, Henri IV christened it by charging across on his steed; the bronze equestrian statue of the king was melted down during the Revolution but replaced in 1818. Decorated with striking carved heads, the bridge was unique for its time in that it had no houses built upon it. It has 12 arches and a span of 275 m (912 ft) extending both sides of the island. *Map M3*

7 Palais de Justice

Stretching across the west end of the Ile de la Cité from north to south, the Palais de Justice, along with the Conciergerie, was once part of the Palais de la Cité, seat of Roman rule and the home of the French kings until 1358. It took its present name during the Revolution and the buildings now contain the city's law courts. You can watch the courts in session from Monday to Friday and wander through the public areas, with their many ornate features. The Cour du Mai (May Courtyard) is the area through which prisoners passed during the Revolution on their way to execution.
4 blvd du Palais, 75001 • Map M3 • Open 8:30am–6pm Mon–Fri, 9:30am–6pm Sat • Free

8 Place Dauphine

In 1607 Henri IV transformed this former royal garden into a triangular square and named it after his son, the Dauphin and future King Louis XIII. Surrounding the square were uniformly built houses of brick and white stone; No. 14 is one of the few that retains its original features. One side was destroyed to make way for the expansion of the Palais de Justice. Today this quiet, charming spot is a good place to relax over a drink or meal *(see p73)*. *Map M3*

Pont Neuf and Square du Vert-Galant

Sculptured relief, Palais de Justice

9 St-Louis-en-l'Ile

This lovely Baroque church on Ile St-Louis was designed between 1664 and 1726 by the royal architect Louis Le Vau. The exterior features an iron clock (1741) at the entrance and an iron spire, while the interior, richly decorated with gilding and marble, has a statue of St Louis holding his Crusader's sword. *19 bis rue St-Louis-en-l'Ile, 75004 • Map Q5 • Open 9:30am–1pm, 2–7:30pm daily (until 7pm Sun)*

10 Square du Vert-Galant

The tranquil western tip of the Ile de la Cité, with its verdant chestnut trees, lies beneath the Pont Neuf – take the steps behind Henri IV's statue. This King had a notoriously amorous nature and the name of this peaceful square recalls his nickname, meaning "old flirt". From here there is a wonderful view of the Louvre *(see pp8–11)* and the Right Bank. It is also the departure point for cruises on the Seine on Les Vedettes du Pont-Neuf *(see p165)*. *Map M3*

A Day on the Islands

Morning

Arrive at **Notre-Dame** *(see pp18–21)* by 8am to beat the crowds and appreciate its magnificence, then head for the fragrant Marché aux Fleurs. As well as flowers, you can buy all kinds of garden accessories and seeds. Return to Notre-Dame if you want to ascend the towers, which open at 10am. Take a coffee break at **Le Flore en l'Ile** *(see p73)*, with its views of the cathedral.

The fascinating Crypte Archéologique is worth a half-hour visit, then spend the late morning at **Sainte-Chapelle** *(see pp30–31)*, when the sun beams through the stained-glass windows.

There are plenty of places for lunch, but on a sunny day try **La Rose de France** *(see p73)*, which has terrace seating.

Afternoon

Spend a leisurely afternoon strolling the narrow streets of the Ile St-Louis, which are filled with characterful shops and galleries *(see p72)*.

Wind up with an afternoon treat by visiting **Berthillon,** considered the best ice-cream purveyor in all of France *(see p73)*. With at least 70 delicious varieties of ice cream on offer, ranging from plain vanilla to whisky, and including virtually any fruit you can think of, the hardest part will be choosing. There will be plenty of time to make your choice however, as there will inevitably be a long queue, especially in summer.

Left **Pylones Boutique** Centre **Librairie Ulysse** Right **Boulangerie des Deux Pontss**

TOP 10 Shopping

1 Lafitte
Foie gras and other regional products from the southwest await those looking to indulge in French gastronomy. *8 rue Jean du Bellay, 75004 • Map P4 • Closed Sun & Mon*

2 Jean-Paul Gardil
This boucherie-charcuterie is a carnivore's palace, offering a fantastic choice of cured hams, pâtés and sausages, perfect for a picnic on the pretty Ile St-Louis. *44 rue St-Louis-en-l'Ile, 75004 • Map Q5 • Closed Mon*

3 Librairie Ulysse
Today Paris, tomorrow the world. This eccentric travel bookshop will take you anywhere you want with thousands of titles in French and English – including many on Paris itself. *26 rue St-Louis-en-l'Ile, 75004 • Map Q5 • Closed Sat–Mon*

4 Laguiole
Browse an exhaustive array of knives and cutlery sets from the iconic cutlery brand born in the Aveyron region of southern of France. Look for the famous bee motif on the handles. *44 rue des Deux Ponts, 75004 • Map Q4*

5 Clair de Rêve
This interesting boutique sells curiosities such as puppets, robots and miniature theatres making it an ideal shop if you're looking for a present with a difference. *35 rue St-Louis-en-l'Ile, 75004 • Map Q5*

6 Alain Carion
A wealth of meteorites, fossils and minerals. Some are made into imaginative jewellery. *92 rue St-Louis-en-l'Ile, 75004 • Map Q5 • Closed Sun, Mon*

7 Pylones Boutique
Rubber and painted metal are used to create the whimsical jewellery and accessories here, along with novelty gifts. *57 rue St-Louis-en-l'Ile, 75004 • Map Q5*

8 Boulangerie des Deux Ponts
You won't be able to resist the freshly baked bread at this old-fashioned bakery. *35 rue des Deux-Ponts, 75004 • Map Q5 • Closed Wed, Thu, Aug*

9 Arche de Noé
Translated as Noah's Ark, this is a treasure trove for children's gifts, with a good selection of old-fashioned toys. *70 rue St-Louis-en-l'Ile, 75004 • Map Q5*

10 La Ferme Saint Aubin
Cheese in all shapes and sizes from all over France. An aromatic delight. *76 rue St-Louis-en-l'Ile, 75004 • Map Q5 • Closed Mon*

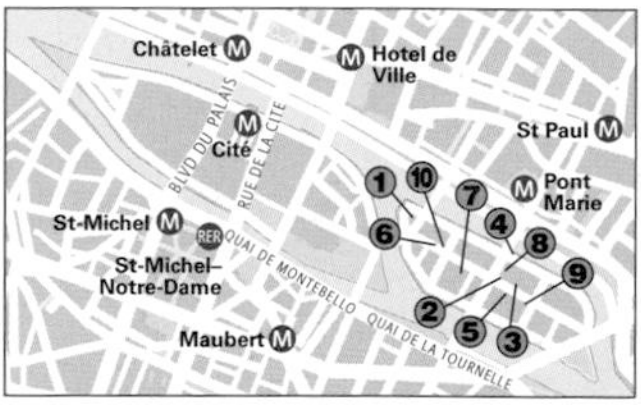

For more on shopping in Paris **See p169**

Price Categories

For a three-course meal for one with half a bottle of wine (or equivalent meal), taxes and extra charges	€	under €30
	€€	€30–€40
	€€€	€40–€50
	€€€€	€50–€60
	€€€€€	over €60

Left **La Rose de France** Right **Taverne Henry IV**

TOP 10 Places to Eat

1 Isami
One of the best Japanese restaurants in the city, but tiny so book ahead. Good choice of sushi. *4 quai d'Orléans, 75004 • Map P5 • 01 40 46 06 97 • Closed Sun, Mon, Aug (3 wks), 2 weeks Christmas • No disabled access • €€€€*

2 Kitchen Galerie Bis
KGB serves inspired and innovative cuisine in a sleek setting. The menu offers a mix of traditional French dishes with modern global influences. *25 rue des Grands Augustins, 75006 • Map Q5 • 01 46 33 00 85 • Closed Sun, Mon and 4 weeks Jul–Aug • €€€*

3 Les Fous de L'Ile
This modern Parisian bistro serves French classics such as *entrecôte* or steak tartare. It also hosts exhibitions and live concerts. *33 rue des Deux Ponts, 75004 • Map Q4 • 01 43 25 76 67 • Closed Tue L, Sat, Sun, end Feb, Aug • €€*

4 Le Petit Plateau
This tea room is a great lunch spot, as it serves delicious home-made salads, quiches and cakes. *1 quai aux Fleurs, 75004 • Map G5 • 01 44 07 61 86 • Closed D, Sat in winter • No disabled access • €*

5 Brasserie de l'Ile St-Louis
Wooden tables and a rustic look complement hearty Alsace fare such as Tripe in Riesling wine. *55 quai de Bourbon, 75004 • Map P4 • 01 43 54 02 59 • Closed Wed, Aug • No disabled access • €€€*

6 La Rose de France
Lovely terrace and a cosy dining room. *24 pl Dauphine, 75001 • Map M3 • 01 43 54 10 12 • €€*

7 Taverne Henri IV
A fine wine list and simple plates of *charcuterie* or cheese. *13 pl du Pont-Neuf, 75001 • Map M3 • 01 43 54 27 90 • Closed Sat, Sun, Aug • €€*

8 Mon Vieil Ami
A chic interior is the backdrop for dishes such as foie gras. *69 rue St-Louis-en-l'Ile, 75004 • Map Q5 • 01 40 46 01 35 • Closed Mon, Tue, Jan, Aug • No disabled access • €€€€*

9 Le Flore en l'Ile
Go for the views as well as the food in this bistro and tea room, open from breakfast until 1am. *42 quai d'Orléans, 75004 • Map P5 • 01 43 29 88 27 • No disabled access • €€*

10 Berthillon
There is always a queue outside this legendary ice cream shop and tea room. *31 rue St-Louis-en-l'Ile, 75004 • Map G5 • 01 43 54 31 61 • Closed Mon, Tue, 1 week Feb, 1 week Easter, Aug • No credit cards • €*

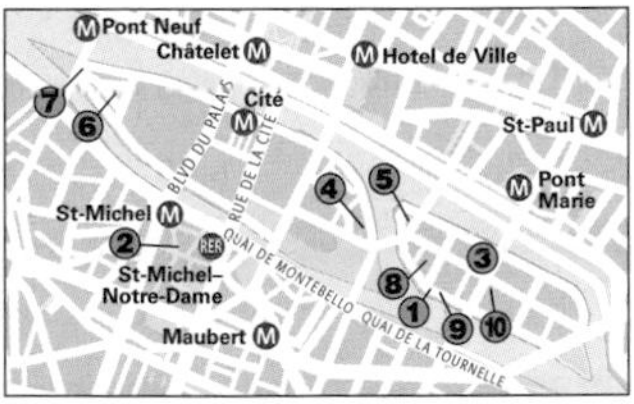

Note: *Unless otherwise stated, all restaurants accept credit cards and serve vegetarian meals*

Left **Stravinsky fountains** Centre **Fashion in Les Halles** Right **One of the cinemas in Forum des Halles**

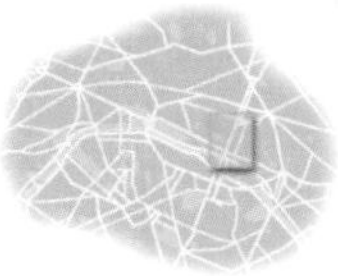

Beaubourg and Les Halles

THE SMALL BUT LIVELY BEAUBOURG QUARTER, brimming with art galleries and cafés, has become a major tourist attraction since the construction of the Centre Georges Pompidou. This inside-out hulk of modern architecture has become the focus of the area since it opened in 1977. Les Halles was the marketplace of Paris for 800 years, its glass-covered pavilions packed with butchers, fishmongers and fruit and vegetable stalls; novelist Emile Zola called it "the belly of Paris". In 1969, the market was demolished and moved to the suburbs to alleviate traffic congestion. The soulless underground shopping mall, Forum des Halles, which replaced it is currently undergoing a large-scale renovation; however most of the bistros and speciality shops are still open for business.

Le Défenseur du Temps

TOP 10 Sights

1. Centre Georges Pompidou
2. Forum des Halles
3. St-Eustache
4. Bourse du Commerce
5. Le Défenseur du Temps
6. Fontaine des Innocents
7. Eglise St-Merri
8. St-Germain l'Auxerrois
9. Musée de la Poupée
10. Tour St-Jacques

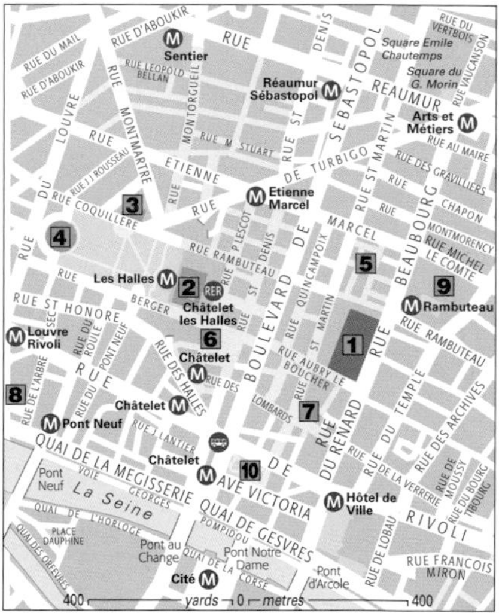

1 Centre Georges Pompidou

See pp26–7.

2 Forum des Halles

Ten years after the original market was demolished, the so-called "largest urban hole in Europe" was filled with this controversial shopping complex. This largely underground maze caters to the young, with music shops and boutiques. Outside, buskers, young people and tourists throng the steps and gardens (not a place to linger at night). Today, it's more of a sore spot than a hotspot and French architect David Mangin has been commissioned to oversee its renovation, which will include a revamped shopping centre, gardens, metro and RER station. This is due to be completed by 2016/2017. *Map N2*

3 St-Eustache

With its majestic arches and pillars, St-Eustache is one of the most beautiful churches in Paris. Although Gothic in design, it took 105 years to build (1532–1637) and its interior decoration reflects the Renaissance style of this time. The church was modelled on Notre-Dame *(see pp18–21)*, with double side aisles and a ring of side chapels. The stained-glass windows made from sketches by Philippe de Champaigne (1631) and the ornate tomb of politician Jean-Baptiste Colbert (1619–83) are highlights. Don't miss the naive sculpture in Chapelle St-Joseph which recalls Les Halles' market days. *2 impasse St-Eustache, 75001 • Map M1 • Open 9:30am–7pm Mon–Fri, 10am–7pm Sat, Sun • Free*

4 Bourse du Commerce

The circular building which houses the Commodities Exchange was erected as a grain market in 1767 and remodelled in the 19th century. It was first covered with a wooden dome, then by subsequent structures of iron and copper. Under today's glass dome, activity in the world commodities market proceeds at a leisurely pace compared to the way other financial centres operate. *2 rue de Viarmes, 75001 • Map M1 • Open 8:30am–6pm Mon–Fri (identification papers are required to visit)*

St-Eustache

Georges Pompidou

Georges Pompidou (1911–74) had the unenviable task of following General de Gaulle as President of France, from 1969 until his death. During his tenure he initiated many architectural developments in Paris, including the controversial but ultimately successful Pompidou Centre, and the less popular scheme to demolish the Les Halles market.

5 Le Défenseur du Temps

The "Defender of Time", Paris's modern public clock, stands in the grim Quartier de l'Horloge (Clock Quarter) shopping area. This fantasy mechanical sculpture of brass and steel by Jacques Monastier is 4 m (13 ft) high and weighs 1 tonne. When the clock strikes the hour, the warrior fends off a savage cockerel, crab or dragon (representing air, water and earth) with his sword, with accompanying sound effects. At noon, 6pm and 10pm he vanquishes all three (when the clock is working). *Rue Bernard-de-Clairvaux, 75003 • Map P2*

6 Fontaine des Innocents

The Square des Innocents is a Les Halles crossroads and a hangout for street performers and young people. It was built atop a cemetery in the 18th century, and two million human remains were transferred to the Catacombs at Denfert-Rochereau. The Renaissance fountain, the last of its era built in the city, was designed by Pierre Lescot and carved by sculptor Jean Goujon in 1547. It originally stood against a wall on rue St-Denis, and was moved to the new square, when the fourth side was added *(see p39)*.
Rues St-Denis & Berger, 75001 • Map N2

7 Eglise St-Merri

Formerly the parish church of the Lombard moneylenders, St-Merri was built between 1520 and 1612, and reflects the Flamboyant Gothic style. Its name is a corruption of St-Médéric, who was buried on this site in the early 8th century. The bell in the church's northwest turret, thought to be the oldest in Paris, dates from 1331 and hung in a chapel that once stood on the site. Other highlights include the decorative west front, the 17th-century organ loft, beautiful stained glass and carved wood panelling.
76 rue de la Verrerie, 75004 • Map P2 • Open noon–6:45pm daily • Free

8 St-Germain l'Auxerrois

When the Valois kings moved to the Louvre palace in the 14th century *(see p8)*, this became the church of the royal family. On 24

St-Germain l'Auxerrois

August 1572, the tolling of its bell was used as the signal for the St Bartholomew's Day Massacre, when thousands of Huguenots who had come to Paris for the wedding of Henri of Navarre to Marguerite of Valois were murdered *(see p20)*. The church features a range of architectural styles, from its flamboyant Gothic façade to its Renaissance choir. Try and visit on Sunday afternoon when there are organ recitals.
2 pl du Louvre, 75001 • Map M2 • Open 8am–7pm Mon–Sat, 9am–8pm Sun • Free

9 Musée de la Poupée

This delightful museum has a superb collection of 300 rare French dolls, including unglazed hand-painted porcelain dolls which were manufactured between 1800 and 1945. The museum explores the function of dolls and their construction. It also features the main doll makers of Germany and France. The museum runs a doll hospital where doll doctor Véronique Derez works miracles on dolls of all ages. *Impasse Berthaud, 75003 • Map P2 • Open 10am–6pm Tue–Sun • Closed public hols • Admission charge*

10 Tour St-Jacques

The late Gothic tower, dating from 1523, is all that remains of the church of St-Jacques-la-Boucherie, once the largest medieval church in Paris and a starting point for pilgrims on their journey to Santiago de Compostela in Spain. In the 17th century the physicist Blaise Pascal used the tower for barometrical experiments. The church was pulled down after the Revolution. Visitors can explore the lower floors of the tower and visit the gardens around the base.
39 rue de Rivoli, 75004 • Map N3

A Day in Les Halles

Morning

Start your day with breakfast at the **Le Zimmer Café** *(1 pl du Châtelet, 01 42 36 74 03)* before admiring some of Picasso's paintings at the **Centre Georges Pompidou** *(see pp26–7)* where the temporary exhibits are also well worth a look. If you need refreshment after all that art, it has to be **Georges**, the chic brasserie at the top of the centre with good views and a choice of drinks, snacks or main meals.

On leaving the centre turn right into the Quartier de l'Horloge to catch the noon battle of the **Défenseur du Temps** clock.

Providing you have booked ahead, lunch at the 1912 bistro **Benoit** *(see p81)*, whose lunchtime menu is far cheaper than in the evening. After lunch visit the **Eglise St-Merri**.

Afternoon

Pass the **Fontaine des Innocents** as you head for Les Halles, but first go into the church of **St-Eustache** *(see p75)*, which was the place of worship of the market workers at the old Les Halles. You could then spend the rest of the afternoon shopping at the vast, if somewhat unprepossessing **Forum des Halles** *(see p75)*.

Stop for a drink at Tour de Montlhéry, more commonly known as **Chez Denise** *(see p81)*. It's packed at mealtimes, but by late afternoon you might be lucky enough to get a seat and be ready to try their famous Gâteau Marguerite with strawberries and cream.

Left **Le Christ Inn's Bistrot** Right **Sculpture outside St-Eustache church**

TOP 10 Memories of Les Halles

1 Le Christ Inn's Bistrot
Dating back to the early 20th century, this ornate former working men's café/bar, decorated with historic tiles and murals, has only a small dining room so book in advance. *15 rue Montmartre, 75001 • Map F3*

2 Au Pied de Cochon
This 24-hour brasserie still serves dishes that used to appeal to the earthy tastes of market workers, including pigs' trotters *(see p81)*.

3 St-Eustache Sculpture
The naive sculpture by Raymond Mason in the church's Chapelle St-Joseph is a tribute to the beloved market. Its colourful figures depict *The Departure of Fruit and Vegetables from the Heart of Paris, 28 February 1969.*

4 Rue Montorgueil
The colourful market (Tuesday to Sunday) along this cobbled street is a reminder of the old Les Halles and is frequented by many Paris chefs. *Map N1*

5 Stöhrer
One of the loveliest old-fashioned patisseries in the city, founded in 1730 by a pastry chef who had worked for Louis XV. *51 rue Montorgueil, 75002 • Map N1*

6 Bistrot d'Eustache
A visit here is like stepping back into the jazz spots of Paris in the 1930–40s. It offers good, reasonably priced brasserie fare and live music on Friday and Saturday. *37 rue Berger, 75001 • Map N2*

7 La Fresque
This wonderful restaurant used to be a fishmongers. An original fresco of a fishing scene still decorates the back room. *100 rue Rambuteau, 75001 • Map N1*

8 Dehillerin
Since 1820, everyone from army cooks to gourmet chefs has come here for copper pots, cast-iron pans and cooking utensils. *18 rue Coquillière, 75001 • Map M1*

9 Duthilleul et Minart
For more than 100 years this shop has sold French work clothes and uniforms such as chef's hats and watchmaker's smocks. *14 rue de Turbigo, 75001 • Map P1*

10 A La Cloche des Halles
This wine bar literally rings with history. The "cloche" is the bronze bell whose peal once signalled the beginning and end of the market day. *28 rue Coquillière, 75001 • Map M1*

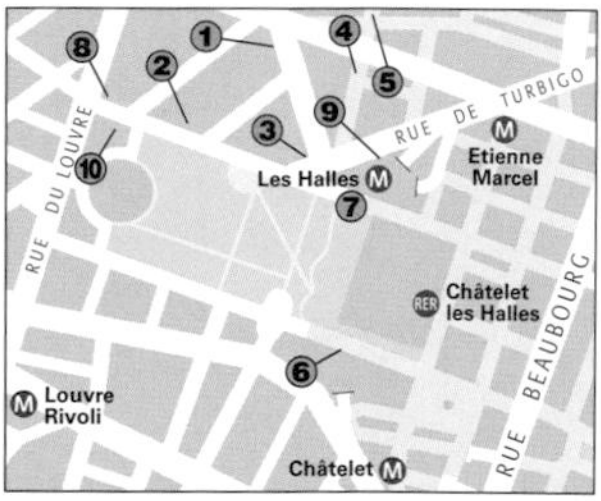

Left **Typical Paris beer bar** Centre **Le Sous-Bock** Right **Au Trappiste**

TOP 10 Beer Bars

1 Le Sous-Bock
A good place for *moules* (mussels), with 200 types of beer to wash them down with. There are also 40 whiskies.
49 rue St-Honoré, 75001 • Map M2

2 Quigley's Point
Right in front of Eglise St-Eustache, this friendly Irish pub serves beer from Holland, Germany, Ireland and Britain.
5 rue du Jour, 75001 • Map M1

3 Hall's Beer Tavern
Although situated in a fairly touristy street, this is a relaxed and friendly place with a good selection of draught beers, including La Chouffe and Duvel.
68 rue St-Denis, 75001 • Map N2

4 Le Bogman
Formerly the Goblot d'Argent, this bar may have changed name and location, but it retains an Irish pub feel, with a dartboard and live music on Tuesdays. *2 rue de la Petite Truanderie, 75001 • Map N1*

5 The Frog and Rosbif
For homesick English or Anglophiles, this is the place to find real ale (brewed downstairs) and fish and chips, play pub quizzes, read English newspapers and watch live football and rugby matches.
116 rue St-Denis, 75002 • Map F3

6 McBrides
A popular place to watch football, this friendly Irish sports bar attracts homesick expats with its fried breakfasts. Enjoy live music on Sunday nights.
54 rue St-Denis, 75001 • Map F4
• 01 40 26 46 70

7 Au Trappiste
Among the many beers on tap, sample Jenlain, a French brew, and the Belgian Hoegaarden. Food is also served. *4 rue St-Denis, 75001 • Map F3*

8 Guinness Tavern
Fourteen beers are on tap in this Irish bar with live music every night and a bigger Irish concert once a month. The party really kicks off after 10pm. *31 bis rue des Lombards, 75004 • Map N2*

9 Café Oz
A range of Australian beers and wines combined with archetypal Outback decor makes this rowdy bar popular with antipodean expatriates and French patrons alike. *18 rue St-Denis, 75001 • Map F3*

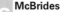

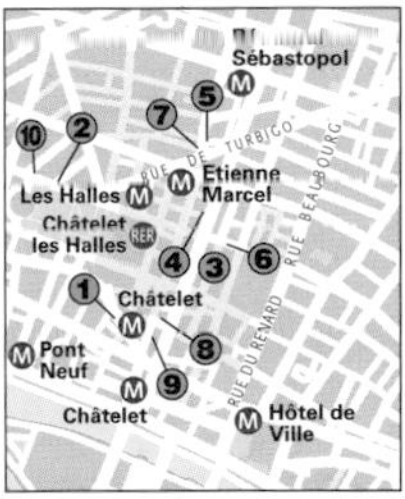

10 La Taverne de Maître Kanter
Part of a chain of Alsatian-style taverns, this is a good place to relax over a pint of French beer. Food is also served. *16 rue Coquillière, 75001 • Map F3*
• 01 42 36 74 24

For more cafés and bars **See pp52–3**

Left **View of Les Halles c.1870-80**

Top 10 Historical Events in Les Halles

1 Roman Era
A marketplace was first established on the Right Bank of the Seine in a place then called Les Champeaux.

2 10th Century
A larger market for meat, fruit and vegetables is known to have existed in the part of Paris which is now Les Halles.

3 1183
The market is enlarged by King Philippe Auguste, who built shelters for the market traders near St-Eustache church *(see p75)*. This date is generally accepted as the founding of Les Halles as the city's market.

4 1850s
Twelve huge iron and glass market halls are built. Napoleon III declares that Les Halles is essential to Paris life.

5 1965
Work begins on a modern wholesale market south of Paris, at Rungis.

6 1969
The central Paris market is closed and moved to Rungis, partly to ease the traffic congestion that was by now too much for the centre of the city.

7 1971
The old buildings are demolished and digging begins, to create for a time what is known as the *trou des Halles* (the hole of Les Halles).

8 Mid-1970s
As well as the shopping malls, gardens are created and buildings next to the cleared space can be seen properly for the first time, including the church of St-Eustache.

9 1977
The Forum des Halles opens and ensures that the area remains as busy as ever, although the goods for sale (high fashion, CDs, fast food) have changed considerably since the market's early days.

10 2010
Massive renovation and restructuring begins; the renovation is scheduled to be completed by 2016/2017 and the area is expected to undergo a complete face-lift.

St-Eustache

For more on shopping in Paris **See p169**

Above **Au Pied de Cochon**

Price Categories

For a three-course meal for one with half a bottle of wine (or equivalent meal), taxes and extra charges	€	under €30
	€€	€30–€40
	€€€	€40–€50
	€€€€	€50–€60
	€€€€€	over €60

TOP 10 Places to Eat

1 Dans le Noir

For brave souls only, this pitch-black restaurant provides a unique dining experience. ✆ *51 rue Quincampoix, 75004 • Map F4 • 01 42 77 98 04 • Closed lunch Sun–Wed • No disabled access • €€€€*

2 Au Pied de Cochon

Long-time Les Halles favourite. If your taste is not for offal, there are options such as oysters and steak. Open 24 hours a day. ✆ *6 rue Coquillière, 75001 • Map M1 • 01 40 13 77 00 • €€€*

3 Benoit

Super-chef Alain Ducasse's smart bistro in Paris, which has one Michelin star but erratic service. ✆ *20 rue St-Martin, 75004 • Map P1 • 01 42 72 25 76 • Closed Aug • €€€€€*

4 L'Ambassade d'Auvergne

Auvergne cooking, with lots of pork and cabbage dishes. Shared tables; good for solo diners. ✆ *22 rue du Grenier-St-Lazare, 75003 • Map P1 • 01 42 72 31 22 • Closed Sun, Mon • Limited disabled access • €€*

5 Tour de Montlhéry, Chez Denise

A Les Halles legend for its huge portions and convivial air. Book in advance. ✆ *5 rue des Prouvaires, 75001 • Map N2 • 01 42 36 21 82 • Closed Sat, Sun, mid-Jul–mid-Aug • €€€*

6 Le Tambour

This 24-hour bistro draws a lively crowd with its friendly service and hearty French fare. ✆ *41 rue Montmartre, 75002 • Map N1 • 01 42 33 06 90 • €€*

7 Café Beaubourg

The terrace here overlooks the Pompidou Centre. Steak tartare is a house special. ✆ *43 rue St-Merri, 75004 • Map P2 • 01 48 87 63 96 • No disabled access • €€*

8 Spring

American chef Daniel Rose offers a fixed menu, which includes dishes made with fresh ingredients from the market. Book in advance. ✆ *6 rue Bailleul, 75001 • Map M2 • 01 45 96 05 72 • €€€€€*

9 Restaurant Georges

Sleek design and a great view make this museum restaurant a great choice for a glamorous night out. ✆ *Centre Georges Pompidou, 19 rue Beaubourg, 75004 • Map G4 • 01 44 78 47 99 • Closed Tue • €€€€*

10 Le Hangar

Hidden down a street near the Pompidou, this small, friendly bistro is no secret to locals, who keep returning for the fabulous food, such as steak tartare, foie gras and *moelleux au chocolat*. ✆ *12 Impasse Berthaud, 75003 • Map G4 • 01 42 74 55 44 • Closed Sun, Mon • €€€*

Note: *Unless otherwise stated, all restaurants accept credit cards and serve vegetarian meals*

Left **Place des Vosges street sign** Centre **Place de la Bastille** Right **Maison de Victor Hugo**

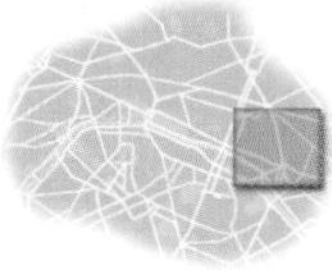

Marais and the Bastille

FOR MANY, THE MARAIS IS THE MOST ENJOYABLE quarter of Paris, with its mansions, museums and medieval lanes, but the district was little more than a muddy swamp until Henri IV built the place Royale (now place des Vosges) in 1605. Following its notoriety as the birthplace of the Revolution, the Bastille district sank into oblivion, until artists and designers arrived in the 1990s. Its streets are now home to the city's liveliest nightspots.

TOP 10 Sights

1. Musée Picasso
2. Musée Cognacq-Jay
3. Place des Vosges
4. Musée Carnavalet
5. Place de la Bastille
6. Marché d'Aligre
7. The Passages
8. Rue de Lappe
9. Maison Européenne de la Photographie
10. Maison de Victor Hugo

Bastille passage

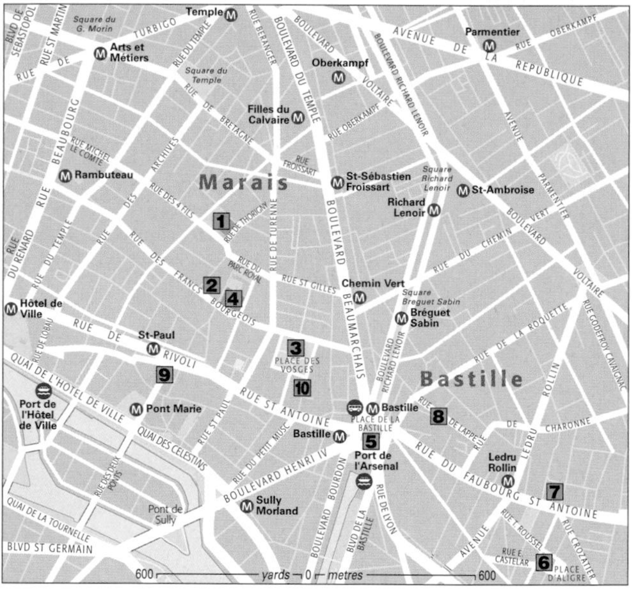

1 **Musée Picasso**

When the Spanish-born artist Pablo Picasso died in 1973, his family donated thousands of his works to the French state in lieu of estate taxes. Thus Paris enjoys the largest collection of Picassos in the world. Housed in the beautifully restored Hôtel Salé *(see p90)*, the museum's extensive collection displays the range of his artistic development, from his Blue and Pink Periods to Cubism, and reveals his proficiency in an astonishing range of techniques and materials *(see p36)*.

5 rue de Thorigny, 75003 • Map R2 • check website for opening times • Admission charge (free first Sun of month) • www.musee-picasso.fr

2 **Musée Cognacq-Jay**

This small but excellent museum portrays the sophisticated French lifestyle in the so-called Age of Enlightenment, which centred around Paris. The 18th-century art and furniture on display were once the private collection of Ernest Cognacq and his wife, Louise Jay, founders of the Samaritaine department store. It is superbly displayed in the Hôtel Donon, an elegant late 16th-century town mansion *(see p35)*. *8 rue Elzévir, 75003 • Map Q3 • Open 10am–6pm Tue–Sun • www.cognacq-jay.paris.fr*

3 **Place des Vosges**

Paris's oldest square is also one of the most beautiful in the world. The square was commissioned by Henri IV. Its 36 houses with red-gold brick and stone façades, slate roofs and dormer windows were laid out with striking symmetry in 1612. Originally built for silk workers, the likes of Cardinal Richelieu (1585–1642) and playwright Molière (1622–73) quickly moved in and it remains an upper-class residential address. But everyone can enjoy a stroll around the area and the art galleries under the arcades. *Map R3*

4 **Musée Carnavalet**

Devoted to the history of Paris, this museum sprawls through two mansions, the 16th-century Carnavalet and 17th-century Le Peletier de Saint-Fargeau. The former was the home of Madame de Sévigné, the famous letter-writer, from 1677 to 1696 and a gallery here portrays her life. The extensive museum contains period rooms filled with art and portraits. Revolutionary artifacts and memorabilia of 18th-century philosophers Rousseau and Voltaire can be found *(see p34)*.

23 rue de Sévigné, 75003 • Map R3 • Open 10am–6pm Tue–Sun • www.carnavalet.paris.fr

5 **Place de la Bastille**

Today this notorious square has become a busy traffic circle. Originally, the Bastille was a fortress built by Charles V to

Musée Cognacq-Jay

The Jewish Quarter

The Jewish Quarter, centred around rues des Rosiers and des Écouffes, was established in the 13th century and has attracted immigrants since the Revolution. Many Jews fled here to escape persecution in Eastern Europe, but were arrested during the Nazi Occupation. Since World War II, Sephardic Jews from North Africa have found new homes here.

defend the eastern edge of the city, but it soon became a jail for political prisoners. Angry citizens, rising up against the excesses of the monarchy, stormed the Bastille on 14 July 1789 *(see p45)*, setting off the French Revolution, and destroyed this hated symbol of oppression. In its place is the bronze Colonne de Juillet (July Column), 52 m (171 ft) high and crowned by the Angel of Liberty, which commemorates those who died in the revolutions of 1830 and 1848. Looming behind it is the Opéra Bastille, once the largest opera house in the world, which opened on the bicentennial of the Revolution in 1989. *Map H5*

6 Marché d'Aligre

Set around an old guardhouse and clocktower, the wonderful Aligre market is a melting pot of Parisians from all walks of life. It dates back to 1643 and was once as important as the more famous Les Halles *(see p75)*. In the gourmet covered market you'll see everything from rows of pheasants to a whole wild boar hanging from the stalls. North African traders give the outdoor produce market an ethnic flare. The flea market dates back to the days when nuns distributed second-hand clothing to the poor *(see p55)*. *place d'Aligre • Map H5 • Open until 1pm Tue–Sat, to 2pm Sun*

7 The Passages

The Bastille has been a quarter of working-class artisans and craft guilds since the 17th century and many furniture makers are still located in these small alleyways, called *passages*. The rue du Faubourg-St-Antoine is lined with shops displaying a striking array of both traditional period furniture and modern designs, but don't neglect to visit the narrow *passages*, such as the Passage de l'Homme, running off this and other streets

Rue de Lappe

in the Bastille. Many artists and craftspeople have their ateliers (workshops) in these atmospheric alleys. ⊗ *Map H5*

8 Rue de Lappe

Once famous for its 1930s dance halls *(bals musettes)*, rue de Lappe is still the Bastille's after-dark hotspot. This short, narrow street is filled with bars, clubs, restaurants and cafés, and positively throbs with music. Crowds of hip night-owls trawl the cobblestones looking for action, and spill into the adjoining rue de la Roquette and rue de Charonne where there are even more trendy bars and restaurants. ⊗ *Map H5*

9 Maison Européenne de la Photographie

This excellent gallery showcasing contemporary European photography opened in 1996 in an early 18th-century mansion, Hôtel Hénault de Cantorbre. The restoration is a mix of historic features and modern spaces that show off its permanent collection and changing exhibitions of items from its archives.
⊗ 5–7 rue de Fourcy, 75004 • Map Q3 • Open 11am–8pm Wed–Sun • Admission charge (free Wed after 5pm & for under 8s) • www.mep-fr.org

10 Maison de Victor Hugo

French author Victor Hugo (1802–85) lived on the second floor of the Hôtel de Rohan-Guéménée, the largest house on the place des Vosges, from 1832 to 1848. He wrote most of *Les Misérables* here *(see p46)* and many other works. In 1903 the house became a museum of his life. *⊗ 6 pl des Vosges, 75004 • Map R4 • Open 10am–6pm Tue–Sun • Closed public holidays • Admission charge for exhibitions • www.musee-hugo.paris.fr*

A Day in the Marais

Morning

Begin the morning at the **Musée Carnavalet** *(see p85)*, to beat the crowds and allow enough time to view the impressive collections. There is also a lovely garden courtyard. Afterwards, walk to the place des Vosges. Stand in the centre near the fountains to take in the whole square.

Have a coffee at Ma Bourgogne *(19 pl des Vosges • 01 42 78 44 64)*, right on the square. Afterwards, tour the **Maison de Victor Hugo,** then go to the southwest corner of the square, through a wooden door to the pretty garden of the **Hôtel de Béthune-Sully** *(see p90)*. Then walk to place de la Bastille.

A good lunch choice is **Brasserie Bofinger** *(see p65)*, with its ornate decor and true Parisian feel.

Afternoon

The **place de la Bastille** *(see p85)* is something of a traffic nightmare, but take time to admire the column in the centre and contemplate the events that happened here when this was the site of the city's dreaded prison. Walk around the square and along rue Faubourg-St-Antoine, a now fashionable shopping street. Turn off down some of the passageways to see the furniture-makers and craft workshops that have a long history in the area.

From here it's not far to the **Gare de Lyon** and dinner in style beneath the chandeliers and frescoes of **Le Train Bleu** *(20 blvd Diderot • 01 43 43 09 06)*.

Left **Isabel Marant** Right **Antoine et Lili**

TOP 10 Shops

1 Izraël
Also called the "World of Spices", this is a treasure trove of the world's best food and drink. Tiny but packed with meat, cheese, wine, rum, dates, honey, mustard…it has to be seen. *30 rue François-Miron, 75004 • Map P3*

2 BHV
The Bazar de l'Hôtel de Ville is an upmarket all-round shopper's paradise at which you can track down everything from DIY products to stylish underwear. *52–64 rue de Rivoli, 75004 • Map F4*

3 Antoine et Lili
Vibrant and eclectic clothes for women inspired by tzigane and Oriental styles using colourful natural fabrics. *51 rue des Francs-Bourgeois, 75004 • Map Q3*

4 Autour du Monde
Stylish clothes and objects for the home from French designer Bensimon. The canvas sneakers in pastel colours for kids and adults are a classic. *8, 12 rue des Francs Bourgeois, 75003 • Map G4 • 01 42 77 16 18*

5 Florence Kahn
This shop offers a range of cakes with freshly baked rye bread and a deli. *24 rue des Ecouffes, 75004 • Map Q3*

6 Fleux
This concept store is dedicated to contemporary Parisian interior design, with furniture and innovative home accessories. *39 rue Sainte Croix de Bretonnerie, 75004 • Map P2*

7 Isabel Marant
A designer starting to get a lot of recognition outside Paris, her work is hip but elegant. *16 rue de Charonne, 75011 • Map H5*

8 Sessùn
This is the flagship store of the young French womenswear label, which produces chic, edgy clothes and accessories. *34 rue de Charonne, 75011 • Map H5*

9 Merci
This trendy, three-storey concept store stocks clothes, homeware and stationery. It is also home to three cafés. *111 blvd Beaumarchais, 75003 • Map H4 • 01 42 77 00 33*

10 Emery & Cie
Stylish, coloured ceramics, tiles, lamps and other goods, run by an interior decorator. *18 passage de la Main d'Or, 75011 • Map H5*

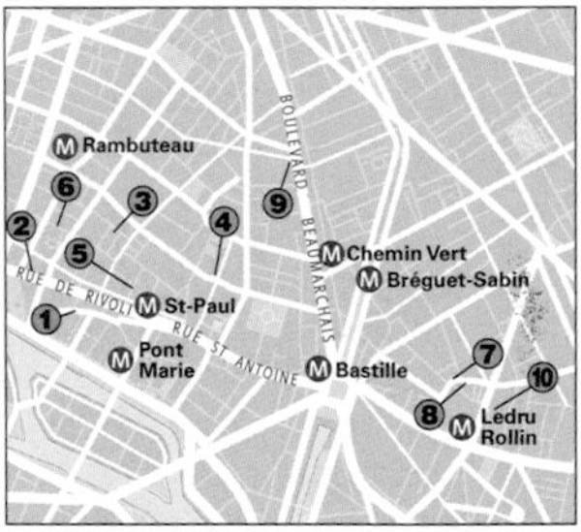

For more on shopping in Paris **See p169**

Left **Mariage Frères** Right **L'Arbre à Lettres**

TOP 10 Specialist Shops

1 Fragonard
If you can't visit this perfume maker's factory in the south of France, pick up some soaps and scents in their fragrant boutique. *51 rue des Francs-Bourgeois, 75004 • Map Q2*

2 Mariage Frères
This famous tea house was founded in 1854 and sells all kinds of blends, as well as tea-making paraphernalia. *6 rue du Bourg-Tibourg, 75004 • Map Q3*

3 Goumanyat
Paris's top chefs stock up on herbs, spices and teas here. This is a great place to find an interesting food gift or souvenir. *3 rue Dupuis, 75003 • Map R1 • 01 44 78 96 74*

4 Pasta Linea
Visit for fresh pasta dishes all made in-house from organic flour. Not much seating, but the leafy place des Vosges is nearby. *9 rue de Turenne, 75004 • Map G4 • Closed Sun, Mon, Aug*

5 Village Saint-Paul
This wonderful maze of art galleries, fine antiques and design shops is located behind Eglise Saint-Paul. *Between rue St-Paul and rue des Jardins St-Paul, 75004 • Map R4*

6 L'Art du Bureau
If your desk is your altar, you'll find everything you could possibly need here, and it's all in the most modern designs. In fact, this shop is worth visiting for the design aspects alone. *47 rue des Francs-Bourgeois, 75004 • Map R3*

7 L'Arbre à Lettres
A beautiful bookshop; its content is on the serious side, focusing on fine arts, literature and human sciences. *56 rue du Faubourg-St-Antoine, 75012 • Map H5*

8 A l'Olivier
Since 1822, this shop has specialized in all kinds of oil, from the finest olive oil to other Provençal specialities. *23 rue de Rivoli, 75004 • Map H5*

9 Papeterie Saint Sabin
Parisian stationery shops are a class apart, and here you will find stylish notebooks, pens, pads and other tasteful items. *16 rue St-Sabin, 75011 • Map H4*

10 Jacques Genin
This trendy chocolatier sells unique combos alongside a selection of some of the best caramels and fruit jellies. *133 rue de Turenne, 75003 • Map G3*

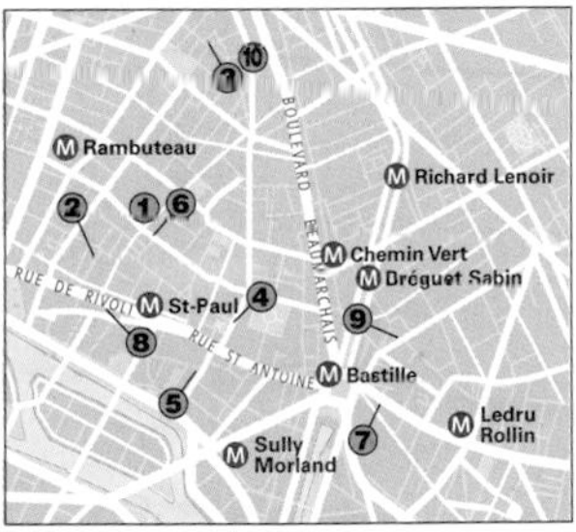

Left **Hôtel de Sens** Centre **Hôtel de Soubise** Right **Hôtel de Lamoignon**

TOP 10 Mansions

1 Hôtel de Coulanges
This mansion boasts beautiful early 18th-century architecture, although the right wing dates from the early 1600s. ✎ *35 rue des Francs-Bourgeois, 75004 • Map Q2 • Open only for concerts*

2 Hôtel Salé
Built in 1656–9 for Aubert de Fontenay, a salt-tax collector, this mansion is now the home of the Musée Picasso *(see p85)*.

3 Hôtel Guénégaud
Designed by the architect François Mansart in the mid-17th century, this splendid mansion houses a Hunting Museum. ✎ *60 rue des Archives, 75003 • Map P3 • Open 11am–6pm Tue–Sun • Admission charge*

4 Hôtel de Beauvais
The young Mozart performed at this 17th-century mansion. Notice the balcony decorated with goats' heads. ✎ *68 rue François-Miron, 75004 • Map P3 • Closed to the public*

5 Hôtel de Béthune-Sully
This 17th-century mansion was home to the Duc de Sully, chief minister to Henri IV. It now houses the French National Monuments administration. ✎ *62 rue St-Antoine, 75004 • Map R4 • Closed to the public except gardens*

6 Hôtel de Sens
One of Paris's few medieval mansions. Henri IV's wife Marguerite de Valois *(see p20)* lived here after their divorce. It is now home to a fine arts library. ✎ *1 rue Figuier, 75004 • Map Q4 • Closed to the public*

7 Hôtel de St-Aignan
The plain exterior hides an enormous mansion within. It is now the Museum of Jewish Art and History. ✎ *71 rue du Temple, 75003 • Map P2 • Open 11am–6pm Mon–Fri, 10am–6pm Sun • Admission charge • www.mahj.org*

8 Hôtel de Soubise
Along with the adjacent Hôtel de Rohan, this mansion houses the national archives. ✎ *60 rue des Francs-Bourgeois, 75003 • Map Q2 • Open 10am–12:30pm, 2–5:30pm Wed–Fri, 2–5:30pm Sat & Sun • Admission charge*

9 Hôtel de Lamoignon
Built in 1584 for the daughter of Henri II. ✎ *24 rue Pavée, 75004 • Map Q3 • Closed to the public*

10 Hôtel de Marle
The Swedish Institute is located here. ✎ *11 rue Payenne, 75003 • Map G4 • Open noon–6pm Tue–Sun • Closed mid-Jul–end Aug*

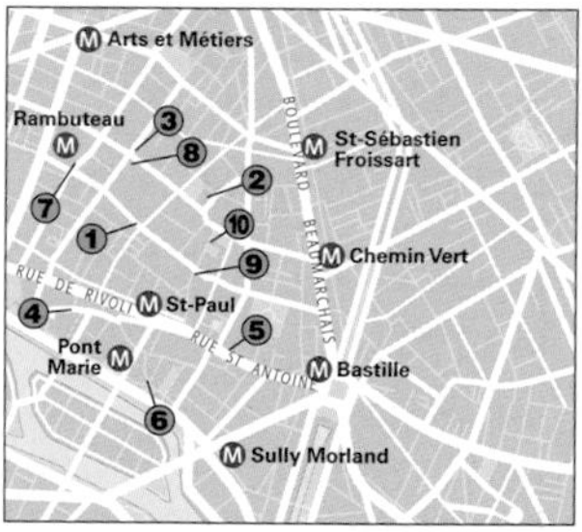

For more historic buildings in Paris **See pp42–3**

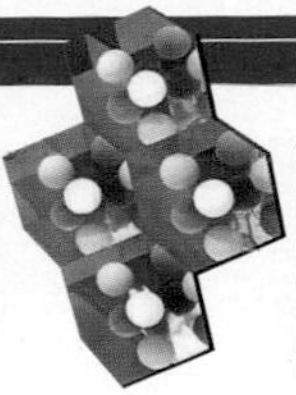

Left **Galerie Patrick Seguin** Centre **Galerie Lavignes-Bastille** Right **Galerie Nikki Diana Marquardt**

Top 10 Galleries

1 Galerie Marian Goodman
Housed in a 17th-century mansion, this gallery is a slice of New York. Artists include Jeff Wall and video-maker Steve McQueen. *79 rue du Temple, 75003 • Map P2 • Open 11am–7pm Tue–Sat • Closed Aug*

2 Galerie Akié Arichi
Eclectic exhibitions covering photography, sculpture and paint, often with an Asian influence. *26 rue Keller, 75011 • Map H5 • Open 2:30–7pm Tue–Sat • www.galeriearichi.com*

3 Galerie Alain Gutharc
Alain Gutharc devotes his space to the work of young, contemporary artists. *7 rue St Claude, 75003 • Map H4 • Open 11am–1pm, 2–7pm Tue–Sat • www.alaingutharc.com*

4 Galerie Daniel Templon
A favourite among the French contemporary art establishment, exhibiting big, international names as well as talented newcomers. *30 rue Beaubourg, 75003 • Map P2 • Open 10am–7pm Mon–Sat • www.danieltemplon.com*

5 Galerie Karsten Greve
A leading international gallery with top names in modern and contemporary art and photography. *5 rue Debelleyme, 75003 • Map R2 • Open 10am–7pm Tue–Sat*

6 Galerie Patrick Seguin
This gallery features stylish 20th-century furniture and architecture. *5 rue des Taillandiers, 75011 • Map H4 • Open 10am–7pm Tue–Sat*

7 Galerie Lavignes-Bastille
Narrative figuration, Op Art and new artists are featured here. *27 rue de Charonne, 75011 • Map H5 • Open 2–7pm Tue–Sat • www.lavignesbastille.com*

8 Galerie Thaddeus Ropac
A major contemporary gallery showcasing new international artists. *7 rue Debelleyme, 75003 • Map Q1 • Open 10am–7pm Tue–Sat • www.ropac.net*

9 Galerie Yvon Lambert
A stalwart of contemporary art in Paris, this gallery hosts changing exhibitions and photography. *108 rue Vieille du Temple, 75003 • Map Q1 • Open 10am–1pm, 2:30–7pm Tue–Fri, 10am–7pm Sat • www.yvon-lambert.com*

10 Galerie Nikki Diana Marquardt
This gallery contains politically motivated artworks executed in all types of art media. *9 pl des Vosges, 75004 • Map R3 • Open 11am–7pm Mon–Sat • www.galerienikkidianamarquardt.com*

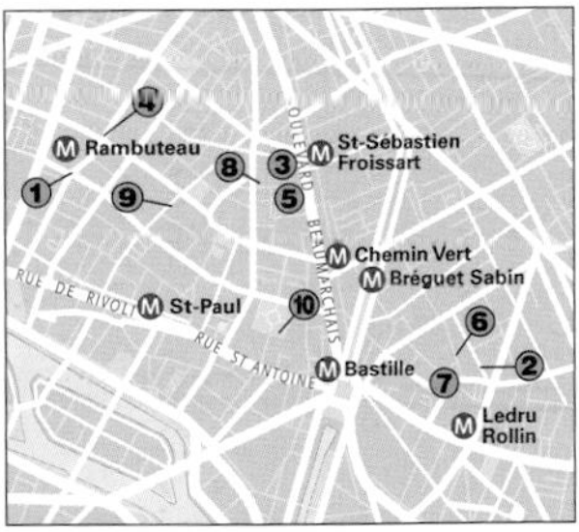

Left **Le Square Trousseau** Right **Pop In**

TOP 10 Fashionable Hang-outs

1 Zéro Zéro
It doesn't get much cooler than this den-like bar with wood panelling and flowered wallpaper. Though not listed on the menu, cocktails are a speciality. *89 rue Amelot, 75011 • Map H4*

2 Andy Wahloo
Located in one of Henri IV's former mansions, pop art and Oriental decor form a backdrop for some of the city's most fashionable soirées. *69 rue des Gravilliers, 75003 • Map Q1*

3 La Perle
This popular bistro is one of the capital's most famous hang-outs, drawing a fashionable crowd in the evening. *78 rue Vieille du Temple, 75003 • Map Q2 • 01 42 72 69 93*

4 Bataclan
This venerable concert hall attracts international artists as well as household French names. The adjoining bar provides beer and meals. *50 boulevard Voltaire, 75011 • Map H4*

5 Pop In
This shabby-chic bar cum nightclub has cheap drinks, friendly staff, a cool crowd and funky DJs. It is open on Sundays. *105 rue Amelot, 75011 • Map H4*

6 Café de l'Industrie
This fashionable and sizeable café has three rooms where the walls are lined with paintings and old-fashioned artifacts. The food is cheap but pretty good, and the later it gets the better the buzz *(see p53)*. *16 rue St-Sabin, 75011 • Map H4*

7 Grazie
This Italian pizzeria with an industrial loft-style decor attracts a hip crowd. *91 blvd Beaumarchais, 75003 • Map H4 • 01 42 78 11 96*

8 Le Panic Room
Top Parisian DJs set the tone at this quirky bar offering fancy cocktails, a smoking room and cellar dance floor. *101 rue Amelot, 75011 • Map H4*

9 Le Square Trousseau
This media haunt in the Bastille district serves breakfast, lunch and dinner and has a lovely heated terrace. *1 rue Antoine-Vollon, 75012 • Map H5*

10 Le Progrès
The pavement terrace of this corner café in the trendy Northern Marais fills up during Paris Fashion Week. *1 rue de Bretagne, 75003 • Map R2 • 01 42 72 01 44*

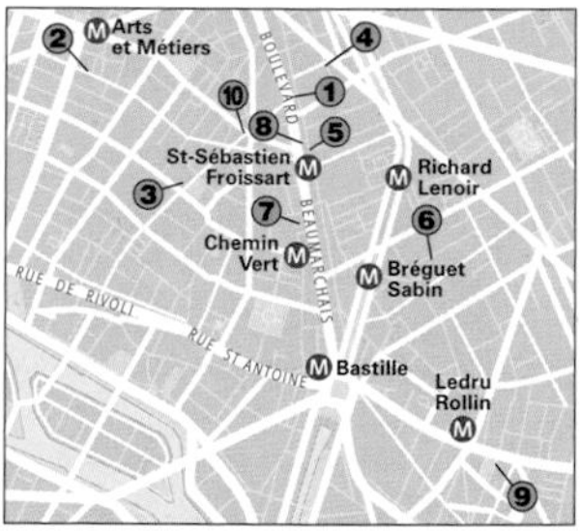

For more bars in Paris **See pp52–3**

Left **La Gazzetta**

Price Categories

For a three-course	€	under €30
meal for one with half	€€	€30–€40
a bottle of wine (or	€€€	€40–€50
equivalent meal), taxes	€€€€	€50–€60
and extra charges	€€€€€	over €60

TOP 10 Places to Eat

1 L'Ambroisie

The finest service matches the finest of food. The wine list is renowned and the chocolate tart is out of this world. Reserve in advance. *9 pl des Vosges, 75004 • Map R3 • 01 42 78 51 45 • Closed Sun, Mon • €€€€€*

2 Café des Musées

A traditional bistro, which serves classic French dishes such as steak tartare and *crème brûlée.* *49 rue de Turenne, 75003 • Map R2 • 01 42 72 96 17 • No disabled access • €€*

3 Patisserie Carette

Salads and sandwiches, as well as delicious cakes, feature at this patisserie and tea room on the picturesque place des Vosges. *25 pl des Vosges, 75003 • Map G4 • 01 48 87 94 07 • €*

4 Au Vieux Chêne

Hidden down a side street, this atmospheric bistro is a treat. Expect updated French classics such as duck *pot-au-feu* with foie gras. *7 rue Dahomey, 75011 • 01 43 71 67 69 • Closed Sat, Sun, Aug • €€€*

5 La Gazzetta

Inventive, contemporary dishes, such as venison, polenta, dried figs and dandelion leaves are served in a Neo-Art Deco setting. *29 rue de Cotte, 75012 • Map H5 • 01 43 47 47 05 • Open Tue–Sat • €€€€*

6 Breizh Café

An award-winning crêperie with a contemporary take on both savoury and sweet Breton pancakes. *109 rue Vieille du Temple, 75003 • Map G4 • 01 42 72 13 77 • Closed Mon, Tue • €€*

7 Le Baron Rouge

Cold meats, cheeses and oysters are served in an authentic setting by the Aligre Market. *1 rue Théophile-Roussel, 75012 • Map H5 • 01 43 43 14 32 • Closed Mon, Sun D • €*

8 Chez Paul

This old bistro has a fairly simple but delicious menu. Book ahead. *13 rue de Charonne, 75011 • Map H5 • 01 47 00 34 57 • €€*

9 Septime

This modern restaurant serves dishes such as cress and sorrel risotto and veal tartare. Book ahead. *80 rue de Charonne, 75011 • Map H5 • 01 43 67 38 29 • €€*

10 L'As du Fallafel

This is the best falafel joint in the city. The "special" with aubergine and spicy sauce is a must. *34 rue des Rosiers, 75004 • Map Q3 • 01 48 87 63 60 • Closed Fri D, Sat • €*

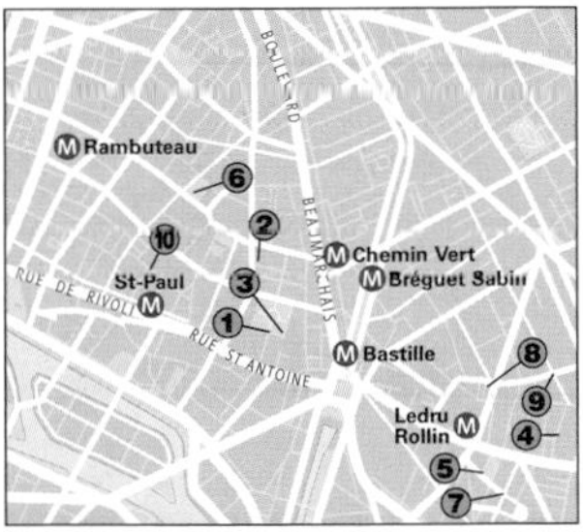

Note: *Unless otherwise stated, all restaurants accept credit cards and serve vegetarian meals*

Left **Musée du Louvre** Centre **Café Marly, Louvre** Right **Musée Nationale de la Mode et du Textile**

Tuileries and Opéra Quarters

THESE TWO QUARTERS *were once the province of the rich and the royal. Adjoining the Tuileries Gardens is the largest museum in the world, the Louvre, while the grand opera house gives the second quarter its name. The place de la Concorde is one of the most historic sites in the city.*

Top 10 Sights

1. Musée du Louvre
2. Rue de Rivoli
3. Place de la Concorde
4. Jardin des Tuileries
5. Musée des Arts Décoratifs
6. Art Nouveau Museum
7. Palais-Royal
8. Place Vendôme
9. Opéra National de Paris Garnier
10. Place de la Madeleine

Opéra de Paris Garnier

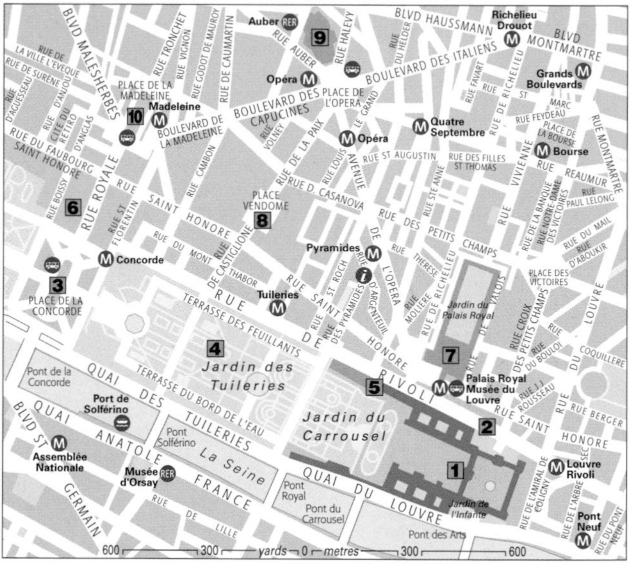

1 Musée du Louvre

See pp8–10.

2 Rue de Rivoli

Commissioned by Napoleon and named after his victory over the Austrians at Rivoli in 1797, this grand street links the Louvre with the Champs-Elysées *(see p103)*. It was intended as a backdrop for victory marches but was not finished until the 1850s, long after the emperor's death. Along one side, railings replaced the old Tuileries walls, opening up the view, while opposite, Neo-Classical apartments sit atop the long arcades. These are now filled with a mix of shops, selling luxury goods or tourist souvenirs. *Map M2*

3 Place de la Concorde

This historic octagonal square, covering more than 8 ha (20 acres), is bounded by the Tuileries Gardens on one side and marks the starting point of the Champs-Elysées on the other. It was built between 1755–75 to designs by architect Jacques-Ange Gabriel as the grand setting for a statue of Louis XV, but by 1792 it had become the place de la Révolution and its central monument was the guillotine. Louis XVI, Marie-Antoinette and more than 1,000 others were executed here *(see p70)*. In 1795, in the spirit of reconciliation, it received its present name. The central obelisk, 23 m (75 ft) tall and covered in hieroglyphics, is from a 3,300-year-old Luxor temple, and was a gift from Egypt, erected in 1833. Two fountains and eight statues representing French cities were also added. On the north side of the square are the mansions Hôtel de la Marine and Hôtel Crillon, also by Gabriel. *Map D3*

Arcades on rue de Rivoli

4 Jardin des Tuileries

These gardens *(see p38)* were first laid out as part of the old Tuileries Palace, which was built for Catherine de Médici in 1564 but burned down in 1871. André Le Nôtre redesigned them into formal French gardens in 1664. At the Louvre end is the Arc de Triomphe du Carrousel, erected by Napoleon in 1808. Here is also the entrance to the underground shopping centre, the Carrousel du Louvre. Nearby, sensuous nude sculptures by Aristide Maillol (1861–1944) adorn the ornamental pools and walkways. At the far end is the hexagonal pool, the Jeu de Paume gallery *(see p36)* and the Musée de l'Orangerie *(see p37)*, famous for its giant canvases of Monet waterlilies. *Map J2*

5 Musée des Arts Décoratifs

This huge collection covers the decorative arts from the Middle Ages to the 20th century. With over 100 rooms, the many highlights include the Medieval and Renaissance rooms, the Art Deco rooms and a superb jewellery collection. Also in the same building is the Musée Nationale de la Mode et du Textile with displays of fashion, textiles, posters and advertising ephemera in changing temporary exhibitions. *107 rue de Rivoli, 75001 • Map M2 • Open 11am–6pm Tue–Sun (until 9pm Thu) • Admission charge • www.lesartsdecoratifs.fr*

Storming of the Tuileries

Looking at the Tuileries Gardens now, where children play and lovers stroll, it is hard to imagine the scenes that took place here on 20 June 1792. The palace and gardens were invaded by French citizens seeking to overthrow the monarchy. This was finally achieved on 10 August, when the Tuileries Palace was sacked and Louis XVI overthrown.

6 Art Nouveau Museum

This small museum (which is part of the famous Maxim's restaurant) houses Pierre Cardin's impressive Art Nouveau collection. The 750 works of art, designed by big names such as Tiffany, Toulouse-Lautrec, Galle Massier and Marjorelle, are set in a re-created 1900s apartment. A guided visit can be combined with dinner in the glamorous restaurant. *3 rue Royale, 75008 • Map D3 • Open 2–5:30pm Wed–Sun, guided tours 2pm (in English), 3:15pm, 4:30pm • Adm • www.maxims-musee-artnouveau.com*

7 Palais-Royal

In the late 18th century extensive changes were made under the dukes of Orléans. The architect Victor Louis was commissioned to build 60 uniformly styled houses around three sides of the square and the adjacent theatre, which now houses the Comédie Française *(see p59)*. Today the arcades house specialist shops, galleries and restaurants, and the courtyard and gardens contain modern works of art *(see p43)*. *Pl du Palais-Royal, 75001 • Map L1 • Open Oct–Mar: 7am–8:30pm daily; Apr–May: 7:30am–10:15pm daily; Sep: 7am–9:30pm daily • Public access to gardens and arcades only*

8 Place Vendôme

Jules Hardouin-Mansart, the architect of Versailles *(see p151)*, designed the façades of this elegant royal square for Louis XIV in 1698. Originally intended for foreign embassies, bankers soon moved in and built lavish dwellings. It remains home to jewellers and financiers today.

Palais Royal courtyard

Opéra de Paris Garnier façade

The world-famous Ritz hotel was established here at the turn of the 20th century. It is currently closed for renovations until 2016. The central column, topped by a statue of Napoleon, is a replica of the one destroyed by the Commune in 1871. *Map E3*

9 Opéra National de Paris Garnier

Designed by Charles Garnier for Napoleon III in 1862, Paris' opulent opera house took 13 years to complete. A range of styles from Classical to Baroque incorporates stone friezes and columns, statues and a green, copper cupola. The ornate interior has a Grand Staircase, mosaic domed ceiling over the Grand Foyer and an auditorium with a ceiling by Marc Chagall. There's even an underground lake – the inspiration for Gaston Leroux's Phantom of the Opera – sadly closed to visitors *(see p58)*. *Pl de l'Opéra, 75009 • Map E2 • 01 71 25 24 23 • Open 10am–5pm daily (closes at 1pm on day of matinee performances; closed public hols) • Admission charge • www.operadeparis.fr*

10 Place de la Madeleine

Surrounded by 52 Corinthian columns, the huge Classical style La Madeleine church *(see p40)* commands this elegant square. On the east side a colourful flower market is held Tuesday to Saturday. The square is surrounded by some of the most upmarket *épiceries* (food stores) and speciality shops in the city *(see p98)*. *Map D3*

A Day in the Tuileries

Morning

Visiting the **Louvre** *(see pp8–11)* takes planning, and you should get there at least 15 minutes before opening (unless you've already bought your ticket). Spend the whole morning and pick up a map as you enter so that you can be sure to see the main highlights. Have a morning coffee in the elegant Richelieu, Denon or Mollien cafés within the museum.

From the Louvre, either visit the Carrousel du Louvre's underground shops or walk along **rue de Rivoli** towards **place de la Concorde** *(see p95)*. This end of the street is filled with souvenir shops but avoid the overpriced cafés and turn right to rue Mondovi for a good lunch at Lescure, a little rustic bistro *(7 rue de Mondovi • 01 42 60 18 91 • Closed Sat, Sun)*.

Afternoon

After being indoors all morning, get some fresh air in the **Jardin des Tuileries** *(see p95)* then walk down to **place de la Madeleine** to spend the afternoon shopping in its many food stores, or visit the **Art Nouveau Museum** and admire its decorative arts collection. Later, take tea in the restaurant of one of the best shops, **Hédiard** *(see p98)*.

Spend the evening attending a classical music concert at **L'église de la Madeleine** *(see p40)* or watching a performance at **L'Opéra Garnier**. Finish the day with a delicious gastronomic dinner at Michelin-starred **Senderens** *(see p99)*.

Left **Fauchon biscuits** Right **La Maison du Miel honey**

TOP 10 Food Shops

1 Hédiard
Founded in 1854, this world food emporium features a cornucopia of fruits and vegetables, exotic spices and oils and a host of other gourmet delights. *21 pl de la Madeleine, 75008 • Map D3*

2 Fauchon
The king of Parisian *épiceries* (grocers). The mouth-watering window displays are works of art and tempt you inside for pastries, exotic fruits and some 3,500 other items. *26–30 pl de la Madeleine, 75008 • Map D3*

3 Au Verger de la Madeleine
Rare vintage wines are the speciality at this store. The owner will help you find a wine to match the year of any special occasion. *4 blvd Malesherbes, 75008 • Map D3*

4 Caviar Kaspia
The peak of indulgence. Caviars from around the world, plus smoked eels, salmon and other fishy fare. *17 pl de la Madeleine, 75008 • Map D3*

5 La Maison de la Truffe
France's finest black truffles are sold here during the winter truffle season. Preserved truffles and other delicacies can be savoured in the shop or at home. *19 pl de la Madeleine, 75008 • Map D3*

6 La Maison du Miel
The "house of honey", family-owned since 1908, is the place to try speciality honeys, to spread on your toast or your body in the form of soaps and oils. *24 rue Vignon, 75009 • Map D3*

7 Boutique Maille
The retail outlet for one of France's finest mustard-makers. Fresh mustard served in lovely ceramic jars and seasonal limited edition mustards are available. *6 pl de la Madeleine, 75008 • Map D3*

8 La Maison du Chocolat
A superb chocolate shop, which offers fine chocolates and pastries including eclairs, tarts and macaroons. *8 blvd Madeleine, 75009 • Map E3 • 01 47 42 86 52*

9 Betjeman and Barton
This tea shop offers some 250 varieties from all over the world, as well as wacky teapots. *23 blvd Malesherbes, 75008 • Map D3*

10 Ladurée
A splendid *belle époque* tea salon that has been serving the best macaroons in Paris since 1862. *16 rue Royale, 75008 • Map D3*

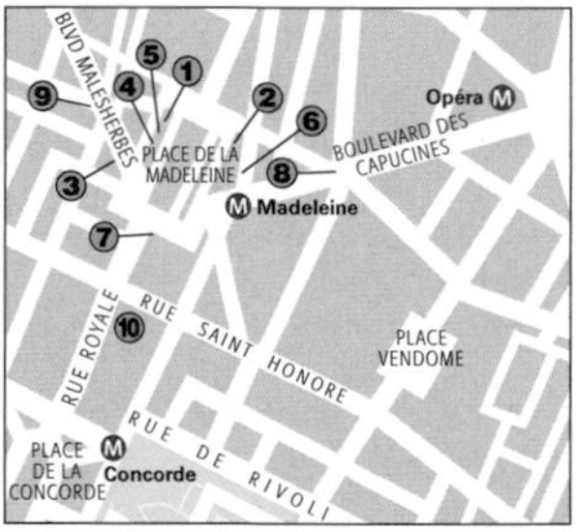

For more on shopping in Paris **See p169**

Price Categories

For a three-course meal for one with half a bottle of wine (or equivalent meal), taxes and extra charges	€	under €30
	€€	€30–€40
	€€€	€40–€50
	€€€€	€50–€60
	€€€€€	over €60

Left **Senderens** Right **Le soufflé**

TOP 10 Places to Eat

1 Le Soufflé
A wide choice of soufflés, from savoury leek to sweet passionfruit, are on offer here. *36 rue du Mont Thabor, 75001 • Map E3 • 01 42 60 27 19 • Closed Sun • €€€*

2 Le Meurice
Try the herbed lamb and semolina roasted with lemon and capers at this three-starred Michelin establishment. *228 rue de Rivoli, 75001 • Map E3 • 01 44 58 10 55 • Closed Sat & Sun • €€€€€*

3 Le Grand Véfour
This beautiful 18th-century restaurant with two Michelin stars is a gourmet treat. *17 rue de Beaujolais, 75001 • Map E3 • 01 42 96 56 27 • Closed Fri D, Sat, Sun, Aug, some of Dec • No disabled access • €€€€€*

4 Senderens
Chef Alain Senderens maintains a two Michelin star status and superb quality food. *9 pl de la Madeleine, 75008 • Map D3 • 01 42 65 22 90 • Closed Aug & public hols • No disabled access • €€€€€*

5 Le Zinc d'Honoré
Join the lunchtime business crowds and the evening theatre-goers for well-priced bistro cuisine. *36 pl du Marché St-Honoré, 75001 • Map E3 • Open daily • €€*

6 Higuma
This no-frills Japanese noodle house serves great value food. *32 bis rue Sainte-Anne, 75001 • Map E3 • 01 47 03 38 59 • €*

7 A Casaluna
Traditional Corsican specialities such as baked aubergines with goat's cheese are served at this charming restaurant. *6 rue Beaujolais, 75001 • Map E3 • 01 42 60 05 11 • No disabled access • €€€*

8 Willi's Wine Bar
This cosy bar and adjacent dining room – Macéo – is a popular haunt for lovers of modern French food and wines from small producers. *13 rue des Petits-Champs, 75001 • Map E3 • 01 42 61 05 09 • Closed Sun, 10 days Aug • €€€*

9 Restaurant du Palais Royal
Contemporary French food is served in the bucolic Palais Royal gardens *(see p39)*. *110 galerie de Valois, 75001 • Map E3 • 01 40 20 00 27 • No disabled access • €€€€*

10 Verjus
Book in advance for the set, six-course gourmet dinner in the intimate dining room, or enjoy a lighter bite in the wine bar. *752 rue de Richelieu, 75001 • Map E3 • 01 42 97 54 40 • Closed Sat & Sun • €€–€€€€€*

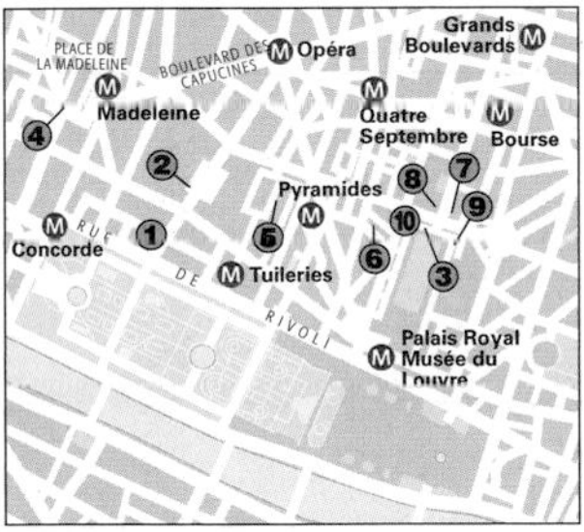

Note: *Unless otherwise stated, all restaurants accept credit cards and serve vegetarian meals*

BON
Bon
Bon
Bon

Left **Arc de Triomphe** Right **Palais de L'Elysée**

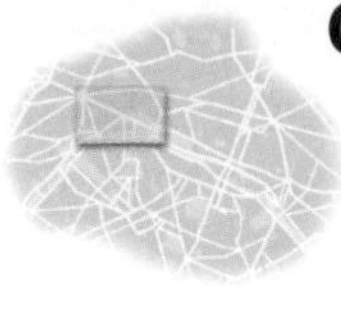

Champs-Elysées Quarter

THE CHAMPS-ELYSEES IS UNDOUBTEDLY *the most famous street in Paris and the quarter that lies around it is brimming with wealth and power. It is home to the president of France, great* haute couture *fashion houses, embassies and consulates, and the five-star hotels and fine restaurants frequented by the French and foreign élite. The Champs-Elysées itself runs from the place de la Concorde to the place Charles de Gaulle, which is known as* L'Etoile *(the star) because of the 12 busy avenues that radiate out from it. It is the most stately stretch of the so-called Triumphal Way, built by Napoleon, where Parisians celebrate national events with parades or mourn at the funeral cortèges of the great and good.*

TOP 10 Sights

1. Arc de Triomphe
2. Avenue des Champs-Elysées
3. Grand Palais
4. Petit Palais
5. Pont Alexandre III
6. Palais de la Découverte
7. Rue du Faubourg-St-Honoré
8. Avenue Montaigne
9. Palais de l'Elysée
10. Musée Jacquemart-André

Home of La Marseillaise

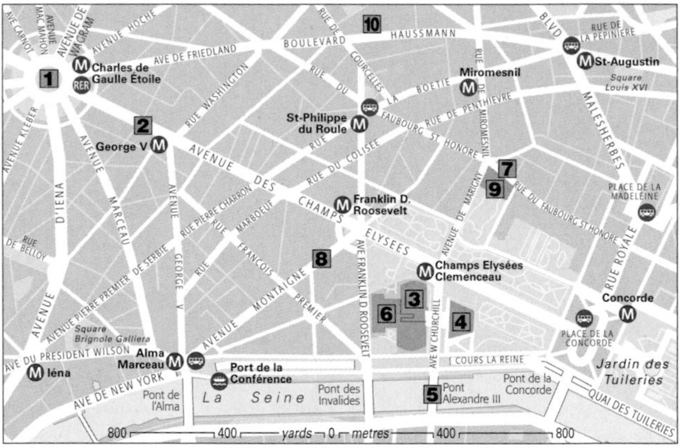

Preceding pages **French patisseries**

de Triomphe

e pp24–5.

venue des Champs-Elysées

e of the most famous enues in the world came into eing when the royal gardener André Le Nôtre planted an arbour of trees beyond the border of the Jardin des Tuileries in 1667 *(see p95)*. First called the Grand Cours (Great Way), it was later renamed the Champs-Elysées (Elysian Fields). In the mid-19th century the avenue acquired pedestrian paths, fountains, gas lights and cafés, and became the fashionable place for socialising and entertainment. Since the funeral of Napoleon in 1840, this wide thoroughfare has also been the route for state processions, victory parades and other city events. The Rond Point des Champs-Elysées is the prettiest part, with chestnut trees and flower beds. Formerly touristy parts have been revamped but flagship stores of international brands have made for less interesting shopping. A walk along the avenue is still an essential Paris experience. *Map C3*

3 Grand Palais

This immense *belle époque* exhibition hall was built for the Universal Exhibition in 1900. Its splendid glass roof is a landmark of the Champs-Elysées. The façade, the work of three architects, is a mix of Art Nouveau ironwork, Classical stone columns and a mosaic frieze, with bronze horses and chariots at the four corners of the roof. The Galleries du Grand Palais host temporary art exhibitions. *3 ave du Général-Eisenhower, 75008 • Map D3 • 01 44 13 17 17 • Opening hours vary according to exhibition • Closed 1 May • Admission charge depending on exhibition • www.grandpalais.fr*

4 Petit Palais

The "little palace" echoes its neighbour in style. Set around a semi-circular courtyard, with Ionic columns and a dome, the building now houses the Musée des Beaux-Arts de la Ville de Paris. This includes medieval and Renaissance art, 18th-century furniture and a collection of 19th-century paintings. *Ave Winston Churchill, 75008 • Map D3 • 01 53 43 40 00 • Open 10am–6pm Tue–Sun (to 8pm Thu for temporary exhibitions) • www.petitpalais.paris.fr*

Avenue des Champs-Elysées

La Marseillaise

The stirring French national anthem was written in 1792 by a French army engineer named Claude Joseph Rouget de Lisle. He lived for a time in this district, at 15 rue du Faubourg-St-Honoré. The rousing song got its name from the troops from Marseille who were prominent in the storming of the Tuileries during the Revolution *(see p45)*.

5 Pont Alexandre III

Built for the 1900 Universal Exhibition to carry visitors over the Seine to the Grand and Petit Palais, this bridge is a superb example of the steel architecture and ornate Art Nouveau style popular at the time. Named after Alexander III of Russia, who laid the foundation stone, its decoration displays both Russian and French heraldry. The bridge creates a splendid thoroughfare from the Champs-Elysées to the Invalides *(see p48)*. *Map D3*

6 Palais de la Découverte

Set in a wing of the Grand Palais, this museum showcasing scientific discovery was created by a Nobel Prize-winning p for the World's Fair of 193 exhibits focus on invention innovation in the sciences, f biology to chemistry, to astron and physics, with interactive exhibits and demonstrations (th magnetism show is especially spectacular). There is also a planetarium, while the Planète Terre (Planet Earth) rooms examine global warming. *Ave Franklin-D.-Roosevelt, 75008 • Map D3 • Open 9:30am–6pm Tue–Sat, 10am–7pm Sun • Closed 1 Jan, 1 May, 14 Jul, 22 Jul, 25 Dec • Admission charge*

Pont Alexandre III

7 Rue du Faubourg-St-Honoré

Running roughly parallel to the Champs-Elysées, this is Paris's equivalent of Fifth Avenue, Bond Street or Rodeo Drive. From Christian Lacroix and Versace to Gucci and Hermès, the shopfronts read like a *Who's Who* of fashion. Even if the prices may be out of reach, window-shopping is fun. There are also elegant antiques and art galleries. Look out for swallows that nest on many of the 19th-century façades. *Map D3*

8 Avenue Montaigne

In the 19th century the Avenue Montaigne was a night-life hotspot. Parisians danced the night away at the Mabille Dance Hall until it closed in 1870 and Adolphe Sax made music with his newly invented saxophone in the Winter Garden. Today this chic avenue is a rival to the rue Faubourg-St-Honoré as the home to more *haute couture* houses such as Christian Dior and Valentino. There are also luxury hotels, top restaurants, popular cafés, and the Comédie des Champs-Elysées and Théâtre des Champs-Elysées. *Map C3*

Rue du Faubourg-St-Honoré

9 Palais de l'Elysée

Built in 1718, after the Revolution this elegant palace was turned into a dance hall, then, in the 19th century, became the residence of Napoleon's sister Caroline Murat, followed by his wife Empress Josephine. His nephew, Napoleon III, also lived here while plotting his 1851 coup. Since 1873 it has been home to the president of France. For this reason, it is worth noting that the palace guards don't like people getting too close to the building *(see p42)*. *55 rue du Faubourg-St-Honoré, 75008 • Map D3 • Closed to the public*

10 Musée Jacquemart-André

This fine display of art and furniture, once belonging to avid art collectors Edouard André and his wife Nélie Jacquemart, is housed in a late 19th-century mansion. It is best known for its Italian Renaissance art, including frescoes by Tiepolo and Paolo Uccello's *St George and the Dragon* (*c.*1435). The reception rooms feature the art of the 18th-century "Ecole française", with paintings by François Boucher and Jean-Honoré Fragonard. Flemish masters are in the library. *158 blvd Haussmann, 75008 • Map C2 • 01 45 62 11 59 • Open 10am–6pm daily (to 8:30pm Mon & Sat for temporary exhibits) • Adm • www.musee-jacquemart-andre.com*

A Day of Shopping

Morning

The **Champs-Elysées** *(see p103)* is an area for leisurely strolls. Begin by window-shopping along one side of the **avenue Montaigne**, where Prada, Nina Ricci, Dior and many more have their flagship stores – the area oozes money. Have a break in the Bar des Théâtres, where fashion names and the theatre crowd from the Comédie des Champs-Élysées across the street sometimes hang out *(6 ave Montaigne • 01 47 23 34 63)*.

Return up the other side of avenue Montaigne to the Champs-Elysées, for the stroll to the Arc de Triomphe. Here you will find many flagship shops of world-famous brands. Call ahead for a table at **Le Cinq** to splurge on lunch *(see p109)*.

Afternoon

Continuing up the Champs-Elysées, look past the showrooms and fast food outlets to note the many interesting buildings that house them.

Take the underpass to the **Arc de Triomphe** *(see pp24–5)* and climb to the top for the views, which are superb at dusk when the avenues light up. Walk or take the metro to the **rue du Faubourg St-Honoré**, for more designer shops.

For tea and cakes, **Ladurée**, located a short walk away at 75 Avenue des Champs-Elyseés, is a wonderfully elegant experience.

Left **Avenue de Marigny** Centre **Avenue Franklin-D.-Roosevelt** Right **25 Avenue Montaigne**

TOP 10 International Connections

1 Avenue de Marigny
American author John Steinbeck lived here for five months in 1954 and described Parisians as "the luckiest people in the world". *Map C3*

2 8 Rue Artois
Here, in September 2001, the legendary Belgian mobster François Vanverbergh – godfather of the French Connection gang – fell victim to a drive-by assassin as he took his afternoon mineral water. *Map C2*

3 37 Avenue Montaigne
Having wowed Paris with her comeback performances, iconic German actress and singer Marlene Dietrich spent her reclusive final years in a luxury apartment here. *Map C3*

4 Pont de l'Alma
Diana, Princess of Wales, was killed in a tragic accident in the underpass here in 1997. Her unofficial monument nearby attracts thousands of visitors each year *(see p48)*. *Map C3*

5 31 Avenue George V, Hôtel George V
A roll-call of rockers – from the Rolling Stones and Jim Morrison to J-Lo and Ricky Martin – have made this their regular Paris home-from-home. *Map C3*

6 Hôtel d'Elysée-Palace
Mata Hari, the Dutch spy and exotic dancer, set up her lair in Room 113 before finally being arrested outside 25 Avenue Montaigne. *Map C3*

7 37 Avenue George V
Franklin D. Roosevelt and his new bride visited his aunt's apartment here in 1905. He was later commemorated in the name of a nearby avenue. *Map C3*

8 49 Avenue des Champs-Elysées
Author Charles Dickens may well have had "the best of times and the worst of times" when he resided here from 1855–6. Ten years earlier he had also lived at 38 Rue de Courcelles. *Map C3*

9 114 Avenue des Champs-Elysées
Brazilian aviation pioneer Alberto Santos-Dumont planned many of his amazing aeronautical feats – notably that of circling the Eiffel Tower in an airship in 1901 – from this address. *Map C2*

10 102 Boulevard Haussmann
Hypochondriac author Marcel Proust lived in a soundproofed room here, turning memories into a masterwork. *Map D2*

Left **Student riots, 1968** Right **Bastille Day celebrations**

TOP 10 Events on the Champs-Elysées

1 1616
Paris's grand avenue was first laid out when Marie de Médici, wife of Henri IV, had a carriage route, the Cours-la-Reine (Queen's Way), constructed through the marshland along the Seine.

2 1667
Landscape gardener Le Nôtre lengthened the Jardin des Tuileries to meet the Cours-la-Reine, and opened up the view with a double row of chestnut trees, creating the Grand Cours.

3 1709
The avenue was re-named the Champs-Elysées (Elysian Fields). In Greek mythology, the Elysian Fields were the "place of ideal happiness", the abode of the blessed after death.

4 1724
The Duke of Antin, overseer of the royal gardens, extended the avenue to the heights of Chaillot, the present site of the Arc de Triomphe *(see pp24–5)*.

5 1774
Architect Jacques-Germain Soufflot lowered the hill of the Champs-Elysées by 5 m (16 ft) to reduce the steep gradient, therefore making an easier and safer passage for residents' horses and carriages.

6 26 August 1944
Parisians celebrated the liberation of the city from the German Nazi Occupation of World War II with triumphant processions and festivities.

7 30 May 1968
The infamous student demonstrations of May 1968, when student protests against state authority spilled over into riots and massive gatherings. De Gaulle and his supporters held a huge counter-demonstration here, marking a turning point in the uprising.

8 12 November 1970
The death of President Charles de Gaulle was an immense event in France, as he had been the single most dominant French political figure for 30 years. He was honoured by a silent march along the Champs-Elysées.

9 14 July 1989
The parade on Bastille Day marking the bicentennial of the Revolution, was a dazzling display of folk culture and avant-garde theatre. It was a distinct change from the usual military events, and was organized by Mitterand's Culture Minister, Jack Lang.

10 12 July 1998
Huge, ecstatic crowds packed the Champs-Elysées to celebrate France's football team winning the World Cup. People came from all over Paris to join in the festivities that captured the nation's imagination.

Left **Christian Dior bag** Centre **Chanel** Right **Boutique Prada**

TOP 10 Designer Shops

1 Christian Dior
The grey and white decor, with silk bows on chairs, makes a chic backdrop for fashions from lingerie to evening wear. *30 ave Montaigne, 75008 • Map C3*

2 Chanel
Chanel classics, from the braided tweed jackets to two-toned shoes as well as Lagerfeld's more daring designs, are displayed in this branch of the main rue Cambon store. *51 ave Montaigne, 75008 • Map C3*

3 Givenchy
This fashion house has been synonymous with Parisian style since the 1930s. Shop for women's and men's ready-to-wear outfits here. *28 rue Faubourg St-Honoré 75008 • Map C3 • 01 44 31 50 00*

4 Balenciaga
This world-famous label is known for its modern creations, which are now designed by Alexander Wang. *10 ave George V, 75008 • Map C3 • 01 47 20 21 11*

5 Boutique Prada
A stylish boutique offering clothes and accessories from the latest collection. *10 ave Montaigne, 75008 • Map C3*

6 Joseph
Renovated by the leading architect Raed Abilama, this shop stocks the Joseph brand and a selection of other designer labels. *14 ave Montaigne, 75008 • Map C3*

7 Jil Sander
A minimal and modern store, just like the clothes it sells. Sander's trouser suits, cashmere dresses and overcoats in neutral colours are displayed on two floors. *56 ave Montaigne, 75008 • Map C3*

8 Chloé
Simple, classy, ready-to-wear designer womens' clothes and accessories are sold in this minimalist temple of feminine chic. *44 ave Montaigne, 75008 • Map C3*

9 Eres
A range of luxury swimwear and lingerie in subtle colours and with a certain Parisian sensuality, are beautifully displayed in this elegant boutique. *40 ave Montaigne, 75008 • Map C3 • 01 47 23 07 26*

10 Barbara Bui
High-end Parisian fashion designer Barbara Bui has been creating elegant womenswear since the 1980s. Lovely neutral colours and luxury fabrics are available here. *50 ave Montaigne, 75008 • Map C3 • 01 42 25 05 25*

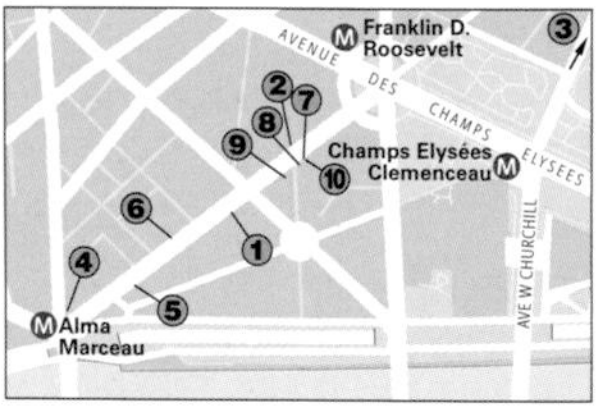

For more on shopping in Paris **See p169**

Price Categories		
For a three-course meal for one with half a bottle of wine (or equivalent meal), taxes and extra charges	€	under €30
	€€	€30–€40
	€€€	€40–€50
	€€€€	€50–€60
	€€€€€	over €60

Above **Plaza Athénée**

TOP 10 Places to Eat

1 Alain Ducasse au Plaza Athénée

Superchef Alain Ducasse's flagship restaurant. Langoustines with caviar is just one mouthwatering bite. *Hôtel Plaza Athénée, 25 ave Montaigne, 75008 • Map C3 • 01 53 67 65 00 • Closed Mon–Wed L, Sat, Sun, Aug, some of Dec • €€€€€*

2 Le Mini Palais

A modern French restaurant with a beautiful terrace. Try the duck fillet and foie gras burger, with truffle sauce. *Grand Palais, ave Winston Churchill, 75008 • Map D3 • 01 42 56 42 42 • €€€€€*

3 Le Café Artcurial

Good soups and sandwiches, served in a grand auction house. *7 rond-point des Champs-Elysées, 75008 • Map C3 • 01 53 75 15 22 • €*

4 Epicure

At the elegant Hotel Le Bristol, diners can choose from a multi-Michelin-starred menu. *112 rue Faubourg St-Honoré, 75008 • Map D2 • 01 53 43 43 40 • €€€€€*

5 Taillevent

One of the city's best dining experiences. The menu changes often, relying on fresh, seasonal ingredients *(see p64)*. *15 rue Lamennais, 75008 • Map C3 • 01 44 95 15 01 • Closed Sat, Sun, Aug • €€€€€*

6 Gagnaire

Chef Pierre Gagnaire is legendary for his artistry for blending flavours, such as lamb cutlets with truffles. *6 rue Balzac, 75008 • Map C3 • 01 58 36 12 50 • Closed Sat, Sun, Aug, 1 week Dec–Jan • No disabled access • €€€€€*

7 Tokyo Eat

This trendy restaurant, housed in a contemporary art museum, serves fruity smoothies and fusion food. *Palais de Tokyo, 13 ave du Président-Wilson, 75016 • Map B3 • 01 47 20 00 29 • Closed Tue • €€€*

8 Bread and Roses

A fabulous tea salon and bakery. Great for breakfast or lunch. *25 rue Boissy d'Anglas, 75008 • Map D3 • 01 47 42 40 00 • Closed Sun • €€€*

9 L'Atelier des Chefs

This cooking school offers a range of classes in French, from €15 for a lunchtime session, after which you get to eat the meal you've made. *10 rue de Penthièvre, 75008 • Map D2 • 01 53 30 05 82 • Closed Sun • www.atelierdeschefs.fr*

10 Le Cinq

The George V's *(see p106)* two Michelin-starred restaurant serves French cuisine with a fresh twist. *31 ave George V, 75008 • Map C3 • 01 49 52 70 00 • €€€€€*

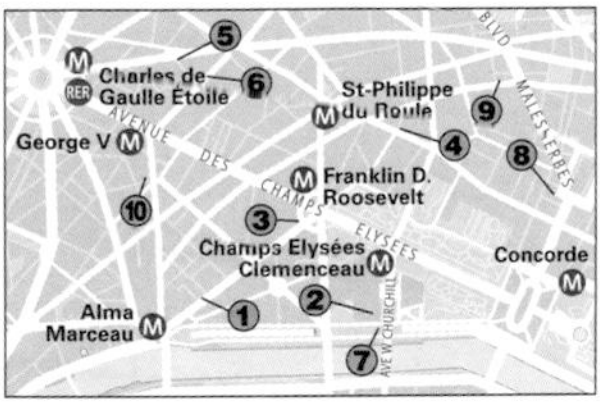

Note: *Unless otherwise stated, all restaurants accept credit cards and serve vegetarian meals*

Left **Dôme church** Centre **Pont Alexandre III** Right **Champs-de-Mars**

Invalides and Eiffel Tower Quarters

TWO OF PARIS'S BEST-KNOWN LANDMARKS, *the golden-domed Hôtel des Invalides and the Eiffel Tower, are found in these quarters. Large parts of the area were created in the 19th century, when there was still room to construct wide avenues and grassy esplanades. To the east of the Invalides are numerous stately mansions now converted into embassies, and the French parliament. Jean Nouvel's musée du quai Branly is a striking feature beside the Seine.*

TOP 10 Sights

1. Hôtel des Invalides
2. Eiffel Tower
3. Les Egouts
4. Musée de l'Armée
5. Musée Rodin
6. musée du quai Branly
7. Rue Cler
8. Ecole Militaire
9. UNESCO
10. Assemblée Nationale

***The Thinker*, Musée Rodin**

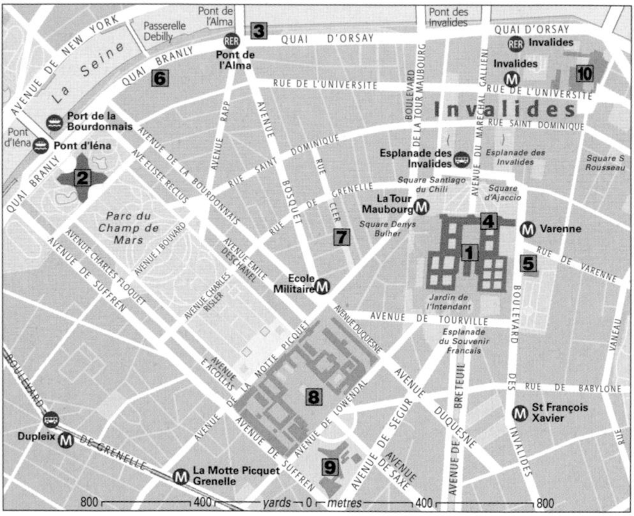

1 Hôtel des Invalides

See pp32–3.

2 Eiffel Tower

See pp16–17.

3 Les Egouts

In a city of glamour and grandeur, the sewers *(égouts)* of Paris are an incongruously popular attraction. They date from the Second Empire (1851–70), when Baron Haussmann was transforming the city *(see p45)*. The sewers, which helped to sanitize and ventilate Paris, are considered one of his finest achievements. Most of the work was done by an engineer named Belgrand. The 2,100-km (1,300-mile) network covers the area from Les Halles to La Villette – if laid end-to-end the sewers would stretch from Paris to Istanbul. An hour-long tour includes a walk through some of the tunnels, where you'll see water pipes and various cables. The Paris Sewers Museum, which is situated in the sewers beneath the Quai d'Orsay on the Left Bank, tells the story of the city's water and sewers, from their beginnings to the present day. There is also an audio-visual show. *Opposite 93, quai d'Orsay, 75007 • Map C4 • Open May–Sep: 11am–5pm Sat–Wed; Oct–Apr: 11am–4pm Sat–Wed • Closed 1 Jan, two weeks mid-Jan, 25 Dec • Admission charge*

General Foch, Musée de l'Armée

4 Musée de l'Armée

The Army Museum contains one of the largest and most comprehensive collections of arms, armour and displays on military history in the world. There are weapons ranging from pre-historic times to the end of World War II, representing countries around the world. Housed in the Hôtel des Invalides, the galleries occupy the old refectories in two wings on either side of the courtyard. The museum's ticket price includes entry to the Musée des Plans-Reliefs, the Historial Charles de Gaulle, the Musée de L'Ordre de la Libération and Napoleon's Tomb *(see p114)*. *Hôtel des Invalides, 75007 • Map C4 • Open 10am–6pm Wed–Mon, (until 9pm Tue & 5pm in winter) • Closed 1 Jan, 1 May, 25 Dec • Admission charge*

5 Musée Rodin

An impressive collection of works by the sculptor and artist Auguste Rodin (1840–1917) is housed in a splendid 18th-century mansion, the Hôtel Biron *(see p116)*, where he spent the last nine years of his life. The rooms display his works roughly chronologically, including his sketches and watercolours. Masterpieces such as *The Kiss* and *Eve* are displayed in the airy rotundas. One room is devoted to works by his talented model and muse, Camille Claudel, and Rodin's personal collection of paintings by Van Gogh, Monet and other masters hang on the walls. The museum's other

Young Napoleon

The most famous alumnus of the Ecole Militaire was Napoleon Bonaparte, who was admitted as a cadet, aged 15, in 1784 and deemed "fit to be an excellent sailor". He graduated as a lieutenant in the artillery, and his passing-out report stated that "he could go far if the circumstances are right". The rest, as they say, is history.

highlight is the gardens, the third-largest private gardens in Paris, where famous works such as *The Thinker*, *Balzac* and *The Gates of Hell* stand among the lime trees and rose bushes. *79 rue de Varenne, 75007 • Map C4 • Open 10am–5:45pm Tue–Sun (until 8:45pm Wed) • Admission charge • www.musee-rodin.fr*

6 musée du quai Branly

The aim of this museum is to showcase the arts of Africa, Asia, Oceania and the Americas. The collection boasts nearly 300,000 artifacts, of which 3,500 are on display, including a fantastic array of African instruments, Gabonese masks, Aztec statues and 17th-century painted animal hides from North America (once the pride of the French royal family). Designed by Jean Nouvel, the building is an exhibit in itself: glass is ingeniously used to allow the surrounding greenery to act as a natural backdrop to the collection. *37 quai Branly, 75007 • Map B4 • Open 11am–7pm Tue–Sun (until 9pm Thu–Sat) • Closed 1 May, 25 Dec • Admission charge*

7 Rue Cler

The cobblestone pedestrianized road that stretches south of rue de Grenelle to avenue de La Motte-Picquet is the most exclusive street market in Paris. Here greengrocers, fishmongers, butchers, and wine merchants sell top-quality produce to the well-heeled residents of the area. Tear yourself away from the mouth-watering cheeses and pastries, however, to feast your eyes on the Art Nouveau buildings at Nos. 33 and 151. *Map C4*

8 Ecole Militaire

At the urging of his mistress Madame Pompadour, Louis XV approved the building of the Royal Military Academy in 1751. Although its purpose was to educate the sons of impoverished officers, a grand edifice was designed by Jacques-Ange

musée du quai Branly

Gabriel, architect of the place de la Concorde *(see p95)* and the Petit Trianon at Versailles, and completed in 1773. The central pavilion with its quadrangular dome and Corinthian pillars is a splendid example of the French Classical style. *1 pl Joffre, 75007 • Map C5 • Open to the public by special permission only (apply in writing)*

9 UNESCO

The headquarters of the United Nations Educational, Scientific and Cultural Organization (UNESCO) were built in 1958 by an international team of architects from France (Zehrfuss), Italy (Nervi) and the United States (Breuer). Their Y-shaped building of concrete and glass may be unremarkable, but inside, the showcase of 20th-century art by renowned international artists is well worth a visit. There is a huge mural by Picasso, ceramics by Joan Miró, and a 2nd-century mosaic from El Djem in Tunisia. Outside is a giant mobile by Alexander Calder and a peaceful Japanese garden. *7 pl de Fontenoy, 75007 • Map C5 • 01 45 68 10 00 • By appointment only • Free*

10 Assemblée Nationale

Built for the daughter of Louis XIV in 1722, the Palais Bourbon has housed the lower house of the French parliament since 1827. The Council of the Five Hundred met here during the Revolution, and it was the headquarters of the German Occupation during World War II. Napoleon added the Classical riverfront façade in 1806 to complement La Madeleine *(see p97)* across the river. *33 quai d'Orsay, 75007 • Map D4 • Open for tours only (identity papers compulsory); advance reservation required, see www.assemblee-nationale.fr • Free*

A Day Around the Invalides Quarter

Morning

Begin the day with an early morning visit to the **Musée Rodin** *(see p111)*. A magnificent collection of Rodin's works are displayed both indoors and outside in the attractive garden. There are also excellent temporary exhibitions. Stop for a coffee at the garden café with its leafy terrace.

Move on to the **Hôtel des Invalides** *(see pp32–3)* next door to see Napoleon's Tomb and the **Musée de l'Armée** *(see p111)*. From here, walk along the esplanade towards the Seine and the **Pont Alexandre III** *(see p104)*, turning left before the river on to rue Saint-Dominique. Stop here for lunch at **Les Cocottes de Constant** *(see p117)*, which serves good, fresh meals.

Afternoon

After lunch, follow the rue de l'Université to the **musée du quai Branly** where you can enjoy the fascinating collections of tribal art and superb modern architecture. The Café Branly, located in the museum's restful gardens, is the perfect place to stop and enjoy a cup of tea.

Make sure you book ahead, by phone or online, for a late-afternoon visit to the **Eiffel Tower** *(see pp16–17)*. The views are spectacular at dusk. Splash out on dinner at the world-famous **Le Jules Verne** restaurant on level 2, or head back to the Branly museum, and its rooftop restaurant **Les Ombres** *(see p117)*.

Left ***The Abdication of Napoleon* (1814), François Pigeot** Right **Suit of armour**

TOP 10 Musée de l'Armée Exhibits

1 Modern Department (1648–1792)

The modern royal army, from its birth under Louis XIV to the training of Revolutionary soldiers, is related through objects such as some fine early rifles.

2 Modern Department (1792–1871)

Displays here cover the beginnings of the Revolution to the Paris Commune, including the personal belongings of Napoleon I.

3 Ancient Armoury Department

The third-largest collection of armoury in the world is on show in the northeast refectory. Assembled over a 40-year period since the 1960s, these items had been lost since the Revolution.

4 17th-Century Murals

In the Ancient Armoury Department, restored 17th-century murals by Joseph Parrocel celebrate Louis XIV's military conquests.

5 The World Wars

Two rooms on the second floor are devoted to World War I and World War II. Documents, uniforms, maps, photographs and other memorabilia bring the conflicts of both wars to life, often to disturbing effect.

6 Banners and Trophies

A small collection of 17th–20th-century military banners is displayed in the east wing.

7 Historial of Charles de Gaulle

This state-of-the-art display on the life of the former wartime president is in the Cour d'Honneur, Orient wing.

8 Musée des Plans Reliefs

On the fourth floor of the east wing is a collection of relief models of French towns showing the development of fortifications from the 17th century onwards.

9 Artillery

Over 800 cannons are displayed inside and in front of the museum.

10 Salle Orientale

This collection of arms and armour reflects the military styles of different nations.

***Verdun* (1917), Felix Vallotton, Two World Wars**

For the Musée de l'Armée **See p111**

Left **View from the Eiffel Tower** Right **Pont Alexandre III and Hôtel des Invalides**

TOP 10 Views

1 Top of the Eiffel Tower
There is nowhere in Paris to match the view from the top of the tower, so hope for good weather. With the cityscape and the sparkling waters of the Seine below, it is the highlight of any visit *(see pp16–17)*. *Map B4*

2 Pont d'Iéna
There is no bad approach to the Eiffel Tower, but the best is from the Trocadéro direction, walking straight to the tower across the Pont d'Iéna. *Map B4*

3 Base of the Eiffel Tower
Everybody wants to race to the top, but don't neglect the view from the ground. Looking directly up at the magnificent structure makes one appreciate the feat of engineering all the more *(see pp16–17)*. *Map B4*

4 Eiffel Tower at Night
To usher in the Millennium the tower was "robed" in lights and since then there have been a variety of lighting displays. For five minutes every hour, from dusk to midnight, the whole edifice twinkles. *Map B4*

5 Saxe-Breteuil Market
This old street market in avenue de Saxe is a little off the usual tourist track, but the view of the Eiffel Tower above the fruit and vegetable stalls is totally Parisian and will especially appeal to photographers. *Map D5 • 7am–2:30pm Thu, 7am–3pm Sat*

6 Pont Alexandre III
Flanked by impressive gilded statues, superb views can be enjoyed from this magnificent bridge *(see p48)*. *Map D4*

7 Musée Rodin Gardens
The golden Dôme church gleams through the trees that line these delightful gardens. *Map D5*

8 Hôtel des Invalides
The majestic gilded dome above Napoleon's tomb dominates the skyline. It is a particularly superb sight when seen from the river on a sunny morning *(see pp32–3)*. *Map D4*

9 Pont de la Concorde
The Egyptian obelisk at the centre of place de la Concorde *(see p95)* is at its most impressive from the bridge. *Map D4*

10 musée du quai Branly
Jean Nouvel's bold, colourful building is best seen from the riverside. Note the striking "Green Wall" at the west end *(see p112)*. *Map B4*

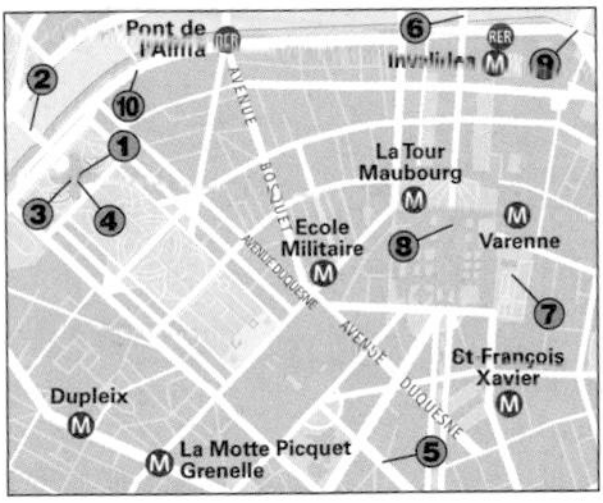

Left **Hôtel de Biron** Right **Hôtel de Villeroy**

Top 10 Mansions

1 Hôtel Biron
Built in 1730, from 1904 this elegant mansion was transformed into state-owned artists' studios. Among its residents was Auguste Rodin (1840–1917). After the sculptor's death the house became the Musée Rodin *(see p111)*.

2 Hôtel de Villeroy
Built in 1724 for Charlotte Desmarnes, an actress, it is now the Ministry of Agriculture.
78–80 rue de Varenne, 75007 • Map D4 • Closed to the public

3 Hôtel Matignon
One of the most beautiful mansions in the area is now the official residence of the French prime minister. *57 rue de Varenne, 75007 • Map D4 • Closed to the public*

4 Hôtel de Boisgelin
Built in 1732 by Jean Sylvain Cartaud, this mansion has housed the Italian Embassy since 1938.
47 rue de Varenne, 75007 • Map D4 • Call 01 49 54 03 00 for appointment

5 Hôtel de Gallifet
This attractive mansion was built between 1776 and 1792 with Classical styling. It is now the Italian Institute. *50 rue de Varenne, 75007 • Map D4 • Galleries open 10am–6pm daily*

6 Hôtel d'Estrées
Three floors of pilasters feature on this 1713 mansion. Formerly the Russian embassy, Czar Nicolas II lived here in 1896. It is now a government building.
79 rue de Grenelle, 75007 • Map B5 • Closed to the public

7 Hôtel d'Avaray
Dating from 1728, this mansion belonged to the Avaray family for nearly 200 years. It became the Dutch Embassy in 1920. *85 rue de Grenelle, 75007 • Map B5 • Closed to the public*

8 Hôtel de Brienne
This mansion houses the Ministry of Defence. Napoleon's mother lived here from 1806–17.
14–16 rue St Dominique, 75007 • Map D4 • Closed to the public

9 Hôtel de Noirmoutiers
Built in 1724, this was once the army staff headquarters. It now houses ministerial offices.
138–140 rue de Grenelle, 75007 • Map B5 • Closed to the public

10 Hôtel de Monaco de Sagan
Now the Polish Embassy, this 1784 mansion served as the British Embassy until 1825. *57 rue St-Dominique, 75007 • Map D4 • Closed to the public*

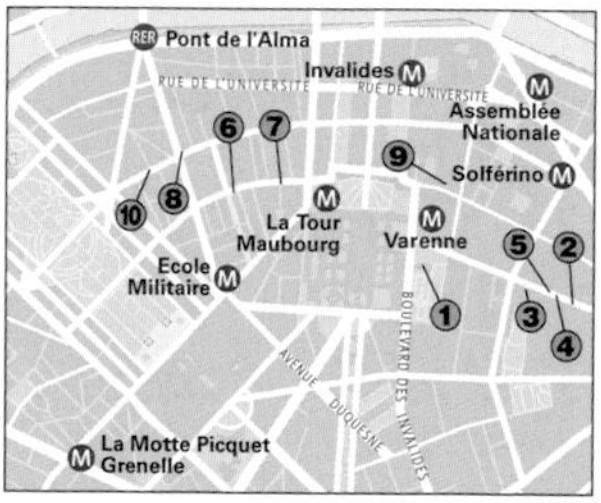

For more historic buildings in Paris **See pp42–3**

Price Categories

For a three-course meal for one with half a bottle of wine (or equivalent meal), taxes and extra charges	€	under €30
	€€	€30–€40
	€€€	€40–€50
	€€€€	€50–€60
	€€€€€	over €60

Above **Le Jules Verne**

TOP 10 Places to Eat

1 Le Jules Verne
Book a window table for the view and then sit back and enjoy the fine food from Alain Ducasse. A reservation is required for dinner. *2nd Level, Eiffel Tower, Champ-de-Mars, 75007 • Map B4 • 01 45 55 61 44 • No disabled access • €€€€€*

2 Le Casse-Noix
A charming restaurant serving desserts such as *île flottante* (meringue floating on vanilla custard). *56 rue de la Fédération, 75015 • Map B5 • 01 45 66 09 01 • Closed Sat & Sun • No disabled access • €€€*

3 L'Arpège
Among the best restaurants in the city. Chef Alain Passard produces exquisite food. *84 rue de Varenne, 75007 • Map D4 • 01 47 05 09 06 • Closed Sat, Sun • No disabled access • €€€€€*

4 Le Violin d'Ingres
Chef Stéphane Schmidt is another shining star. The seasonal menu offers classic French cuisine with a modern twist. *135 rue Saint-Dominique, 75007 • Map C4 • 01 45 55 15 05 • €€€€€*

5 Café Constant
Chef Christian Constant serves modern French fare that changes seasonally. *139 rue Saint-Dominique, 75007 • Map C4 • 01 47 53 73 34 • Closed Mon • No disabled access • €€*

6 Thoumieux
Inventive cuisine by former Crillon chef Jean-François Piège, in an historical setting. *79 rue Saint-Dominique, 75007 • Map C4 • 01 47 05 49 75 • €€€€*

7 L'Ami Jean
Inventive dishes such as marinated scallops with ewe's milk cheese. *27 rue Malar, 75007 • Map C4 • 01 47 05 86 89 • Closed Sun, Mon • No disabled access • €€€€*

8 Les Cocottes de Constant
Star chef Christian Constant's French take on a diner, with bar seating and delicious food. *135 rue Saint-Dominique, 75007 • Map C4 • 01 45 50 10 31 • €€*

9 Les Ombres
Fine food from rising star Sebastien Tasset. Ask for a table with a view of the famous Eiffel Tower. *27 quai Branly, 75007 • Map B4 • 01 47 53 68 00 • €€€€€*

10 La Fontaine de Mars
Sumptuous classic dishes such as foie gras are served at this archetypal French restaurant. *129 rue Saint-Dominique, 75007 • Map C4 • 01 47 05 46 44 • €€€€€*

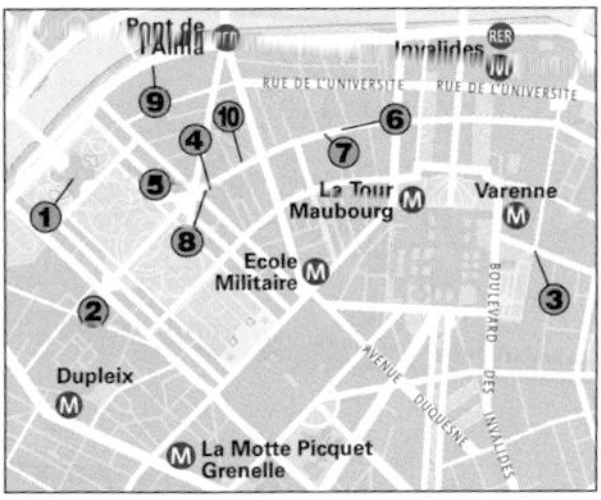

Note: Unless otherwise stated, all restaurants accept credit cards and serve vegetarian meals

Left **Musée d'Orsay** Centre **Panthéon** Right **St-Sulpice**

St-Germain, Latin and Luxembourg Quarters

THIS AREA OF THE LEFT BANK IS *possibly the most stimulating in Paris. St-Germain-des-Prés, centred around the city's oldest church, is a synonym for Paris's café society, made famous by the writers and intellectuals who held court here in the first half of the 20th century. Although it's more touristy today, a stroll around the back streets reveals lovely old houses plastered with plaques noting famous residents. The Latin Quarter takes its name from the Latin spoken by students of the Sorbonne until the Revolution. The scholastic centre of Paris for more than 700 years, it continues to buzz with student bookshops, cafés and jazz clubs. It was also the site of a Roman settlement and remains from that era can be seen in the Musée du Moyen-Age. The area's western boundary is the bustling boulevard Saint-Michel and to the south is the tranquil greenery of the Luxembourg Quarter.*

Jardin du Luxembourg

Top 10 Sights

1. Musée d'Orsay
2. Panthéon
3. Jardin du Luxembourg
4. St-Sulpice
5. La Sorbonne
6. Musée du Moyen Age
7. Boulevard St-Germain
8. Boulevard St-Michel
9. Quai de la Tournelle
10. Musée Maillol

1 Musée d'Orsay

See pp12–15.

2 Panthéon

See pp28–9.

3 Jardin du Luxembourg

This 25-ha (60-acre) park is a swathe of green paradise on the very urban Left Bank. The formal gardens are set around the Palais du Luxembourg *(see p43)*, with broad terraces circling the central octagonal pool. A highlight of the garden is the beautiful Medici Fountain *(see p39)*. Many of the garden's statues were erected during the 19th century, among them the monument to the painter Eugène Delacroix and the statue of Ste Geneviève, patron saint of Paris. There is also a children's playground, open-air café, a bandstand, tennis courts, a puppet theatre and even a bee-keeping school *(see p38)*. ✎ *Map L6*

4 St-Sulpice

Begun in 1646, this enormous church unsurprisingly took 134 years to build. Its Classical façade by the Florentine architect Giovanni Servandoni features a two-tiered colonnade and two incongruously matched towers. Notice the two holy water fonts by the front door, made from huge shells given to François I by the Venetian Republic. *Jacob*

Medici Fountain, Jardin du Luxembourg

Clock, La Sorbonne

Wrestling with the Angel and other splendid murals by Delacroix (1798–1863) are in the chapel to the right of the main door. ✎ *2 rue Palatine, pl St-Sulpice, 75006 • Map L5 • Open 7:30am–7:30pm daily • Free*

5 La Sorbonne

Paris's world-famous university *(see p43)* was founded in 1253 and was originally intended as a theology college for poor students. It soon became the country's main centre for theological studies. It was named after Robert de Sorbon, confessor to Louis IX. Philosophers Thomas Aquinas (c.1226–74) and Roger Bacon (1214–92) taught here; Italian poet Dante (1265–1321), St Ignatius Loyola (1491–1556), the founder of the Jesuits, and church reformer John Calvin (1509–64) are among its list of alumni. Its tradition for conservatism led to its closure during the Revolution (it was reopened by Napoleon in 1806) and to the student riots of 1968 *(see p45)*. ✎ *47 rue des Ecoles, 75005 • Map M5 • 01 40 46 21 11 • Group tours only, Mon–Fri and one Sat each month (advance booking) • Admission charge*

Jazz on the Left Bank

Jazz has been played in Paris, especially on the Left Bank, since the 1920s. Numbers of black musicians moved here from the US as they found France less racially prejudiced, and Paris became a second home for many jazz musicians such as Sidney Bechet *(see p63)*. The city has never lost its love of jazz, nor jazz its love for the city.

6 Musée National du Moyen Age

This impressive mansion was built by the abbots of Cluny at the end of the 15th century and now houses a magnificent collection of art, from Gallo-Roman antiquity to the 15th century. It adjoins the ruins of 2nd-century Roman baths *(thermes)* with their huge vaulted *frigidarium* (cold bath). Nearby are the 21 carved stone heads of the kings of Judea from Notre-Dame, decapitated during the Revolution. The museum's highlight is the exquisite *Lady and the Unicorn* tapestry series, representing the five senses *(see p34)*. *6 pl Paul-Painlevé, 75005 • Map N5 • Open 9:15am–5:45pm Wed–Mon • Closed 1 Jan, 1 May, 25 Dec • Admission charge • www.musee-moyenage.fr*

7 Boulevard St-Germain

This famous Left Bank boulevard runs for more than 3 km (2 miles) anchored by the bridges of the Seine at either end. At its heart is the church of St-Germain-des-Prés, established in 542, although the present church dates from the 11th century. Beyond the famous cafés, Flore and Les Deux Magots *(see p125)*, the boulevard runs west past art galleries, bookshops and designer boutiques to the Pont de la Concorde. To the east, it cuts across the Latin Quarter through the pleasant street market in the place Maubert, to join the Pont de Sully which connects to the Ile St-Louis *(see p69)*. *Map J3*

8 Boulevard St-Michel

The main drag of the Latin Quarter was created in the late 1860s as part of Baron Haussmann's city-wide makeover *(see p45)*, and named after a chapel that once stood near its northern end. It's now lined with a lively mix of cafés, clothes shops and cheap restaurants. Branching off to the east are rues de la Harpe and de la Huchette, which date back to medieval times. The

Boulevard St-Germain

Quai de la Tournelle

latter is an enclave of the city's Greek community, with many *souvlaki* stands and Greek restaurants. In the place St-Michel is a huge bronze fountain that depicts St Michael killing a dragon. ⓢ *Map M4*

9 Quai de la Tournelle

From this riverbank, just before the Pont de l'Archevêché there are lovely views across to Notre-Dame. The main attraction of this and the adjacent Quai de Montebello, however, are the dark-green stalls of the *bouquinistes* *(see p122)*. The Pont de la Tournelle also offers splendid views up and down the Seine. ⓢ *Map P5*

10 Musée Maillol

Dina Vierny, who modelled for the artist Aristide Maillol (1861–1944) from the ages of 15 to 25, went on to set up this foundation dedicated largely to his works. Set in an 18th-century mansion, it features sculpture, paintings, drawings, engravings and terracotta works. The museum puts on two temporary exhibitions per year, and there are also drawings by masters of French Naive art, including Degas, Matisse and Picasso. ⓢ *59–61 rue de Grenelle, 75007 • Map J4 • Open 10:30am–7pm daily (to 9:30pm Fri) • Closed 1 Jan, 25 Dec • Admission charge • www.museemaillol.com*

A Day on the Left Bank

Morning

This area is as much about atmosphere as sightseeing, so take time to soak up some of that Left Bank feeling. Begin on the **quai de la Tournelle**, strolling by the booksellers here and on the adjacent quai de Montebello, which runs parallel to rue de la Bûcherie, home to **Shakespeare and Company** *(see p122)*.

From here head south down any street away from the river to the busy **boulevard St-Germain**. Turn right for two famous cafés, the **Flore** and **Les Deux Magots**, and stop for a break *(see p125)* among the locals talking the morning away.

Cut your way south to the rue de Grenelle and the **Musée Maillol**, a delightful lesser-known museum. Then enjoy lunch at **L'Épi Dupin** *(see p127)*, a popular bistro, which attracts a mix of locals and travellers.

Afternoon

The later you reach the **Musée d'Orsay** *(see pp12–15)* the less crowded it will be. Spend an hour or two exploring the collection. The most popular displays are the Impressionists on the upper level.

After the museum visit, enjoy tea and a cake at **Christian Constant** *(see p123)*, one of the best chocolate-makers in Paris. Or if it's dinner time, stay at the Musée d'Orsay and indulge in their set menu (Thu only).

Left **Bouquinistes** Right **San Francisco Book Co.**

Top 10 Booksellers

1 Shakespeare and Company
Bibliophiles spend hours in the rambling rooms of Paris's renowned English-language bookshop. There are regular readings in English and French. *37 rue de la Bûcherie, 75005 • Map N5*

2 Bouquinistes
The green stalls of the booksellers *(bouquinistes)* on the quays of the Left Bank are a Parisian landmark. Pore over the posters, old postcards, magazines, hardbacks, paperbacks, comics and sheet music. *Map N5*

3 Musée d'Orsay Bookshop
As well as its wonderful collections, the museum has a bewilderingly large and busy art bookshop *(see pp12–15)*.

4 La Hune
Renowned literary hangout. Good collections on art, photography and literature. *170 boulevard St-Germain, 75006 • Map K4*

5 Gibert Jeune
A cluster of bookshops that sell everything from travel guides and French literature to cookery books and children's stories. *3 and 5 place St-Michel, 27 quai St-Michel, 30–34 blvd St-Michel, 75006*

6 Album
Specialist in comic books, which are big business in France, from Tintin to erotica. *8 rue Dante, 75005 • Map L4*

7 Librairie Présence Africaine
Specialist on books on Africa, as the name suggests. Good information point, too, if you want to eat African food or hear African music. *25 bis rue des Écoles, 75005 • Map P6 • Closed Aug*

8 San Francisco Book Co.
This hodge-podge of all genres carries exclusively used English books at reasonable prices. *17 rue Monsieur le Price, 75006 • Map M5*

9 Librairie Maeght
Specialist in books on art adjoining the Maeght art gallery, with a good collection of posters, postcards and other items. *42 rue du Bac, 75007 • Map N5*

10 Abbey Bookshop
This quirky, Canadian-owned shop offers books in French and English and serves up coffee with maple syrup. *29 rue de la Parcheminerie Paris, 75005 • Map N5*

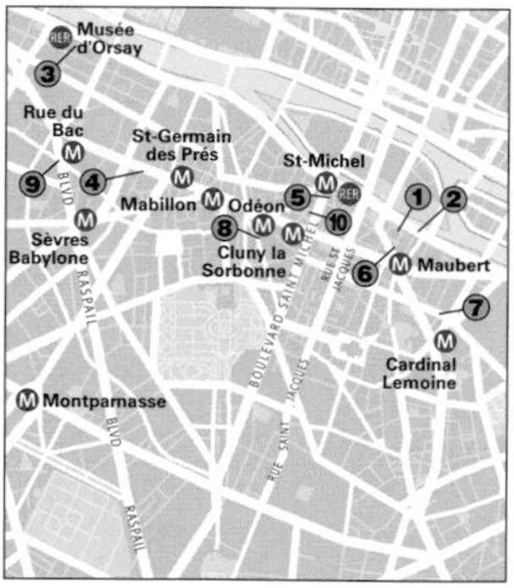

For more on shopping in Paris **See p169**

Left **Paris chocolatier** Right **Patisserie**

TOP 10 Specialist Food Shops

1 Patrick Roger
One of a new generation of *chocolatiers*, Patrick Roger already has legions of fans thanks to his lifelike sculptures and ganache-filled chocolates. *108 boulevard St Germain, 75006 • Map F5 • Closed Sun*

2 Christian Constant
Famous French chef Christian Constant's chocolate shop offers ganache, truffles and filled chocolates of all different flavours. *37 rue d'Assas, 75006 • Map E5 • 01 53 63 15 15*

3 Jean-Paul Hévin
Another very distiguished *chocolatier*. Elegant, minimalist presentation and superb flavour combinations. *3 rue Vavin, 75006 • Map E6 • Closed Sun, Mon, Aug*

4 Poilâne
Founded in the 1930s, this tiny bakery produces rustic, naturally leavened loaves in a wood-fired oven. *8 rue du Cherche-Midi, 75006 • Map E5 • Closed Sun*

5 La Dernière Goutte
The owners of this English-speaking wine shop, which specializes in bottles from small producers, also run the nearby wine bar Fish. *6 rue Bourbon Le Château, 75006 • Map E5*

6 Debauve & Gallais
This shop dates from 1800 when chocolate was sold for medicinal purposes. *30 rue des Sts-Pères, 75007 • Map K4 • Closed Sun*

7 Pierre Hermé Paris
Here are some of the city's very finest cakes and pastries, including innovative flavoured macarons. *72 rue Bonaparte, 75006 • Map L5*

8 Ryst Dupeyron
Wine shop specializing in fine Bordeaux, rare spirits and champagne. *79 rue du Bac, 75007 • Map N5 • Closed Sun, Mon am*

9 Sadaharu Aoki
Aoki cleverly incorporates Japanese flavours such as yuzu, green tea and black sesame into intoxicating classic French pastries that taste as good as they look. *35 rue de Vaugirard 75006 • Map E5 • Closed Mon*

10 Gérard Mulot
Here you'll find some of the finest pastries in Paris, along with some truly miraculous macarons. *76 rue de Seine, 75006 • Map L4 • Closed Wed*

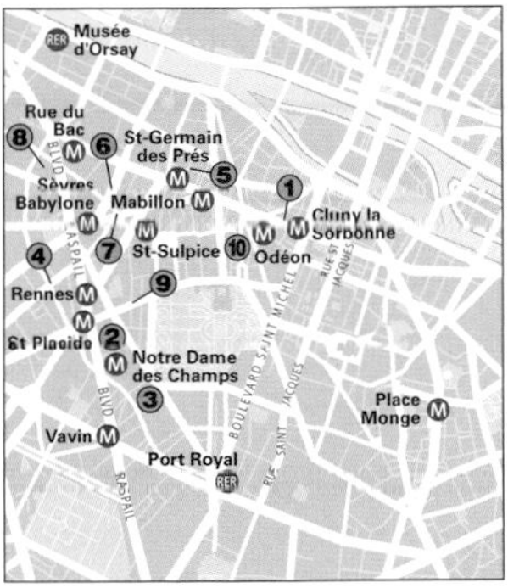

Left **Le 10 Bar** Right **Pub Saint Germain**

Top 10 Late-Night Bars

1 Le 10 Bar
This incredibly lively sangria bar has been a neighbourhood institution since 1955. Happy hour 6–8pm. *10 rue de l'Odéon, 75006 • Map L5*

2 Café de la Mairie
An old-fashioned Parisian café, which offers great views of St-Sulpice Church from its pavement terrace. Open until 2am daily except Sunday. *8 pl St-Sulpice, 75006 • Map K5*

3 Prescription Cocktail Club
The expertly-mixed drinks are the main attraction at this chic and hip cocktail bar. *23 rue Mazarine, 75006 • Map L4*

4 Pub Saint Germain
Sip drinks until dawn at this pub *à la français*. It has tables and lounge areas on three floors. *17 rue Ancienne Comédie, 75006 • Map L4*

5 L'Assignat
Pleasant, bright family-run L'Assignat is full of regulars propping up the bar with a beer or a glass of wine. *7 rue Guénégaud, 75006 • Map L3 • Closed Sun*

6 Mezzanine
The lounge bar of the legendary Alcazar *(see p127)* is the place to be seen. Drinks are not expensive given the buzz and the wonderful location. *Alcazar, 62 rue Mazarine, 75006 • Map L3*

7 Curio Parlor
Cosy private alcoves and low lighting make this the perfect place to relax. *16 rue des Bernardins, 75005 • Map P5 • Closed Sun & Mon*

8 Le Bob Cool
Close to St-Michel, this shabby-chic bar plays host to thirsty local nighthawks as well as trendier partygoers on late-night cocktails. *15 rue des Grands Augustins, 75006 • Map M4 • Closed Sun*

9 Coolin
An Irish bar that appeals to drinkers, talkers and listeners of all ages, who like their draught Guinness with a blarney chaser. *15 rue Clément, 75006 • Map L4*

10 Playtime Cocktails
Inside the Artus Hotel, this cosy bar serves up an array of fun cocktails, or you could have the bartender personally design your own. *34 rue de Buci, 75006 • Map L4*

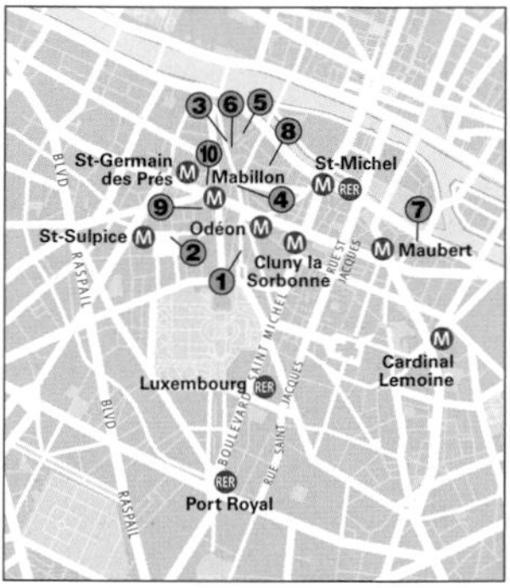

For more cafés and bars in Paris **See pp52–3**

Left **Café de Flore** Right **Shakespeare and Company**

TOP 10 Literary Haunts

1 La Palette

This café has been patronized by the likes of Henry Miller, Apollinaire and Jacques Prévert. *43 rue de Seine, 75006 • Map L4 • Open 8am–2am daily*

2 Les Deux Magots

This was home to the literary and artistic élite of Paris as well as a regular haunt of Surrealists such as François Mauriac *(see p52)*. *6 pl St-Germain-des-Prés, 75006 • Map K4 • Open 7:30am–1am daily*

3 Café de Flore

Guillaume Apollinaire founded his literary magazine, *Les Soirées de Paris*, here in 1913 *(see p52)*. *172 blvd St-Germain, 75006 • Map K4 • Open 7am–2am daily*

4 Le Procope

The oldest café in Paris, this was a meeting place for writers such as Voltaire, Balzac and Zola. *13 rue de l' Ancienne-Comédie, 75006 • Map L4 • Open 11:30am–midnight Sun–Wed, 11:30am–1am Thu–Sat)*

5 Brasserie Lipp

Ernest Hemingway pays homage to this café in *A Moveable Feast*. André Gide was also a customer. *151 blvd St-Germain, 75006 • Map L4 • Open 9am–1am daily*

6 Hotel Pont Royal

Henry Miller drank here at the time of writing his *Tropic of Capricorn* and *Tropic of Cancer*. *5–7 rue de Montalembert, 75007 • Map J3 • Open 7am–midnight daily*

7 Shakespeare and Company

This renowned bookshop was once described by novelist Henry Miller as a "wonderland of books" *(see p122)*.

8 Le Sélect

F. Scott Fitzgerald and Truman Capote were among many American writers who drank in this café. *99 blvd du Montparnasse, 75006 • Map E6 • Open 7am–2am Mon–Fri (to 3am Sat & Sun)*

9 La Coupole

Opened in 1927, this former coal depot was transformed by artists into a lavish Art Deco brasserie. It attracted such luminaries as Louis Aragon and Françoise Sagan *(see p157)*.

10 Le Petit St-Benoît

Camus, de Beauvoir and James Joyce once took their daily coffee here. *4 rue St Benoît, 75006 • Map K3 • Open noon–2:30pm, 7–10:30pm Tue–Sat*

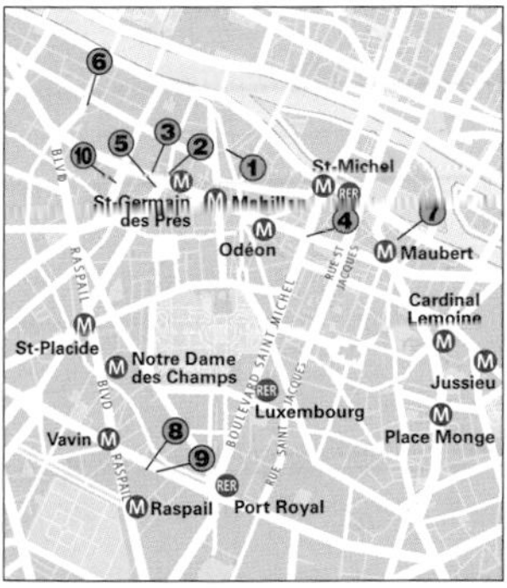

For more on writers in Paris **See p47**

Left **Rue de Buci market** Right **Parisian patisserie**

Top 10 Picnic Providers

1 Rue de Buci Market
Head for this chic daily market where you'll find the very best regional produce, wine and pastries *(see p54)*. *Map L4*

2 Poilâne
The best bread, made from the recipe of the late king of bread-makers, Lionel Poilâne.
8 rue du Cherche-Midi, 75006 • Map J5

3 Maubert Market
A small market specializing in organic produce every Tuesday, Thursday and Saturday morning. A good place to pick up olives, cheese, tomatoes and fruit.
Pl Maubert, 75006 • Map N5

4 Fromagerie Androuet
One of the oldest cheese shops in Paris, where the cheese is aged onsite. *134 rue Mouffetard, 75005 • Map D5 • Closed Sun pm & Mon*

5 Naturalia
For a fully organic picnic, look no further: excellent breads, wines, cheeses, hams, fruits, desserts and much more. *36 rue Monge, 75005 • Map N6 • Closed Sun*

6 Marché Raspail
This food market is held on Tuesday, Friday and Sunday (when it is all organic) mornings. Superb produce but pricey. *Blvd Raspail, 75006 • Map J4*

7 Bon
Wonderful patisserie and chocolatier, with a good line in small fruit tarts, and chocolates in the shape of the Eiffel Tower.
159 rue St-Jacques, 75005 • Map N5 • Closed Mon

8 La Grande Epicerie de Paris
Hunt for treasures such as Breton seaweed butter and *coucou de Rennes* at the food hall in Le Bon Marché *(see p55)*.
Le Bon Marché, 38 rue de Sèvres, 75007 • Map D5

9 Le Pirée
Delicious, freshly prepared Greek and Armenian specialities, such as stuffed vegetables and honey-soaked cakes, are sold here.
47 blvd St-Germain, 75005 • Map N5

10 Kayser
If you don't want to make up your own picnic then try a ready-made sandwich from the bakery. Mouthwatering combinations include goat's cheese with pear.
14 rue Monge, 75005 • Map P6

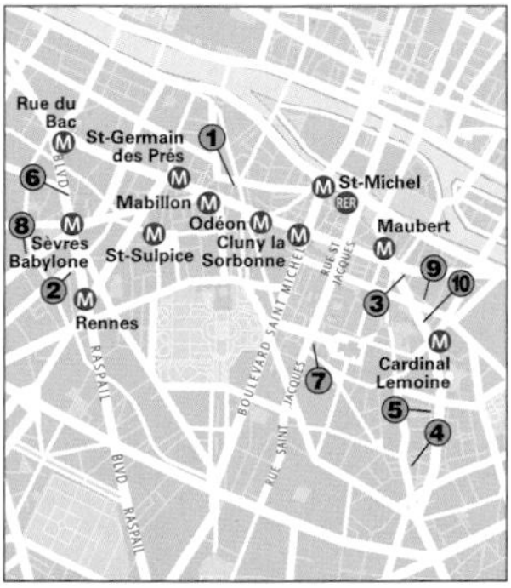

For more shops and markets in Paris **See pp54–5**

Price Categories

For a three-course	€	under €30
meal for one with half	€€	€30–€40
a bottle of wine (or	€€€	€40–€50
equivalent meal), taxes	€€€€	€50–€60
and extra charges	€€€€€	over €60

Above **Alcazar**

TOP 10 Places to Eat

1 L'Épi Dupin
The dishes, such as scallop risotto, are sublime but be sure to reserve a table in advance. *11 rue Dupin, 75006 • Map J5 • 01 42 22 64 56 • Closed Sat, Sun, Mon L, Aug • €€€*

2 La Tour d'Argent
This historic restaurant with fine views of Notre-Dame serves duckling as the speciality. *15 quai de la Tournelle, 75005 • Map P5 • 01 43 54 23 31 • Closed Sun, Mon, Aug • €€€€€*

3 Les Bouquinistes
Creative cooking is served at this bistro, owned by Guy Savoy, on the banks of the Seine. *53 quai des Grands-Augustins, 75006 • Map M4 • 01 43 25 45 94 • Closed Sat L, Sun, Aug • No disabled access • €€€€*

4 Alcazar
A stylish brasserie with a mix of French, Asian and British food. *62 rue Mazarine, 75006 • Map L3 • 01 53 10 19 99 • €€€€*

5 Lapérouse
Classic French cuisine served in a setting unchanged since 1766. *51 quai des Grands-Augustins, 75006 • Map M4 • 01 43 26 68 04 • Closed Sat L, Sun, Aug • €€€€€*

6 L'Atelier Maître Albert
Spit-roasted meats and signature dishes by top chef Guy Savoy. Aim for a table in front of the giant fireplace. *1 rue Maître Albert, 75005 • Map F5 • 01 56 81 30 01 • Closed Sat L, Sun L over Christmas • €€€€*

7 La Bastide Odéon
A taste of Provence in an elegant setting. Try the risotto with scallops. *7 rue Corneille, 75006 • Map L5 • 01 43 26 03 65 • No disabled access • €€€*

8 Le Pré Verre
Dine on classic French cooking with Asian flourishes. *8 rue Thénard, 75005 • Map F5 • 01 43 54 59 47 • Closed Sun, Mon, Aug, 25 Dec–1 Jan • €€*

9 Les Papilles
Pick your wine straight off the shelves to accompany the stunning menu *(see p64)*. *30 rue Gay Lussac, 75005 • Map F6 • 01 43 25 20 79 • Closed Sun, Mon, Aug, 25 Dec–1 Jan • No disabled access • €€€*

10 Au Moulin à Vent
One of the best bistros in Paris, with frogs' legs on the menu. *20 rue des Fossés-St-Bernard, 75005 • Map P6 • 01 43 54 99 37 • Closed Sat L, Sun, Mon, Aug • €€€€*

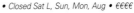

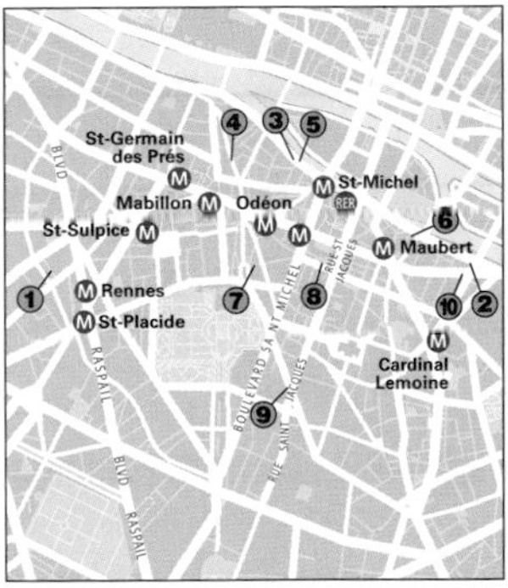

Note: *Unless otherwise stated, all restaurants accept credit cards and serve vegetarian meals*

Left **Jardin des Plantes** Centre **Natural History Museum** Right **Institut du Monde Arabe**

Jardin des Plantes Quarter

TRADITIONALLY ONE OF THE MOST PEACEFUL areas of Paris, the medicinal herb gardens which give the quarter its name were established here in 1626. It retained a rural atmosphere until the 19th century, when the city's population expanded and the surrounding streets were built up. Near the gardens is the Arènes de Lutèce, a well-preserved Roman amphitheatre. The rue Mouffetard, winding down the hill from the bustling place de la Contrescarpe, dates from medieval times and has one of the best markets in the city. The area is also home to a sizeable Muslim community, focused on the Institut du Monde Arabe cultural centre and the Paris Mosque. In contrast to the striking Islamic architecture are the grey slab 1960s buildings of Paris University's Jussieu Campus.

Riding a stone hippopotamus at the Ménagerie

Top 10 Sights

1. Jardin des Plantes
2. Muséum National d'Histoire Naturelle
3. Ménagerie
4. Institut du Monde Arabe
5. Mosquée de Paris
6. Rue Mouffetard
7. Arènes de Lutèce
8. Place de la Contrescarpe
9. St-Médard
10. Manufacture des Gobelins

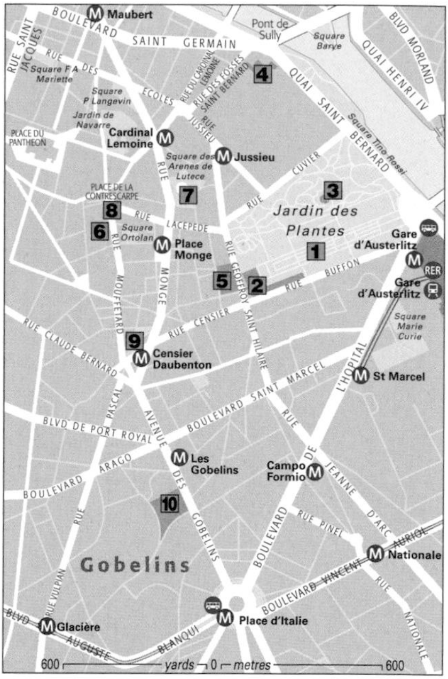

1 Jardin des Plantes

The 17th-century royal medicinal herb garden was planted by Jean Hérouard and Guy de la Brosse, physicians to Louis XIII. Opened to the public in 1640, it flourished under the curatorship of Comte de Buffon. It contains some 6,500 species, and 10,000 plants. There is also a Cedar of Lebanon that was planted in 1734, a hillside maze, and Alpine and rose gardens *(see p132)*. *57 rue Cuvier, 75005 • Map G6 • 01 40 79 30 00 • Open 8am–5:30pm daily, 7:30am–8pm summer*

2 Muséum National d'Histoire Naturelle

Separate pavilions in the Jardin des Plantes house exhibits on anatomy, fossils, geology, mineralogy and insects. The Grande Galerie de l'Evolution *(see p60)* is a magnificent collection of stuffed African mammals, a giant whale skeleton and an endangered species exhibit *(see p34)*. *57 rue Cuvier, 75005 • Map G6 • Pavilions: open 10am–5pm Wed–Mon; Evolution Gallery: open 10am–6pm Wed–Mon • Closed 1 May • Admission charge • www.mnhn.fr*

3 Ménagerie

The country's oldest public zoo was founded during the Revolution to house the surviving animals from the royal menagerie at Versailles. Other animals were donated from circuses and abroad, but during the Siege of Paris in 1870–71 *(see p45)* the unfortunate creatures were eaten by hungry citizens. A favourite with children *(see p60)*, the zoo has since been restocked. *Jardin des Plantes, 75005 • Map G6 • Open 9am–5pm daily • Admission charge*

Minaret, Mosquée de Paris

4 Institut du Monde Arabe

This institute was founded in 1980 to promote cultural relations between France and the Arab world. The stunning building (1987) designed by architect Jean Nouvel *(see musée du quai Branly p112)* features a southern wall of 240 photo-sensitive metal screens that open and close like camera apertures to regulate light entering the building. The design is based on the latticed wooden screens of Islamic architecture. Inside is a museum featuring Islamic artworks, from 9th-century ceramics to contemporary art, and a tea salon and restaurant. *1 rue des Fossés-St-Bernard, pl Mohammed V, 75005 • Map G5 • 01 40 51 38 38 • Open 10am–6pm Tue–Sun (until 9:30pm Fri & 7pm Sun) • Admission charge • www.imarabe.org*

5 Mosquée de Paris

Built in 1922–6, the mosque complex is the spiritual centre for Parisian Muslims *(see p41)*. The beautiful Hispano-Moorish decoration, particularly the grand patio, was inspired by the Alhambra in Spain. The minaret soars nearly 33 m (100 ft). There is also an Islamic school, tea room and Turkish baths, open to men and women on separate days. *2 bis pl du Puits-de-l'Ermité, 75005 • Map G6 • Tours: 9am–noon, 2–6pm Sat–Thu; closed Islamic hols • Admission charge*

French North Africa

France has always had close connections with North Africa, though not always harmonious. Its annexation of Algeria in 1834 led to the long and bloody Algerian War of Liberation (1954–62). Relations with Tunisia, which it governed from 1883 to 1956, and Morocco, also granted independence in 1956, were better. Many North Africans now live in Paris.

6 Rue Mouffetard

Although the rue Mouffetard is famous today for its lively street market held every Tuesday to Sunday *(see p55)*, it has an equally colourful past. In Roman times this was the main road from Paris to Rome. Some say its name comes from the French word *mouffette* (skunk), as a reference to the odorous River Bièvre (now covered over) here waste was dumped by tanners and weavers from the nearby Gobelins tapestry factory. Though no longer poor or Bohemian, the neighbourhood still has lots of character, with its 17th-century mansard roofs, old-fashioned painted shop signs and affordable restaurants. In the market you can buy everything from Auvergne sausage to horse meat and ripe cheeses. *Map F6*

Arènes de Lutèce

7 Arènes de Lutèce

The remains of the 2nd-century Roman amphitheatre from the settlement of Lutetia *(see p44)* lay buried for centuries and were only discovered in 1869 during construction of the rue Monge. The novelist Victor Hugo, concerned with the preservation of his city's historic buildings, including Notre-Dame *(see p21)*, led the campaign for the restoration. The original arena would have had 35 tiers and could seat 15,000 spectators for theatrical performances and gladiator fights. *47 rue Monge, 75005 • Map G6 • Open 9am–9:30pm daily (summer); 8am–5:30pm daily (winter) • Free*

8 Place de la Contrescarpe

This bustling square has a village community feel, with busy cafés and restaurants and groups of students from the nearby university hanging out here after dark. In medieval times it lay outside the city walls, a remnant of which still stands. Notice the memorial plaque above the butcher's at No. 1, which marks the site of the old Pine Cone Club, a café where François Rabelais and other writers gathered in the 16th century. *Map F5*

9 St-Médard

The church at the bottom of rue Mouffetard dates back to the 9th century, when it was a parish church dedicated to St Médard, counsellor to the Merovingian kings. The present church, completed in 1655, is a mixture of Flamboyant Gothic and Renaissance styles. Among the fine paintings inside is the 17th-century *St Joseph Walking with the Christ Child* by Francisco de Zurbarán. The churchyard was the scene of hysterical fits in the 18th century, when a cult of "*convulsionnaires*" sought miracle cures at the grave of a Jansenist deacon. *141 rue Mouffetard, 75005 • Map G6 • Open 8am–noon, 2:30–7pm Tue–Sat; 8am–2:30pm, 4–8:30pm Sun • Free*

10 Manufacture des Gobelins

This internationally renowned tapestry factory was originally a dyeing workshop, founded by the Gobelin brothers in the mid-15th century. In 1662, Louis XIV's minister Colbert set up a royal factory here and gathered the greatest craftsmen of the day to make furnishings for the palace at Versailles *(see p151)*. You can see the traditional weaving process on a guided tour. *42 ave des Gobelins, 75013 • Metro Gobelins • Guided visits: 3:30pm Wed & Sun, 4pm Thu, 2:30pm & 4pm Sat, open for temporary exhibitions only 11am–6pm Tue–Sun • Tickets must be bought prior to visit at a branch of FNAC*

A Day in the Gardens

Morning

If it's a fine morning get an early start and enjoy a stroll in the **Jardin des Plantes** *(see p129)* before the city gets truly busy. The **Muséum National d'Histoire Naturelle** *(see p129)* doesn't open until 10am, but the garden is close enough to **rue Mouffetard** to enable you to enjoy the fabulous market, which gets going by about 8am. Don't forget to take your eyes off the stalls every now and then to see the splendid old buildings on this medieval street. Then return to the museum and its Evolution Gallery.

From the gardens it is a short walk to the **place de la Contrescarpe**. Enjoy this friendly square before walking down the rue Mouffetard for a coffee at one of its many cafés. Once revived, walk down to the bottom of the road to see the church of **St-Médard** on your left.

Turn left along rue Monge to the **Arènes de Lutèce**. A couple of minutes away is a little bistro, **Le Buisson Ardent** *(see p133)*, which is ideal for lunch.

Afternoon

You can spend part of the afternoon at the **Institut du Monde Arabe** *(see p129)*, exploring its beautiful Islamic artworks, before walking down to admire the Moorish architecture of the **Mosquée de Paris** *(see p129)*. Finish the day with a mint tea at the Café de la Mosquée *(pl du Puits-de-l'Ermité • 01 43 31 18 14)*.

Left **Flowers in the Jardin des Plantes** Right **Dinosaur model**

TOP 10 Jardin des Plantes Sights

1 Dinosaur Tree
One of the trees in the Botanical Gardens is a *Ginkgo biloba*, which was planted in 1795, but the species is known to have existed in exactly the same form in the days of the dinosaurs, 125 million years ago.

2 Cedar of Lebanon
This magnificent tree was planted in 1734, and came from London's Botanic Gardens in Kew, although a story grew up that its seed was brought here all the way from Syria in the hat of a scientist.

3 Rose Garden
Having only been planted in 1990 and so relatively modern compared to the other gardens, the beautiful *roseraie* has some 170 species of roses and 180 rose bushes on display. Spectacular when they are in full bloom in spring and summer.

4 Rock Gardens
One of the stars of the Botanical Gardens, with more than 3,000 plants from the world's many diverse Alpine regions. There are samples from Corsica to the Caucasus, Morocco and the Himalayas.

5 Sophora of Japan
Sent to Paris under the label "unknown seeds from China" by a Jesuit naturalist living in the Orient, this tree was planted in 1747, first flowered in 1777, and still flowers today.

6 Iris Garden
An unusual feature is this designated garden which brings together more than 400 different varieties of iris.

7 Dinosaur Model
Outside the Palaeontology Gallery, which is crammed with precious dinosaur skeletons, is a huge dinosaur model of a stegosaurus *(see p60)*.

8 Nile Crocodile
The crocodile in the Reptile House now has a better home than he once did. This creature was found in 1998, when he was six months old, in the bathtub of a Paris hotel room, left behind as an unwanted pet!

9 Greenhouses
Otherwise known as *Les Grandes Serres*, these 19th-century greenhouses were at one time the largest in the world. Today, they house a prickly Mexican cacti garden and a tropical winter garden kept at a constant 22°C (74°F) and 80 per cent humidity.

10 Young Animal House
One of the zoo's most popular features for children is this house where young creatures, which for one reason or another cannot be looked after by their natural parents, are raised. Once they reach adulthood they are returned to their natural habitat.

For the Jardin des Plantes **See p129**

Price Categories

For a three-course meal for one with half a bottle of wine (or equivalent meal), taxes and extra charges	€	under €30
	€€	€30–€40
	€€€	€40–€50
	€€€€	€50–€60
	€€€€€	over €60

Above **L'Avant-Goût**

TOP 10 Places to Eat

1 Le Petit Pascal

This family-run, provincial-style bistro, popular with locals at dinner, has a menu of regional dishes that changes daily. *33 rue Pascal, 75013 • Metro Gobelins • 01 45 35 33 87 • Closed Sat, Sun, Aug • €€*

2 Léna et Mimile

Those in the know avoid the touristy restaurants around rue Mouffetard to savour a meal at this ambitious bistro with a peaceful terrace. *32 rue Tournefort, 75005 • 01 47 07 72 47 • €€€*

3 Au Petit Marguery

One for meat lovers, with plenty of steak, veal and game on the menu. Boisterous atmosphere. *9 blvd de Port-Royal, 75013 • Map F6 • 01 43 31 58 59 • €€€€*

4 Le Buisson Ardent

This creative bistro is a romantic night-time destination serving classic French dishes with a twist. Set menus offer good value. *25 rue Jussieu, 75005 • Map G6 • 01 43 54 93 02 • Closed Sun D (brunch only Sun) • €€€*

5 La Truffière

A 17th-century building, a wood fire and welcoming staff all make for a great little bistro. Naturally, the menu features truffles. *4 rue Blainville, 75005 • Map F6 • 01 46 33 29 82 • Closed Sun, Mon • €€€€€*

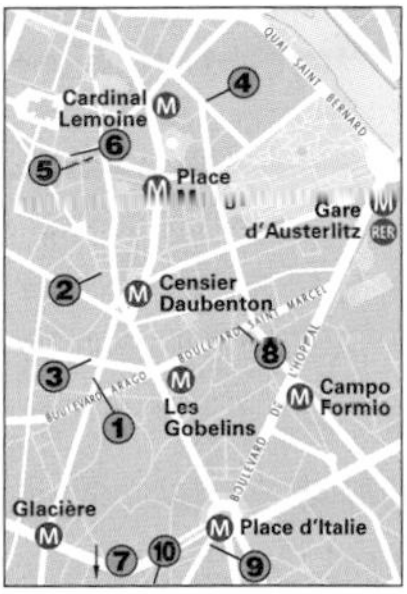

6 L'Agrume

This restaurant is popular for its affordable five-course fixed-price menu. *15 rue des Fossés Saint-Marcel, 75005 • Map G6 • 01 43 31 86 48 • No disabled access • Closed Sun–Tue • €€€€*

7 Chez Paul

Not the best place for vegetarians, with *pot au feu*, tongue and other meaty delights, but there is also fish. *22 rue de la Butte-aux-Cailles, 75013 • Metro Place d'Italie • 01 45 89 22 11 • €€€*

8 Au Coco de Mer

Spicy Seychelles cuisine, plus a "beach hut" terrace with soft sand. Vegetarians should book ahead. *34 blvd St-Marcel, 75005 • Map G6 • 06 81 57 29 29 • Closed Sun, Mon L, Aug • €€*

9 L'Avant-Goût

Small and noisy with tables crammed together. Try the *pot au feu* or apple flan, if available, though the menu changes daily. *26 rue Bobillot, 75013 • Metro Place d'Italie • 01 53 80 24 00 • Closed Sun, Mon • €€€*

10 Chez Gladines

A lively place with waiters running around serving huge portions of Basque cuisine. Arrive early to get a table. *30 rue des Cinq Diamants, 75013 • 01 45 80 70 10 • Closed Jul • No credit cards • €*

***Note:** Unless otherwise stated, all restaurants accept credit cards and serve vegetarian meals*

Left **Jardins du Trocadéro** Center **Cinéaqua** Right **Café Carette**

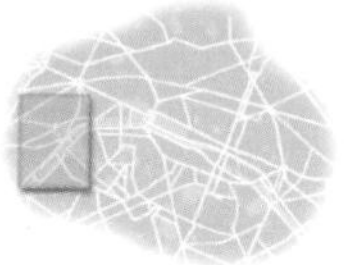

Chaillot Quarter

CHAILLOT WAS A SEPARATE VILLAGE *until the 19th century, when it was swallowed up by the growing city and bestowed with wide avenues and lavish mansions during the Second Empire building spree* (see p45). *Its centrepiece is the glorious Palais de Chaillot which stands on top of the small Chaillot hill, its wide white-stone wings embracing the Trocadéro Gardens and its terrace gazing across the Seine to the Eiffel Tower. Behind the palace is the place du Trocadéro, laid out in 1858 and originally called the place du Roi-de-Rome (King of Rome), the title of Napoleon's son. The square is ringed with smart cafés, overlooking the central equestrian statue of World War I hero Marshal Ferdinand Foch. Many of the elegant mansions in this area now house embassies, and there are numerous fine dining spots. To the west are the exclusive residential neighbourhoods of the Parisian bourgeoisie.*

TOP 10 Sights

1. Palais de Chaillot
2. Cinéaqua
3. Musée de la Marine
4. Cité de l'Architecture et du Patrimoine
5. Musée d'Art Moderne de la Ville de Paris
6. Cimetière de Passy
7. Jardins du Trocadéro
8. Musée du Vin
9. Maison de Balzac
10. Musée National des Arts Asiatiques-Guimet

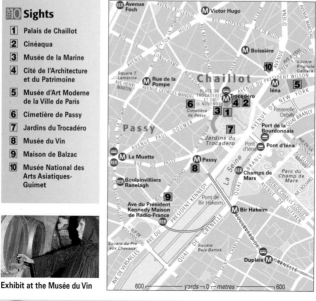

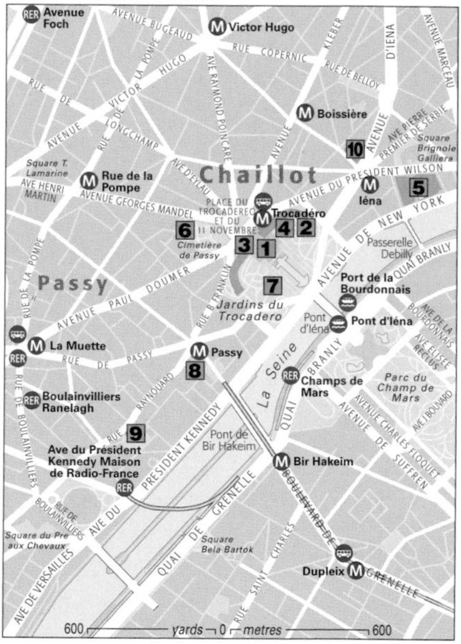

Exhibit at the Musée du Vin

1 Palais de Chaillot

The fall of his empire scuppered Napoleon's plans for an opulent palace for his son on Chaillot hill, but the site was later used for the Trocadéro palace, built for the Universal Exhibition of 1878. It was replaced by the present Neo-Classical building with its huge colonnaded wings for the prewar exhibition of 1937. The two pavilions house three museums, including the Musée de la Marine *(see below)*. The broad terrace is the domain of souvenir sellers and skateboarders by day, while at night it is crowded with tourists admiring the splendid view of the Eiffel Tower across the Seine. Two bronzes, *Apollo* by Henri Bouchard and *Hercules* by Pommier, stand to the front of the terrace. Beneath the terrace is the 1,200-seat Théâtre National de Chaillot. *17 pl du Trocadéro, 75016 • Map B4*

2 Cinéaqua

Originally built in 1878 for the Universal Exhibition, Paris's fascinating aquarium is home to over 10,000 species, including seahorses, stonefish and some spectacular sharks and rays. Built into a former quarry, the site has been designed to blend in with the Chaillot hillside. There is also a futuristic cinema complex showing nature films, and a Japanese restaurant. *Ave Albert de Mun, 75016 • Map B4 • Open 10am–7pm daily • Closed 14 Jul • Admission charge • www.cineaqua.com*

3 Musée de la Marine

Three hundred years of French naval history is the focus of this museum, whether in war, trade and commerce, or industries such as fishing. The displays range from naval art to

Palais de Chaillot

science to maritime adventure and popular legends and traditions. Among the highlights is an outstanding collection of model ships, from the feluccas of ancient Egypt, to medieval galleys and nuclear submarines. You can also watch craftsmen at work on the models. Napoleon's royal barge is also on show *(see p35)*. *Palais de Chaillot, 17 pl du Trocadéro, 75016 • Map B4 • Open 11am–6pm Wed–Mon (to 7pm Sat & Sun) • Closed 1 Jan, 1 May, 25 Dec • Admission charge • www.musee-marine.fr*

4 Cité de l'Architecture et du Patrimoine

Occupying the east wing of the Palais Chaillot, this museum is a veritable ode to French architectural heritage, showcasing its development through the ages as well as contemporary architecture. The Galerie des Moulages (Medieval to Renaissance) contains moulded portions of churches and great French cathedrals such as Chartres. The Galerie Moderne et Contemporain includes a reconstruction of an apartment designed by Le Corbusier, and architectural

General Foch

General Ferdinand Foch (1851–1929), whose statue stands in the centre of place du Trocadéro, was the commander-in-chief of the Allied armies by the end of World War I. His masterful command ultimately led to victory over the Germans in 1918, whereupon he was made a Marshal of France and elected to the French Academy.

designs from 1990 onwards. The gallery in the Pavillon de Tête has a stunning collection of murals copied from medieval frescoes. *Palais de Chaillot, 75116 • Map B4 • Open 11am–7pm Wed–Mon (until 9pm Thu) • Closed 1 Jan, 1 May, 14 Jul, 25 Dec • 01 58 51 52 00 • Admission charge • www.citechaillot.fr*

5 Musée d'Art Moderne de la Ville de Paris

This modern art museum is housed in the east wing of the Palais de Tokyo, built for the 1937 World Fair. Its permanent collection includes such masters as Chagall, Picasso, Modigliani and Léger; further highlights include Raoul Dufy's enormous mural *The Spirit of Electricity* (1937), and Picabia's *Lovers (After the Rain)* (1925). The museum also showcases up-and-coming artists in the west wing. *11 ave du Président-Wilson, 75016 • Map B4 • Open 10am–6pm Tue–Sun (until 10pm Thu during temporary exhibitions) • Closed public hols • 01 53 67 40 00 • Permanent collection free; temporary exhibitions admission charge • www.mam.paris.fr*

6 Cimetière de Passy

This small cemetery covers only 1 ha (2.5 acres), yet many famous people have been laid to rest here with the Eiffel Tower as their eternal view *(see p138)*. It is worth a visit just to admire the striking sculptures on the tombs. *Pl du Trocadéro (entrance rue du Commandant Schloessing) 75016 • Map A4*

7 Jardins du Trocadéro

Designed in 1937, the tiered Trocadéro Gardens descend gently down Chaillot hill from the palace to the Seine and the Pont d'Iéna. The centrepiece of this 10-ha (25-acre) park is the long rectangular pool lined with stone and bronze statues, including *Woman* by Georges Braque (1882–1963). Its illuminated fountains are spectacular at night. With flowering trees, walkways and bridges over small streams, the gardens are a romantic place for a stroll *(see p39)*. *Map B4*

Cimetière de Passy

8 Musée du Vin

The vaulted 14th-century cellars where the monks of Passy once made wine are an atmospheric setting for this wine museum. Waxwork figures depict the history of the wine-making process, and there are displays of wine paraphernalia. There are tasting sessions, wine for sale and a restaurant. *5 square Charles-Dickens, rue des Eaux, 75016 • Map A4 • Open 10am–6pm Tue–Sun • Admission charge • www.museeduvinparis.com*

9 Maison de Balzac

The writer Honoré de Balzac *(see p46)* rented an apartment here from 1840–44, and assumed a false name to avoid his many creditors. He worked on several of his famous novels here, including *La cousine Bette* and *La comédie humaine*. The house is now a museum displaying first editions and manuscripts, personal mementoes and letters, and paintings and drawings of his friends and family as well as housing temporary exhibitions. *47 rue Raynouard, 75016 • Map A4 • Open 10am–6pm Tue–Sun • Closed public hols • Admission charge for temporary exhibitions • www.balzac.paris.fr*

10 Musée National des Arts Asiatiques-Guimet

One of the world's foremost museums of Asiatic and Oriental art, founded in 1889. The Khmer Buddhist temple sculptures from Angkor Wat are the highlight of a fine collection of Cambodian art. Guimet's original collection tracing Chinese and Japanese religion from the 4th to 19th centuries is also on display, as are artifacts from India, Indonesia and Vietnam. *6 pl d'Iéna, 75016 • Map B3 • Open 10am–6pm Wed–Mon • Closed 1 Jan, 1 May, 25 Dec • Admission charge • www.guimet.fr*

A Day in Chaillot

Morning

It would be hard to imagine a better start to a day in Paris than going to the **Palais de Chaillot** *(see p135)* and seeing the perfect view it has across the Seine to the **Eiffel Tower** *(see pp16–17)*. Then tour the fascinating collections of the **Cité de l'Architecture** *(see pp135–6)* and, if marine history is your thing, the **Musée de la Marine** *(see p135)*, both in the palace. Outside the palace, take a break in the Café du Trocadéro *(8 pl du Trocadéro • 01 44 05 37 00)* and watch the comings and goings in the square.

Afterwards, head along rue Benjamin Franklin and rue Raynouard, where you will find first the **Musée du Vin** and the **Maison de Balzac**. Walk to the far side of the Maison de Radio France building for a brunch or lunch at **Zebra Square** *(see p139)*.

Afternoon

Revived, walk back along the Seine towards the Palais de Chaillot, and head up to the place d'Iéna to the refurbished and much improved **Musée National des Arts Asiatiques-Guimet** for its spectacular Eastern artworks.

By now you will definitely be in need of a rest, so return to the place du Trocadéro for a coffee at the Café Kléber No. 4 *(01 47 27 86 65)*. End the day in the peaceful **Cimetière de Passy** before an unforgettable dinner overlooking the lights of the city at the stylish **Le Jules Verne** *(see p117)*.

Left **Manet bust** Centre **Debussy's grave** Right **Fernandel's grave**

Top 10 Graves in Cimetière de Passy

1 Edouard Manet
Born in Paris in 1832, Manet became the most notorious artist in the city when works such as *Olympia* and *Le Déjeuner sur l'Herbe (see p12)* were first exhibited. He died in Paris in 1883.

2 Claude Debussy
The French composer (1862–1918) achieved fame through works such as *Prélude à l'Après-midi d'un Faune* and *La Mer*, and was regarded as the musical equivalent of the Impressionist painters.

3 Berthe Morisot
The French Impressionist artist was born in Paris in 1841, posed for Edouard Manet and later married his lawyer brother Eugène. She never achieved the fame of the male Impressionists and died in Paris in 1895.

4 Fernandel
The lugubrious French film actor known as Fernandel was born in Marseille in 1903 and made more than 100 films in a career that lasted from 1930 until his death in Paris in 1971.

5 Marie Bashkirtseff
This Russian artist became more renowned as a diarist after her death from tuberculosis in 1884. Despite living for only 24 years she produced 84 volumes of diaries and their posthumous publication created a sensation due to their intimate nature.

6 Henri Farman
The French aviator was born in Paris in 1874 and died here in 1958. He was the first man to make a circular 1-km (0.5-mile) flight, and the first to fly cross-country in Europe. His gravestone shows him at the controls of a primitive plane.

7 Antoine Cierplikowski
The grave of this fairly obscure artist of the 1920s attracts attention because of its immensely powerful sculpture of a man and woman joined together and seeming to soar from the grave to the heavens.

8 Comte Emanuel de las Cases
Born in 1766, this historian and friend of Napoleon shared the emperor's exile on the island of St Helena and recorded his memoirs. The Comte himself died in Paris in 1842.

9 Gabriel Fauré
The French composer, probably best known today for his *Requiem*, was a great influence on the music of his time. He died in Paris in 1924, at the age of 79.

10 Octave Mirbeau
The satirical French novelist and playwright was also an outspoken journalist. Born in 1848, he died in Cheverchemont in 1917 and his body was brought to Passy for burial.

For Cimetière de Passy **See p136**

Price Categories

For a three-course meal for one with half a bottle of wine (or equivalent meal), taxes and extra charges	€	under €30
	€€	€30–€40
	€€€	€40–€50
	€€€€	€50–€60
	€€€€€	over €60

Left **Maison Prunier** Right **Le Relais du Parc**

Top 10 Places to Eat

1 Le Relais du Parc
The fixed-price lunch menu, which changes seasonally, is a bargain. *55–57 ave Raymond Poincaré, 75016 • Map B3 • 01 44 05 66 10 • Closed Sat L, Sun, Aug • €€€€€*

2 Le Jamin
Former Guy Savoy disciple Alain Pras presides over this elegant, formal restaurant, offering an inventive approach to French classics, and good vegetarian options. *32 rue de Longchamp, 75016 • Map A3 • 01 45 53 00 07 • Closed Sat L, Sun, Aug • No disabled access • €€€€€*

3 Le Bistrot du Chineur
A tiny, friendly bistro serving good value, thoughtfully prepared cuisine. Advance reservation essential. *5 impasse des Carrières, 75016 • Map A4 • 01 42 88 17 70 • Closed D, Sat, Sun, Mon • €*

4 L'Astrance
Pascal Barbot serves fusion food at its best. Book a month in advance. *4 rue Beethoven 75116 • Map B4 • 01 40 50 84 40 • Closed Sat, Sun, Mon • No disabled access • €€€€€*

5 Maison Prunier
Fish dishes reign at this restaurant with 1930s decor. *16 ave Victor-Hugo, 75016 • Map B3 • 01 44 17 35 85 • Closed Sun, Aug • No disabled access • €€€€€*

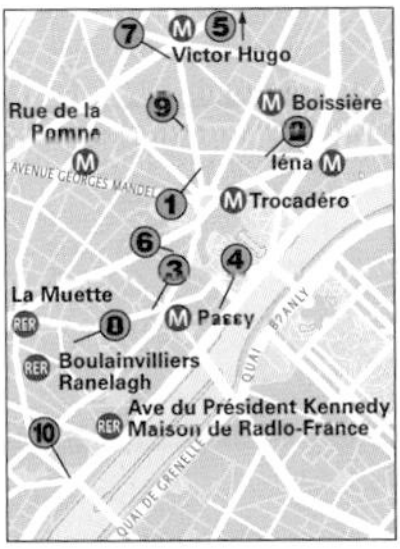

6 Comme des Poissons
This tiny Japanese sushi restaurant serves good food at reasonable prices, so book ahead. *22 rue de la Tour, 75016 • Map A4 • 01 45 20 70 37 • Closed Mon, Aug • €*

7 Le Petit Rétro
Cosy atmosphere in this 1900s bistro and affordable prices. *Blanquette de Veau* is delicious. *5 rue Mesnil, 75016 • Map B3 • 01 44 05 06 05 • Closed Sat, Sun, Aug • No disabled access • €€€*

8 Le Bistrot des Vignes
Unpretentious little bistro of the type everyone hopes to find in Paris. *1 rue Jean-Bologne, 75016 • Map B4 • 01 45 27 76 64 • No disabled access • €€€*

9 La Table Lauriston
Serge Barbey believes in the best ingredients prepared simply. La Table Lauriston is a hit with local gourmets who tuck into his gargantuan steak and rum-doused *baba* in the jewel-toned dining room. *129 rue Lauriston, 75116 • Map A3 • 01 47 27 00 07 • Closed Sun, Sat L, Aug, 1 wk over Christmas • €€€€*

10 Zebra Square
This is a media hangout as it's next to France's public service radio network. Sunday brunches are popular. *3 pl Clément-Ader, 75016 • Map A4 • 01 44 14 91 91 • €€€€€*

Note: *Unless otherwise stated, all restaurants accept credit cards and serve vegetarian meals*

Left **Sacré-Coeur** Centre **Espace Montmartre Salvador Dalí** Right **Place Pigalle**

Montmartre and Pigalle

PAINTERS AND POETS, *from Picasso to Apollinaire, put the "art" in Montmartre, and it will forever be associated with their Bohemian lifestyles of the late 19th and early 20th centuries. There are plenty of artists around today too, painting quick-fire portraits of tourists in the place du Tertre. The area's name comes from "Mount of Martyrs", commemorating the first bishop of Paris, St Denis, who was decapitated here by the Romans in AD 250. Parisians, however, call it the "Butte" (knoll) as it is the highest point in the city. Throngs of tourists climb the hill for the stupendous view from Sacré-Coeur, crowding the main square, but you can still discover Montmartre's charms along the winding back streets, small squares and terraces. Below the hill, Pigalle, once home to dance halls and cabarets, has largely been taken over by sleazy sex shows along the boulevard de Clichy.*

Streetside painter, Montmartre

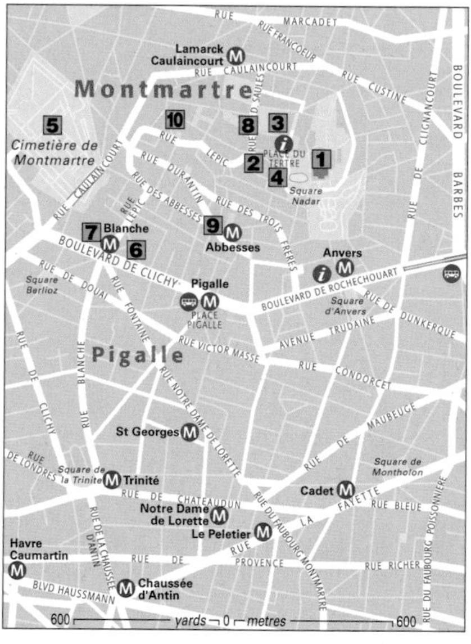

Top 10 Sights

1. Sacré-Coeur
2. Espace Montmartre Salvador Dalí
3. Musée de Montmartre
4. Place du Tertre
5. Cimetière de Montmartre
6. Musée d'Erotisme
7. Moulin Rouge
8. Au Lapin Agile
9. Place des Abbesses
10. Moulin de la Galette

1 Sacré-Coeur

See pp22–3.

2 Espace Montmartre Salvador Dalí

The Dalí works here may not be the artist's most famous or best, but this museum is still a must for any fan of the Spanish Surrealist *(see p144)*. More than 300 of his drawings and sculptures are on display amid high-tech light and sound effects, including Dalí's voice, which create a "surreal" atmosphere. There are also bronzes of his memorable "fluid" clocks *(see p37)*. *11 rue Poulbot, 75018 • Map F1 • Open 10am–6pm daily (Jul–Aug to 8pm) • Admission charge • www.daliparis.com*

3 Musée de Montmartre

The museum is set in Montmartre's finest townhouse, known as Le Manoir de Rose de Rosimond after the 17th-century actor who once owned it. From 1875 it provided living quarters and studios for many artists. Using drawings, photographs and memorabilia, the museum presents the history of the Montmartre area, from its 12th-century convent days to the present, with an emphasis on the Bohemian lifestyle of the *belle époque*. There is even a re-created 19th-century bistro, as well as lovely gardens where Renoir painted. *12 rue Cortot, 75018 • Open 10am–6pm daily • Admission charge • www.museedemontmartre.fr*

4 Place du Tertre

At 130 m (430 ft), Montmartre's old village square, whose name means "hillock", is the highest point in the city. Any picturesque charm it might once have had is now sadly hidden under the tourist-trap veneer of overpriced restaurants and portrait artists hawking their services, although the fairy lights at night are still atmospheric. No. 21 houses the Old Montmartre information office, with details about the area. Nearby is the church of St-Pierre de Montmartre, all that remains of the Benedictine abbey which stood here from 1133 until the Revolution. *Map F1*

5 Cimetière de Montmartre

The main graveyard for the district lies beneath a busy road in an old gypsum quarry, though it's more restful than first appears when you actually get below street level. The illustrious tombs, many with ornately sculpted monuments, packed tightly into this intimate space reflect the artistic bent of the former residents, who include composers Hector Berlioz and Jacques Offenbach, writers Stendhal and Alexandre Dumas, Russian dancer Nijinsky and the film director François Truffaut. *20 ave Rachel, 75018 • Map E1*

Sculpture of writer Marcel Aymé

The Montmartre Vineyards

It's hard to imagine it today, but Montmartre was once a French wine region said to match the quality of Bordeaux and Burgundy. There were 20,000 ha (50,000 acres) of Parisian vineyards in the mid-18th century, but today just 1,000 bottles of wine are made annually from the remaining 2,000 vines in Montmartre, and sold for charity.

6 Musée de l'Erotisme

With more than 2,000 items from around the world, this museum presents all forms of erotic art from painting, sculpture, photos and drawings to objects whose sole purpose seems to be titillation. It's all tastefully presented, however, reflecting the sincere interest of the three collectors who founded the museum in 1997 to explore the cultural aspects of eroticism. The displays range from spiritual objects of primitive cultures to whimsical artworks. *72 blvd de Clichy, 75018 • Map E1 • Open 10am–2am daily • Admission charge • www.musee-erotisme.com*

7 Moulin Rouge

The Moulin Rouge ("red windmill") is the most famous of the *belle époque* dance halls which scandalized respectable citizens and attracted Montmartre's artists and Bohemians. Henri de Toulouse-Lautrec immortalized the era with his sketches and posters of dancers such as Jane Avril, some of which now grace the Musée d'Orsay *(see p13)*. Cabaret is still performed here *(see p58)*. *82 blvd de Clichy, 75018 • Map E1 • Shows daily at 9pm & 11pm (dinner at 7pm) • www.moulinrouge.fr*

8 Au Lapin Agile

This *belle époque* restaurant and cabaret was a popular hang-out for Picasso, Renoir, and poets Apollinaire and Paul Verlaine. It took its name from a humorous painting by André Gill of a rabbit *(lapin)* leaping over a cooking pot, called the "Lapin à Gill". In time it became known by its current name ("nimble rabbit") *(see p58)*. *22 rue des Saules, 75018 • Map F1 • Open 9pm–1am Tue–Sun • www.au-lapin-agile.com*

Au Lapin Agile

Moulin de la Galette

9 Place des Abbesses

This pretty square lies at the base of the Butte, between Pigalle and the place du Tertre. Reach it via the metro station of the same name to appreciate one of the few original Art Nouveau stations left in the city. Designed by the architect Hector Guimard, it features ornate green wrought-iron arches, amber lanterns and a ship shield, the symbol of Paris, on the roof. Along with Porte Dauphine, it is the only station to retain its original glass roof. A mural painted by local artists winds around the spiral staircase at the entrance. But don't walk to the platform, take the elevator – it's the deepest station in Paris, with 285 steps. *Map E1*

10 Moulin de la Galette

Montmartre once had more than 30 windmills, used for pressing grapes and grinding wheat; this is one of only two still standing. During the siege of Paris in 1814 its owner, Pierre-Charles Debray, was crucified on its sails by Russian soldiers. It became a dance hall in the 19th century and inspired paintings by Renoir and Van Gogh *(see p144)*. It is now a restaurant, but it can be admired from outside, and rue Lepic is worth a visit for its shops and restaurants. *83 rue Lepic, 75018 • Map E1*

A Day in Montmartre

Morning

As with all the city's busy attractions, the sooner you get to **Sacré-Coeur** *(see pp22–3)* the more you will have it to yourself – it opens at 8am. Later in the morning, enjoy the bustle of Montmartre with tourists having their portraits painted by the area's street artists in the **place du Tertre** *(see p141)*. There are plenty of places to choose for a coffee, but the one most of the artists frequent is the Clairon des Chasseurs *(3 pl du Tertre • 01 42 62 40 08)*.

For art of a more surreal kind, pay a visit to the **Espace Montmartre Salvador Dalí** *(see p141)*. Head down rue des Saules to continue the artistic theme with lunch at La Maison Rose *(2 rue de l'Abreuvoir • 01 42 57 66 75)*. Utrillo once painted this pretty pink restaurant.

Afternoon

After lunch, the **Musée de Montmartre** *(see p141)* is nearby, as are the Montmartre Vineyards, and the little Cimetière St Vincent where you will find Maurice Utrillo's grave.

Head back up to rue Lepic to see the **Moulin de la Galette** before heading towards the boulevard de Clichy. Here you will see the sleazy side of Pigalle life, although the **Musée de l'Erotisme** is a more tasteful interpretation.

To the east is a great bar for an apéritif, La Fourmi *(74 rue des Martyrs • 01 42 64 70 35)*. Then end the day with a show at the world-famous **Moulin Rouge** cabaret.

Left **Dalí sculpture** Centre **Pablo Picasso** Right **Moulin de la Galette, Renoir**

TOP 10 Artists who Lived in Montmartre

1 Pablo Picasso
Picasso (1881–1973) painted *Les Demoiselles d'Avignon* in 1907 while living at the Bateau-Lavoir. It is regarded as the painting which inspired the Cubism movement, which he launched with fellow residents Georges Braque and Juan Gris.

2 Salvador Dalí
The Catalan painter (1904–89) came to Paris in 1929 and held his first Surrealist exhibition that year. He kept a studio in Montmartre, and his work is now celebrated in the Espace Montmartre Salvador Dalí *(see p141)*.

3 Vincent Van Gogh
The Dutch genius (1853–90) lived for a time on the third floor of 54 rue Lepic. Many of his early paintings were inspired by the Moulin de la Galette windmill *(see p143)*.

4 Pierre-Auguste Renoir
Renoir (1841–1919) is another artist who found inspiration in the Moulin de la Galette, when he lived at 12 rue Cortot. For a time he laid tables at Au Lapin Agile *(see p142)*.

5 Edouard Manet
Manet (1832–83) frequented Montmartre's artist haunts and scandalized the art world with his paintings of nudes, including the famous *Olympia* *(see p13)*.

6 Maurice Utrillo
Utrillo (1883–1955) often painted the Auberge de la Bonne-Franquette, an atmospheric depiction of old Montmartre. His mother was the artist Suzanne Valadon and they both lived at 12 rue Cortot, now the Musée de Montmartre *(see p141)*.

7 Henri de Toulouse-Lautrec
More than any other artist, Toulouse-Lautrec (1864–1901) is associated with Montmartre for his sketches and posters of dancers at the Moulin Rouge and other dance halls. They epitomize the era to this day *(see p13)*.

Toulouse-Lautrec

8 Raoul Dufy
The painter Dufy (1877–1953) lived at Villa Guelma on the boulevard de Clichy from 1911 to 1953, when he was at the height of his career.

9 Amedeo Modigliani
The Italian painter (1884–1920) and sculptor arrived in Paris in 1906, when he was 22, and was greatly influenced by Toulouse-Lautrec and the other artists on the Montmartre scene.

10 Edgar Degas
Edgar Degas was born in Paris in 1834 and lived in the city for the whole of his life, most of the time in Montmartre. He died here in 1917 and is buried in the Montmartre cemetery *(see p141)*.

Left **Art Brut, Halle Saint Pierre** Right **Rue de Poteau market**

Top 10 Places to Escape the Crowds

1 St-Jean l'Evangéliste de Montmartre
This 1904 church is a clash of styles, from Moorish to Art Nouveau. *21 rue des Abbesses, 75018 • Map E1 • Open daily • Free*

2 Montmartre City Hall
On display in this building are two Utrillo paintings. *1 pl Jules-Joffrin, 75018 • Metro Jules Joffrin*

3 Hameau des Artistes
This little hamlet of artists' studios is private, but no one will mind if you take a quiet look round. *11 ave Junot, 75018 • Map E1*

4 Musée de la Vie Romantique
Writer George Sand was a frequent visitor to this house, which is now devoted to her works. *16 rue Chaptal, 75009 • Map E1 • Open 10am–6pm Tue–Sun • Adm charge for temporary exhibitions*

5 Musée Gustave Moreau
The former home of Symbolist artist Moreau displays a large collection of his works. *14 rue de La Rochefoucauld, 75009 • Map E2 • Open 10am–12:45pm, 2–5:15pm Wed–Mon (all day Fri–Sun) • Admission charge • www.musee-moreau.fr*

6 Halle Saint Pierre
A fascinating cultural centre that exhibits naive folk art as well as Art Brut. *2 rue Ronsard, 75018 • Map F1 • 01 42 58 72 89 • Open 10am–6pm daily (until 7pm Sat, from 11am Sun) • Closed public hols • Admission charge*

7 Cité Véron
This cul-de-sac is home to the Académie des Arts Chorégraphiques, a prestigious dance school. *92 blvd de Clichy, 75018 • Map E1*

8 Square Suzanne-Buisson
Named after a World War II Resistance fighter, this square is a romantic spot. *Map E1*

9 Rue de Poteau Market
This great food market is a long way from the tourist crowds. *Metro Jules Joffrin*

10 Crypte du Martyrium
This simple, peaceful 19th-century chapel is said to be on the spot where St Denis, patron saint of Paris, was beheaded by the Romans in AD 250. *11 rue Yvonne-Le-Tac, 75018 • Map F1 • 01 42 23 48 94 • Open 3–6pm Fri*

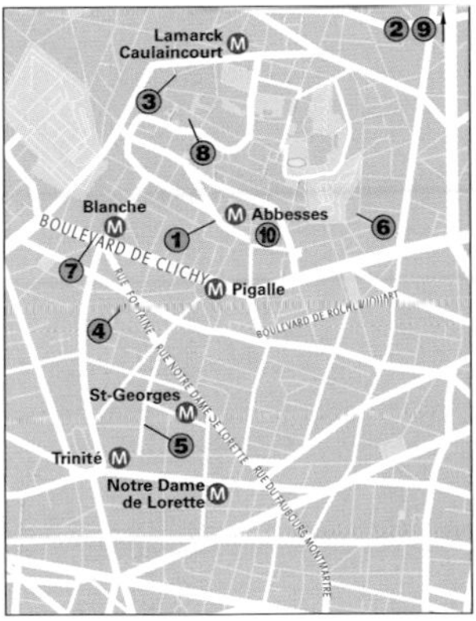

Left **Au Lapin Agile** Right **Moulin Rouge**

Top 10 Cabarets and Clubs

1 Au Lapin Agile
Poets and artists not only drank in this cabaret club, some such as Renoir and Verlaine also laid tables. Picasso even paid his bill with one of his Harlequin paintings *(see p142)*.

2 Moulin Rouge
As old as the Eiffel Tower (1889) and as much a part of the Parisian image, today's troupe of 60 Doriss Girls are the modern versions of Jane Avril and La Goulue *(see p142)*. *82 boulevard de Clichy, 75018 • Map E1*

3 Autour de Midi et Minuit
Tuck into delicious bistro food before heading into the small vaulted cellar for a jazz concert. *11 rue Lepic, 75018 • Map E1 • Closed Sun, Mon, end Feb, Aug*

4 Le Carmen
This trendy hangout offers excellent cocktails and hosts themed nights featuring live music. *34 rue Duperré, 75009 • Map E1 • 01 45 26 50 00 • Closed Sun–Wed, Aug*

5 La Nouvelle Eve
One of the lesser-known cabaret venues. Its intimate nature does not undermine the professionalism of the shows. *25 rue Fontaine, 75009 • Map E1*

6 Le Bus Palladium
This 60s club hosts concerts with an alternative/rock vibe. *6 rue Pierre Fontaine, 75009 • Map E1 • 01 45 26 80 35 • Closed Sun, Mon*

7 Cabaret Michou
Outrageous drag artists and a legendary compère whose behaviour can never be predicted, this is close to the original spirit of Montmartre cabaret. *80 rue des Martyrs, 75018 • Map E1*

8 Folies Pigalle
This former strip club is now a leading dance venue and popular among the gay community. *11 pl Pigalle, 75018 • Map E1*

9 La Machine du Moulin Rouge
This venue next to the Moulin Rouge hosts both club nights and concerts. *90 boulevard de Clichy, 75018 • Map E1*

10 Le Divan du Monde
World music is played here, live and DJ, with regular dance events and concerts too. *75 rue des Martyrs, 75018 • Map E1*

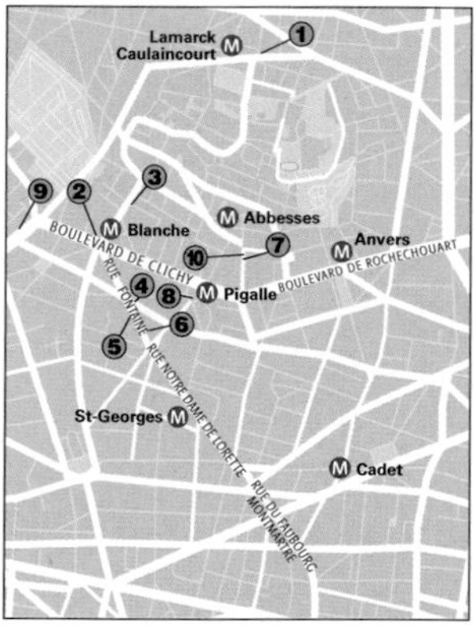

For more jazz clubs in Paris See pp62–3

Left **Café Burq**

Price Categories

For a three-course meal for one with half a bottle of wine (or equivalent meal), taxes and extra charges	€	under €30
	€€	€30–€40
	€€€	€40–€50
	€€€€	€50–€60
	€€€€€	over €60

TOP 10 Places to Eat

1 Café Burq

A genuine Montmartre bistro with a trendy clientele. Roasted Camembert with honey is a favourite. *6 rue Burq, 75018 • Map E1 • 01 42 52 81 27 • Closed L, Sun, 1 wk Christmas • No disabled access • €€*

2 Le Miroir

The emphasis here is on classic French fare with a seasonal menu. *94 rue des Martyrs, 75018 • Map E1 • 01 46 06 50 73 • No disabled access • Closed Sun & Mon • €€€*

3 Table d'Eugène

This chic restaurant serves gastronomic cuisine for a very reasonable price. *18 rue Eugène Sue, 75018 • 01 42 55 61 64 • Closed Sun, Mon, Aug • €€*

4 Restaurant Jean

This restaurant boasts fine contemporary cuisine and a Michelin star. *8 rue St-Lazare, 75009 • Map F1 • 01 48 78 62 73 • Open daily (brunch only Sat & Sun) • €€€€*

5 Le Pétrelle

A restaurant with an offbeat, eccentric decor, an intimate atmosphere and a menu using only local produce. *34 rue Pétrelle, 75009 • Map F1 • 01 42 82 11 02 • Closed Sun, Mon, 1st week May, Aug • €€€*

6 Rose Bakery

The square quiches, carrot cakes and sticky puddings have made this eatery legendary. *46 rue des Martyrs, 75009 • Map F2 • 01 42 82 12 80 • Closed D, Mon • €*

7 Charlot "Roi des Coquillages"

Art Deco brasserie, specializing in seafood. *81 boulevard de Clichy, 75009 • Map E1 • 01 53 20 48 00 • No disabled access • €€€*

8 Le Cul de Poule

Bistro offering modern French dishes and a good selection of wines. *53 rue des Martyrs, 75009 • Map F2 • 01 53 16 13 07 • Closed Sun L, a few weeks from Dec–Jan • €€*

9 Hotel Amour

The cosy restaurant in this hip hotel serves Anglo-inspired food. *8 rue de Navarin, 75009 • Map F2 • 01 48 78 31 80 • €€*

10 Chamarré de Montmartre

Creative Mauritanian-French fusion food is served on a terrace at this fine dining restaurant. *52 rue Lamarck, 75018 • Map E1 • 01 42 55 05 42 • No disabled access • €€€€*

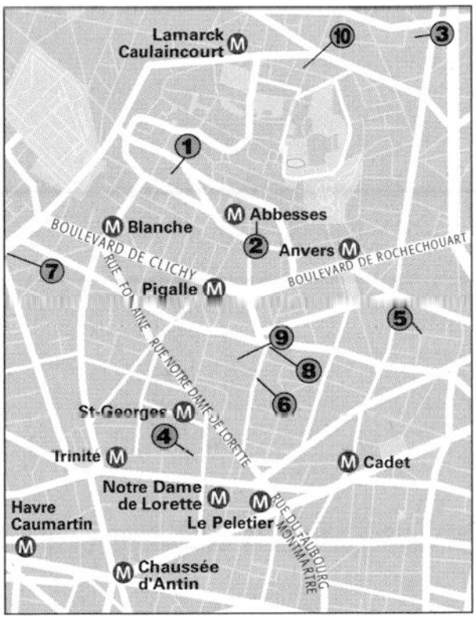

Note: *Unless otherwise stated, all restaurants accept credit cards and serve vegetarian meals.*

Left **Bois de Boulogne** Centre **Cimetière Père-Lachaise** Right **Parc Monceau**

Greater Paris

CENTRAL PARIS HAS MORE THAN ENOUGH *on offer to keep any visitor occupied, but if time permits you should make at least one foray out of the centre, whether your interest is in the sumptuous Palace of Versailles, former home of the "Sun King" Louis XIV, or in the Magic Kingdom of Disneyland® Paris. The excellent metro system makes for easy day trips to the area's two main parks, the Bois de Boulogne and the Bois de Vincennes, for a wide range of outdoor activities, from boating to riding or in-line skating, or just strolling amid pleasant greenery. In contrast to these bucolic pleasures is the cutting-edge modern architecture of La Défense. Visually stunning, it comprises Paris's stylish business district to the west of the city, with added attractions in its exhibition centres. Two large cemeteries outside the centre are worth a visit for their ornate tombs.*

TOP 10 Sights

1. Versailles
2. Disneyland® Paris
3. La Défense
4. Bois de Vincennes
5. Bois de Boulogne
6. Parc de la Villette
7. Montparnasse
8. Cimetière du Père Lachaise
9. Parc Monceau
10. Musée Marmottan-Claude Monet

Sculptures, Versailles

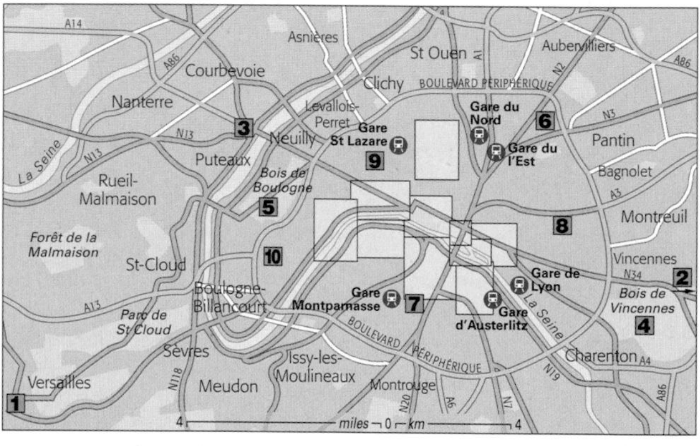

Preceding pages **Versailles gardens**

1 Versailles

The top day-trip from Paris has to be Versailles. This stunning chateau, begun by Louis XIV in 1664, is overwhelming in its opulence and scale. Plan what you want to see and arrive early, as even a full day may not be long enough. Much of the palace is only accessible by guided tour *(see p154)*. Buy a Versailles Passport online to avoid the queues. *Versailles, 78000 • RER line C to Versailles-Rive Gauche • Château open Apr–Oct: 9am–6:30pm Tue–Sun; Nov–Mar: 9am–5:30pm Tue–Sun; gardens open 8am–8:30pm daily (to 6pm winter) • Closed public hols • Admission charge • www.chateauversailles.fr*

2 Disneyland® Paris

Visitors with children will probably have no choice about whether they visit the Paris branch of Disneyland or not. However, even parents will enjoy the hi-tech workings and imagination behind such attractions as "Pirates of the Caribbean" and "The Haunted House" *(see p60)*. The Walt Disney Studios® Park involves visitors interactively through film, with a professional stunt show at the end and special effects rides. *Marne-la-Vallée • RER line A to Marne-la-Vallée Chessy/ Disneyland • Open Sep–Jun: 9am–8pm daily; Jul–Aug: 9am–11pm daily (Studios Sep–Jun: 9am–6pm daily; Jul–Aug: 9am–8pm daily); times vary for Walt Disney Studios® Park • Admission charge • www.disneylandparis.com*

3 La Défense

French vision and flair coupled with Parisian style are clearly shown by this modern urban development. This business and government centre was purposely built to the west of the city to allow the centre to remain unmarred by skyscrapers. More than just offices, however, the area is also an attraction in its own right, with stunning sights such as the Grande Arche, a cube-like structure with a centre large enough to contain Notre-Dame, and surrounded by artworks, a fountain, cafés and restaurants. *Metro Esplanade de la Défense or RER line A to Grande-Arche-de-la-Défense*

4 Bois de Vincennes

Southeast of the city lies the Bois de Vincennes, which has several lakes, boating facilities, lovely formal gardens, a Buddhist centre, a zoo and an amusement park. The Château de Vincennes was a royal residence before Versailles and has the tallest keep in Europe. The more energetic can walk here all the way from the Bastille along the Promenade Plantée, formerly a railway viaduct. *Vincennes, 94300 • Metro Château de Vincennes/RER Vincennes • Park: open dawn–dusk daily; château: Sep–Apr: 10am–5pm; May–Aug: 10am–6pm • Closed public hols • www.chateau-vincennes.fr*

Grande Arche, La Défense

The Treaty of Versailles

France, Great Britain, the USA, Italy and the German Republic negotiated this agreement after World War I at Versailles, which required Germany to demilitarize parts of its territory, reduce the size of its army, abolish conscription, cease trading in military equipment and to pay compensation. The Treaty was signed on 28 June 1919.

5 Bois de Boulogne

This enormous park is the Parisians' favourite green retreat, especially on summer weekends when its 865 ha (2,135 acres) can become crowded. There is plenty to do, apart from simply walking and picnicking, such as cycling, riding, boating or visiting the various attractions. These include parks within the park, two race courses *(see p51)* and an art and folk museum. The park is open 24 hours a day, but avoid after dark. *Map A2*

6 Parc de la Villette

More than just a park, this landscape was created in 1993 to a futuristic design. It provides the usual park features of paths and gardens, but modern sculptures, zany park benches and several major hi-tech attractions offer a different edge. These include the interactive science museum, the Cité des Sciences et de l'Industrie, a 60-seater mobile hydraulic cinema, an Omnimax cinema, play areas for younger children and a music institute *(see p60)*. *30 ave Corentin-Cariou, 75019 • Metro Porte de Pantin • 01 40 03 75 75 • Opening times vary depending on the attraction • Admission charge for certain attractions • www.villette.com*

7 Montparnasse

Montparnasse's location is highly visible due to the 209-m (685-ft) Tour du Montparnasse which offers spectacular views. Five minutes' walk away is the area's main draw, the Cimetière du Montparnasse, where the great writers Maupassant, Sartre, de Beauvoir, Baudelaire and Samuel Beckett are buried *(see p156)*. For breathtaking views of Paris by night visit the rooftop restaurant "Le Ciel de Paris". *Metro Gare Montparnasse • Tour du Montparnasse: open 9:30am–11:30pm daily (winter until 10:30pm, 11am Sat & Sun); admission charge • Cemetery: open 8:30am–5:30pm daily; free • www.tourmontparnasse56.com*

Cimetière du Montparnasse

8 Cimetière du Père Lachaise

This is the most visited cemetery in the world, largely due to rock fans who come from around the world to see the grave of the legendary singer Jim Morrison of The Doors. There are about one million other graves here, in some 70,000 different tombs, including those of Chopin, Oscar Wilde, Balzac, Edith Piaf, Colette, Molière and Delacroix *(see p156)*. There are maps posted around the cemetery to help you find these notable resting places, or a more detailed plan can be bought at kiosks in the grounds. *16 rue du Repos • Metro Père-Lachaise • 01 55 25 82 10 • Open 8am–5:30pm Mon–Fri, 8:30am–5:30pm Sat, 9am–5:30pm Sun (Mar–Nov: to 6pm) • Free*

9 Parc Monceau

This civilized little park is no further from the city centre than Montmartre, yet it goes unnoticed by many visitors. It was created in 1778 by the Duc de Chartres and is still frequented by well-heeled residents. The grounds are full of statues and an air of well-being *(see p38)*. *Blvd de Courcelles, 75008 • Metro Monceau*

10 Musée Marmottan-Claude Monet

Paul Marmottan was an art historian and his 19th-century mansion now houses the world's largest collection of works by Claude Monet *(see p13)*, including his *Impression Soleil Levant* which gave the Impressionist movement its name. The collection was donated by the artist's son in 1966, and includes the artist's collection of works by Renoir and Gauguin. *2 rue Louis-Boilly, 75016 • Metro Muette • Open 10am–6pm Tue–Sun (to 8pm Thu) • Adm charge • www.marmottan.com*

A Taste of Greater Paris

Morning

You won't cover Greater Paris in a day, and **Disneyland® Paris** and **Versailles** *(see p151)* both need at least a day.

If you want variety, go to **Montparnasse** by metro. In front of the busy mainline station, is the Tour Montparnasse – take a trip to the top to admire the view and then enjoy a coffee break in the Panoramic Bar.

When you leave, walk down boulevard Edgar Quinet. On your right is the entrance to the **Cimetière du Montparnasse**. An hour should be plenty of time here.

Walk towards the Vavin metro station to the historic café/brasserie **La Coupole** *(see p157)*, to have lunch.

Afternoon

Take the metro at Vavin, changing at Réaumur Sébastopol, to **Cimetière du Père Lachaise** and explore the city's other great cemetery. Spend one or two hours searching out the famous names buried here and admiring the architecture of the monuments. Have a coffee afterwards at a neighbourhood café, Le Saint Amour *(2 ave Gambetta • 01 47 97 20 15 • Metro Père-Lachaise)*. From Père-Lachaise it is again just one change on the metro, at Nation, to the **Bois de Vincennes**, where you can spend the late afternoon in the park and admire the château.

Left **Marble courtyard** Right **Palace gardens**

Top 10 Versailles Sights

1 The Hall of Mirrors
The spectacular 70-m (233-ft) long Galerie des Glaces (Hall of Mirrors) has been magnificently restored. It was in this room that the Treaty of Versailles was signed in 1919, to formally end World War I.

2 Chapelle Royale
The Royal Chapel is regarded as one of the finest Baroque buildings in the country. Finished in 1710, the elegant, white marble Corinthian columns and numerous murals make for an awe-inspiring place of prayer.

3 Salon de Venus
In this elaborate room decorated mainly in marble, a statue of Louis XIV, the creator of Versailles, stands centre stage, exuding regal splendour beneath the fine painted ceiling.

4 Queen's Bedroom
Nineteen royal infants were born in this opulent room, which has been meticulously restored to exactly how it appeared when it was last used by Marie-Antoinette in 1789.

5 Marble Courtyard
Approaching the front of the palace across the vast open forecourt, visitors finally reach the splendour of the black-and-white marble courtyard, which is the oldest section of the palace. The north and south wings were added later.

6 L'Opéra
The opulent opera house was built in 1770 for the marriage of the *dauphin*, the future Louis XVI, to Marie-Antoinette. The floors were designed so that they could be raised to stage level during special festivals.

7 Le Trianon
In the southeast corner of the gardens Louis XIV and Louis XV had the Grand and Petit Trianon palaces built as "private" retreats. Marie-Antoinette was given Petit Trianon by Louis XVI.

8 Palace Gardens
The palace gardens feature many walkways, landscaped topiary, fountains, pools, statues and the Orangery, where exotic plants were kept in the winter. The magnificent Fountain of Neptune is situated to the north of the North Wing.

9 Salon d'Apollon
Louis XIV's throne room is, naturally, one of the palace's centrepieces, and features a suitably regal portrait of the great Sun King. Dedicated to the god Apollo, it strikingly reflects the French monarchy's divine self-image.

10 Stables of the King
The magnificent stables have been restored and they now house the famous Bartabas equine academy.

Not all sights are open at once, so check upon arrival

Left **Boating on lake** Right **Cycling in the Bois de Boulogne**

Top 10 Bois de Boulogne Features

1 Parc de Bagatelle
Differing garden styles feature in this park, including English and Japanese, though the major attraction is the huge rose garden, best seen in June.

2 Pré Catelan
This park-within-a-park is at the very centre of the Bois. Its lawns and wooded areas include a magnificent 200-year-old beech tree and the idyllic, eponymous restaurant *(see p157)*.

3 Jardin d'Acclimatation
The main children's area of the Bois incorporates a small amusement park, a zoo with a farm and a pets' corner, and a Herb Museum aimed especially at children *(see p60)*.

4 Lakes
Two long, thin lakes adjoin each other. The larger of the two, confusingly called Lac Inférieur (the other is Lac Supérieur) has boats for hire and a motor boat to take you to the islands.

5 La Grande Cascade
This man-made waterfall was a major undertaking when the park was built, requiring concrete to be shipped down the Seine.

6 Stade Roland Garros
The legendary home of French clay-court tennis hosts the glamorous French Open each year in June.

7 Château de Longchamp
At the same time as he re-designed central Paris *(see p45)*, Baron Haussmann landscaped the Bois de Boulogne. This château was given to him as a thank-you from Napoleon III.

8 Shakespeare Garden
Inside Pré Catelan park is a little garden planted with all the trees, flowers and herbs mentioned in the plays of Shakespeare. There is a lovely open-air theatre.

Shakespeare Garden

9 Jardin des Serres d'Auteuil
This 19th-century garden has a series of greenhouses where ornamental hothouse plants are grown. In the centre is a palm house with tropical plants.

10 Horse-Racing
The Bois is home to two race courses. To the west is the Hippodrome de Longchamp, where flat racing takes place including the Prix de l'Arc de Triomphe *(see p57)*; in the east, the Hippodrome d'Auteuil holds steeplechases.

For more on the Bois de Boulogne **See p152**

Left **Père Lachaise cemetery** Centre **Jim Morrison's grave** Right **Edith Piaf's tomb**

Top 10 Graves

1 Jim Morrison, Père Lachaise Cemetery

The American lead singer of The Doors rock band spent the last few months of his life in Paris and died here in 1971. Fans still hold vigils at his grave, which is covered with scrawled messages from all over the world.

2 Oscar Wilde, Père Lachaise Cemetery

The Dublin-born author and wit died in 1900, after speaking his alleged last words in his Paris hotel room: "Either that wallpaper goes, or I do." His tomb is unmissable, with a huge monument by Jacob Epstein.

3 Fredéric Chopin, Père Lachaise Cemetery

The Polish composer was born in 1810 but died in Paris at the age of 39. The statue on his tomb represents "the genius of music sunk in grief".

4 Edith Piaf, Père Lachaise Cemetery

The "little sparrow" was born in poverty in the Belleville district of Paris in 1915, less than 1,500 m (5,000 ft) from where she was buried in 1963 in a simple black tomb *(see p63)*.

5 Marcel Proust, Père Lachaise Cemetery

The ultimate chronicler of Paris, the writer was born in the city in 1871. He is buried in the family tomb *(see p47)*.

6 Samuel Beckett, Montparnasse Cemetery

The Irish-born Nobel Prize-winning writer settled in Paris in 1937, having previously studied here. He died in 1989 and his gravestone is a simple slab, reflecting the writer's enigmatic nature *(see p47)*.

7 Jean-Paul Sartre and Simone de Beauvoir, Montparnasse Cemetery

Joined together in death as in life, even though they never lived together, their joint grave is a remarkably simple affair. Both of these philosophers were born, lived and died in Paris.

8 Guy de Maupassant, Montparnasse Cemetery

The great French novelist and short-story writer died in Paris in 1893, and his grave with its luxuriant growth of shrubs stands out because of the open book carving *(see p46)*.

9 Charles Baudelaire, Montparnasse Cemetery

The poet who shocked the world with his frank collection of poems *Les Fleurs du Mal* was born in Paris in 1821 and died here in 1867.

10 Charles Pigeon Family, Montparnasse Cemetery

This charming and touching grave shows Charles Pigeon and his wife in bed, reading by the light of the gas lamp he invented.

For Greater Paris cemeteries **See pp152–3**

Price Categories

For a three course meal for one with half a bottle of wine (or equivalent meal), taxes and extra charges	€	under €30
	€€	€30–€40
	€€€	€40–€50
	€€€€	€50–€60
	€€€€€	over €60

Left **Le Dôme**

TOP 10 Places to Eat

1 Le Pré Catelan

Tucked away in the Bois de Boulogne *(see p152)* is this high-class dining pavilion. Romantic setting and elegant service. *Route de Suresnes, Bois de Boulogne, 75016 • Metro Porte Maillot • 01 44 14 41 14 • Closed Sun, Mon, 2 weeks winter, 1 week Oct, Aug • €€€€€*

2 Gordon Ramsay au Trianon

Celebrity chef Gordon Ramsay's protegé Simone Zanoni is the chef at this two Michelin-starred restaurant. *1 blvd de la Reine, Versailles • RER line C to Versailles • 01 30 84 55 56 • Closed D Fri & Sat, Sun, Mon, Aug • €€€€€*

3 Le Resto du Roi

Close to the chateau, this informal bistro serves classic dishes. Specialities include duck foie gras with fresh fig compote or salmon smoked with birch branches. *1 ave de Saint-Cloud, Versailles • 01 39 50 42 26 • Closed Wed, D Mon, Tue & Sun • €*

4 La Coupole

Near the Cimetière de Montparnasse *(see p152)*, this Parisian landmark has an eclectic menu. *102 blvd du Montparnasse, 75014 • Map E6 • 01 43 20 14 20 • €€€€*

5 La Closerie des Lilas

With its piano bar and terrace, this is a Montparnasse institution. The brasserie is cheaper and the steak tartare is recommended. *171 blvd du Montparnasse, 75006 • Map E6 • 01 40 51 34 50 • €€€€*

6 Le Dôme

Montparnasse's prime fish restaurant, once frequented by Sartre. Great food and grand decor. *108 blvd du Montparnasse, 75014 • Map E6 • 01 43 35 25 81 • Closed Sun & Mon Aug • €€€€€*

7 La Gare

If visiting the Bois de Boulogne, include La Gare on the itinerary. This stylish brasserie in a former railway station has a summer terrace. *19 chaussée de la Muette, 75016 • Metro La Muette • 01 42 15 15 31 • €€€*

8 Le Baratin

A local favourite in Belleville, this bistro serves modern French cuisine with excellent wines. The fixed-price lunch is particularly popular. *3 rue Jouye-Rouve, 75020 • 01 43 49 39 70 • Closed Sun & Mon • No disabled access • No vegetarian options • €*

9 Le Chapeau Melon

This natural wine shop turns into a charming diner by night. There is a fixed menu with a great selection of wines. *92 rue Rébeval, 75019 • 01 42 02 68 60 • Closed Mon, Tue, 2 weeks Aug • €€*

10 Relais d'Auteuil

At the southern end of the Bois de Boulogne is this gourmet restaurant. Sea bass in a pepper crust is one delicious speciality. *31 blvd Murat, 75016 • Metro Michel-Ange-Molitor • 01 46 51 09 54 • Closed L Sat, Sun, Mon • Closed Aug • €€€€€*

***Note:** Unless otherwise stated, all restaurants accept credit cards and serve vegetarian meals*

STELLA ARTOIS
BAR
SANDWICH
TURC
RAITEUR
AP
ASIE
RESTIGE
01 43 31 80 73
SUBLIME !

STREETSMART

Left **Parisian hotel** Centre **Parisian restaurant** Right **French perfume**

TOP 10 Planning Your Trip

1 When to Go
April in Paris may be a cliché but it is still a good time to visit. Spring and autumn are both pleasant and there are plenty of parks and tree-lined boulevards to enjoy. Although certain restaurants close in August, when most Parisians take their holidays, there is still plenty to see and do.

2 Choosing an Area
The Left Bank is a good choice if you like a Bohemian atmosphere of cafés and student life. The Marais has many museums, shops and restaurants and the Opéra and Louvre quarters are central to everything. To save money, stay just outside the centre and use the excellent yet cheap metro.

3 Choosing a Hotel
If space is important, ask about the size of the rooms: some can be very cramped. It is also worth checking whether the rooms face busy, noisy roads and what is the hotel's nearest metro station. Ask if there is an elevator to all floors, as in some older buildings this may not be the case.

4 Choosing a Restaurant
If you like to eat well, or want to try a particular restaurant, phone and book a few weeks ahead of your visit. If you decide to take pot luck, the city is full of good places to eat. Remember many restaurants close on Mondays, at weekends and in August.

5 What to See
Don't expect to see the whole of Paris on a weekend visit – you would not even see the whole of the Louvre in this time *(see pp8–11)*. Even on a longer visit, don't be over-ambitious: leave time for wandering the streets or relaxing in a bar or café, the way the Parisians do. It's all part of the experience.

6 What to Pack
The weather can be unpredictable, so allow for unexpected cold or wet spells at almost any time of year by bringing a pullover, umbrella and comfortable shoes. Parisians are casual but chic, so take a few smart outfits for dining out. Only the most expensive restaurants require men to wear a tie.

7 How much Money to Take
You can use the major credit cards (Visa, MasterCard, American Express) almost everywhere, and there are cash dispensers (ATMs) all over Paris which display symbols of cards they accept. Make sure you have a few euros in cash when you arrive, however, to pay for metro tickets or a taxi. *Bureaux de change* offices also abound throughout the city.

8 Passports and Visas
No visa is required for citizens of EU countries, the USA, Canada, Australia or New Zealand if you are staying for less than three months, although your passport will need to be valid for at least three months beyond the end of your stay. Citizens of other countries should consult their French embassy or consulate for information before travelling.

9 Customs
For EU citizens there are no limits on goods that can be taken into or out of France, provided they are for your personal use. Outside the EU, you may import the following allowances duty-free: 200 cigarettes or equivalent in tobacco; 4 litres of wine, or 2 litres of wine plus 1 litre of spirits; 60ml of perfume and 250ml of eau de toilette; €350 worth of other items.

10 Travelling with Children
Parisians dislike *enfants terribles*, so always try to ensure good behaviour. Some hotels allow kids to sleep free in family rooms *(see p179)*. Children are seldom seen in restaurants at night, but there are plenty of child-friendly alternatives.

For hotels in Paris **See pp172–9**

Left **Metro exit sign** Right **Restaurant prices**

TOP 10 Things to Avoid

1 Crime
Paris is a reasonably safe city. Muggings are rare, but theft and pick-pocketing are common so take sensible precautions. Avoid Les Halles, the Bois de Boulogne and Vincennes after dark, and quiet sections of the metro and the RER after 9pm.

2 Health Costs
EU travellers with a European Health Insurance Card (EHIC) get free or reimbursed healthcare, otherwise it is best to have private insurance. For minor problems, ask a pharmacist (look for the green cross). If one is closed, the address of the nearest open pharmacy will be shown in the window.

3 Beggars
Do not confuse the genuine homeless (known as "SDFs") with organized beggars at the top tourist spots who should be avoided and ignored. Metro buskers are usually "legit" and often talented.

4 Pickpockets
Pickpockets do frequent busy tourist places and public transport so keep a watchful eye on your belongings. Men should never keep their wallet in a back pocket and women should make sure their handbags are closed and held firmly in front of them if possible.

5 Taking the Wrong Metro
To avoid taking the wrong route, check the number of the line you want on a map and the name of the end station for the direction in which you wish to travel. All signs in metro stations work in this way and the system is simple. There is always a panel on the wall just before you reach the platform; this panel will have a list of the train's destinations, so you can double check *(see p164)*. The RER can be quite confusing and is best avoided for trips in the city centre.

6 Transport Fines
Hold on to your metro, RER or bus ticket for the whole of your journey in case an inspector asks to see it. Remember to validate or show your ticket when boarding a bus.

7 Tourist Traps
In general, avoid the tourist-targeted brasseries with their multilingual *menus touristiques*, flags of the world and photographs of the food on offer. The places where the locals eat will be far better.

8 Hidden Charges in Cafés or Bars
When paying a bill, check if service is included – it usually is. If you want to save money, take your drink or snack at the counter. Prices are lower and no tip is expected.

9 Over-Tipping
Restaurants and cafés normally include a 10–15 per cent service charge, so only leave a further small gratuity for very good service. Taxi drivers should get 10–15 per cent but this is not obligatory. Porters can be tipped €2–3 per bag and chambermaids a similar amount per day, usually left at the end of your stay.

10 Queues
Paris's top sights have made strenuous efforts to reduce their notorious queues for tickets. Almost all sights now sell their tickets in advance at their websites and sometimes for specific times (such as the Eiffel Tower). Otherwise, arrive early or take advantage of late-night openings *(nocturnes)*.

Queues to enter Notre-Dame

Left **Eurostar train** Centre **Ice cream parlour in Gare du Nord** Right **Orlyval high-speed train**

10 Arriving in Paris

1 Eurostar

Eurostar trains arrive at Gare du Nord, slightly north of the city centre. The station is served by three metro lines and three RER lines, and has a taxi rank outside, usually manned by assistants to help newly arrived visitors.

2 Gare du Nord Facilities

Gare du Nord is a large station with several places to eat and drink and shops selling books, newspapers and snacks. The metro station is reached from the concourse and is clearly signposted. There is also a tourist office by the Grandes Lignes exit.

3 CDG Airport

Roissy-Charles-de-Gaulle Airport is the arrival point for most international flights, 23 km (14 miles) northeast of the city centre. Its main terminals are some distance apart, so check which one you require when returning. A 24-hour English-language information service is available. *CDG information: 39 50.*

4 Connections from CDG Airport

CDG is connected to central Paris by Air France and Roissy bus services, and (the easiest option) the RER train line B3. This links with Gare du Nord, Les Halles and St Michel. Taxis take about 30 minutes to the city centre, sometimes more, and cost about €55.

5 Orly Airport

Orly is 14 km (8.5 miles) south of the city centre and is used by French domestic services and some international airlines. It has two terminals: Orly-Sud is mainly for international flights; Orly-Ouest is for domestic flights. English-language information is available 6am–11:30pm. *Orly information: 39 50.*

6 Connections from Orly Airport

Air France coaches run to and from Etoile, Invalides and Montparnasse metro and mainline stations. The high-speed Orlyval shuttle train serves both Orly terminals from Antony on RER line B4. Metro signs to Orly on RER C refer to Orly town – avoid. Taxis take about 30 minutes and cost about €30.

7 Beauvais Tillé Airport

Beauvais Tillé Airport is some 70 km (43 miles) north of Paris and is used by low-cost airlines. There is a connecting bus link with Porte Maillot metro station; allow at least an hour for the journey.

8 Arriving by Road

All motorways from whichever direction eventually link with Paris's Boulevard Périphérique (Inner Ring Road). Access to central Paris is via different exits *(portes)*, so drivers should always check their destination before setting off and know which exit they will need.

9 Parking

To park on the street you will need the nerves and ability of a local. Meters take the pre-paid *carte* only, which is available from tobacconists *(tabac)*. Otherwise use one of the many underground car parks in the city, which are clean and safe. For prepaid parking visit www.parkingsdeparis.com.

10 Arriving by Bus

The main operator, Eurolines, has services from the UK, Ireland, Germany and several other European countries. Coaches arrive at Gare Routière International, east of the city centre but are linked to the metro from the Galliéni station on Line 3.

Eurolines long-distance bus

For information on getting around Paris **See p164**

Left **Paris tourist office sign** Right **Parisian listings magazines**

TOP 10 Sources of Information

1 French Tourist Offices
The French Tourist Office has branches in many major international cities.

2 Office de Tourisme de Paris
The main office is near the Pyramides metro station. It is well stocked with brochures, and has hotel and tour reservation services.
25 rue des Pyramides, 75001 • Map E3 • Open 10am–7pm Mon–Sat, 11am–7pm Sun (9am–7pm Jun–Oct) • Closed 1 May • www.parisinfo.com

3 Espace du Tourisme d'Ile de France
This tourist facility serves Paris and the wider Ile de France region, and is the best source of advice and information on visiting places outside the city. It has offices in airports and train stations and a useful website. • *www.nouveau-paris-ile-de-france.fr*

4 Websites
Two official sites are the Paris City Hall (www.paris.fr) and the city tourist office (www.parisinfo.com), with lots of information and links in French and English. Most major attractions such as the Musée du Louvre (www.louvre.fr) also have their own sites.

PARIS Convention and Visitors Bureau Tourist Office

5 Magazines
If you are able to read French, try the free, weekly *A Nous Paris*, which is available in metro stations, and the *Sortir* insert in the weekly magazine *Télérama*.

6 Officiel des Spectacles & Pariscope
These two events guides can be bought at newspaper stands and are ideal if you want more general information about current exhibitions.

7 Paris Voice
This monthly magazine is published by the American Church and aimed at US residents in Paris. Available from English-language bookshops, it is a good source of information on what is happening in the city. It also has a website. • *www.parisvoice.com*

8 Bonjour Paris electronic newsletter
This email newsletter and website, entirely in English, provides fascinating articles and up-to-date information on cultural activities as well as restaurant openings and closings in the city. The newsletter is released at least once a week to provide the most current information. • *www.bonjourparis.com*

9 Libraries
Public libraries are found all over Paris and all of them are free to enter. Most have selections of newspapers and magazines, as well as notices that may be useful to visitors. Only Paris residents, however, can borrow material.

10 Newspapers
Foreign newspapers are available on the day of publication in many newsagents. The *International Herald Tribune* is published from Paris. French-speakers can also keep in touch with world events via France's national publications such as *Le Monde* or *Libération*, or the city's own paper, *Le Parisien*.

French Tourist Offices Overseas

www.franceguide.com

UK
Lincoln House, 300 High Holborn, London WC1V 7JH • 0906 8244 123 (60p/min)

USA
825 Third Ave, 29th floor, New York, NY 10022

Australia
25 Bligh St, Level 13, Sydney, NSW 2000 • 02 9231 5244

Canada
1800 Ave McGill College, Suite 1010, Montréal, QUE H3A 3J6 • 514 288 2026

Left **Metro sign** Centre **Locator map outside a metro station** Right **Walking in Paris**

Top 10 Getting Around Paris

1 Metro
The Paris metro system is cheap and efficient. The network is comprehensive and the service is very frequent. The service operates from roughly 5:30am–12:30am (until 1:30–2am Fri, Sat and the evening before bank holidays) and exact times for each line are given at stations. *www.ratp.fr*

2 RER
The RER train system (5am–12:30am; to 1:30am Fri, Sat and the evening before public holidays) has only five lines, but the network goes further into the suburbs. Metro tickets are only valid on RER trains in Zone 1. If travelling further, you must buy a separate RER ticket (subject to change).

3 Buses
Buses run from approximately 6:30am–8:30pm, although some services operate through the night (Noctilien Buses). A *Grand Plan de Paris* available from metro stations shows all bus routes. Metro tickets are valid in Zones 1 and 2, but you cannot switch between bus and metro on the same ticket. Bus stops show the line route.

Parisian bus

4 Taxis
Remember that taxis may not always stop if you hail them on the street. The best method is to head for one of the 470 taxi ranks (look for the taxi icon on a blue background), or ask your hotel or restaurant to call for one. Many drivers will not take more than three people, to avoid front-seat passengers. Fares are not expensive but there may be a charge for extra luggage.

5 Arrondissements
Paris is divided into 20 *arrondissements* (districts), which radiate out in a clockwise spiral from the centre. The first is abbreviated to 1er (Premier) and follow on as 2e, 3e (Deuxième, Troisième) etc. The postal address for the first district is 75001, and again these follow on – the second district is 75002.

6 Asking Directions
The Parisians' reputation for rudeness is unjustified. Most are polite and will try to help even if you do not speak French (many Parisians speak English). Politeness and an effort to speak French are always appreciated, so be sure to begin with "*Excusez-moi*" ("Excuse me").

7 Cycling
Paris is an excellent city for cyclists. You can hire bikes via Allovelo or Parisvelosympa, or try the self-service scheme Vélib'. Bike stands are found every 300 metres (330 yards) and payment can be made online or by credit card at the access terminals, which operate in eight languages. *www.allovelo.com; www.parisvelosympa.com; www.velib.paris.fr*

8 Rollerblading
Parisians are mad about rollerblading and on Friday nights and Sunday afternoons organized *balades* (outings) often take place, beginning at Montparnasse. *www.pari-roller.com*

9 Boat
The Batobus runs year round and its eight stops link all the major sights on the river. Boats run every 20–25 minutes, from 10am–9:30pm (until 7pm in winter). One-day, two-day and five-day passes are great value if you plan on making more than one journey. *08 25 05 01 01, www.batobus.com*

10 Walking
Central Paris is fairly compact, and even a walk from the Arc de Triomphe to the Bastille should only take an hour. Be sure to look up to see the beautiful old buildings – and down to avoid the evidence of Parisian dogs.

Left **Canal tour boat** Centre **Pedestrian walk sign** Right **Bus tour**

Top 10 Guided Tours

1 Boat Tours

The long-established Bateaux-Mouches operate daily with regular day and evening dinner cruises. *Bateaux-Mouches: 01 42 25 96 10, www.bateaux-mouches.fr • Bateaux Parisiens: 01 76 64 14 66, www.bateauxparisiens.com • Vedettes de Paris: 01 44 18 19 50, www.vedettesdeparis.com • Les Vedettes du Pont Neuf: 01 46 33 98 38, www.vedettesdupontneuf.fr*

2 Walking Tours

Tours are available on a wide range of themes and in several languages. Secrets of Paris, Paris Walks and Context travel are three of the leading English-language companies. Also check out the website www.paris-expat.com *Context travel: www.contexttravel.com • Paris Walks: 01 48 09 21 40, www.paris-walks.com • Secrets of Paris: www.secretsofparis.com*

3 Cycle Tours

Several companies offer guided cycling tours, with multilingual guides, including night-time tours and medieval Paris tours. For the less energetic, Segway Tours hire out electric scooters. *Paris à Vélo: 01 48 87 60 01, www.parisvelosympa.com • Fat Tire Bike Tours: 01 56 58 10 54, www.fattirebiketours.com • City Segway Tours: 01 56 58 10 54, www.citysegwaytours.com*

4 Canal Tours

Less well-known than river trips, these tours take you into the fascinating backwaters of the Paris canal system. A fabulous light show by artist Keiichi Tahara is displayed on the underground section of the Canal St-Martin.

Sign for Paris canal tour

Canauxrama and Navettes de la Villette: 01 42 39 15 00, www.canauxrama.com • Paris Canal: 01 42 40 96 97, www.pariscanal.com

5 Bus Tours

Numerous bus tours are available – the main tourist office on rue des Pyramides *(see p163)* is the best place to begin. Tours usually last up to two hours but many of the companies allow you to hop on and off at any of their stops.

6 Gourmet Tours

Promenades Gourmandes offers tours of Paris markets, food shops and other foodie haunts (English available). Or try a personalized, self-guided itinerary from Edible Paris. *Edible Paris: www.edible-paris.com • Promenades Gourmandes: 01 48 04 56 84, www.promenadesgourmandes.com*

7 Wine Tours

O-Chateau organizes day trips and tours from Paris to several wine regions including Champagne. They also offer tasting cruises along the Seine. *68 rue Jean-Jacques Rousseau, 75001 • Map M1 • 01 44 73 97 80 • www.o-chateau.com*

8 Shopping and Fashion Tours

Pay a guide to direct you to the best shops. You can then choose from a range of themes including Made in France, along the Left Bank and Unique Boutique in the Marais district. *Chic Shopping Paris: 06 77 65 08 01, www.chicshoppingparis.com*

9 Themed Tours

American company Paris Through Expatriate Eyes runs several tours, revealing many secrets even Parisians don't know. Visit www.parisinfo.com for other tour operators. *Paris Through Expatriate Eyes: 06 70 98 13 68, www.paris-expat.com*

10 Sports Tour

Sports fans can take a guided one hour tour of the huge and world-famous arena, the Stade de France. *Stade de France: 08 92 70 09 00 • Various tours available (except on event days) • www.stadefrance.com*

Left **Paris bus** Centre **Budget hotel** Right **Eating at the bar**

TOP 10 Paris on a Budget

1 Public Transport

There is a bewildering array of discount travel passes available *(see p168)*, so be sure to study them to find the best one for you. Visitors can buy one-, two-, three- and five-day passes (called a Paris Visite ticket), with options for different zones and savings on the entrance fees to some sights. *www.ratp.fr*

2 Hostels, Apartments and Camping

It is perfectly feasible to find accommodation in central Paris for €40–50 per night. Even cheaper options include the following hostel groups. *www.hostelbookers.com • FUAJ: 01 44 89 87 27, www.fuaj.com • Camping du Bois de Boulogne: 01 45 24 30 00, www.campingparis.fr • St Christopher's Inn: www.st-christophers.co.uk • Perfectly Paris Apartments: www.perfectlyparis.com*

3 Bed-and-Breakfast

Several companies offer rooms with Parisian families on a bed-and-breakfast basis. Most are located either centrally or close to a metro station, and can cost as little as €30 per person per night, if sharing. *Alcove & Agapes: 01 44 85 06 05, www.bed-and-breakfast-in-paris.com • Good Morning Paris: 01 47 07 28 29, www.goodmorningparis.fr*

Paris metro sign

4 Cheap Eats

For a coffee or snack, standing at the bar is cheaper than sitting down. In restaurants, the *prix-fixe* (fixed-price) menus offer good deals and the *plat du jour* (dish of the day) is usually inexpensive. If you want to sample fine dining, do it at lunchtime when it's often cheaper.

5 Cheap Seats

Half-price theatre and concert tickets are available for same-day performances only from kiosks at place de la Madeleine *(see p97)*. Cinemas usually offer discounts in the mornings, and on Wednesdays.

6 Cheap Treats

All national museums, including the Louvre, Musée Picasso and Musée d'Orsay, are free on the first Sunday of each month. Early evening admission for the various *nocturnes* (late-night openings) is also cheaper. The Paris City Passport, available from tourist offices, offers reductions for certain sights, shops and tours.

7 Sightseeing Passes

The Paris Museum Pass gives unlimited visits to museums and monuments throughout Paris, and a two-day pass costs €39 for adults. The Paris Pass provides access to many attractions along with free transport on the metro, buses and RER. A two-day adult pass costs €110. Visit the websites for further details and other available rates. *www.parismuseumpass.fr; www.parispass.com*

8 Breakfast

Most hotels charge separately for breakfast and what is on offer varies widely, from bread and jam to a lavish buffet. You can save money by opting out and choosing a small snack in a café or boulangerie instead.

9 Churches

Although church interiors are free, there may be a charge for towers, crypts etc. If passing a church, take a look to see if any free or inexpensive lunchtime or evening concerts are being advertised.

10 Concessions

State-run national museums are free all year round for everyone under 18 and for those under 26 who are from the EU (ID may be required). Other groups, such as senior citizens, also enjoy special rates.

For budget hotels in Paris **See p175**

Left **Paris taxi** Right **Musée d'Orsay**

TOP 10 Paris for the Disabled

1 Tourist Office Leaflets
The main tourist office in Paris *(see p163)* has information leaflets on facilities for the disabled. Their website also has useful addresses. *www.parisinfo.com*

2 Useful Organizations
Both the Association des Paralysés de France (APF) and the Groupement pour l'Insertion des Personnes Handicappées Physiques (GIHP) provide information on disabled facilities in Paris. *APF: 17 blvd Auguste Blanqui, 75013, 01 40 78 69 00, www.apf.asso.fr • GIHP: 32 rue du Paradis, 75010, 01 43 95 66 36, www.gihpnational.org*

3 Guided Tours
The Paris City Hall organizes numerous specialized tours of the city's parks, gardens and cemeteries for people with disabilities, including special visits for the blind. *City Hall: 01 43 28 47 63*

4 Itineraries
For those with wheelpower who want to go it alone in central Paris, APF have detailed information on negotiating various quarters of the city *(see above for address). Paris comme sur des roulettes* is also a useful guide with maps colour coding the quality of the pavements on given routes, access to public conveniences etc. *Editions Dakota, 45 rue St-Sébastien, 75011* (€8.99), *or from FNAC and large newsagents.*

5 Travel Agents
Tourism for All, in the UK, has a useful list of specialist tour operators. Sage Travelling offers a variety of packages and assistance. *Tourism for All: 0303 303 0146, outside UK +44 1539 814 683, www.tourismforall.org.uk • Sage Travelling: 1-888-645-7920, www.sagetraveling.com*

6 Metro/RER
Few stations are easily accessible for wheelchairs and most require a station member of staff to operate lifts to avoid either stairs or escalators. Line 14, however, is wheelchair accessible. Main metro and RER stations have a leaflet on transport facilities, called *Handicaps et Déplacements en Région Ile-de-France.*

7 Buses
Paris buses are being equipped with access for wheelchairs, and all buses already have seats reserved for disabled and elderly persons, war veterans and pregnant women.

8 Taxis
It is a legal requirement for taxi drivers to help people with disabilities to get in and out of their vehicle, and to carry guide dogs as passengers. This does not mean that all taxis are able to carry wheelchairs, so do check when booking. *Taxi G7 has a special service for clients in wheelchairs: 01 47 39 00 91*

9 Hotels
Many older hotels are unsuitable for people with mobility problems as they are without elevators, so it is essential that you check before booking. Newer hotels and the modern hotel chains are usually wheelchair accessible, but always ask when making a reservation.

10 Attractions
While some of the older museums and monuments are not accessible for people in wheelchairs, most museums and galleries are, and they also increasingly cater for those with special needs. Wheelchair uses enter the Louvre on an open lift under the pyramid. APF publishes a guide to disabled access in Paris's museums, theatres and cinemas *(see Useful Organizations).*

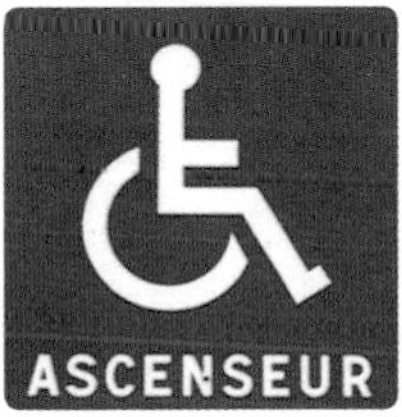

Wheelchair access sign

Left **Metro carnet tickets** Centre **Navigo Découverte** Right **Paris Visite**

Top 10 Tickets

1 Metro Tickets

Metro tickets can be bought in batches of 10 *(un carnet)*, which offer considerable savings on the price of a single ticket. Each ticket is valid for one journey in the central zones, no matter how many changes are made. They must be stamped when you enter the metro and retained until you leave *(see p161)*. If staying for a few days, consider buying a *Navigo Découverte* (photo ID needed) or a *Paris Visite* card, which offer savings at some attractions too *(see p166)*.

2 Bus Tickets

One type of ticket serves all bus and metro routes and Zones 1 and 2 of the RER network. As with the metro, you must time-stamp your ticket when boarding the bus and keep it until the end of the journey. You will be fined if you are not in possession of a valid ticket.

3 RER Tickets

Using metro and bus tickets in Zone 1 of the RER network makes for a convenient way to get around. See the station maps for the extent of these zones.

4 SNCF Train Tickets

Tickets issued by the RATP (Régie Autonome des Transports Parisiens) are not valid on the mainline SNCF (Société Nationale des Chemins de Fer) services, France's national rail network. To find out about services to suburban stations, including Versailles *(see p151)*, ring the General Information and reservations line. *SNCF information: 3635 (special number) • www.sncf.com*

5 Theatre Tickets

These can be bought at the box office of the theatre, by telephone or at ticket agencies (including FNAC stores). Some theatres offer reduced-price tickets for students or stand-by seats 15 minutes before the performance. There is also a half-price ticket kiosk *(see p166)*.

6 Cinema Tickets

Prices are average for a European city, but ask about discounts that may be available for students, over-60s and families. Admission prices on Wednesdays are sometimes reduced. Larger cinemas take credit card reservations over the phone and online.

7 Clubs

Admission prices are high at all Paris clubs and are often increased at weekends or after midnight, but women can sometimes get in at a reduced rate or for free. The admission charge may include a first drink, but subsequent drinks will usually be pricey.

8 Tickets for Attractions

Some concessionary and discount tickets are available *(see p166)*. The Museum Pass saves queueing if you are planning to visit many of the major museums *(see pp34–5)*. Some museums have online booking, and the Louvre has automatic ticket machines *(see p8)*. Turning up early is another option.

9 Ticket Touts

Like elsewhere, Paris has its ticket touts, and the usual rules apply. It may get you tickets for an in-demand event, but be wary of forgeries and exorbitantly increased prices. Some Parisians carry a sign outside venues saying; "*cherche une place*" ("looking for a seat"), which sometimes gets a ticket at face-value from someone with one to spare.

10 Ticket Agencies

Tickets for concerts and theatre shows are sold at the main tourist information centre at 25 rue des Pyramides as well as at ticket agencies all around the city, including at several branches of the FNAC chain of CD/book/movie stores. There is a booking fee for using agencies. *FNAC, 74 ave des Champs-Elysées • Map C3 • Open 10am–11:45pm Mon–Sat, noon–11:45pm Sun • www.fnactickets.com*

Left **Paris chocolate shop** Centre **Street market stall** Right **Souvenir biscuit tins**

TOP 10 Shopping

1 Shopping Hours

Department stores and chain boutiques are usually open from 9:30am–7pm Monday to Saturday. Late-night shopping is on Thursdays until 9pm. Private boutiques often don't open until 10 or 11am, and may be closed during holidays, on Mondays and/or between noon and 2pm, but many open on Sundays. Most food shops are open on Sunday morning.

2 Taxes

Different rates of sales tax (TVA) apply to most goods, varying between 5–25 per cent and are generally included in the stated price. No refunds are available on purchases of food, wine or tobacco. On other goods, tax can be refunded to non-EU citizens who spend more than €175 in one shop. Ask the store for the appropriate form.

3 Food

Shops such as Maille, Hédiard, Fauchon and Ladurée sell beautifully packaged delicacies. Ask to have your pungent French cheeses vacuum packed *(sous vide)*. Place de Madeleine has several top-quality delis *(see p98)*, or try one of the street markets for fresh produce.

4 Clothes

Paris is one of the world centres of fashion and is home to all the top names *(see p108)*, but don't forget to look out for the independent designers and labels often found nowhere else, such as Antoine et Lili *(see p88)*. For vintage clothes try Espace Kiliwatch (64 rue Tiquetonne) and Didier Ludot in the Palais-Royal's arcades *(see p96)*.

5 Lingerie

French fashion isn't all on the surface. Designers also produce beautiful lingerie or you can try specialist firms such as Lejaby, Lise Charmel, Aubade (available from good department stores) or Carine Gilson (18 rue de Grenelle).

6 Perfume and Cosmetics

The Marionnaud and Sephora chains offer a huge variety of scents and make-up brands. Prices are usually reasonable too. For something different try Clara Molloy (Memo Boutique, 60 rue des Saints-Pères) or Les Parfums de Rosine (Palais-Royal).

Designer shoes

7 Department and Concept Stores

Galeries Lafayettes, Au Printemps and Le Bon Marché are worth a visit just for their *Belle Epoque* interiors *(see p54)*. Concept stores are recent arrivals – try L'Eclaireur (26 Champs-Elysées), which sells clothes and hosts art exhibitions and events, or Merci *(see p88)*.

8 Bric-a-brac, Books and Prints

The flea market at Saint-Ouen *(see p55)* is good for bric-a-brac, while the Marché Malassis gallery stocks a range of 20th-century treasures. The *bouquinistes* by the Seine sell vintage posters and postcards. Shakespeare and Company is the place for rare books *(see p122)*.

9 Music

The FNAC chain of shops stock a huge range of CDs, books, videos and computer software. The all-purpose department store BHV also has a selection of French and international CDs for those who still seek them.

10 Stationery

French stationery can be exquisite and even chains such as Plein Ciel sell beautiful notebooks, diaries and address books. Independent shops include Magna Carta (101 rue du Bac), while Lamartine (118 rue de la Pompe) sells G. Lalo's superb products.

For more shops in Paris **See pp54–5**

Left **Bureau de change** Centre **Paris postbox** Right **Newspapers on sale**

TOP 10 Banking & Communications

1 Currency

The euro (€), the single European currency, is now operational in 17 of the 27 member states of the EU, including France. Euro banknotes have seven denominations: 5, 10, 20, 50, 100, 200 and 500. There are also eight coin denominations: €1 and €2, and 50, 20, 10, 5, 2 and 1 cents (also referred to as centimes). Both notes and coins are valid and interchangeable within each of the 17 countries. Check on exchange rates against your own currency at the time of travel.

2 Credit Cards

These are widely accepted throughout Paris and you should have no difficulty paying for most things with plastic. The only exception is American Express because of the heavy commission it incurs. The Visa card is the most widely used.

Parisian public telephone

3 Cash Dispensers (ATMs)

There are cash dispensers all over Paris, and each one indicates the cards it accepts. Many of them also operate in several languages. If you know your PIN number, obtaining cash in this way is very easy.

4 Changing Money

Bureaux de Change exist throughout Paris, especially near tourist hotspots. Many banks also have either a *bureau de change* or foreign desk. "No commission" signs can be misleading, as they probably mean an unfavourable rate.

5 Post Offices

The main post offices in the heart of Paris are at 52 rue de Louvre (open 24 hours) and 71 ave des Champs-Elysées. They do not exchange currency or travellers' cheques but will exchange international postal cheques, giros and money orders. For simple letters and postcards, you can buy stamps at a *tabac* (tobacconist) rather than try to find a post office. Not all of them advertise the service, but if they sell postcards it is worth asking. Some hotels and newsagents also sell postage stamps.

6 Telephones

Paris phone numbers begin with 01 or 09 and have eight subsequent digits, usually written in four sets of two digits. If calling Paris from overseas, drop the zero from "01". Most public telephones require a *télécarte* (phonecard), which can be bought from post offices, metro stations, tobacconists and a few other outlets. Mobile phone numbers begin with 06.

7 Mobile Phones

Check the roaming rates with your mobile operator before your trip. Pay as you go SIM cards can be bought for unlocked phones and topped up at tobacconists.

8 Internet Access

Internet cafés are becoming less common as free Wi-Fi hotspots take over, and many cafés provide free Wi-Fi access. Find a complete list at www.cafes-wifi.com.

9 Newspapers and Magazines

A wide choice of the major foreign newspapers is available on the day of publication throughout Paris. The closer you are to the Champs-Elysées, the more you will see. The popular *International Herald Tribune* is published in Paris.

10 Television and Radio

Most hotels subscribe to multilingual cable and satellite channels, which vary the diet of French-language entertainment.

Left **Pedestrian stop sign** Centre **Paris police car** Right **Pharmacy sign**

TOP 10 Security & Health

1 Crossing the Road
Take care when crossing Paris's roads. French drivers are not known for respecting pedestrians, though a red light will usually – although not always – make them stop. Pedestrians do not have automatic priority on a crossing, unless lights are also in their favour. On pedestrian crossings, motorists often have the right to turn right, so always look before you start to cross.

2 Pickpockets
Gangs of pickpockets do frequent tourist spots such as the Eiffel Tower and the Arc de Triomphe, as well as wandering the metro system. Some are amateur gangs and easy to spot, but others are more subtle so guard your belongings at all times.

3 Mugging
Mugging is less of a problem in Paris than in other big cities, but it can happen. Try not to travel alone late at night and avoid unlit streets. Try to avoid long changes between metro lines too: better a longer journey than an unfortunate experience. The main stations you should avoid at night are Les Halles and Gare du Nord.

4 Police
There are a number of police stations in central Paris. These are listed in the phone book, or call the Préfecture Centrale for details. All crimes should be reported, if only for insurance purposes. *Préfecture Centrale: 01 53 71 53 71 • Open 24 hours*

5 Women Travellers
Parisian men are generally courteous. A firm rebuttal usually halts unwanted attention. If not, try to seek the help of another man: they do not like to see a woman being pestered.

6 Insurance
Paris medical treatment is very good but it can be expensive, so be sure to have good health insurance. Visitors from EU countries should be equipped with a European Health Insurance card to avoid emergency fees. All other nationalities should take out private insurance. Report all crimes or lost property, and keep a copy of the statement you make to the police.

7 Hospitals
English-speaking visitors might want to contact the British or the American Hospitals, both open 24 hours a day. Paris hospitals are listed in the phone book, or call Hôpital Assistance Publique. *British Hospital: 01 46 39 22 22 • American Hospital: 01 46 41 25 25 • Hôpital Assistance Publique: www.aphp.fr*

8 Ambulances
If you need an ambulance, dial the emergency number. Fire stations also have ambulances and are qualified to carry out first aid.

9 Pharmacies
A green cross indicates a pharmacy (chemist). They are usually open between 9am–7pm Monday to Saturday. At other times, the address of the duty pharmacy will probably be displayed, or contact the local *gendarmerie*. Pharmacies will also give doctors' details.

10 Dentists
These are listed in the Paris *Pages Jaunes (Yellow Pages)* under *Dentistes*. In a dire emergency, a service called SOS Dentistes will provide a house call, but be prepared to pay a large amount for this. A large dental practice is at the Centre Médical Europe. *SOS Dentistes: 87 blvd Port Royal, 01 43 37 51 00 • Centre Médical Europe: 44 rue d'Amsterdam, 01 42 81 93 33*

Emergency Numbers

Police
112; 17

Ambulance (SAMU)
15

Fire Department
18

Left **The Westin Paris** Centre **Renaissance le Parc Trocadero** Right **Meurice**

Top 10 Luxury Hotels

1 Plaza Athénée

Surrounded by designer shops *(see p108)* is this venerable but thoroughly modernized hotel, famed for its old-world air of luxury and its immaculate service. Alain Ducasse has a dazzling restaurant in the hotel *(see p109)*. *25 ave Montaigne, 75008 • Map C3 • 01 53 67 66 65 • www.plaza-athenee-paris.com • €€€€€*

2 Four Seasons George V

One of the most luxurious and fashionable hotels in Paris, the George V combines period features with modern amenities. Bedrooms are spacious, beautifully decorated and have marble bathrooms. The restaurant, Le Cinq *(see p109)*, has become one of "the" places to eat. *31 ave George V, 75008 • Map C3 • 01 49 52 70 00 • www.fourseasons.com/paris • €€€€€*

3 The Westin Paris

A world away from the usual anonymity of chain hotels, being set in a 19th-century building designed by Charles Garnier and overlooking the Tuileries *(see p95)*. The original atmosphere has been retained, but the rooms offer everything you would expect from a Westin hotel. *3 rue de Castiglione, 75001 • Map E3 • 01 44 77 11 11 • www.westin.com • €€€€€*

4 Mandarin Oriental

Centrally located on one of Paris's most fashionable streets, Rue Saint-Honoré, the interiors of this hotel boast Art Deco with Oriental influences. The rooms and suites are luxurious and spacious. *251 rue Saint-Honoré, 75001 • Map E3 • 01 70 98 78 88 • www.mandarinoriental.com/paris • €€€€€*

5 Meurice

The sumptuous antique decor of the Meurice may not be original, but you would never know it. The fading hotel has been completely restored, creating spacious guest rooms and state-of-the-art facilities, as well as interiors by Philippe Starck. And the location could not be better. *228 rue de Rivoli, 75001 • Map E3 • 01 44 58 10 15 • www.lemeurice.com • €€€€€*

6 Renaissance Le Parc Trocadero

The façade of this 1912 mansion conceals a beautiful flower-filled courtyard, while the interior decor combines the feel of the old with the design of the new. Its restaurant, Le Relais du Parc *(see p139)*, is one of the best dining venues in the area. *55–59 ave Raymond Poincaré, 75016 • Map B3 • 01 44 05 66 66 • www.parisrenaissance.com • €€€€*

7 Shangri-La Paris

Housed in the former home of Napoleon's grand-nephew, this fabulous hotel is located in the chic 16th arrondisement. Most of the rooms have impressive views of the Eiffel Tower. *10 ave d'Iéna, 75116 • Map A3 • 01 80 27 19 35 • www.shangri-la.com • €€€€€*

8 Hôtel Raphaël

One of the city's finest hotels. The antique decor is reflected in the rooms but they have been fully modernized in terms of facilities. Higher floors have stunning Parisian views. *17 ave Kleber, 75016 • Map B3 • 01 53 64 32 00 • www. raphael-hotel.com • €€€€€*

9 Le Royal Monceau

This Paris branch of the Raffles hotel chain features interiors by Philippe Starck and two superb restaurants. *37 ave Hoche, 75008 • Map C2 • 01 42 99 88 00 • www.raffles.com/paris • €€€€€*

10 Westminster

This hotel was built in the 18th century and was named after the Duke of Westminster who used to stay here. The rooms combine modern facilities with elegant English-style furnishings. *13 rue de la Paix, 75002 • Map E3 • 01 42 61 57 46 • www.warwickwestminsteropera.com • €€€€*

***Note:** Unless otherwise stated, all hotels accept credit cards, have en-suite bathrooms and air conditioning*

Price Categories

For a standard, double room per night (with breakfast if included), taxes and extra charges.		
	€	under €100
	€€	€100–€150
	€€€	€150–€250
	€€€€	€250–€350
	€€€€€	over €350

Left **Brighton** Right **Hôtel du Panthéon**

TOP 10 Hotels in Great Locations

1 Hôtel Edouard VII

An elegant boutique hotel with eclectic design features and oodles of charm. Most rooms have the bonus of breath-taking balcony views over the spectacular Opéra National de Paris Garnier *(see p97)*. *39 avenue de l'Opéra, 75002 • Map E3 • 01 42 61 56 90 • www.edouard7hotel.com • info@edouard7hotel.com • €€€€€*

2 Brighton

Enjoy the rue de Rivoli, within walking distance of many attractions, without paying the usual prices associated with this location. This old hotel has been completely refurbished, ask for one of the rooms with a view over the Tuileries opposite *(see p95)*, or of the Eiffel Tower *(see pp16–17)*. *218 rue de Rivoli, 75001 • Map K1 • 01 47 03 61 61 • www.paris-hotel-brighton.com • €€€*

3 Bristol

Prices reflect the luxury standards and location, close to the Faubourg St-Honoré. Rooms are large and fitted out with antique furniture and spacious, marble bathrooms, as well as all the latest modern facilities. There are also two restaurants. *112 rue du Faubourg-St-Honoré, 75008 • Map D3 • 01 53 43 43 00 • www.lebristolparis.com • resa@lebristolparis.com • €€€€€*

4 Hôtel du Jeu de Paume

Tucked away on the Ile St-Louis is this beautiful old building with beams. Some rooms overlook a peaceful courtyard. Rooms are small but the friendly atmosphere makes up for everything. *54 rue St-Louis-en-l'Ile, 75004 • Map Q5 • 01 43 26 14 18 • www.jeudepaumehotel.com • info@jeudepaumehotel.com • €€€€*

5 Hôtel des Deux-Iles

To stay on one of the Seine islands is a treat, and to do it in this hotel is a double treat. The bedrooms may be small, due to the building's 17th-century origins, but the cheerful decor, the intimacy (only 17 rooms) and the hidden patio with its flowers and fountain more than compensate. *59 rue St-Louis-en-l'Ile, 75004 • Map Q5 • 01 43 26 13 35 • www.hoteldesdeuxiles.com • No disabled access • €€€*

6 Hôtel d'Orsay

Art-lovers will enjoy this hotel, right by the magnificent Musée d'Orsay *(see pp12–15)*. The hotel's modern bright colours are strikingly offset with antique furniture here and there. Several more expensive suites are also available. *93 rue de Lille, 75007 • Map J2 • 01 47 05 85 54 • www.paris-hotel-orsay.com • €€€*

7 Hôtel du Panthéon

A small, charming hotel set in an 18th-century building right by the Panthéon *(see pp28–9)*. *19 place du Panthéon, 75005 • Map N6 • 01 43 54 32 95 • www.hoteldupantheon.com • reservation@hoteldupantheon.com • €€€€*

8 Pavillon de la Reine

The best hotel in the Marais, right on the place des Vosges *(see pp84–7)*. Lovely rooms, a spa and a quiet courtyard. *28 pl des Vosges, 75003 • Map R3 • 01 40 29 19 19 • www.pavillon-de-la-reine.com • contact@pavillon-de-la-reine.com • €€€€€*

9 Hôtel de la Place du Louvre

A hotel that provides its guests with a superb view of the Louvre *(see pp10–13)*. The rooms cleverly mix the historical with the modern. *21 rue des Prêtres-St-Germain-l'Auxerrois, 75001 • Map M2 • 01 42 33 78 68 • www.paris-hotel-place-du-louvre.com • No disabled access • €€€*

10 Hôtel Castille

This elegant hotel near place Vendôme is just a couple of steps away from the original Chanel store. It also boasts an Italian restaurant, L'Assaggio. *33 rue Cambon, 75001 • Map E3 • 01 44 58 44 58 • www.castille.com • €€€€€*

Left **Hôtel Bellechasse** Centre **Aviatic Hôtel** Right **Hôtel d'Aubusson**

Top 10 Romantic Hotels

1 Hôtel d'Aubusson

The rooms in this 17th-century building are spacious and many of them have beams. In winter there is a log fire in the guests' lounge. *33 rue Dauphine, 75006 • Map M4 • 01 43 29 43 43 • www.hoteldaubusson.com • €€€€*

2 Hôtel Particulier Montmartre

Housed in a former private residence, this hotel's rooms are individually decorated in stunning Baroque style. *23 ave Junot, Pavillon D, 75018 • Map E1 • 01 53 41 81 40 • www.hotel-particulier-montmartre.com • No disabled access • €€€€€*

3 Aviatic Hôtel

A stylish hotel that bubbles with the delightful atmosphere of the Left Bank. Ask them to pack a picnic for you for a romantic stroll around the nearby Jardin du Luxembourg *(see p119)*. *105 rue de Vaugirad, 75006 • Map D6 • 01 53 63 25 50 • www.aviatic.fr • welcome@aviatic.fr • No disabled access • €€€€*

4 L'Hôtel

This hotel has come up in the world since Oscar Wilde expired here, having uttered the famous words, "My wallpaper and I are fighting a duel to the death. One or the other of us has to go." Fashionable as it has become, with stylish decor by Jacques Garcia and a Michelin-starred restaurant, the hotel still has a quirky charm. *13 rue des Beaux-Arts, 75006 • Map E4 • 01 44 41 99 00 • www.l-hotel.com • €€€€€*

5 Hôtel Bellechasse

The fabulously opulent rooms at this hotel were designed by Christian Lacroix. Special packages, such as *Pour Une Nuit*, include a 3pm checkout, champagne and other indulgent treats. The hotel is located just a few minutes' walk from the Musée d'Orsay. *8 rue de Bellechasse, 75007 • Map J2 • 01 45 50 22 31 • www.lebellechasse.com • No disabled access • €€€€€*

6 Five Hotel

Fibre-optic lighting creates a glittering atmosphere in many of this boutique hotel's 24 rooms. Guests can choose from nine colours, ranging from tranquil black to cheerful plum-and-pink, and five "olfactory ambiences" by Esteban. The Five has already established a reputation as the perfect lovers' getaway. *3 rue Flatters, 75005 • 01 43 31 74 21 • www.thefivehotel.com • €€*

7 Hôtel Costes

Book a first-floor room overlooking the courtyard for a romantic place to stay. Low lighting and dark furniture add to the mood, as does the Oriental-style swimming pool and trendy restaurant. *239 rue St-Honoré, 75001 • Map E3 • 01 42 44 50 00 • www.hotelcostes.com • €€€€€*

8 Le Relais Christine

This historic mansion with a spa offers a backstreet haven from the St-Germain bustle. Opt for a terraced room overlooking the secluded garden and take breakfast in the vaulted room which was once an abbey's refectory. *3 rue Christine, 75006 • Map M4 • 01 40 51 60 80 • www.relais-christine.com • No disabled access • €€€€*

9 Hôtel Lancaster

Pampering is paid for here, but the investment pays off with huge rooms in a 19th-century mansion just a stroll from the Champs-Elysées. *7 rue de Berri, 75008 • Map C3 • 01 40 76 40 76 • www.hotel-lancaster.fr • reservations@hotel-lancaster.fr • €€€€€*

10 Hôtel Caron de Beaumarchais

Wooden beams, candlelight, a log fire, authentic decor and sparkling crystal chandeliers evoke the essence of 18th-century romance. Rooms are beautiful and guests are truly pampered. *12 rue Vieille-du-Temple, 75004 • Map R2 • 01 42 72 34 12 • www.carondebeaumarchais.com • hotel@carondebeaumarchais.com • No disabled access • €€*

Price Categories

For a standard, double room per night (with breakfast if included), taxes and extra charges.	€	under €100
	€€	€100–€150
	€€€	€150–€250
	€€€€	€250–€350
	€€€€€	over €350

Left **Hôtel des Grandes Écoles** Right **Hôtel Lenox Montparnasse**

TOP 10 Budget Hotels

1 Hôtel des Grandes Écoles

A secret hideaway in a lovely part of Paris, the three buildings that make up this 51-room hotel are set around a garden. The rooms are attractively decorated and the location is perfect as a base for exploring the Latin Quarter. ✆ *75 rue du Cardinal-Lemoine, 75005 • Map P6 • 01 43 26 79 23 • www.hotel-grandes-ecoles.com • No air conditioning • €€*

2 Hôtel Lenox Montparnasse

The flower-filled Lenox is close to Montparnasse cemetery *(see p151)*. The rooms are clean, with modern facilities. Some are on the small side so ask for a larger room if you don't like being too cramped: there is also a top-floor suite. ✆ *15 rue Delambre, 75014 • Map D6 • 01 43 35 34 50 • www.hotellenox.com • No disabled access • €€€*

3 Hôtel Saint-André-des-Arts

This charmingly modest hotel offers ancient exposed beams and a Left Bank location at bargain prices. The rooms are tiny, but for a cheap bolt-hole and truly Parisian Bohemian feel, it can't be beaten. ✆ *66 rue St-André-des-Arts, 75006 • Map M4 • 01 43 26 96 16 • hsaintand@wanadoo.fr • No air conditioning • No disabled access • €*

4 Hôtel Amour

Situated just below Montmartre, this extremely trendy vintage hotel and bistro has medium-sized rooms decorated with cutting edge photography and pop art (bare bottoms and more much are in evidence). As it is on a quiet residential street, guests can experience Parisian Bohemia without the usual crowds. ✆ *8 rue Navarin, 75009 • Map F1 • 01 48 78 31 80 • www.hotelamourparis.fr • €€€*

5 Grand Hôtel Lévêque

The only thing grand about this hotel is its name, but it remains a favourite for budget accommodation in Paris. Almost all rooms have fans, phone, TV and a hairdryer. ✆ *29 rue Cler, 75007 • Map C4 • 01 47 05 49 15 • www.hotel-leveque.com • info@hotel-leveque.com • No disabled access • €*

6 Hôtel du Cygne

This lovely hotel is housed in a restored 17th-century building and has 20 rooms. It is centrally located, just a five-minute walk away from Forum Les Halles. Free Wi-Fi is available in all the rooms. ✆ *8 rue du Cygne, 75001 • Map N1 • 01 42 60 14 16 • Not all en-suite • No air conditioning • No disabled access • €€*

7 Le Caulaincourt Square Hôtel

Part budget hotel, part hostel, with a friendly atmosphere and access to the sights of Montmartre. ✆ *2 square Caulaincourt, 75018 • Map E1 • 01 46 06 46 06 • www.caulaincourt.com • No air conditioning • No disabled access • €*

8 Mama Shelter

Created by well-known designer Philippe Starck, this trendy hotel offers stylish and affordable rooms. The lively restaurant is very popular with guests. ✆ *109 rue de Bagnolet, 75020 • 01 43 48 48 48 • www.mamashelter.com • €€*

9 St Christopher's Inn Paris

This hostel offers mixed as well as single-sex dorms, private twins with shared bathrooms and private doubles. ✆ *159 rue de Crimée, 75019 • Map H1 • 01 40 34 34 40 • www.st-christophers.co.uk/paris-hostels • Not all en-suite • €*

10 Ermitage Hôtel

A wonderful family-run hotel in Montmartre. Some rooms have views over the city, others overlook a garden, and the furniture is antique or retro. ✆ *24 rue Lamarck, 75018 • Map E1 • 01 42 64 79 22 • www.ermitagesacrecoeur.fr • No credit cards • No air conditioning • No disabled access • €€*

***Note:** Unless otherwise stated, all hotels accept credit cards, have en-suite bathrooms and air conditioning*

Left **Hôtel de Seine** Right **Hôtel de Banville**

TOP 10 Medium-Priced Hotels

1 La Régence Étoile Hôtel

Very reasonably priced for its standard and location (a short walk from the Arc de Triomphe), the Régence has plush public areas and modern bedrooms with TVs, direct-dial phones, mini-bars and safe. *24 ave Carnot, 75017 • Map B2 • 01 58 05 42 42 • www.laregenceetoile.com • No disabled access • €€€*

2 Hôtel d'Angleterre

Hemingway once stayed in this long-established hotel. Most rooms are a good size with high ceilings, and some are decorated with antiques. The standard rooms are small so book a superior one at extra cost. *44 rue Jacob, 75006 • Map N5 • 01 42 60 34 72 • www.hotel-dangleterre.com • No air conditioning • No disabled access • €€€*

3 L'Abbaye Saint-Germain

This 16th-century former convent has a cobbled courtyard in a quiet location near St-Sulpice *(see p41)*. It is perfect for exploring much of the Left Bank, and is a haven to return to afterwards. The 44 rooms are all different, the best being the top-floor suites with their rooftop views. *10 rue Cassette, 75006 • Map K5 • 01 45 44 38 11 • www.hotel-abbaye.com • hotel-abbaye@wanadoo.fr • No disabled access • €€€€*

4 Hôtel de Seine

Timbered rooms indicate the old-world nature of this mansion, close to the Jardin du Luxembourg. Some rooms have balconies. *52 rue de Seine, 75006 • Map L5 • 01 46 34 22 80 • www.hoteldeseine.com • No disabled access • €€€*

5 Hôtel Notre-Dame Maître Albert

Situated in a quiet street opposite Notre-Dame, close to the Latin Quarter and the Marais, this hotel combines modern design with beams and stone walls. *19 rue Maitre-Albert, 75005 • Map N5 • 01 43 26 79 00 • www.hotel-charme-notredame.com • No disabled access • €€€*

6 Hôtel Le Clos Médicis

Built in 1773 for the Médici family, ancient beams and artworks now combine with modern design. Rooms are small, but compensations are the garden, adjacent bar, and the location in a quiet street off boulevard St-Michel. *56 rue Monsieur-le-Prince, 75006 • Map M5 • 01 43 29 10 80 • www.hotelclosmedicisparis.com • message@closmedicis.com • 1 room suitable for disabled guests • €€€*

7 Hotel des Trois Poussins

This hotel is in the Pigalle area but is well away from the sleazy side. Some rooms are small, but the higher they go, the better the view. *15 rue Clauzel, 75009 • Map E1 • 01 53 32 81 81 • www.les3poussins.com • h3p@les3poussins.com • €€€*

8 Le Citizen

This eco-hotel with modern decor boasts lovely views over the fashionable Canal St-Martin. There are 12 comfortable rooms. A wide choice of restaurants is available nearby. *96 quai de Jenmapes, 75010 • Map H2 • 01 83 62 55 50 • www.lecitizenhotel.com • €€€*

9 Hôtel Saint-Paul

This 17th-century building has antique furniture, beams and some four-poster beds. Several rooms have great views over Paris and the Sorbonne *(see p119)*. *43 rue Monsieur-le-Prince, 75006 • Map M5 • 01 43 26 98 64 • www.hotelsaintpaulparis.fr • contact@hotelsaintpaulparis.com • €€€*

10 Hôtel de Banville

This wonderful 1928 mansion may be away from the centre but it oozes class and is filled with antiques. Several bedrooms have balconies. *166 boulevard Berthier, 75017 • Metro Porte de Clichy • 01 42 67 70 16 • www.hotelbanville.fr • €€€*

***Note:** Unless otherwise stated, all hotels accept credit cards, have en-suite bathrooms and air conditioning*

Left **Hotel Résidence Lord Byron** Right **Hôtel Chopin**

Price Categories

For a standard,	€	under €100
double room per	€€	€100–€150
night (with breakfast	€€€	€150–€250
if included), taxes	€€€€	€250–€350
and extra charges.	€€€€€	over €350

TOP 10 Famous-Name Hotels

1 Hôtel Esmeralda

The proximity to Notre-Dame gives the hotel its name. Ask for a room with a cathedral view, and be prepared for a Bohemian atmosphere. The area is noisy and the rooms are not modernized, although they all have en-suite bathrooms. *4 rue St-Julien-le-Pauvre, 75005 • Map P4 • 01 43 54 19 20 • www.hotel-esmeralda.fr • No air conditioning • No disabled access • €€*

2 Résidence Lord Byron

Located just off the Champs-Elysées, this is an inexpensive hotel in an expensive area, with a pleasant courtyard garden for summer breakfasts. Top floor rooms have good views. *5 rue Chateaubriand, 75008 • Map C2 • 01 43 59 89 98 • www.hotel-lordbyron.fr • lordbyron@hotel-lordbyron.fr • €€€*

3 Hôtel Balzac

Fashionably chic, this luxurious hotel has a restaurant and a basement bar, both popular with the locals. The hotel's 57 rooms and 13 apartments are simply but tastefully decorated, with terraced suites offering great views of the Eiffel Tower. *6 rue Balzac, 75008 • Map C2 • 01 44 35 18 00 • www.hotelbalzac.com • reservation-balzac@jjwhotels.com • €€€€€*

4 Hôtel Chopin

Hidden away in one of the city's *passages (see p50)*, the Chopin opened in 1846. At this price don't expect the best facilities, but it is a pleasant place to stay and the rooms are comfortable. Ask for an upper room for more light. *46 passage Jouffroy, 10 blvd Montmartre, 75009 • Map F2 • 01 47 70 58 10 • www.hotelchopin.fr • No air conditioning • No disabled access • €€*

5 Hôtel Langlois

Originally opened in 1897, this quaint *belle époque* hotel has large, individually decorated rooms, all en-suite, and a modern lift. It is located near the Gustave Moreau Museum and the Opéra National de Paris Garnier is within walking distance. *63 rue Saint-Lazare, 75009 • 01 48 74 78 24 • www.hotel-langlois.com • No disabled access • €€*

6 Hôtel Flaubert

Terrific value, slightly out of the centre but not far from the metro. New owners have smartened it up and the lush garden is a delight. Room sizes vary. *19 rue Rennequin, 75017 • Map C1 • 01 46 22 44 35 • www.hotelflaubert.com • paris@hotelflaubert.com • €€*

7 Hôtel Baudelaire Opéra

The French writer Baudelaire lived here in 1854, and today it makes a good bargain find in this central area. Rooms are brightly decorated, although most of them are small. *61 rue St-Anne, 75002 • Map H4 • 01 42 97 50 62 • www.hotel-baudelaire.com • resa@hotel-baudelaire.com • No air conditioning • No disabled access • €€€*

8 The W

Ideally located next to the Paris Opera, the W brings its trendy and modern flair to Paris with 91 ultra-chic rooms and suites. Nab one with a view of the opera house. . *4 rue Meyerbeer, 75009 • Map E2 • 01 77 48 94 94 • www.wparisopera.com • €€€€€*

9 Hôtel Galileo

Tasteful decor and a walled garden, all just a short walk from the Arc de Triomphe. *54 rue Galilée, 75008 • Map B2 • 01 47 20 66 06 • www.galileo-paris-hotel.com • €€€€*

10 Grand Hôtel Jeanne d'Arc

You could pass a whole weekend in Paris without wandering far from this well-equipped hotel, surrounded as it is by Marais attractions. *3 rue de Jarente, 75004 • Metro St Paul • 01 48 87 62 11 • www.hoteljeannedarc.com • information@hoteljeannedarc.com • No air conditioning • €€*

Left **Hotel Square** Centre **Hôtel du Quai Voltaire** Right **Le Notre-Dame St-Michel**

TOP 10 Rooms with a View

1 Hôtel Bourgogne et Montana
Stylish hotel, with the Musée d'Orsay *(see pp12–15)* and the Invalides close by. Rooms have empire-style furnishings with Kenzo-designed wallpaper. Some top-floor rooms have views across the Seine. *3 rue de Bourgogne, 75007 • Map D4 • 01 45 51 20 22 • www.bourgogne-montana.com • No disabled access • €€€€*

2 Artus Hôtel
Indulge yourself in the food shops of the Rue de Buci *(see p123)*, then indulge yourself even more back in this hotel – especially if you have booked the suite with a Jacuzzi from which there are views of the Latin Quarter. *34 rue de Buci, 75006 • Map L4 •01 43 29 07 20 • www.artushotel.com • info@artushotel.com • No disabled access • €€€€*

3 Hotel Square
Ultra-chic boutique hotel with 22 rooms and views over Paris. The Zebra Square is a cool restaurant *(see p139)*. *3 rue de Boulainvilliers, 75016 • Map A5 • 01 44 14 91 90 • www.hotelsquare.com • reservation@hotelsquare.com • €€€€€*

4 Hôtel du Quai Voltaire
Impressionist artist Camille Pissarro (1830–1903) painted the view of the Seine and Notre-Dame visible from most of the guest rooms here. Rooms are small, but the warm welcome and the location more than make up for that. *19 quai Voltaire, 75007 • Map K2 • 01 42 61 50 91 • www.quaivoltaire.fr • No air conditioning • No disabled access • €€*

5 Hôtel des Grands Hommes
Great upper floor views of the Panthéon *(see pp28–9)* from this intimate 30-room hotel in an 18th-century house. The rooms are reasonably sized. *17 pl du Panthéon, 75005 • Map N6 • 01 46 34 19 60 • www.hoteldesgrandshommes.com • No disabled access • €€€€*

6 Terrass Hôtel
Located in Montmartre, the Terrass has fabulous views over Paris which can be enjoyed from its rooftop terrace. Most rooms in this early 19th-century building have air conditioning. There is a bar, restaurant and other facilities. *12–14 rue Joseph-de-Maistre, 75018 • Map E1 • 01 44 92 34 14 • www.terrass-hotel.com • reservation@terrass-hotel.com • €€€€*

7 Le Notre-Dame St-Michel
A great location right by the Seine with magnificent views of Notre-Dame, the bright decor by Christian Lacroix here makes up for the size of the rooms. There are also three suites. *1 quai St Michel, 75005 • Map N4 • 01 43 54 20 43 • www.hotelnotredameparis.com • info@hotelnotredameparis.com • No disabled access • €€€€*

8 Les Rives de Notre-Dame
The view of Notre-Dame from this 10-room hotel is arguably the best in Paris. The spacious and modern rooms have charming wooden beams. *15 quai St-Michel, 75005 • Map N4 • 01 43 54 81 16 • www.rivesdenotredame.com • hotel@rivesdenotredame.com • No disabled access • €€€€*

9 Hôtel Régina
Across the rue de Rivoli from the Louvre *(see pp8–11)* with views of the Tuileries and the Louvre, this is a splendid old hotel. *2 pl des Pyramides, 75001 • Map K1 • 01 42 60 31 10 • www.regina-hotel.com • €€€€€*

10 Radisson Blu Le Metropolitan
Five upper suites offer striking views onto the Eiffel Tower; the best has a giant bull's-eye window. Lower-floor rooms have good, but less spectacular, balcony views. *10 place de Mexico, 75016 • Map A3 • 01 56 90 40 04 • www.radissonblu.com • €€€€*

***Note:** Unless otherwise stated, all hotels accept credit cards, have en-suite bathrooms and air conditioning*

Left **Relais St-Germain** Right **Fleurie**

Price Categories

For a standard, double room per night (with breakfast if included), taxes and extra charges.	€	under €100
	€€	€100–€150
	€€€	€150–€250
	€€€€	€250–€350
	€€€€€	over €350

Top 10 Family-Friendly Hotels

1 Hôtel Baltimore
Part of the Accor hotel chain and situated between the Trocadéro and the Arc de Triomphe, the Baltimore caters well for families with good facilities and a friendly attitude. Rooms and suites are elegant. *88 bis avenue Kléber, 75016 • Map B3 • 01 44 34 54 54 • www.accorhotels.com • €€€€*

2 Relais St-Germain
A delightful hotel in a 17th-century town house right in the heart of the Left Bank. The Musée du Louvre, Musée d'Orsay and Notre-Dame cathedral are all within walking distance, and the Jardin du Luxembourg is nearby for when the children simply want to play in the park. *9 carrefour de l'Odéon, 75006 • Map L4 • 01 43 29 12 05 • www.hotel-paris-relais-saint-germain.com • No disabled access • €€€€*

3 Relais du Louvre
Right by the Louvre, this great family hotel offers a self-catering apartment for five, plus several family suites and communicating rooms, as well as a host of "extras" for small children. *19 rue des Prêtres-Saint-Germain-l'Auxerrois, 75001 • Map M2 • 01 40 41 96 42 • www.relaisdulouvre.com • contact@relaisdulouvre.com • No disabled access • €€€*

4 Fleurie
Children under 12 sleeping in their parents' room stay free in this smart but lively St-Germain hotel. A small charge is made for over 12s. Satellite TV, Wi-Fi and air conditioning in each room, and a huge buffet breakfast. *32–4 rue Grégoire de Tours, 75006 • Map L4 • 01 53 73 70 00 • www.hotel-de-fleurie.fr • bonjour@hotel-de-fleurie.fr • No disabled access • €€€*

5 Pullman Paris Montparnasse
Facilities here include family rooms with two double beds. Children's entertainment is laid on during Sunday brunch. *19 rue du Commandant René Mouchotte, 75014 • Map D6 • 01 44 36 44 36 • www.pullmanhotels.com • €€€*

6 Hôtel de l'Université
This 17th-century St-Germain mansion has several apartments with two rooms and small terraces. *22 rue de l'Université, 75007 • Map K3 • 01 42 61 09 39 • www.hoteluniversite.com • hoteluniversite@wanadoo.fr • €€€*

7 Hôtel des Arts
This hotel is an excellent choice for families on a budget, with triple rooms and cots available. The hotel is in one of Paris's passages *(see p50)*. *7 Cité Bergère, 6 rue du Faubourg Montmartre, 75009 • Map F2 • 01 42 46 73 30 • www.hoteldesarts.fr • contact@hoteldesarts.fr • No air conditioning • No disabled access • €*

8 Hôtel St-Jacques
Numerous Left Bank attractions are near this comfortable hotel with triple-bed rooms and cots available. All rooms are en-suite and have a TV. *35 rue des Écoles, 75005 • Map N5 • 01 44 07 45 45 • www.paris-hotel-stjacques.com • hotelsaintjacques@wanadoo.fr • €€€*

9 Hôtel Residence Romance Malesherbes
A collection of intriguing studios with kitchenettes makes up for the slightly out-of-centre location. Parc Monceau and a good market are nearby. *129 rue Cardinet, 75017 • Map D1 • 01 44 15 85 00 • www.hotel-romance.com • hotel@hotel-romance.com • No air conditioning • No disabled access • €€€*

10 Hotel Ibis Bastille Opéra
Right in the heart of the Bastille district, this no-frills chain hotel offers triple-bed rooms or doubles with a child's bed. Rooms are small but well-equipped and are cheaper at weekends. *15 rue Breguet, 75011 • Map H5 • 01 49 29 20 20 • www.ibishotel.com • €€*

For Paris for children **See pp60–61**

General Index

Acknowledgements

Authors
Donna Dailey and Mike Gerrard are award-winning journalists, specializing in travel, food and wine, and have written more than 30 guidebooks between them. Mike Gerrard's *Time for Food* guide to Paris for Thomas Cook won the Benjamin Franklin Award for best new guidebook in 2001. Their work has appeared in international publications such as the *Times*, *Washington Post* and *Global Adventure*.

Produced by Book Creation Services Ltd, London

Project Editor Zoë Ross
Art Editor Alison Verity
Designer Anne Fisher
Picture Research Monica Allende
Proofreader Stewart J Wild
Index Hilary Bird
Revisions Team
Kim Laidlaw Adrey, Claire Baranowski, Sonal Bhatt, Anna Brooke, Louise Cleghorn, Simon Davis, Nicola Erdpresser, Fay Franklin, Anna Freiberger, Rhiannon Furbear, Lydia Halliday, Kaberi Hazarika, Lily Heise, Victoria Heyworth-Dunne, Paul Hines, Laura Jones, Bharti Karakoti, Kim Laidlaw Adrey, Louise Rogers Lalaurie, Maite Lantaron, Delphine Lawrance, Carly Madden, Hayley Maher, Nicola Malone, Sam Merrell, Claire Naylor, Jane Oliver-Jedrzejak, Helen Partington, Susie Peachey, Bryan Pirolli, Quadrum Solutions, Rada Radojicic, Tamiko Rex, Philippa Richmond, Ellen Root, Laura de Selincourt, Beverly Smart, Rebecca Taylor, Graham Tearse, Conrad van Dyk, Nikhil Verma, Beatriz Waller, Sophie Warne, Dora Whitaker.
Additional Contributor Rosa Jackson
Main Photographer Peter Wilson
Additional Photography Kim Laidlaw Adrey, Max Alexander, Marta Bescos, Michael Crockett, Robert O'Dea, Britta Jaschinski, Oliver Knight, Neil Lukas, Eric Meacher, Rough Guides/James McConnachie, Jules Selmes, Tony Souter, Valerio Vincenzo, Steven Wooster.

Illustrator Chris Orr & Associates
Cartography Dominic Beddow, Simonetta Giori (Draughtsman Ltd)

At Dorling Kindersley:
Senior Editor Marcus Hardy
Senior Art Editor Marisa Renzullo
Cartography Co-ordinator Casper Morris
Senior DTP Designer Jason Little
Production Joanna Bull, Marie Ingledew
Publishing Manager Kate Poole
Senior Publishing Manager Louise Bostock Lang
Director of Publishing Gillian Allan

Special Assistance
The authors would like to thank Eurostar and Room Service for help with their travel arrangements.

Picture Credits
a-above; b-below/bottom; c-centre; f-far; l-left; r-right; t-top

Works of art on the pages detailed have been reproduced with the permission of the following copyright holders:

Eiffel Tower illuminations Pierre Bideau 16-7; *Sculpture Palais Royale Courtyard* Pol Bury @ADAGP, Paris and DACS, London 2011 96b; *Espace Montmartre* Salvador Dali © Kingdom of Spain, Gaia - Salvador Dali Foundation, DACS, London 2011 140tc; *Sculpture* Salvador Dali © Kingdom of Spain, Gaia - Salvador Dali Foundation, DACS, London 2011 144tl; *Lip Sofa* Salvador Dali © Kingdom of Spain, Gaia - Salvador Dali Foundation, DACS, London 2011 37c; *L'Ecoute* Henri de Miller ©ADAGP, Paris and DACS, London 2011 78tr; *Stravinsky Fountain* Niki de Saint Phalle and Jean Tinguely ©ADAGP, Paris and DACS, London 2011 27tr, 39r, 74tl.

The publishers would like to thank the following individuals, companies and picture libraries for permission to reproduce their photographs:
AFP, London: 56tl, 56b; AGENCE REPUBLIC: 168tc; AKG, London:17tr, 20tl, 21tr, 29cr, 44tl, 44tr, 45t, 45c 47c, 47b, 58b, 63t, 63b,128tc,135t, *Mona Lisa* by Leonardo da Vinci 6ca, 11t, 34tl, *The Raft of the Medusa* by Theodore Gericault 9t, *Leonardo da Vinci portrait* 11c, *Picnic on the Grass* by Manet 12b, *Empress Josephine* by Pierre Paul Prud'hon 20tc, *Capture* by Anton von Werner 23cr, *Tableau de Guerre Interprete* by Vallotton 114b, Erich Lessing: 10t, 10b,107tl, *The Lace-Maker* by Vermeer 9c, *Van Gogh Bedroom in Arles* by Van Gogh 12-13c, 36tl, *Statues of Dancers* by Degas 13tr, *Cafe des Hauteurs* by Toulouse-Lautrec 13cr, *Blue Waterlilies* by Monet 13b, © Succession H Matisse/DACS, London 2011 *Sorrow of the King* by Matisse, ALAMY IMAGES: Bildarchiv Monheim GmbH/Florian Monheim 3tl, 19c; Chad Ehlers 135tr, Matthew Richardson 171tc; ALCAZA RESTAURANT: 127tl; MAX ALEXANDER: 4-5; ANTOINE ET LILI: 88tr; ART ARCHIVE: Musée Carnavalet Paris/ Dagli Orti *Interior of Pantheon Church Paris* by Boilly 28-29c, Musee d'Orsay, Paris/Dagli Orti *Blue Dancers* by Degas 14tl, *La Belle Angela* by Gaugin 14tr, *Cathedral at Rouen* by Monet 15t, *Dance at Moulin de la Galette* by Renoir 15b, 144b, *General Ferdinand Foch* 111b; L'ATELIER DE JOEL ROBUCHON: Gerard Bedeau 65cr; L'ATELIER MAITRE ALBERT: Eric Brissaud 127tr; AVIATIC HOTEL: 174c. HOTEL BANVILLE: 176tr; BRIDGEMAN ART LIBRARY: 26–27c, 45b, 46tr, 47t, Musee d'Armee, Paris 114tr, *The Succession of Louis XIII* by Gianni 44b, Roger Viollet, Paris 114tl. CAVEAU DE LA HUCHETTE Gary Wiggins performing 62b; CHRISTOPHE CAZARRE: 165 tr; CINEAQUA: 134tc; CORBIS: 33t. GALERIE NIKKI DIANA MARQUARDT: 91tr; A GAZZETTA: 93; GETTY IMAGES: The Bridgeman Art Library/Felix Benoist 80t; The Bridgeman Art Library/Giradon/Musee Marmottan Portrait of Napoleon Bonaparte (1769-1821) (oil on canvas), Jean Pierre Franque (1774-1860) 29tr; RONALD GRANT ARCHIVE: 59t, 59c, 59b. LA HALLE SAINT PIERRE: *Untitled* Stavroula Feleggakis 145tl. HOTEL LE BELLECHASE: 174tl. HOTEL D'AUBUSSON: 174tr. LE JULES VERNE: Eric Laignel 64tc. LA MAISON DRUNIER: 139tl; MUSEE NATIONALE DE LA MODE ET DU TEXTILE: Diego Zitelli 94tr. MUSEE DU QUAI BRANLY: 112b. PYLONES: 72tl. LE RELAIS DU PARC: 139tc; RESTAURANT LA ROSE DE FRANCE: 73tl; SAN FRANCISCO BOOK COMPANY: 122tr; LE SOUFFLÉ: 99tc; SENDERENS: Roberto Frankenburg 99tl; LE SOUS-BOCK: Tarek Nini 79tc; STARWOOD HOTELS AND RESORTS: 62tl. TOPHAM PICTUREPOINT: 21b, 46t, 56tr, 57b, 144tc, 144b, 150cr, 154tl, 154 tr, 162tl, J.Brinon/STR 107tr, Daniel Frasnay 63b.
All other images are © DK. For further information see www.dkimages.com.

Phrase Book

In Emergency

Help!	**Au secours!**	*oh sekoor*
Stop!	**Arrêtez!**	*aret-ay*
Call a doctor!	**Appelez un médecin!**	*apuh-lay uñ medsañ*
Call an ambulance!	**Appelez une ambulance!**	*apuh-lay oon oñboo-loñs*
Call the police!	**Appelez la police!**	*apuh-lay lah poh-lees*
Call the fire brigade!	**Appelez les pompiers!**	*apuh-lay leh poñ-peeyay*

Communication Essentials

Yes/No	**Oui/Non**	*wee/noñ*
Please	**S'il vous plaît**	*seel voo play*
Thank you	**Merci**	*mer-see*
Excuse me	**Excusez-moi**	*exkoo-zay mwah*
Hello	**Bonjour**	*boñzhoor*
Goodbye	**Au revoir**	*oh ruh-vwar*
Good night	**Bonsoir**	*boñ-swar*
What?	**Quel, quelle?**	*kel, kel*
When?	**Quand?**	*koñ*
Why?	**Pourquoi?**	*poor-kwah*
Where?	**Où?**	*oo*

Useful Phrases

How are you?	**Comment allez-vous?**	*kom-moñ talay voo*
Very well,	**Très bien,**	*treh byañ*
Pleased to meet you.	**Enchanté de faire votre connaissance.**	*oñshoñ-tay duh fehr votr kon-ay-sans*
Where is/are...?	**Où est/sont...?**	*oo ay/soñ*
Which way to...?	**Quelle est la direction pour...?**	*kel ay lah deer-ek-syoñ poor*
Do you speak English?	**Parlez-vous anglais?**	*par-lay voo oñg-lay*
I don't understand.	**Je ne comprends pas.**	*zhuh nuh kom-proñ pah*
I'm sorry.	**Excusez-moi.**	*exkoo-zay mwah*

Useful Words

big	**grand**	*groñ*
small	**petit**	*puh-tee*
hot	**chaud**	*show*
cold	**froid**	*frwah*
good	**bon**	*boñ*
bad	**mauvais**	*moh-veh*
open	**ouvert**	*oo-ver*
closed	**fermé**	*fer-meh*
left	**gauche**	*gohsh*
right	**droit**	*drwah*
entrance	**l'entrée**	*l'on-tray*
exit	**la sortie**	*sor-tee*
toilet	**les toilettes**	*twah-let*

Shopping

How much does this cost?	**C'est combien s'il vous plaît?**	*say kom-byañ seel voo play*
I would like ...	**je voudrais...**	*zhuh voo-dray*
Do you have?	**Est-ce que vous avez?**	*es-kuh voo zavay*
Do you take credit cards?	**Est-ce que vous acceptez les cartes de crédit?**	*es-kuh voo zaksept-ay leh kart duh kreh-dee*
What time do you open?	**A quelle heure êtes-vous ouvert?**	*ah kel urr voo zet oo-ver*
What time do you close?	**A quelle heure êtes-vous fermé?**	*ah kel urr voo zet fer-may*
This one.	**Celui-ci.**	*suhl-wee-see*
That one.	**Celui-là.**	*suhl-wee-lah*
expensive	**cher**	*shehr*
cheap	**pas cher, bon marché,**	*pah shehr, boñ mar-shay*
size, clothes	**la taille**	*tye*
size, shoes	**la pointure**	*pwañ-tur*
white	**blanc**	*bloñ*
black	**noir**	*nwahr*
red	**rouge**	*roozh*
yellow	**jaune**	*zhohwn*
green	**vert**	*vehr*
blue	**bleu**	*bluh*

Types of Shop

antique shop	**le magasin d'antiquités**	*maga-zañ d'oñteekee-tay*
bakery	**la boulangerie**	*booloñ-zhuree*
bank	**la banque**	*boñk*
bookshop	**la librairie**	*lee-brehree*
cake shop	**la pâtisserie**	*patee-sree*
cheese shop	**la fromagerie**	*fromazh-ree*
chemist	**la pharmacie**	*farmah-see*
department store	**le grand magasin**	*groñ maga-zañ*
delicatessen	**la charcuterie**	*sharkoot-ree*
gift shop	**le magasin de cadeaux**	*maga-zañ duh kadoh*
greengrocer	**le marchand de légumes**	*mar-shoñ duh lay-goom*
grocery	**l'alimentation**	*alee-moñta-syoñ*
market	**le marché**	*marsh-ay*
newsagent	**le magasin de journaux**	*maga-zañ duh zhoor-no*
post office	**la poste, le bureau de poste, le PTT**	*pohst, booroh duh pohst, peh-teh-teh*
supermarket	**le supermarché**	*soo pehr-marshay*
tobacconist	**le tabac**	*tabah*
travel agent	**l'agence de voyages**	*l'azhoñs duh vwayazh*

Sightseeing

abbey	**l'abbaye**	*l'abay-ee*
art gallery	**la galerie d'art**	*galer-ree dart*
bus station	**la gare routière**	*gahr roo-tee-yehr*
cathedral	**la cathédrale**	*katay-dral*
church	**l'église**	*l'aygleez*
garden	**le jardin**	*zhar-dañ*
library	**la bibliothèque**	*beebleeo-tek*
museum	**le musée**	*moo-zay*
railway station	**la gare (SNCF)**	*gahr (es-en-say-ef)*
tourist information office	**renseignements touristiques, le syndicat d'initiative**	*roñsayn-moñ toorees-teek, sandee-ka d'eenee-syateev*
town hall	**l'hôtel de ville**	*l'ohtel duh veel*

Staying in a Hotel

Do you have a vacant room?	**Est-ce que vous avez une chambre?**	*es-kuh voo-zavay oon shambr*
double room,	**la chambre à deux**	*shambr ah duh*

with double bed	**personnes, avec un grand lit**	*pehr-son avek un groñ lee*
twin room	**la chambre à deux lits**	*shambr ah duh lee*
single room	**la chambre à une personne**	*shambr ah oon pehr-son*
room with a bath, shower	**la chambre avec salle de bains, une douche**	*shambr avek sal duh bañ, oon doosh*
I have a réservation.	**J'ai fait une reservation.**	*zhay fay oon rayzehrva-syoñ*

Eating Out

Have you got a table?	**Avez-vous une table libre?**	*avay-voo oon tahbl duh leebr*
I want to reserve a table.	**Je voudrais réserver une table.**	*zhuh voo-dray rayzehr-vay oon tahbl*
The bill please.	**L'addition s'il vous plaît.**	*l'adee-syoñ seel voo play*
Waitress/ waiter	**Madame, Mademoiselle/ Monsieur**	*mah-dam, mah-demwahzel/ muh-syuh*
menu	**le menu, la carte**	*men-oo, kart*
fixed-price menu	**le menu à prix fixe**	*men-oo ah pree feeks*
cover charge	**le couvert**	*koo-vehr*
wine list	**la carte des vins**	*kart-deh vañ*
glass	**le verre**	*vehr*
bottle	**la bouteille**	*boo-tay*
knife	**le couteau**	*koo-toh*
fork	**la fourchette**	*for-shet*
spoon	**la cuillère**	*kwee-yehr*
breakfast	**le petit déjeuner**	*puh-tee deh-zhuh-nay*
lunch	**le déjeuner**	*deh-zhuh-nay*
dinner	**le dîner**	*dee-nay*
main course	**le plat principal**	*plah prañsee-pal*
starter, first course	**l'entrée, le hors d'oeuvre**	*l'oñ-tray, or-duhvr*
dish of the day	**le plat du jour**	*plah doo zhoor*
wine bar	**le bar à vin**	*bar ah vañ*
café	**le café**	*ka-fay*

Menu Decoder

baked	**cuit au four**	*kweet oh foor*
beef	**le boeuf**	*buhf*
beer	**la bière**	*bee-yehr*
boiled	**bouilli**	*boo-yee*
bread	**le pain**	*pan*
butter	**le beurre**	*burr*
cake	**le gâteau**	*gah-toh*
cheese	**le fromage**	*from-azh*
chicken	**le poulet**	*poo-lay*
chips	**les frites**	*freet*
chocolate	**le chocolat**	*shoko-lah*
coffee	**le café**	*kah fay*
dessert	**le dessert**	*deh-ser*
duck	**le canard**	*kanar*
egg	**l'oeuf**	*l'uf*
fish	**le poisson**	*pwah-ssoñ*
fresh fruit	**le fruit frais**	*frwee freh*
garlic	**l'ail**	*l'eye*
grilled	**grillé**	*gree-yay*
ham	**le jambon**	*zhoñ-boñ*
ice, ice cream	**la glace**	*glas*
lamb	**l'agneau**	*l'anyoh*
lemon	**le citron**	*see-troñ*
meat	**la viande**	*vee-yand*
milk	**le lait**	*leh*
mineral water	**l'eau minérale**	*l'oh meeney-ral*
oil	**l'huile**	*l'weel*
onions	**les oignons**	*leh zonyoñ*
fresh orange juice	**l'orange pressée**	*l'oroñzh press-eh*
fresh lemon juice	**le citron pressé**	*see-troñ press-eh*
pepper	**le poivre**	*pwavr*
pork	**le porc**	*por*
potatoes	**les pommes de terre**	*pom-duh tehr*
rice	**le riz**	*ree*
roast	**rôti**	*row-tee*
salt	**le sel**	*sel*
sausage, fresh	**la saucisse**	*sohsees*
seafood	**les fruits de mer**	*frwee duh mer*
snails	**les escargots**	*leh zes-kar-goh*
soup	**la soupe, le potage**	*soop, poh-tazh*
steak	**le bifteck, le steack**	*beef-tek, stek*
sugar	**le sucre**	*sookr*
tea	**le thé**	*tay*
vegetables	**les légumes**	*lay-goom*
vinegar	**le vinaigre**	*veenaygr*
water	**l'eau**	*l'oh*
red wine	**le vin rouge**	*vañ roozh*
white wine	**le vin blanc**	*vañ bloñ*

Numbers

0	**zéro**	*zeh-roh*
1	**un, une**	*uñ, oon*
2	**deux**	*duh*
3	**trois**	*trwah*
4	**quatre**	*katr*
5	**cinq**	*sañk*
6	**six**	*sees*
7	**sept**	*set*
8	**huit**	*weet*
9	**neuf**	*nerf*
10	**dix**	*dees*
11	**onze**	*oñz*
12	**douze**	*dooz*
13	**treize**	*trehz*
14	**quatorze**	*katorz*
15	**quinze**	*kañz*
16	**seize**	*sehz*
17	**dix-sept**	*dees-set*
18	**dix-huit**	*dees-weet*
19	**dix-neuf**	*dees-nerf*
20	**vingt**	*vañ*
30	**trente**	*tront*
40	**quarante**	*karoñt*
50	**cinquante**	*sañkoñt*
60	**soixante**	*swasoñt*
70	**soixante-dix**	*swasoñt-dees*
80	**quatre-vingts**	*katr-vañ*
90	**quatre-vingt-dix**	*katr-vañ-dees*
100	**cent**	*soñ*
1,000	**mille**	*meel*

Time

one minute	**une minute**	*oon mee-noot*
one hour	**une heure**	*oon urr*
half an hour	**une demi-heure**	*urr duh-me urr*
one day	**un jour**	*urr zhorr*
Monday	**lundi**	*luñ-dee*
Tuesday	**mardi**	*mar-dee*
Wednesday	**mercredi**	*mehrkruh-dee*
Thursday	**jeudi**	*zhuh-dee*
Friday	**vendredi**	*voñdruh-dee*
Saturday	**samedi**	*sam-dee*
Sunday	**dimanche**	*dee-moñsh*

Index of Main Streets